THE NORTH SPY

Yankee Doodle Spies series

S. W. O'Connell

Lanyard Press
Leesburg Virginia

Other Books by S.W. O'Connell

The Patriot Spy
The Cavalier Spy
The Winter Spy
The Reluctant Spy
The Lafayette Circle
Envoy of the Lord

S.W. O'Connell's books are available for kindle and in print at
Amazon.com

The North Spy

Lanyard Press
Leesburg, Virginia 20176

First Edition, December 2022

ISBN: 978-1-7376636-7-6

Cover art by Jennifer Gibson http://www.jennifergibson.ca/

Map by Bryon Line

Printed in the United States of America.

Acknowledgments

Some talented people helped develop this story. This able group includes Paul Harpin, a former military history professor at the United States Military Academy; Susan Harrison and John Swift, both retired Army Military Intelligence officers; John Molino, author, retired Army officer, and suspense author; Paul Savitsky, retired Army officer, and fellow authors L.J. Litton and F.W. Abel. Thanks also to Bryon Line, retired Army intelligence officer, whose map will help orient the reader to the setting.

For Phil Fazio

"I will go before thee and make the crooked paths straight."

Isaiah 45:2

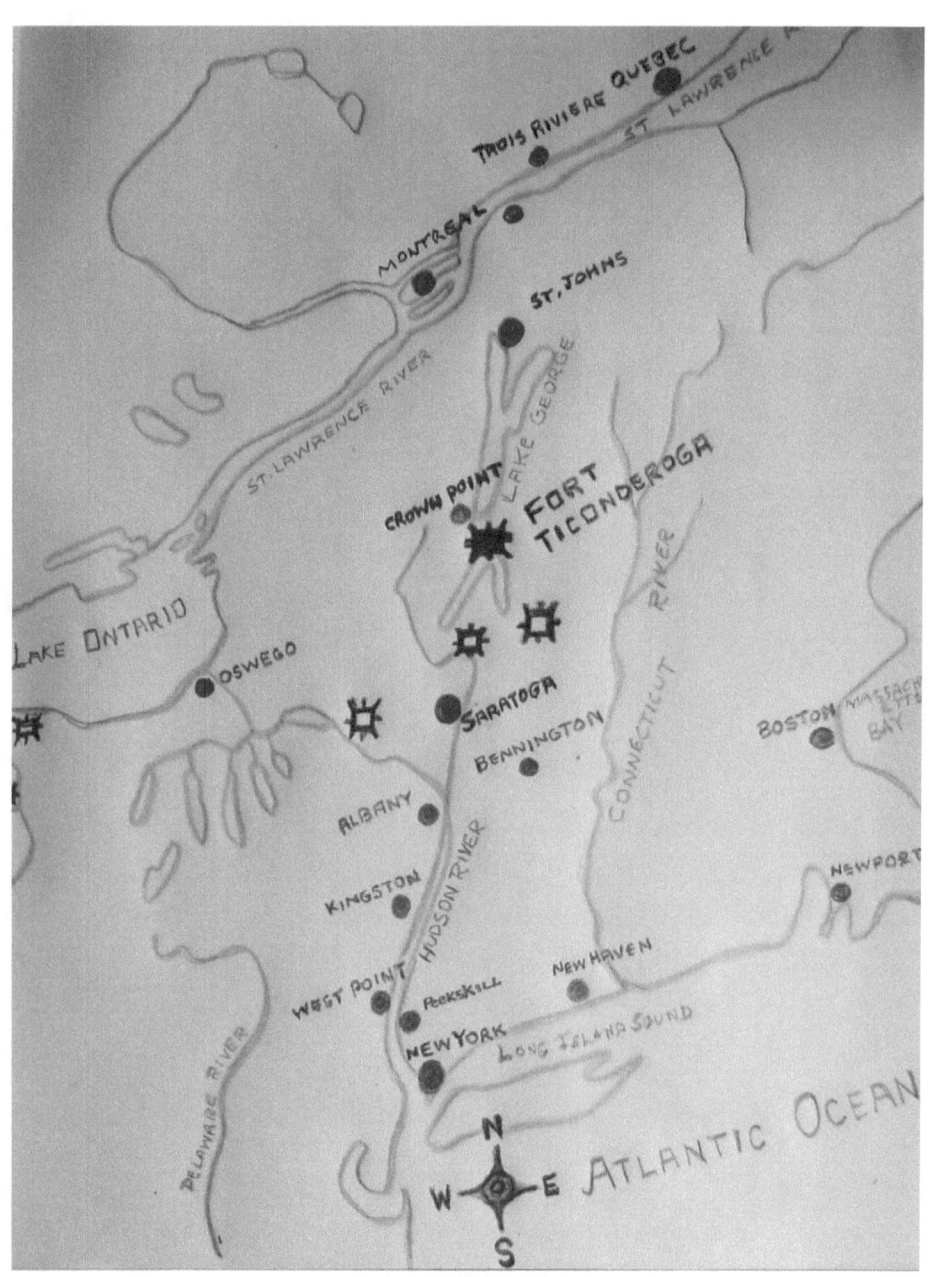

Map New York and Canada 1777

Prologue

May 1777

The American war for independence entered its third year in a stalemate, but one favoring the British, who held the strategic position in New York. General and Commander-in-Chief George Washington's Continental Army huddled behind the Watchung Mountains of northern New Jersey, and for now, Philadelphia, the new nation's capital, remains safe. Slowly, ever so slowly, reinforcements from the states trickle in and gradually swell the Continental Army's depleted ranks. Washington's immediate fear is a direct thrust on the capital when the spring campaign season opens. So, he feverishly prepares for another British juggernaut. One which he fears this time may not stop at the Delaware River.

Neither Washington nor the British commander-in-chief, General Sir William Howe, knew that a change was imminent. The British general, John Burgoyne, had returned to England and secretly proposed a new strategy to Lord George Germain, Minister for the Colonies and the man charged by King George III with bringing the rebels to their knees. Frustrated with Howe's laconic ways, Germain acquiesced to Burgoyne's plan, which was bold and complex.

Washington's "Intelligence Advisor," Colonel Robert Fitzgerald, suspects a shift in British strategy, but he cannot get Washington to envision a significant change by the predictable General Howe. However, news arrives in a letter from an agent in Paris, causing Washington to risk sending a spy north - into Canada. Without hesitation, the man he decides to send is Lieutenant Jeremiah Creed of the 2nd Continental Dragoons. The mission: confirm that General John Burgoyne is preparing an attack south into New York to seize the entire Hudson River valley and split the rebellious colonies in two.

S.W. O'Connell

Chapter 1

Snake Hill, New Jersey, May 1777

Lieutenant Jeremiah Creed scanned the valley through the brass barrel of his spyglass. His body ached and chilled from hours of lying prone in the tree line. Slowly, he stretched his legs and pulled at the hem of the worn-out greatcoat that served as his ground cloth. He could feel a wet, cold seeping through a slush-encrusted soil from the long winter frost.

Below him, the Hackensack River twisted northeast, then bent sharply to the west and wended to the north behind him. He watched from high ground that towered over 150 feet above the meadowlands. *Snake Hill! Aptly named.*

Creed smiled mischievously. He forgot who told him the massive ridge, an Indian burial ground, was named for the numerous black snakes that slithered through its dense grass in search of the sun's warming rays. Before the war, it was a place for felons to hide, conspirators to conspire, and illicit lovers to rendezvous. Roy Harry was all of those.

Now the hill served as an important observation point for the Continental Army. Garrisoned by a platoon of the County Militia, the mountain became a key watchpost and a popular starting point for espionage against the British garrison at Brunswick.

Creed withdrew the brass tube from his eye, turned back, and gazed down the lightly wooded trail. Private Thomas Jeffries stood patiently holding their horses. *Good, patient men. The lads had sat watch through the night. Most others would be asleep now. But not the lads.*

Creed looked down the ridge of the hill. A squad of militiamen in a skirmish line just below him played nervously with their weapons. They kept glancing back at him, anxious for orders. He knew they were worried.

They had a right to be anxious, Creed thought. "Where in Jesus's name is Harry?"

Creed made a hasty sign of the cross for taking the Lord's name and losing his temper. He, of all people, should have remembered that nothing ever went quite as planned in warfare.

And especially not for his platoon of selected Continental Dragoons who served as the army's espionage unit. Creed's "White Knights" had achieved feats that saved the Army and the Cause from defeat. Despite their past success, they now came under the command of Major Benjamin Tallmadge, General Washington's new chief of intelligence operations.

Before Tallmadge's arrival, Creed and his men operated independently. However, Washington sought better coverage of the British Army and, more importantly, its base of operations in New York. Therefore, when Congress approved his request to add a dragoon regiment to expand the Continental Army, he cleverly used one of its troops as his expanded intelligence unit—notably under Tallmadge's command.

Creed put the brass tube to his eye and scanned the flat land to the south. The return plan called for Harry to cross the river east of Newark at Brown's Ferry. He would head east toward Douw's Ferry, then turn northwest, where a boat crewed by Private Elias Parker and a pair of militiamen waited to transport him back to the right bank of the Hackensack at the foot of Snake Hill.

Where the hell is Harry?

To Creed, the mission was simple. Harry had dispatched a spy, a one-time line crosser whose mission was to deliver produce to a commissariat contractor named Pawley. Tallmadge wanted Creed to expand his operations by recruiting and training a new network of low-level agents.

Their first recruit was Delbert Greene, a freed black who made his living bartering with the small farmers along the lower Hackensack Valley. The British took for granted that the blacks in America supported the crown over the locals, who enslaved and suppressed them. But there were exceptions, especially in the north.

Then Creed spotted them. A small pony-drawn cart with two occupants rolled steadily from the west. Greene sat at the reins with Harry riding beside him, musket at the ready.

A quick glint of metal to the south caught his attention. He swiveled the spyglass. More than a dozen men pressed forward on powerful horses that pounded their way along the far side of the river. They wore the red jackets, black helmets, and white breeches of British dragoons. But Harry and Greene seemed oblivious of their followers.

Creed cupped his hands to his mouth. "Harry is on the way back, but he is in danger. We must get down to the river now."

Thomas Jeffries and Jonathan Beall scurried out of the brush with firelocks firmly held.

"Lads, Harry and our agent have been spotted. They can't see their pursuers because of the sunken road."

"The horses are ready, sir," Jeffries replied.

Creed shook his head. "No time to take the trail. We must go straight down this slope and rally the militia. They can cover our crossing. Let's go."

Creed grabbed his German rifle and bounded down the steep hillside with his men scurrying behind. They struggled down the hill, feet kicking stones in all directions and faces feeling the bee-sting-like smack of branches.

When they reached the militia along the lower ridge, they stopped to catch their breath. The cool spring day seemed suddenly quite warm.

Creed waved to the sergeant in charge. "British dragoons pursue our friends below. Move your men above the riverbank and cover us as we cross."

The sergeant spat a bit of chew on the ground. "Are you mad, crossing into the face of British regulars?"

Creed's eyes narrowed. "If ye have fears, save them for me, not the British. Now, do as I order!"

Minutes later, they scrambled into the boat with his own Elias Parker at the helm. Creed sent the skiff's militia crew back to join their mates. They would have little stomach rowing across to certain death.

"Shove off," Creed said. They struggled into the thwarts, grabbed hold of the oars, and, as one began, steady strokes.

The sound of powerful hooves smacking along the muddy ground and a swirl of curses resounded across the water. They heard the *pop – pop – pop* of muskets echo from behind them as the buzz of musket balls whirled over their heads.

Creed smiled grimly. "The militia is covering us. The lads didn't run."

They intensified their strokes.

"Keep pulling until we hit the bank. Then grab your firelocks and form a "V" behind me. Five yards separation."

The boat slammed into the bank with a thump that nearly tipped them into the mudflats. Parker, a strong former sailor and fisherman from the Chesapeake, was the first over the bulwark. He scrambled to the top of the six-foot embankment and, panting from exhaustion, took a knee.

A resounding Huzzah rolled across the flat bottomland. The British were just 200 yards from the cart. But Greene and Harry finally saw them. Greene had the ponies trotting across the muddy fields with a snap of the reins. Creed thought they might make it. But his heart sank when the cart suddenly stopped, its wheels firmly mired in the loamy mud.

Creed turned to his men. "They are undone if we don't distract the horsemen. On my command, present, fire!"

The barrels spewed flame and smoke across the field, but all missed the mark. A trained sharpshooter with a rifled musket might hit his target at 150 yards, and an ordinary musket was almost worthless beyond eighty unless firing in a volley.

The dragoons calmly shifted into a skirmish line and trotted towards Creed's band with sabers brightly flashing in the sunlight.

"Took the bait! Form line, on me. Load double ball and fix bayonets. We'll give them one good volley at ten yards."

They rammed home their powder and ball. A series of clicks secured their blades. They stepped out in an open line.

"Full cock," Creed commanded. Steady thumbs worked the muskets' hammers back to a full cock. The feel steadied their nerves.

"Firelocks, ready!"

They poised their weapons –Thomas and Parker carried French *fusils*, light muskets. Creed and Jonathan Beall each wielded a German Jaeger rifle with a special sword-bayonet affixed to the barrel.

Creed looked back and saw the militia had already abandoned their position. *Well, they had done as much as could be expected.*

The thumping grew louder, and a trumpet blast cut through the air. Sabers pointed. The dragoons closed to fifty yards, then forty. The hooves made a sucking rather than a pounding sound as they struggled across the muddy field.

"Just a wee bit more, boys," Creed whispered. He waited for the line of horsemen to reach twenty yards.

"Present, fire!"

Dragoons tumbled from their saddles, bodies thumping into the mud. Panicked horses reeled and twisted, but the remaining dragoons coolly charged home.

Creed drew a pistol from his belt and fired into the face of the first trooper to reach him. His horse careened past Creed and over the riverbank. Creed blocked a saber blow from the next dragoon, then drove his blade into the trooper's thigh.

The trooper clutched at the wound. "You bloody rebel bastard!"

"These are Continentals, not militia!" a trooper exclaimed.

"No matter, lad – they are rebels nonetheless," a sergeant replied. "Let them taste the king's steel!"

The dragoons cursed and jeered as their horses swirled around Creed and his men, who stood back-to-back, fending them off with desperate thrusts.

"Yield rebels, or die!"

Blades clashed with an almost musical rhythm. Sabers hacked away, desperately searching for a miscalculation to exploit. Creed knew it was only a matter of time before they were cut to pieces.

The short blast of a trumpet then pierced the air.

Creed's heart skipped a beat. *More dragoons!* He knew it was hopeless, but they had to fight on. He and his men might be treated as war prisoners, but Harry and Greene would hang as spies.

"No surrender! Show them what you can do, lads!"

The dull thump of pistol shots erupted from behind the British. One screamed like a stuck pig and grabbed at a shattered elbow.

The redcoats turned to face the blue jackets of the 2nd Continental Dragoons. The British commander nodded at his trumpeter, whose short staccato blasts recalled the redcoats. The dragoons turned their horses and galloped south along the river.

Creed stood panting and gasping for air.

"What mischief have you gotten yourself into, Jeremiah?"

He looked up into the face of Benjamin Tallmadge. A broad grin crossed his face. "Truth be told, captain – I never saw a man's face as lovely as yours! What brought ye here at this, our hour of need?"

Tallmadge plunged his still-smoking pistol into its holster. "Just more of your Irish luck, Jeremiah. Our morning patrol took us from Preakness to Aquackanonck and then south along the Passaic. We heard the musket fire from Snake Hill and rode to the sound."

"Well, your instincts saved my men."

Tallmadge sniffed the air. "It seems to me that had we not arrived. A few more lobsters would have fallen."

"Kind of ye to say, sir, but the lads were tired and resistance waning. I should say you made our morning."

A rider trotted up and tapped a steel hook to his head. Tallmadge returned the salute. "Sir, the redcoats have scattered. They are likely halfway to Brunswick. Harry and his companion are now in our care."

Tallmadge surveyed the field. "Secure the wounded British and place them on the cart. Round up their horses – they can help extract the vehicle from this mud."

The Troop Sergeant, Simon Beall, nodded and barked orders to the troopers who were already relieving the surviving British of their worldly goods.

Beall, a cousin of Private Jonathan Beall, served under Creed's command as the sergeant of the Maryland First Continental Line company during the Battle of Long Island. American troops accidentally shot the former farrier while he was crossing enemy lines. Tallmadge, then Adjutant of the First Connecticut Continental Line, helped get him to a hospital where his lower arm was amputated. Tallmadge personally requested Simon Beall to serve as troop sergeant when forming his troop.

Cart and prisoners secured, Tallmadge and his troopers spurred their horses down the mud-soaked road.

"No time to waste, lads," Creed said as they disappeared down the road. "We have a river to cross and a mountain to climb before we can find the comfort of our saddles."

***

The Dey House, Preakness, New Jersey

Creed and Tallmadge sat at a table in the front room of the grand mansion. A servant placed a teapot between them, gently handed each a pewter mug, and quietly whisked her way back to the kitchen.

Tallmadge nodded at Creed. "I asked Missus Dey to ensure her servants gave us privacy. One never knows."

Creed considered the house one of the finest he had seen in America. The handsome brick-front home was well-appointed with elegant woodwork, finely polished wooden floors, and bright, sunny rooms. The house sat on a 600-acre estate along Totowa Road, just outside the village of Preakness.

Creed cradled his mug and sniffed at the tea. "Colonel Dey makes a fine host, even while absent with the militia." Theunis Dey was in Hackensack, commanding the Bergen County Militia Regiment.

"His wife, Hester Dey, has some role in that. As gracious a hostess as I have met. She's a Schuyler, you know?"

Creed did not reply. He thought he had left the need for a name and connections behind when he departed Europe to start a new life in America.

"Her husband left her instructions to accommodate us, but I believe His Excellency had something to do with it."

Creed's face broke into an easy smile. "No surprise. He has an eye for the ladies, although his heart belongs to Missus Washington."

"Yes, they are the finest couple in the land. But no, we are here because this location provides an excellent position to collect intelligence on the British."

"We can watch their garrisons at Brunswick and the Amboys while screening the approaches to the Watchung Mountains to the west."

"And it provides easy access to the most direct approaches to the Hudson and British-occupied New York."

The men sipped at their tea while Creed selected one of the fresh scones from a pewter plate next to the teapot.

After a few minutes of quiet, Tallmadge began to speak in a calm voice. "You know, Jeremiah, I didn't seek this command. I expected a promotion would find me commanding an infantry unit in the Connecticut Line."

Creed looked ruefully. "Aye, I, too, started this war in command of a company of Continental light infantry, the finest lads in the world." Creed's eyes welled up with tears. His mind briefly drifted to the memory of his men charging repeatedly against a brigade of British regulars on a hot day. Nearly everyone was killed, but they had saved one-third of the American army on Long Island.

"You were considered the most gallant officer on Long Island, Jeremiah. Do you miss it?" Tallmadge asked.

"Miss what, exactly?"

Tallmadge chuckled. "Why, the infantry! The camps with rows of neat white tents, spit and polish parades, mass formations marching in camaraderie, the gallantry of fighting formations maneuvering in pitched battle – everything."

Creed rubbed his chin. "'Tis true, I did at first, but no longer. The lads, the White Knights, are my unit now. They are, in a manner of speaking, my only family." He looked at Tallmadge. "As are the Second Dragoons."

"Were you orphaned?" Tallmadge asked.

Creed coughed nervously. "In a manner of speaking, yes. Twice, in fact."

Creed overcame his initial anger when told he would not receive command of the special cavalry troop. He met Tallmadge on Long Island, so that helped somewhat. After thinking it through, Creed realized he preferred more direct action than the administration of a mounted company. He had his fill of that in France among the Irish Brigade. Now he liked independent operations and espionage.

The evening sun cast shadows across the carefully scrubbed room. The servant reappeared with hot tea and scones and then slipped away more quickly.

Tallmadge eyed Creed pensively. "So, Jeremiah, how do we proceed?"

Creed raised an eyebrow. "I don't understand. Before, I took orders from His Excellency through the good offices of Colonel Fitzgerald. Now they come from you. 'Tis a simple concept – one even a thick-skulled lad from Cork can abide."

They both laughed. "I am new to all of this, Jeremiah. I value your knowledge and experience in this secret work. I need your advice, as well as your service."

Tallmadge's forthrightness touched Creed. "'Tis the rare man who admits deficiency with subordinates, Major Tallmadge. You have my respect, support, and fondest wishes for a successful command. Besides, you have the instinct for this. Those instincts saved my lads and me today."

"Thank you, Jeremiah. My first order is this: call me Benjamin when not among the men. Please render your report, and we can plan our next move."

Creed spent thirty minutes recounting the past week's activity. He had wasted little time putting his platoon into action. His original White Knights: Privates Jonathan Beall, Elias Parker, and Thomas Jeffries, were joined by Roy Harry and Zeke Branford, who escaped the British imprisonment with Harry.

"How are the new men working out?" Tallmadge asked.

" I've not had a chance to take the measure of them. Both Virginians, Jonathan Carter and Job Coleman, were members of His Excellency's Life Guard. Of the other two, I know little. But they are foreigners, like me."

"I would not deem you foreign."

"Perhaps, but others do. It's alright. Better a foreigner in America than a native in Europe."

"Well, your foreigners are former cavalrymen in the Austrian service. Experience counts. Lord knows we have little of it."

Creed nodded. "Indeed, Jan Karcz is an ex-*Uhlan*. Polish lancers once ruled the east. The other is Thadeus Quill, from County Tyrone. He claims he once served with the Habsburgs' famed O'Reilly Light Horse. They're both excellent horsemen."

"Let's just see how they fight." Tallmadge spread a map on the table before them. "I read some of your reports to Colonel Fitzgerald. Based on your ideas, I have designed a strategy for intelligence activity over the spring campaign."

Creed's eyes widened. "Just the spring campaign? Why not summer?"

Tallmadge leaned back. "Let's take this war one season at a time."

He spread his hands across the map. "We need to recruit people to probe Brunswick and the Amboys. Not to arouse suspicions, mind you. Just to listen passively – as you did, posing as this Root Hog. There will be plenty of stray talk with so many British and camp followers crammed along the Raritan."

Creed smiled. "Stray talk often gleans nuggets to the attentive listener."

***

Creed entered the barn just after eight. He had turned down Missus Dey's gracious offer of a room. He liked to stay with his men while on campaign.

The newly promoted Sergeant Harry greeted him. "While you were enjoying the major's high company, the men have fed and watered the horses, cleaned their gear, and oiled their weapons."

"Did they eat?"

Harry nodded. "Yep. They had just some grilled pigeon washed down with rum and coffee."

"Well, you all did better than me," Creed quipped.

"I didn't have time to thank you and the boys for braving the mountain, river, and redcoats to save my skin," Harry said.

Creed smiled. "Just our duty, Harry. Besides, we needed intelligence. And you would have fought off those dragoons anyway."

Harry put a finger to his mouth. "The damned musket had but one ball."

Creed spread his hands. "We go to war with the munitions we have."

The two rolled into their cloaks and stared up at the ceiling rafters. The smell of dung permeated the place. Somehow, Creed found the aroma pleasing. He heard his horse Finn stirring nearby. His band was together and, for now, safe.

Uncounted minutes later, Creed whispered. "Harry, are you awake?"

"I am now, sir."

Creed smiled to himself. Although a natural leader, Harry hated military protocol. His willing subjection to it was in homage to Creed, who saved him and Zeke Branford from the infamous Sugar House prison in New York.

"Harry...do you ever think of young widow Lozier?"

"Yes. Yes, I do. But only once each day, usually for hours at a time."

Harry had an affair with a young farmwife named Judith Lozier while using her husband's farm as a base of operations against the British. Because of her connection to him, a band of Loyalist Provincials burned the farm. They later hanged her husband in front of her and their son.

Creed sat up. "They say she is near the English Village – that's not so far from here, correct?"

"Correct, sir."

"Well, I can grant you leave."

"I will pass on that. No sense in stirring bad memories. I suppose I caused Judith's ruin in every way a man could."

"More reason to make amends and offer assistance, Harry."

"My duty is here, sir. But what of you? I understand a certain young lady has caught your fancy. Emily, I believe."

"So, the lads are speaking, are they? Well, yes. However, she resides with her Da' – in New York. Our acquaintance was fleeting but sweet."

Harry sat bolt upright. "Why not get her out? Despite the Loyalists and British, you seem good at getting in and out of New York."

Creed sighed softly. "A brave and true patriot she is, but she loves her father, Reginald Stanley, who, although a rabid Loyalist, seems a kind and decent man. She could never abandon him."

"Perhaps things will change. Meanwhile, you seem to find interesting ways to keep the mind focused, and the heart suppressed."

Creed dropped back and gathered his mantle around his shoulders. "Ah, 'tis true. Warfare can be a compelling distraction and an equally powerful attraction."

***

Jonathan Beall quietly crept from the barn. The moonless night turned everything black. *Must be just after midnight.*

He felt his way through the dark until he reached a small circle of tents in the orchard.

His cousin, Simon, sat at a small fire, skillfully rotating a pair of apples on a wooden stick.

"Smells good, sergeant," Jonathan said.

Simon did not look up. "The trick is to cook the juices while avoiding burning the skin. They are done about now. Take one."

Jonathan sat on a small log and nibbled at the fruit.

"They miss you back home, you know," Simon said in a hushed voice. "Have you thought of asking for furlough? Mine did me a world of good."

Jonathan shook his head. "You were invalided, Simon. Anyway, I could not leave Lieutenant Creed and the Knights just now. The spring campaign will lead to summer. Perhaps next winter."

Simon grimaced. "I should hope the war is over by then."

"Lieutenant Creed thinks not. I believe he is right."

Simon stared at the fire. "You know, Jonathan, my time at home changed my outlook."

"In what way? Are you Loyal?"

"Hell no! I will fight to the death for the cause. But I am not so confident we will win. Frederick is torn right down the middle on the war. If other towns are like home, I just cannot see...."

"I watched us defeat the British in two pitched battles and more than a half dozen skirmishes. Over time, people will regain their faith in the cause. The Continental Line has expanded. That brought you here and us together again. I see your arm has healed."

Simon raised his left forearm, revealing a wicked-looking steel hook. He chuckled and scratched his forehead reflexively with the tip. "Thanks to good Yankee shooting! A head scratch and a hook. My two war trophies, eh?"

"Well, our shooting improves with every skirmish and battle. And we have good artillery."

Simon turned serious. "I meant to ask why that boy was here. A unit like this has no place for Negroes, except as stable hands."

Jonathan remained calm. He had heard such talk before. "Lieutenant Creed knows good men. Thomas was a stable hand but also a post rider. He rides better than any man in the unit, except maybe the two new foreigners. Expert with horses and has killed several enemies in close combat. Did I mention his courage? His loyalty? He's only sixteen yet moves among men."

"Well, if Lieutenant Creed and you vouch for him, I suppose I can accept him."

Chapter 2

Jacob Arnold's Tavern, Morristown, New Jersey

A modest fire sputtered and crackled in the great hearth, more to ward off a damp spring chill than provide heat. The Continental Army Headquarters itself sizzled with activity. Orderlies rushed back and forth, ensuring cramped work spaces remained stocked with supplies. A pack of aides and staff officers strained over crude maps, carefully marking locations with a nib or a pencil. Their discussions took on the buzz of a beehive.

Washington entered the room. He glanced around and found Captain Harold Martin hunched over a large maple table covered in paper and strewn with a compass, protractors, and other accouterments of an engineer. As acting chief of cartography for Washington's headquarters, he had his hands full. Martin and his two assistants scoured operational reports for hints of details to flesh out the small stock of maps in the army's possession.

Washington, a former surveyor himself, strode to their table to check their progress.

Martin pointed at the map and turned to one of his officers, a lieutenant from Albany named James Tobias. "Now, Jim, the elevation must be accurate in all cases. Minor errors in distance and direction are tolerable to a point, but water depth and width must be perfect."

"I would think nothing less, sir," Tobias replied with a shrug.

Martin smiled grimly. "Well, you'd be shocked at the fanciful things this army has used as maps. I'll have none of it as long as I am here."

Washington stood watching the interchange. He resisted the urge to jump in and work with them as they transformed information into lines and images on paper.

But after some time, unable to restrain himself, Washington moved toward the table. "Accuracy is indeed key, gentlemen. Accurate and detailed knowledge of the land and water will give a distinct advantage over the enemy's numbers and equipment."

"Indeed, sir," Martin said.

"When I fought the Indians out west, a few hundred warriors with deep knowledge of the wilderness managed to frustrate the entire Virginia militia, which was over a thousand strong."

An aide de camp pattered up to the table with a terrier-like impatience. Washington turned to greet the short officer in the neatly tailored uniform. "What is it, Major?"

"Your Excellency, Colonel Fitzgerald has finished his work and requests to speak with you at your earliest convenience."

Washington nodded. "Thank you, Alexander, no doubt the good colonel and I shall be here for a while, so have an orderly send up coffee. And have the horses ready. I plan to ride out to Chatham before dinner and see General Sullivan on an urgent matter. You may attend."

Alexander Hamilton bowed his head. "As you wish, sir."

Washington bounded up the oak-planked staircase to the second-floor room that served as his sleeping quarters and office.

With spring and the campaign season, the commander-in-chief turned his attention more to operational than administrative matters. Since Martha and the other officers' wives had left winter quarters, Washington held most of his meetings there. He valued the privacy it afforded. And he always feared the threat of spies.

However, Washington steered past his chambers and slipped down the hallway, entering a small bedroom that served as the office of his Senior Intelligence Advisor.

***

Colonel Robert Fitzgerald adjusted his spectacles. He had read the letter three times to ensure he understood its meaning and nuance. He had spent several arduous hours on it. The first part was applying chemicals to enable him to read the invisible ink. Then, he had to convert the coded words the transmitter had written into French. Fitzgerald's French proved equal to the task, but not as quickly as hoped.

A rap on the door disturbed his thoughts. The door creaked slowly open, and Washington stepped into Fitzgerald's chambers. He closed the door behind him and sat on the small divan near the room's cold fireplace.

The commander-in-chief spoke just above a whisper, "Alexander has informed me of our need to meet. I trust your efforts have resulted in some success?"

Fitzgerald arched an eye and removed his glasses in a sign of annoyance. "Indeed, Mister Hamilton." Fitzgerald could not hide his disdain for the newly arrived aide de camp.

Washington frowned defensively. "I selected the young man for his brilliance, not his affability, which, I might add, rivals yours."

"I normally would say *touché*, sir, but I truly feel the comparison lacking."

Washington clasped his knee with both hands. "Perhaps you are both judged unfairly. Alexander is hard-working, wise, and driven. We need young men of his caliber around here."

Fitzgerald unfolded a large sheet of paper. "Well, we seem to have little compunction sending at least one such young man in harm's way."

A knock on the door interrupted. A private of Washington's Life Guard set a pot of steaming coffee and a plate full of biscuits and slices of cold tongue before them.

"Since I am riding this afternoon, I ordered some sustenance for us," Washington said.

Fitzgerald smiled. "My apologies, sir. Winter quarters have made me edgy. Lack of activity – cabin fever, as they say."

Washington nodded. "Indeed. I believe we all suffer somewhat from that disorder. Soon, the campaigns begin, and we will all have our fill of activity."

"I, for one, will welcome the warmer weather. These bones seem to ache more with cold and wet weather."

"And I thought it was young Hamilton who longed for the warmth of the islands. You two have more in common than you think!"

Fitzgerald lowered his eyes in submission to the barb hurled so precisely by his commander-in-chief.

Washington twisted his mouth into a sympathetic smile. "I had not meant to discommode you, sir. Please accept my apology for the remark."

Fitzgerald smiled sheepishly and waved a hand. "No offense taken, Your Excellency. I must strive to be less thin-skinned. A proper intelligence officer must suffer all types of critiques and rebuffs with complete composure. Otherwise, my assessments might become less than candid."

"Of that, I brook no fear. I do not pay you to tell me what I want to hear. Quite the contrary."

They dove into the platter of tongue and biscuit, neither man speaking. When the platter was empty, Fitzgerald removed his spectacles and wiped them clean as he said in a harsh yet subdued voice, "I have decoded the letter from 'Demetrius'- it contains some interesting assertions."

Washington bent forward, his head almost touching Fitzgerald's. "Excellent! What, pray tell, does he assert?"

Fitzgerald chose his words carefully. "A confidential informant... a very close confidante, has picked up rumblings from 'Olympus.' A new plan is underway."

Washington's eyes widened. "A new plan? Do we even know of 'an old plan'?"

Although neither dared mention it, "Demetrius" was the codename for America's newest agent in Paris – Doctor Benjamin Franklin. Franklin, the world's most celebrated scientist, businessman, statesman, and philosopher, had been sent to assist and ultimately replace Silas Dean, who had come under suspicion in Congress. Dean had done good work ordering equipment for the new nation. But Dean's connections were deemed insufficient to take the relationship to the next level – an open alliance. That objective became Franklin's mandate.

"Olympus" was the codename for Great Britain – specifically, the Minister for the Colonies, Lord George Germain.

"It seems 'Demetrius' has taken another mistress, a Madame Reynaud, whose husband has business interests in London and Quebec. Monsieur Reynaud recently returned from a secret visit to London. The ministry summoned him to place a discreet order for various items to supply a force of French Canadians they plan on raising as part of a new campaign."

Fitzgerald paused as Washington sat stone-faced.

Fitzgerald let him absorb the importance of the news, then went on. "French foodstuffs primarily: spices, certain vegetables, wines, calvados, and most importantly, gunpowder."

Washington blanched. "Victuals and gunpowder – a strange mix. What do you make of that?"

"Not so strange. A harsh winter in Canada – they could never feed themselves well without support from across the Atlantic. Our forces in seventy-five destroyed two gunpowder works. Perhaps Sullivan and Arnold's failure had elements of success hitherto unknown to us. Now the British need to call on their erstwhile enemies."

Washington leaned back in his chair. "Ironic. Yet Britain manufactures the best gunpowder in the world. Why call on French largesse?"

"They got an excellent price, for one thing. But more importantly, an increase in orders from their factories heading for Canada might come to the attention of our correspondents in that quarter."

Washington smiled. "They seek to deceive even as they satisfy their parsimony."

Fitzgerald pushed a lock of white hair from his forehead. "Indeed, sir. The hand of General Burgoyne is in this. He impressed Monsieur Reynaud greatly during their meeting in London. It seemed he learned of the charms of Madame Reynaud and offered to write a short play in her honor, in French, of course."

Washington chuckled. "In other words, he lost a great sum at cards and hoped to make the debt good with a few pen strokes."

Fitzgerald peered down his glasses. "And likely bed the woman whom he honors. It will be some time before he gets to pay off the debt and enjoy his spoils. Germain has sent him to Canada to replace Carleton as commander-in-chief, although not as Governor-General."

Washington rubbed his chin. "Canada, why that seems as far removed as France. Perhaps they will try a maritime thrust from there – perhaps at Boston or Rhode Island. Or even New York. Reinforce Howe, perhaps."

Fitzgerald spread a crude map across the desk. "Perhaps. However, I do not believe Burgoyne would be satisfied merely with reinforcing Howe. Nor would he risk getting himself trapped in Boston or Newport. No, I suspect something bolder, more to the dramatic side of his temperament."

Washington slowly shook his head. "A land movement? Over hundreds of miles of wilderness? A British army could never stand the logistical consequences of such a move. It would be as disastrous a campaign as ours back in seventy-five."

Fitzgerald raised a finger. "Not necessarily. Our mistake was the secondary thrust by Arnold through the wilderness of upper New England. His men virtually melted away due to a lack of food. When he joined Montgomery's main force, it was too weak. But the New York route has the advantage of a nearly contiguous waterway to supply Burgoyne's army. It is a maritime highway reaching right to New York itself."

Washington grimaced. "Of course. You are correct. And should Howe march north as Burgoyne marches south, the two forces could meet in the middle. New England might be cut off from the rest of the states, rendering the British the strategic initiative."

Fitzgerald rubbed his hands together nervously. "I fear this is precisely what they intend, Your Excellency."

Washington stared at the scrap of paper. "They must be forbidden from this. I do not have the forces to stop Howe should he thrust north. The Royal Navy can protect and carry him as far north as Haverstraw."

"So, we must stop Burgoyne's move south."

Washington nodded.

"But how and where?" Despite his question, Fitzgerald knew the answer.

Both men looked down at the map, and Washington traced his long finger from New York along the North River, stopping at Albany, the small city more than 120 miles north, where the waterway was called the Hudson.

Fitzgerald nervously traced his finger from Montreal south along the Richelieu River, then along the strategic Lake Champlain towards Albany. Before his finger could reach Washington's, it stopped and rested at a point on the southernmost end of Lake Champlain—just north of Lake George.

A cartographer had marked a large star symbolizing a fortress on a small peninsula jutting into the lake. The name was hastily scrawled just next to it, so the black ink had run, blurring the word derived from the Iroquois Indian name for the site - *Ticonderoga*.

***

The Dey House, Preakness, New Jersey

Washington finished his rounds at eight that evening, but instead of heading back to Morristown, he rode south through the Watchung Mountains. The soft evening sun had gone down, and as he entered Preakness, candlelight from a dozen neat buildings lit up the shadows, guiding his way to the Dey House.

He eased back the reins on his white charger and cantered down a lane. His Life Guards and his aide, Alexander Hamilton, nearly lost him on the trail as they struggled to catch up with one of America's most skilled equestrians.

Washington stopped at a small orchard next to the house. He swung from the saddle and walked past an open area where half a dozen tents stood in a neat line. Behind the tents, but almost invisible in the gathering darkness, he saw the shadows of horses, whose presence was confirmed by the smell of sweat and dung.

Washington whispered to Hamilton, "Remain here. I have business to attend. The Life Guard as well. I suspect that our best cavalry troop should provide me enough protection."

Although new to the staff, Hamilton had already become one of Washington's closest aides, rivaling Tench Tilghman.

Hamilton bowed his head graciously. "My regards to Major Tallmadge and Mister Creed."

Tallmadge snapped to attention when Washington entered his room. "Your Excellency!"

"Excuse the sudden and late arrival, Benjamin. Where is Mister Creed?"

"With his men, sir. Is something wrong?"

Washington slid into a chair and removed his heavy leather gloves. "Please ask him to come right away. We need to talk. I have plans for you, for him."

Tallmadge sent an orderly after Creed. While they waited, Washington revealed his plans for the summer. He and Tallmadge went over their plans for the troop. "Your troop will screen the army. But that is just a subterfuge for its real missions."

"Missions, Your Excellency?"

"You will be busy. Patrolling into British-held territory. Recruiting local spies and informants. And all while servicing communications with Colonel Fitzgerald's spy on Long Island – Mister Jons. And his extraordinary spy in New York, 'Mister Smythe'."

The door swung open, and a tall, dark-haired dragoon officer stepped in. Washington stood and grasped his hand. "Ah, Jeremiah, so glad to see you."

A few minutes later, a servant arrived with a bottle of sherry. Washington himself filled their glasses, and after a short toast, they made quick work of the warm golden beverage.

Washington poured a second round and then pulled the map from his vest. "I have little time for discussion tonight, but I felt it necessary to alert you both. Mister Creed must be dispatched on a mission of the utmost urgency and danger."

Creed smiled. "And that would be unlike what previous missions Your Excellency has seen fit to give me?"

Tallmadge's eyes widened at Creed's flip remark, but Washington returned the smile.

"Point well taken, young man. But this is different. You are to go to Canada."

"Canada?" Creed and Tallmadge burst the word out together.

"Yes, Canada. To observe and report on a new British army said to be forming there. It is the belief of both our good colonel and me that Howe's army poses a mortal threat to the rebellion."

Creed and Tallmadge both nodded.

"However, some in Congress are concerned with the northern front, and I am under increasing pressure to ascertain the level of danger from that quarter. So it is with great regret that I relieve myself of your good services and send you to Canada to observe Burgoyne's army."

"Observe, sir?" Creed asked.

"You must learn its strengths and weaknesses. More importantly, you must learn its objectives. Will it take Albany and link with Howe? Or will it turn east and try a *coups de main* on Boston?"

"Something tells me you already know the answer to that, Your Excellency," Tallmadge said.

"Very perceptive, Major Tallmadge. Colonel Fitzgerald and I have our suspicions. But we need confirmation. I have to decide whether the army needs to defend along a wide front, march to block Howe's advance, or...."

"Seize his base of operations in New York when he marches north?" Tallmadge asked. He did not want to lose Creed but realized this was a strategic gambit that overrode his tactical need.

Washington eyed the young officer. "I like the way you think. All options are on the table – for the British and us."

"Assuming I can get close to this army. 'Tis is a difficult task. But sending timely intelligence to you, sir – across hundreds of miles of wilderness. Even with my men, I just don't see how I can."

"You'll learn more about that later. However, for this mission, you must go alone. And

think of this, if you can delay or disrupt this army's advance. The cause would be all the better for it."

Creed's eyes widened.

Tallmadge could see he was overwhelmed by the scheme.

Creed rubbed his chin nervously. "'Tis truly a wonderful thing to have His Excellency's trust. But how can I...."

Washington put a finger to his lips. "You'll receive detailed instructions from Colonel Fitzgerald."

Creed and Tallmadge each looked incredulously at their commander-in-chief. For a while, neither spoke.

Finally, Creed broke the silence. "When do I leave?"

Washington twisted his gloves in his hands and smiled grimly. "Tomorrow night would not be too soon."

Chapter 3

The *Citadelle*, Quebec, Canada, May 1777

General Guy Carleton, British Governor and commander of His Majesty's forces in Canada, looked out the large bay window of the castle that served as his headquarters.

Spring in Canada brought sound, light, and warmth to the dark and frozen colony. The sun's strengthening rays slowly turned the white landscape green as the long winter's ice floes quickly crackled, snapped, and finally cracked with a cannon-like *boom*. The large, shimmering sheets broke apart to begin the long journey toward the Atlantic.

In the dim morning light, still shrouded in mist, he could see the Saint Lawrence River's cold waters cascading over the rocks in a white foam that embraced the small islands dotting the waterway more than 300 feet below.

Carleton mused on what spring might bring. Since the failed rebel assault on Canada in 1775, the north had become a quiet front. His counterstroke across Lake Champlain was checked by the strange appearance of the American Brigadier General Benedict Arnold, who had recovered from his wounds. To Carleton's dismay, the mad rebel had sufficiently damaged the British and caused them to settle near Trois Rivieres on the south bank of the St. Lawrence.

Carleton had nary a word of praise from London, despite the repulse of what could have been the loss of a hard-won quarter of the realm. *Wolfe may have won Canada, but I damned well saved it.*

And what of Howe? If not for the exploits of the Loyalist Captain McKay, he might not have learned of Howe's victory over Washington on Long Island or his taking of New York and New Jersey. The actions at Trenton and Princeton were but skirmishes compared to those confined by the frozen Canadian winter.

A servant gently pushed the door open. "Sir, your breakfast is served."

Behind the servant strode two *Habitants*, local French Canadians called *Quebecois*. An older man carried a platter of cheese, ham, bread, and assorted jams. The other was a young man with straw-colored hair and disheveled. Carleton focused on him because he brought the morning beverages – a pot of warm cocoa and a bottle of cold apple brandy.

Carleton glanced down on the river and wrapped his nightgown tightly to ward off the morning chill. "Very well, Claude, place the breakfast on the table. I will serve myself."

Claude bowed slightly. "As you wish, *monsieur*."

Then, it caught Carleton's eye. The winter freeze had begun to give way to an early spring thaw, making travel on the mighty seaway more hazardous than usual – a small flotilla of boats fighting the rushing ice floes careening downstream, taking everything with them. However, what caught his attention was a large galley flying the flag of a British general officer in command.

Carleton tugged at the lace cord, and a bell clanged. He would need his manservant to dress him appropriately to receive his visitor.

***

Later that morning, playwright and Major General John Burgoyne, from Sutton in Bedfordshire, strutted into Carleton's office waving a paper signed by Lord George Germain. Carleton's stomach turned, and his chest heaved as he read the orders appointing Burgoyne commander-in-chief of all forces in Canada. That meant he had to provide Burgoyne with all deemed necessary to invade New York.

Although he had little knowledge of the political and military maneuvers that swirled about him, his worst fears were realized. He was paying the price for the ignorance of his isolation. *This damned upstart had wrested control from me.*

Carleton knew Burgoyne all too well — a charming man who moved through the stage, back bench, battlefield, and boudoir with ease. An accomplished playwright and Member of Parliament, Burgoyne had friends everywhere. Unsurprisingly, the widower in his mid-fifties maintained an open relationship with his mistress, opera singer, and courtesan Susan Caufield.

Burgoyne had left Canada after Carleton's campaign into New York fizzled out the previous year. However, the slick Burgoyne escaped recrimination and had set himself up as the savior of the north. *Why, he's more than a rogue. He's a blackguard!*

Carleton folded the paper and roughly placed it in Burgoyne's palm. "So, it seems I have no choice but to support your every desire, eh, Johnny? Well played by the playwright. Or should I say well politicked by the politico?"

Burgoyne sniffed. "Let's say George wants a different approach. Your steady hand here while I sally forth. I incur all the risks, Guy. If I succeed, that is, when I succeed, we share the laurels. If I fail, although hardly likely, I am to blame."

Carleton knew Burgoyne would do everything to minimize his role in the victory but maximize it in failure. "This is a bold scheme, Johnny. It's one thing to slash across the lake. But to go on to Albany...."

"Yes, but the other two prongs are the key ingredient. Barry will cross Lake Ontario and descend on the rebels from the west. Howe will come up from the south."

"Barry Saint Leger should never have been promoted above the rank of captain. And you think Billy Howe will subordinate his role to you? Fantasy, I should say. Pure fantasy."

"George assures me he has given Howe strict orders to cooperate in this venture. It is, withal, our best hope at a victory this year. Perhaps forever. Fresh regiments are coming right behind me. Good German troops under von Riedesel are not the least of them. All totaled, I should have well over five thousand in hand by June."

Carleton frowned. "For this to work, you will need boats, porters, guides, and supplies. Supplies did me in last season."

Burgoyne smiled boyishly. "Ah, that is where you come in, Guy. I am not much at logistical planning, as you know. Grand strategy, bold maneuver, and heroic battle suit me better. Why, I might write a play about all this. I will guarantee you a prominent role." He threw back his head in laughter.

Carleton reddened. "Johnny, you will face the rebels across hundreds of miles of hostile wilderness. Supplying a large force will be almost impossible. These rebels proved resilient, and if what I know of the past few months is true, they have shown they can fight."

"I am going to recruit from the savages. That should check their ardor somewhat. Most will accompany Barry out west, but I plan on a sizeable body of them to serve as my 'light cavalry' in the forests. I started in the light cavalry, as you know. I am quite adept at deploying them."

Carleton grimaced and tightened his fingers on the arms of his chair. "Which tribes do you plan to draw on? Using the savages is a two-edged tomahawk blade, you know. Controlling them might present a problem."

Burgoyne chuckled. "Tribes? Iroquois mostly, I suppose. They make the best fighters. Control a problem? Not for your master politician and playwright. They say the savages have a thing for the dramatic. I intend to exploit that."

Carleton twisted his lips into a sneer. "The world may be your stage, Johnny, but not the North American forests. In any event, it seems I must do what I can to assist."

***

The Dunning House, New York

Lady Dunning tilted the teapot slowly, bending just enough to allow the gold heart adorning her *décolleté* to dangle before her guests. Its finely polished veneer sparkled against the late afternoon sunlight with a dazzling effect that was not diminished by its fleshy backdrop.

The two British officers noted her display with satisfaction. Lady Dunning knew how to entertain with just the right mix of refreshment, good talk, and titillation that never quite crossed the bounds of decorum. She was a lady, after all.

"Quite nice, milady, quite nice indeed," murmured Lieutenant Colonel Sir Horace Stilton, second in command of the New York garrison regiment.

"I am so glad it meets your approbation, Sir Horace," she replied demurely.

"Oh yes, the tea is excellent as well," Stilton replied dryly.

Major Sandy Drummond saw Lady Dunning blush at his double entendre but managed an approving smile at one of the most powerful men in the city.

Drummond knew Stilton stood out from the pack for many reasons, not the least of which was his birth and early years spent on the continent. Son of a retired colonel and a large landholder, Stilton lived as a youth in New York before embarking on a military career in the British army, which earned him rapid promotion.

The small group of New York notables laughed. Edmund Laseby, banker and land speculator, showed just a twinge of jealousy. Everyone knew he had had his eye on the comeliest widow in New York.

Drummond watched Laseby's discomfort with interest. *He's upset because the uniform had begun to break the reticent lady's usual calm.*

But Laseby laughed along. Drummond's file pegged Laseby as a passionate Tory and Loyalist who could never serve in uniform due to age and frequent bouts of gout. He used his considerable wealth to fund several battalions and support the crown in any way he could.

"I believe Sir Horace is referring to your pendant…it shines so in the twilight," Laseby said.

Nobody laughed.

"I was rather referring to the pendant's lovely backdrop," said Stilton.

Everyone laughed again. Although clearly frustrated, Laseby smiled along.

"What news from home have you for us, Sir Horace?" Laseby asked. Although born in New York, Laseby always considered England home.

Stilton sipped the tea. "Nothing good, I can assure you."

Drummond bit his lip. Stilton had the habit of talking too much at social events. As Lord William Howe's chief of intelligence, this caused Drummond quite a bit of discomfort.

Lady Dunning smiled pleasantly. "Surely you don't mean that? Is there plague or famine? Or was high society too much for you?"

Everyone laughed but Laseby, who drew a handkerchief and wiped the beads of sweat from his wrinkled brow.

Drummond breathed a sigh of relief. *Perhaps Stilton will stick to a recount of the latest social gossip.*

He did not.

"Seems Johnny Burgoyne got himself in with George Germain and the other George. Troops we hoped for our use here have been diverted to the north."

"New England?" Laseby asked.

"No, Canada," replied Stilton smugly.

Drummond cursed silently. *Too many of these officers placed their personal agendas above the security of His Majesty's forces.* Hours of painstaking work could be thrust aside to impress an associate, lover, or anyone who might benefit them.

"Or not," Drummond interjected. "Perhaps another try at the Carolinas is in the offing." Sir Henry Clinton had led an ill-fated attempt on South Carolina that the rebels repulsed. Drummond took no small pleasure at throwing the name out, but it forced Stilton to change the subject.

Stilton bristled. "I think we have already spent too much time discussing what might and might not happen, Sandy. Lady Dunning, I should like to learn more about the ball this Saturday."

All knew he served with less than distinction under General Henry Clinton during that campaign—a fact he constantly strove to deflect.

However, now Laseby had added to Stilton's discomfort. "The Carolinas are a backwater, the attack there a mere diversion. Better we allow the rebels to check us, Horace. Canada makes sense as a springboard to New York or New England. The only question is which."

Drummond raised his eyes. Edmund Laseby did not become a rich man through mere luck or chicanery. He was canny and bold. In one statement, he put down Stilton's patron, Clinton, while simultaneously exonerating, if not praising him.

Drummond decided on the offensive. "How would you approach the problem, Mister Laseby?"

Laseby smiled. "Well, Major, a strike south in either direction is fraught with perils. Both require crossing the St. Lawrence, and both have hundreds of miles of mountainous wilderness between Canada and any civilized outpost. Savages still live in considerable numbers along both approaches as well. The campaign season in the north is much shorter than down here."

Drummond rubbed his knee. His wound from Long Island still throbbed. "Do either pose a significant advantage?"

Laseby nodded. "A New England thrust would have Boston as its likely objective. The entire Massachusetts area is awash in some of the most rabid rebels. Even if taken, Boston as an objective puts us at the same as in seventy-five."

In 1775, a great militia army surrounded the British in Boston and kept them pinned there until they hastily evacuated by sea to Halifax, Nova Scotia.

"So, Edmund, you favor our good New York?" Lady Dunning asked.

Laseby beamed with satisfaction when she responded to his remarks. "Yes, milady. The populace is friendlier, including the Indians. And there are good waterways, reaching north to south, enabling the flow of supplies. Even with the shorter campaign season, there are reasonable objectives such as the rebel fort at Ticonderoga, another south of Lake George, and Albany."

Drummond was impressed. It seemed as if the man had read his letter to General Howe.

Lady Dunning batted her eyes. "Albany? Yes, my late husband visited there several times. Shipping interests. A dreary Dutch town on the river."

Laseby placed his teacup on his knee. "Indeed, milady. The rebel base is still strongest in New England. But taking Albany concurrent with a thrust up the Hudson would split the colonies, severing New England from New York and the Jerseys. This would isolate them. Deny the beast of rebellion its moral sustenance, and it will surely wither and die on its own."

Stilton guffawed. "A useless gambit…unless General Howe proceeds north. He may, however, have other plans."

Drummond threw an ugly glance at him. He had already advised Howe that his best opportunity would be a move north in the spring, with or without a thrust from Canada. Drummond's advice was *sub rosa* and *ex officio*, as he was now an intelligence officer, not a line officer. *Could Stilton be intimating otherwise?*

Laseby shook his head, his heavy jowls wiggling like fresh liver. "Only a madman would do otherwise. If I were younger, I would take a commission and convince him of the correct course of action."

Stilton smiled churlishly. "If you did that, sir, you would have to learn to sit a horse properly and lead good men into battle. Such skills are not bought outright but gained through years of tough campaigning."

Laseby's eyes bulged, and his face reddened.

He began to mouth a response, but Lady Dunning spoke. "I am sure Edmund would attain the prerequisite skills in months, not years. But enough of this talk, gentlemen. Will you attend General Howe's ball this Saturday?"

Laseby's face lit up. "Indeed, milady, in fact, I am hosting him."

***

The Beekman House, New York

Klara Stumpf smiled politely at the young subaltern who begged her to dance for the third time. He seemed friendly enough. She also found him attractive. Still, she glanced at Sandy Drummond, her "benefactor." Klara never knew if the major would react negatively to a certain friendship, so she acted coy until she received a signal from him.

Drummond encouraged her to bestow her favors on his superiors. General Clinton danced with her twice. His suggestive manner made her ill at ease, but General Howe, the commander-in-chief, proved a gentleman. It was apparent that his affections lay with Missus Elizabeth Loring.

"I am so sorry, lieutenant, I am quite fatigued," Klara replied.

"Well, I shall persist, Miss Stumpf. You have not seen the last of Stephen Whittington."

Her smile in response did not show the disappointment she felt. The subaltern seemed a likely young man. "And I am sure a future request will fall on more accommodating ears, sir."

"One would hope, Miss Stumpf, although a rejection from you pleases far more than an acceptance from a dozen other ladies." He bowed gracefully and turned away.

Klara sighed.

Drummond grabbed her firmly by the elbow. "Another potential beau, Klara? Do not fret. When the time is right, I will find you a suitable prospect. But not that lad."

The band struck up again—four musicians from the 27th Regiment of Foot dressed in reversed tunics of buff with scarlet turnbacks. One was playing the oboe, another the French horn, and the other two ran bows expertly across well-tuned violins.

General Howe slipped his arm through Elizabeth Loring's and led the party onto the dance floor. Klara could see Loring bedazzling with jewels and a revealing gown, gazing intensely at her partner, outfitted in his scarlet uniform with enough gold, lace, and silver to match her. Slowly, they began the dance's twists, twirls, and bows.

Soon, a group of four couples joined in. They all lined up, bowed deeply, and crossed hands. The musicians struck up a slow reel, and the line began its procession as they whirled to the music.

"General Howe has danced the minuet and jig with Missus Loring. A cotillion should follow," Drummond murmured. "Maybe I should find you a suitable partner for that, Klara."

Klara's stomach sank. She knew he would select someone connected or influential. Worse, she knew her partner would likely not be to her taste. He released her and disappeared into one of the side rooms where the bachelors congregated.

Klara watched from afar as Lady Dunning flirted with several men in uniform. Then she saw a young woman slip through the doorway. Anyone not dancing turned their heads toward her and gazed in various states of admiration, jealousy, or longing. And why not, as this was the most beautiful woman Klara had seen since coming to New York as Drummond's "ward." The most beautiful she had ever seen. And she was sure no one at the ball had ever seen.

***

Emily Stanley stood a moment, taking in the crowd just as they seemed to soak her in. She was used to it. But it always made her uncomfortable and seemed somehow immodest.

She wore a dark green gown with just enough silk and brocade to look elegant. Her jewelry was subtle, and her dark honey hair was casually tossed up without any powder or wig, topped with a tiara of tiny spring flowers. Her tall stature and high cheekbones almost resembled that of a native princess, except her skin shone with a cream hue instead of a coppery tone. Her beautiful ocean-green eyes captivated both men and women, but her modest and gracious demeanor set her apart.

It didn't take long for Lady Dunning to draw Emily into her circle of admirers. Soon, several officers of different ages gathered around her. Like schoolboys, each tried to impress her with his importance to the Army, family connections, or wealth.

Emily nodded and smiled but hesitated before accepting offers to dance and politely declined one or two suggestions of an invitation. In the latter case, she skillfully concealed her disgust so that all her would-be suitors left with the best possible impression of this most beautiful and charming woman.

"My, those fine officers better thank their stars you are not one of Mister Washington's generals," Lady Dunning said with evident admiration.

"Whatever do you mean, milady?" Emily replied.

"You checked their every advance despite an abundance of numbers, my dear," Lady Dunning remarked with a twinkle in her eye.

Emily laughed. "However, they are professionals and, although quite gallant, are much too military in their etiquette. They withdraw tactically rather than risk an outright defeat."

"Well, dear, your dress is stunning. From Paris?"

She could see Lady Dunning missed her point. Before she could reply, Edmund Laseby joined in. "My dear Emily, your arrival has enhanced the evening for all of us. Where is your father tonight?"

"At the hospital, Mister Laseby. Disease takes no holiday. He already sent regrets to General Howe."

Laseby flashed a smile. "No matter. His lovely daughter is no small consolation. Would you grace me with a dance when your card is free?"

Emily bowed her head. "Indeed, sir. I would be delighted. It seems I am free now if it is all right with Lady Dunning."

Laseby turned to Lady Dunning. "With your permission, of course, milady."

Lady Dunning nodded. Laseby took Emily's arm, and they cued up for the next dance.

***

Lady Dunning observed carefully as Emily and Laseby bowed and intertwined their fingers to begin the dance.

Sandy Drummond sidled up beside her and whispered. "If I did not know better, I'd say milady is jealous."

"But you know better, don't you, Sandy?"

"I know Missus Loring wants to meet the young lady. She likes to size up her possible competition."

She clasped her hands and looked pensively. "In William Howe's case, she has none. It is a wonder what hold she has over the general. Many of us blame her for his lassitude. Why, some have opined that she is Washington's best weapon."

Drummond grinned lasciviously. "In that case, General Howe has been wounded many times. But no, his caution is of his own making, and I can assure you that she and her husband are the most loyal subjects."

She grinned coyly and tapped playfully on Drummond's chest. "Apropos belles and balls, when will you let our young Klara fly, Sandy? The poor girl needs her freedom. With so many eligible men about."

His eyes narrowed in a dark glare. "I do this for her protection. Far too many of our officers would seduce a pretty colonial girl and then abandon her at conflict's end."

Lady Dunning's face darkened at his last comment, and she turned away. He could see he had struck a nerve.

***

The phaeton rolled down the lane from the Beekman House at midnight. Emily pondered the night's work as the wheels rattled along the ruts. She had tolerated the evening. After her dance with Laseby, the pack of youngbloods descended on her once more. She agreed to dance with but two. Her choices seemed strange to the throng, who expected her to pick from the high rank or the highborn. She did neither.

The first was an artillery captain who had little money and few connections. However, Captain Richard Hawkins oversaw Howe's ordnance and artificers. He knew the layout of tons of shot and powder, without which the army could not fight. Hawkins was a rare officer who earned his advancement through merit and hard work. Ignored by his peers, he worked long and hard to ensure the army's valuable munitions were safe, secure, and available.

Her other partner was, strangely, an officer of the 17th Light Dragoons named Robin Cheatham. Cheatham, who went by Robbie, was an experienced veteran of little connection beyond his immediate military circle. Neither taciturn nor expansive, Cheatham limited his talk to the niceties of life in New York, such as they were.

However, she did ascertain that his troop had patrol duties north of the city and that his base was near the village of White Plains.

Sometime after midnight, the phaeton pulled up to the Stanley House. *The house should be dark at this hour.* She noticed a light burning in the parlor. *Did Nancy wait up? Has a boarder fallen asleep while reading in the parlor?* She pulled gently on the latch and swung her legs out of the cab.

Emily's elegant slippers had barely touched the ground when the phaeton sped off. As she turned, a pair of strong arms circled her waist and lifted her off her feet.

A familiar voice blew softly in her ear. "'Tis dangerous in these parts at night. A lass should not be returning at such a late hour without a proper escort."

Startled, Emily twisted around and looked straight into the face she would recognize on even the darkest night.

"Jeremi..."

His fingers touched her lips, silencing them. She stared up into his dark eyes, unsure what to think, her heart racing with excitement. Emily was both thrilled and dismayed at his presence, for she knew it meant there was dark business about. *Could Colonel Fitzgerald have told him of my role?*

Creed whispered, "Call me Mister Lawrence, James Lawrence. I am your very newest lodger. Traveling north to raise a Tory company to fight the rebels."

She wanted to reply, but their lips touched, then touched again before she could utter a word. They pressed into a warm embrace the third time that seemed to last forever.

When at length they separated, they stood looking at each other. Her heart was pounding. Finally, she spoke, "I am not so sure it was wise to come here, Jere... I mean, Mister Lawrence. After all..."

He took her in his arms again and kissed her passionately. When they finally paused, Emily glanced about to see if someone might be watching. However, only the faint clicking of crickets broke the night's stillness.

She wondered if she could hide her delight. "Nancy has assigned me a room, which I share with a rather corpulent medical officer."

Emily smiled. "Captain Hargrove. A friend and colleague of my father. Perhaps I can use my influence to find you better accommodations."

***

General Howe also returned late from his gala. However, the commander-in-chief of all British forces in North America did not take a cab or go home alone. As he entered his bedroom, he was accompanied by one of the most beautiful women on the continent, Missus Joshua Loring. Elizabeth Loring was the wife of an enthusiastic Loyalist who used her connection to the generalissimo to secure a lucrative position as head of the commissary for prisoners of war.

Fortunately for all, the mother of two took an immediate liking to the general and enjoyed his company. Her husband's duties took him far enough away for her to socialize with the general's inner circle and bask in New York society's light.

Her gown floated to the floor, and she slipped from her petticoat and stockings in the dark. A butler had turned down the general's bed but, on his orders, had not lit a candle or lamp. Their conversation drifted to Howe's plans for the spring and summer campaigns. He liked talking about military affairs with this young woman. It was something he could never do with his wife back in England.

She removed his wig, and her gentle fingers stroked the back of his neck. "All the talk tonight was of Johnny Burgoyne, William. Do you fear he might eclipse your sun?"

Howe laughed. "Anything is possible, dear. Seriously, I expect little rivalry from that quarter."

"*Rivington's Gazette* seemed very sanguine on his chances."

Howe laughed harder. "They are paid good silver to favor our cause. But good for him, then. However, I have some influence on the gazette's publisher, James Rivington. It is in my interest that eyes turn north. All the more to my advantage when I seize the rebel capital."

"Philadelphia? Really, William? You told me that your directions from Lord Germain were to support General Burgoyne."

Her fingers dug into his shoulder muscles, and he felt tingling down his spine.

"Yes, but he left it to me, dear Bess, to decide how I support him. Since that matter was left to my discretion, I say a thrust at the rebel capital will draw attention from him."

She nibbled at his ear. "Or the other way around? You do want full credit for ending this nonsense."

Howe paused, smiled, and looked at her. "You amaze me, dear Bess."

Chapter 4

Montréal, Canada, May 1777

With a martial flourish, the teams of attendants cranked open the room's long windows, which stretched from the ceiling to the floor. A rush of fresh spring air cleansed the room. General Burgoyne winced as the morning light stabbed his still weary pupils into submission. He had dozed at his desk, and his ink jar had spilled, staining the sleeves of his evening jacket with the black ooze. However, the final draft of the plans for the invasion was untouched. He smiled — a *good omen*.

An amateur playwright and man of letters, Burgoyne knew that even the author's best script needed constant polishing. Once the curtain rose, the director had to improvise and guide the players' every performance.

Burgoyne's problem was at the heart of his plan, which required three bodies of men separated by hundreds of miles of wilderness to orchestrate their efforts in a scheme simple in the telling but complex in executing. But unlike a play, once the campaign started, there would be little opportunity to adjust. So, his plan needed to be something that required little interference.

An attendant placed a tray on the table, and Burgoyne splashed its cold water on his face. "Bring some tea, Justin. And a few scones, if there are any left. "

"Yes, sir. Would you like some cold meats as well?"

"That would be nice. Bring extra and ask Colonel Sinclair to see me."

Lazarus Sinclair, the Adjutant General, directed Burgoyne's staff. Sinclair's appearance deceived those who did not know him well. He was a tall, lanky man with a fussy air about him. He understood logistics and the art of maneuver – two subjects under-appreciated by his peers. He had an annoying twitch, which resulted from a bomb that exploded before him as he led a company of forlorn hope against a French redoubt. Burgoyne relied on him for nearly everything.

A half-hour later, Sinclair stepped into the room.

"Lazarus, I have written my draft ideas for the campaign. I would like to discuss them with you, who shall be privileged to see they are carried out." Burgoyne smiled mischievously.

Many would chafe at being a staff work dog, but Sinclair reveled in it. "Very well, sir. Let's have a look."

Burgoyne related his plan for a triple thrust to split the colonies - linking three armies at the headwaters of the North River, as the Hudson was then called.

"Our force of 8,000 from Montreal shall head south along the Richelieu and make camp at the shores of Lake Champlain – whence we shall sail south and seize Ticonderoga as a springboard for second water thrust down Lake George and onto the Hudson."

Sinclair read the notes and nodded pensively. "I have already ordered as many vessels as these Canadians have to support our logistics by water. With any luck, we should make it to the river by summer's end."

Burgoyne sipped at his tea. "Barry St. Leger with his Loyalists and Indian allies should be within striking distance of Albany."

"Indeed, the ground favors an eastward march along the Mohawk," Sinclair said.

"The last and final piece is coordinating General Howe's part in this," Burgoyne spoke it with less confidence than usual.

Sinclair shook his head and ran his fingers through his hair. "I have made some calculations, sir. He has over twenty-four thousand men. If he sends a mere ten thousand north, we can spring the trap and cut the North River."

Burgoyne grew excited. "Precisely! Why even half that number would make the victory complete and decisive."

"Yes, five thousand might do it. However, maintaining our supply line is the key. And support from the natives, both red and white, is as important as support from General Howe," Sinclair said.

Burgoyne was glad to have Sinclair handle details for him. "I admitted as much to Lord Carleton. Where are you on that effort?"

"I have about half of what I need, but we are scouring for volunteers. I hear they are coming from across the colonies."

Burgoyne frowned. "Would General Howe be as confident of my success as the colonials and the savages? How long before all preparations are in order?"

Sinclair looked up from the papers. "A few weeks should do it, sir. One more convoy of troops is due from Europe. Savages are gathering. Canadians and Loyal Americans are forming. Supply craft loaded. Our only failing is a firm commitment from General Howe and...." Sinclair shuffled the papers as if he expected to find something he knew was not there.

Burgoyne cocked his head. "And what, Lazarus? It seems you have accounted for everything."

Sinclair looked at Burgoyne forlornly. "We could use some good maps, sir."

Burgoyne smiled. "Always a problem in America. Never fear. Our local allies and savages shall guide us. Once on the water, we sail south with the afternoon sun on our right shoulder, Lazarus. You worry about transport and supply. I'll take care of the rest."

***

The Stanley House, New York

The smell of bacon frying and freshly brewed coffee woke Creed from a deep sleep. He faintly heard the clinking of utensils and male voices bantering amiably. *Breakfast in the Stanley dining room.*

Creed quickly sprang from the bed and, finding a washbowl with soap, did his best to clean himself, shave, and tie his dark hair back in a queue. He unfolded a scarlet coat from his bag with dark blue cuffs and trim, white breeches, and black stockings. In minutes, he had dressed into his new *persona*, that of Captain James Lawrence of the Royal Americans.

Fitzgerald had read a small recruiting blurb in Rivington's indicating that a certain Captain James Lawrence would sail to Canada via New York to help recruit a 4th battalion of the Royal American Regiment. The blurb stated the real Lawrence would arrive in the fall, but Fitzgerald thought an early arrival would raise few flags and give Creed enough cover and opportunity to reach the city and meet up with Mister Jons. Jons would help him get to Canada. As a gamble, he had a suitable uniform for Creed.

Creed clambered down the staircase a few minutes later and entered the dining room. He saw Emily pouring coffee for a group of men sitting around the table. She wore a simple cream-colored dress with a crisp white linen apron and headcover. The belle of the ball had transformed herself into a no-nonsense proprietress, but the practical attire only highlighted her good looks. The admiring glances of her guests showed they appreciated her charms as much as her crumpets.

"Good morning, sir." She beamed at Creed. "Gentlemen, may I introduce our newest boarder, Captain James Lawrence?"

A round of harrumphs greeted Creed, who smiled pleasantly and took the last empty chair. Emily placed a platter of buckwheat cakes before him. He swore that she winked for a second, but he turned his head away to avoid any hint of their familiarity.

An officer in the dark blue coat of the artillery waved his fork expansively. "What exactly brings the Royal American Regiment to New York? Are we to be reinforced for General Howe's spring offensive?"

Creed paused. The man had not introduced himself, and he suspected a trap.

"Perhaps." Creed dug into a cake with his fork. "Could you please pass the butter?"

A civilian gentleman who called himself Absher spoke up. "Now, now. You have not introduced yourself to our guest, Jellicoe, yet you are already interrogating him. I read Captain Lawrence's visit in Rivington's, although I believe he was scheduled for the fall."

Creed sipped at his coffee. "That post was a ruse to fool the rebel spies. Plans have changed. Exigencies of war, you know. I am to head north immediately to recruit a company for attachment to General Burgoyne. With luck, the war will be over by the fall."

The men murmured their assent.

Jellicoe turned his head. "Just one company? Hardly worth it, I'd say."

Creed placed his cup on its saucer. "A gesture, to be sure. But someone at Horse Guards thought it a good idea to recruit some Loyal Americans and Canadians into the regiment."

"Why that?" Absher asked.

Creed swallowed a mouthful of cakes. "For some time, all its recruiting has been in Ireland and the continent. Lost its 'Americanness,' they say. A 4th Battalion will form over the next few months."

"So, this will be its First Company," Absher mused.

Creed nodded with a smile. His cover story seemed to take hold. "The thinking is…experience with General Burgoyne will provide the battalion with one crack unit."

"Bah, hardly spit in the ocean." Jellicoe squawked.

Creed shrugged matter-of-factly. "A start."

"Why, but even you admit the fighting will be over by the time you complete your mission," replied Jellicoe.

A major of infantry who had sat silently till then joined the discussion. "One would hope so, Jellicoe. But after all, General Howe is still in overall command."

Creed barely smiled, but the others broke into heavy laughter and guffaws. Howe's tendency to act slowly and deliberately had become a subject of great humor among even his admirers.

Absher waved his fork at the major. "Touché, Haddix! I'm sorry, Lawrence. This is Major Donald Haddix, our Quartermaster."

"*Attached* to the Quartermaster, if you please, Mister Absher." Haddix turned to Creed. "I am with the 27th Foot."

Creed smiled. "Ah, the Inniskillens! A fine regiment indeed. Acquitted themselves well on Long Island, so I understand. Except perhaps their grenadiers…."

Haddix looked at him in exasperation. "It took five companies of rebels to stop their advance, which, had it continued, might have ended the war right there."

Creed raised his eyes. "'Tis a shame they did not."

The grenadier company of the Inniskillens was routed by Creed's small band of desperate Marylanders, but he knew no official account would ever include that fact. As was his way, he finished his meal in a hurry and excused himself.

As he left, Absher turned to Jellicoe. "Nice chap, but damned odd he would arrive here so early."

Haddix sniffed. "Not surprising to me he'd be on his mission quicker than reported."

"Why do you say that?" Absher asked.

"His regiment is not yet under General Howe's command…."

Chuckles erupted around the table.

An hour after breakfast, Creed saw Emily in the parlor. He fought the urge to take her in his arms. Instead, he bowed courteously. "Thank you for the wonderful breakfast, Ma'am."

Her smile melted him. "I shall tell the cook you enjoyed it, Captain Lawrence. Will you join us for dinner?"

"No, ma'am. I have business that will keep me late."

She eyed him knowingly. "Then I'll save some cold supper for you. I shall serve it myself."

"That would be most appreciated, ma'am, but I wouldn't want to trouble you."

"No trouble at all, Captain. We do it often. Many of our guests work into the late hours these days. I suppose it's the war."

"Undoubtedly. I should be back by ten."

"Where are you off to?"

"I have to meet a gentleman to find transportation north. He is over in Brooklyn. Keeps a ship there in the service of His Majesty."

"Oh, really, what is the ship's name?"

"I believe they call it the *Red Hen*."

***

Guldener Adler, **Brooklyn, New York,**

The back of Creed's chair scraped the wall. He looked around the smoke-filled taproom, carefully observing the crowd. The large taproom was filled with uniformed men serving His Majesty. Most seemed to be waiting for or recovering from the attention of the dozen women who worked for its notorious owner, Coos Dederick. The Guldener Adler hadn't changed much since he last crossed its threshold.

Despite the bright noon sunshine, the room was dark and smoky, making it difficult to read the man's face across from him. Not that it mattered. A complex and mysterious character, Cornelius Foch, had come through for him once before. But those were different times. The question was, could he come through again?

"You seem different from our last meeting, Captain Lawrence."

Foch's clipped Dutch accent somehow grated on Creed, but he smiled. "My allegiance has changed."

Foch puffed on his pipe. "You also wore a red uniform last time, although it seems you have been promoted. From mere soldier to officer."

Creed laughed. "*Touche' Meen Heer*. Your insight is excellent. That is one reason why I again sought you out."

Foch had helped Creed and his men escape from British-occupied Brooklyn in the summer of 1776. They had switched uniforms with three renegade British soldiers to blend into the confusion caused by the occupying forces. The British soldiers lay nearby in an unmarked grave.

"Ah, here comes the lovely Griet with our drinks," said Foch.

A serving girl placed two tankards of ale and two glasses of crystal-clear liquid before them. Her dark hair and well-rounded figure looked vaguely familiar to Creed. She eyed him with equal curiosity. He silently thanked God for the *Adler's* midday gloom.

Foch gave her a tweak of the buttocks. "Do not linger among your guests, Griet. It is bad for business. I might report you to Coos."

Griet's dark face whitened visibly at the mention of the name, and she whisked back to the kitchen with a swirl of her cotton skirts.

Dederick owned several taverns, ordinaries, and the like that also served as places of illicit entertainment. He was a well-known and infamous character both on Long Island and the Island of New York.

Foch arched a brow. "Why, you know this girl?"

Creed took a swallow of his ale. "Yes, I had an 'assignation' with Griet in a room right up the stairs. She is more than a waitress."

Creed did not tell him that he had so enthralled her that she provided him with vital information on the British that led him to surmise the launching point for their invasion of New York.

"I suppose if she doesn't recognize me, nobody else will."

Foch shook his head. "Always expect you will be caught at the next turn. It keeps your senses sharpened, and it may be true."

"That's how you have survived this war?"

Foch tilted his head back. "Ha! Not just this war, my friend."

Creed knew better than to ask further.

Foch took a long draught of his ale and then wiped the foam from his mustache with the back of his hand. "So, what is the nature of the business you wish to engage me in?"

"Transport north by ship."

Foch's face was impassive. "I see. And how large a ship do you require? Do I move people or contraband?"

"I need the *Red Hen*, although I cannot be specific about the cargo."

Foch's eyes widened, and he inhaled a soft whistle. "The *Red Hen* is my flagship, office, and home. I rarely use it for long sails these days. I prefer using my longboats and barges to move supplies for the British forces."

"I need it, *Mijneer* Foch."

Foch whistled softly. "This must be serious business then."

"Whenever I come to this town, it is serious business, *Meen Heer*."

"*Ja*. For our mutual friend to send you back here to engage my assistance and jeopardize what I am already doing for him."

"Your purse has suffered little from your service, *Meen Heer*. And in return, you have friends on both sides of the river, so to speak."

Foch glanced down, then raised his eyes until they locked on Creed. "Meet me at the *Red Hen* in two hours. We can talk more discreetly there." The grizzled sailor jerked back his head, downed his shot of *genever*, a potent Dutch gin, and slipped out the back door.

***

The Stanley House

The hands of the hallway clock were closing on midnight when Creed returned. His meeting at the *Red Hen* proved productive. Now the success of his venture depended solely upon the mysterious smuggler's generosity and loyalty.

Foch had agreed to gather volunteers for Creed's muster. There were still many disgruntled and unemployed men on Long Island, many of whom owed Foch favors. Others might be Loyalists, eager for adventure and loot. It didn't matter, since this group would have minimal equipment and no training. He could provide the training. He's experienced at training raw recruits. And, in a way, an enthusiastic but untrained band of colonial volunteers wouldn't raise British suspicion. Instead, regardless of their loyalty, it would play into their prejudices against the Americans.

He stepped softly down the hallway. A glance into the parlor revealed Emily in the corner chair, her head tilted forward in blissful sleep.

How beautiful she looks. Creed grimaced. He had promised to return by ten. She had waited for him, undoubtedly braving the flirtations and amorous glances of more than one male tenant. He tiptoed into the room, found a pillow, and tucked it neatly under her head. Then, he gently stroked her lips in an impulse he could not resist.

"Jeremiah Creed. I would have hoped by now it would be your lips bidding me good night instead of your fingers." Emily's eyes flickered open, and her lips turned in a mild frown.

He flushed at being caught in a schoolboy move. But with relief and joy, Creed gently took her chin into his hand. He whispered, "The name is Lawrence, darlin'. James Lawrence, but you may call me James."

He kissed her lips. She responded with a passion that never failed to surprise him.

"A few more kisses, and we shall have become engaged," he whispered, only in half jest.

Emily shook her head. "I am sorry, Captain Lawrence, but my heart belongs to a gallant lieutenant who wears a different uniform."

Creed's heart jumped in confusion until he caught her meaning. "Very well, darlin', but please call me James."

He kissed her again. After a passionate embrace, she pulled back and stood up, gathering the strands of her honey-colored hair.

"Well now, Capt – James. We have both had a long day. I trust you found your friend and his?"

Emily bit her lip. Her eyes pointed towards the kitchen, where one of the tenants had come down in his nightshirt.

Creed nodded. "Indeed, madam. In a few days, I should have the first platoon of the battalion ready to move north and join General Burgoyne's forces."

Major Donald Haddix emerged from the kitchen, slurping milk from a tin cup as he entered the parlor in a nightshirt and slippers.

Emily averted her eyes to avoid the sight of him in undress.

"I beg your pardon, Miss Stanley. But I have been waiting quite some time for Captain Lawrence to return. I must speak with him alone."

Emily looked visibly disturbed. "A simple request, sir. Most easily fulfilled." She grabbed her skirt tails and swept from the room with the grace of a high-born lady.

Creed was concerned. But he sat calmly in a winged chair with legs crossed. "'Tis an unusual time to talk, sir. But I am at your disposal."

"Let me get to the point then, Captain Lawrence," replied Haddix. "Your mission is, well, quite unusual. This army here may never strike the rebels. Howe talks a good game. Assurances that he will advance north and join Burgoyne. But I know better."

"And how is that, sir?" Creed's tone hid his interest.

"As Quartermaster, I can assure you Sir William could send no more than three or four thousand up the Hudson. The supplies are not being forwarded up the river as they should."

"So, he is staying here in New York to ride out the campaign season?"

Haddix shook his head. "Not likely. Too much pressure from Lord Germain. No, milord wants it his way. Glory, yes, but as little bloodshed as possible."

Creed found the news astounding. But he suspected a trap. "So, are you suggesting I not take a band of Loyalists north but wait for Howe's eventual move? I would need clearance from...."

"By all means, no. You have your orders and your duty. However, I have a young man I would like to have conscripted into your company. A likely lad whose father died in the great fire and whose mother...."

"Is your mistress?" Creed could not resist the barb.

Haddix hung his head in shame.

"No worries, sir. Perfectly understood. War throws people together as much as tears them apart."

Haddix brightened. "Very astute comment, that last bit. Was that Voltaire?"

Creed shook his head. "No, my uncle Maurice. As fine a man as you'll ever meet."

"What regiment is he with," asked Haddix reflexively.

"An Irish regiment." Creed neglected to mention his uncle was with an Irish regiment in the service of France.

"Ah, the 5th Dragoons, I'll wager. You look like you come from a family of cavalrymen."

Creed ignored the comment. "Now, sir, tell me about this lad of yours...."

***

The next day, a young man of seventeen stood before Creed. He was of medium height and build, with a shock of chestnut hair tied back in a loose queue. He wore a faded blue suit with old but clean cotton stockings and practical shoes. He told Creed his name was Bartholomew Saunders but preferred the name Bart.

Creed had borrowed the library of the Stanley House for last-minute preparations. He had not anticipated taking on someone not selected by Foch, but he wanted to draw no undue suspicion from Haddix. He also decided to see the boy for another reason. Creed felt guilty about the death of the boy's father.

The great New York fire of autumn 1776 resulted from a skirmish between Creed's men and a Loyalist band. The resulting conflagration consumed one-third of the city, killed hundreds, and sent thousands fleeing. The town had not yet recovered from its devastation.

"So, tell me, Bart, why do you want to enlist in the Royal Americans? Aren't the New York Loyalist regiments recruiting? Oliver De Lancey would welcome a stout lad like you."

"Father was a patriot, sir. He had planned to flee the city when the British came. But mother remained loyal to the crown and refused to leave. They argued, but father loved her more than the rebel cause and wouldn't leave her behind."

"Odd, you call him a patriot. Most loyal Britons would say rebel," Creed replied. "Why didn't he join the rebel militia?"

"He was a surgeon and had many patients who required his care in the city. So, he remained. To my utter grief, he died in the great fire last year. He was treating victims with burns too horrible to imagine when a fireball consumed the wooden building he used as a hospital."

"But you escaped unharmed?"

Bart's eyes filled with tears. "I normally assisted him, but mother and father, despite their differences, made common cause over me. They sent me north of the city on a contrived errand to ensure I stayed out of harm's way. I was there when the fire broke out."

The boy spoke with little emotion.

"Well, I suppose there are brave and honorable men on both sides of this struggle. The question is, young man, which side do you favor?"

"I grew up neutral. To bridge my parents' differences and show my affection for them both."

"I see." The boy was hard to gauge. "So why go north now?"

"Going north will get me respite from this city and my father's memory. And I suppose I should favor my mother's side now. After all, she is all I have left."

Creed frowned. "His Majesty does not question the motives of those who enlist. Just their willingness to obey their superiors. Can you do that?"

"I have obeyed parents who had differing views. I can obey your orders, sir. If you will have me."

Creed carefully penned something on the paper before him – the unit roster. "Very well. You'll hold the rank of ensign."

"Ensign?" Bart stammered.

"I can see from your demeanor and manner of speech that your parents raised a lad who would serve as an officer in other circumstances."

Bart bowed. "Thank you, sir."

"We depart at dawn. Meet me at the East Slip not less than ten minutes prior. Bring clothes fit for the field and your musket if you have one."

"I have no weapon, sir."

"I thought as much. Bring what surgical tools and medicines your father taught you to use. They will be worth more to us than a twelve-pound cannon."

***

Creed put the last touches on his work at eight that evening. Hungry, he went to the kitchen. He was delighted to see that the boarders had left some food. There was a plate of fried fish and potatoes.

He was debating whether to dig into a piece of fish when Nancy entered the room.

"Ah, Nancy, I was looking for Miss Stanley. I depart early tomorrow and wish to pay my bill and bid her a fond *farewell*."

Creed smiled, and she returned it with a knowing look. Nancy knew that "Captain Lawrence" was the young rebel officer who first came to their house in the summer of 1776 and then came and went under mysterious circumstances. Creed marveled at her loyalty to Emily. She could quickly turn him in and reap a king's ransom. And by not turning him, she risked the gallows.

Nancy's only motivation was the well-being of her mistress. Although Emily and her father had become more esteemed in British and Loyalist circles, neither would fare well if a rebel were found among their lodgers.

Nancy responded with a wide grin. "Miss Em had to go meet someone, sir."

"Ah, a gentleman admirer, I am sure." Creed's voice cracked just a little.

"Something to do with her father, sir. She should be home soon. Take a seat out front and wait. Meanwhile, let me fix some vittles for you, sir. I'll bring a nice plate of fish, potatoes, and fruit from the garden. There is still some claret on the dining room table as well."

"Thank you, Nancy. You are ever the soldier's keeper."

Nancy arched an eyebrow. "Indeed, sir. But I'm just doing what my mistress would expect."

A few minutes later, Creed sat down for what he knew would be his last good meal before leaving. He could hear the muffled voices of Haddix, Absher, and Jellicoe, sitting on the front porch with cigars and port. Their babble was punctuated by frequent laughs, resulting from barbs cast at rebels, Mister Washington, and occasionally, General Howe.

Finally, the cigars were extinguished, and the port bottle was emptied. The men noisily stomped up the stairs to their rooms.

Creed took a pillow and slumped onto the parlor sofa. He had packed his bags and planned to make his way out without disturbing anyone. At ten, Creed awoke to the rumble of wheels coming down the lane. The Percheron's massive hooves thumped on the soft earth and gravel as it pulled Emily's coach.

He watched Emily handle the lines like a London hackney, guiding the Percheron straight into the barn. Creed looked around. When he was sure nobody was about, he made his way to the barn - the site of too many of their farewells.

"You're late getting home, Miss Stanley. The city is no place for a woman to be alone after dark."

He took the traces and unhitched the large draught horse from its harness. Creed patted the Percheron's sweat-foamed shoulder. "Still a stout lad, eh? Taking care of his mistress on her jaunts through New York. Let me rub you down."

Emily smiled. "You miss not having your Finn to ride."

"I do miss Finn, but this lad makes a fine substitute."

He began rubbing the horse down with careful strokes along the animal's contours. A mare in the other stall snorted.

Emily giggled. "That's enough, Pudding. We shall get to you next." She turned to Creed. "Pudding gets jealous."

"Well, who could blame her?"

***

When the horses were watered and fed, Creed and Emily sat on a bale of straw. The dim light from a lantern hanging cast shadows about them. Their heads touched gently.

Creed took her hand in his. "I leave at four, Emily. Taking my new ensign with me."

"New ensign? Are Elias or Jonathan not with you?"

"They can't go where I'm going. I've taken the son of Haddix's mistress on."

Her eyes widened. "Why?"

"'Tis strange, but I agreed to it on impulse. His Da' died in the great fire. So, in some way, I am responsible for his death. Haddix may prove helpful later. He informed me that Howe is not likely to support Burgoyne."

"What did he base that on?" Emily stroked his fingers gently.

"He says the positioning of supplies does not support a northern thrust. Makes sense."

"Did Haddix say where Howe is headed?"

She needed to remember all this for her next report. *'Tis well he knows nothing of my secret work.*

"On that point, he was evasive. More from ignorance than deceit. I suspect Howe has not made a firm plan yet."

"Jeremiah, I just do not understand what this trip north is about."

"Call me James...."

He kissed her hand. She giggled softly.

"Seriously, James. You have risked your life for the cause, but in ways that made sense. This...."

He squeezed her hand tightly. "His Excellency works in strange ways. My orders are to raise a unit under pretext and join Burgoyne's forces. I must reach Canada and accomplish all this before...."

"Before what?"

"Before the real James Lawrence arrives in the fall to recruit for the real Royal Americans. Meanwhile...."

"Meanwhile, what?"

Creed gripped her hand tightly. "I don't know."

"What on earth do you mean?" She felt nervous. He was usually more self-assured. Sometimes too self-assured.

"I cannot say more, Emily. The less you know, the better off you will be. Not just for security, but safety. I trust you with my life and my heart, but it is better for your sake that I say no more."

He had no idea she held deeper secrets than he. She placed her hand on his chest. "I understand. I truly do. But this seems beyond dangerous. You may never return."

"Even if I were not engaged in this enterprise, I may not be able to get back here for many months."

"No matter the wait, I shall be here when you return."

They kissed and huddled silently in each other's arms.

After some time, he said, "There is no lack of young officers to keep your mind off this humble lieutenant."

"What do you mean?"

"I have overheard some things. Your boarders like to speak of your sundry gentlemen callers. They say you are the talk of New York."

Emily's face turned red. Her heart sank. There was no way she could tell him why she had become part of the New York social scene, just as he could not tell her more of his mission. He had no idea of her real place in the war – and he never would.

"I have a father who seems to think I am of age. I humor him. That's all. My heart is with a certain lieutenant from Ireland."

He held her tightly. "Maryland, Emily. I'm from Maryland now."

Chapter 5

Long Island Sound, May 1777

The *Red Hen* raced past Fisher's Island towards the open sea with a stiff wind behind her. Ahead, the watch could already see Block Island and the vast expanse where the Long Island Sound meets the Atlantic Ocean.

Cornelius Foch stood on the brig's small quarterdeck and watched Creed, posing as Captain Lawrence, drilling his newly acquired "command." Already they knew the rudiments of musketry, close drill, and the bayonet. The men also learned the correct procedures for loading and presenting their flintlocks, opening and closing ranks, and using the bayonet.

Foch was amazed at what Creed had accomplished in such a short time. Creed acquired twenty British new land muskets with bayonets, ball, and powder. He found British uniforms, although they lacked the dark blue turnbacks of the Royal American Regiment. Most importantly, his men thought they had joined an actual British unit.

Foch cupped his hands to his mouth. "We'll be in the open sea soon. Time to stand down, Captain Lawrence. I'll need your men to help with the lines."

"A quarter-hour more, Captain Foch." Creed turned to the new command. "Sergeant O'Ballance, have the men clean and store their weapons before releasing them to Captain Foch's control. Sea air will melt the finest steel to rust if not kept well oiled."

"Aye, sir," O'Ballance replied.

Creed skipped up the short ladder to the deck where Foch stood with his pipe in hand.

"Handy work, Captain Lawrence. I had no idea you could motivate men so quickly."

Creed grinned. "You mean men such as these, don't you?"

Foch waved the pipe. "I said I'd bring you men, but not British grenadiers. Most come from the lower sort in Brooklyn, Flatbush, and Jamaica. Out of work farmhands, stevedores, or day laborers."

"I am thankful for that. I would have thought the British occupation, our occupation, would have ensured work for all and more."

Foch puffed on his pipe. "A man must want to work, Captain Lawrence."

"A man must want to fight. And that, Captain Foch, is something I cannot teach."

"*Ja*, the English beat it into their men and then use drink to soften the blows of their discipline. The Germans, especially the Hessians, are raised like cattle from birth. Respond well to basic commands and the lash."

"Indeed, however, Americans, whether loyal or patriot, only fight if they trust their leaders. That trust must be earned. That's my real task between here and Canada."

Foch spat a piece of tobacco. The wind caught it, and some of the brown goo blew into his face. He wiped it casually from his whiskers.

"Your Sergeant O'Ballance seems to know his business," Foch said. "Where did you find him?"

"My ensign there, young Bart Saunders, brought him to South Slip. Had some military experience – six years with the 50th Foot."

"So your sergeant is a deserter?"

"Not exactly. Horse Guards saw fit to break up the regiment. Most of the men were assigned to other regiments to fill out losses. The officers and many sergeants went back to Britain to form new units. O'Ballance, if that is his real name, was close enough to the end of his enlistment to get mustered out."

"Bah, how can the English win if they let such men depart on technicalities?"

"Well, it seems a serious case of the pox added to the incentive on his part and the king's."

Foch bent over in laughter. "So, your hazardous mission depends in no small part on a pox-ridden ex-soldier whose name you have not confirmed?"

"'Tis a challenge indeed, *Meen Heer*. But he can teach men how to hold a firelock and march. That suits my purpose for now."

Bart Saunders approached and affected a salute. "The men are heading below to oil their weapons, sir."

"Are your firelock and sword cleaned and oiled, Mister Saunders?"

Bart stood with his short-barreled musket, a *fusil*, and his short officer's sword, a hanger in each hand. "Why, not yet, sir."

"'Tis an officer's place to attend to things martial faster than the men. Repair below and get to it. Then report to me."

This man knows how to move men, Foch thought.

They were well into the Atlantic and beating northwards towards Nova Scotia by morning's end. Creed's band had finished the morning drill and were helping the crew with the lines, swabbing the decks, or working in the galley.

Foch was concerned about his mariners. Good, experienced men, but they were sullen. This voyage north would bring danger and promised little in the way of profit. The *Red Hen* carried ten hogsheads of rum, a dozen barrels of flour, and twice that of corn. But his men knew there would be little Canadian fur to be had for this paltry exchange.

The wind had stiffened and shifted southerly, and the *Red Hen* was running fast.

"'Tis a marvel how you can make this old brig seem to skip across the waves, *Herr* Foch," Creed bit into an apple and gazed to the east.

"*Ja*, I have been able to coax much out of my *Red Hen*," Foch said grimly. "Smuggling is a grave offense in peace or war. However, thanks to certain arrangements I have made, we travel under British authority. So, we have nothing to fear from the Royal Navy."

"Excellent."

"Not so excellent. I received this authority because I have English postal bags aboard. If the pirates catch us, they will skewer us for it and our lack of booty."

"Pirates? Are you serious?"

"Well, they call themselves by other names. You know – privateers, corsairs, even buccaneers. It is all the same to us, honest merchant seamen."

"Honest merchant seaman?" Creed asked sarcastically.

Foch reddened, then laughed. "Well, honest enough. But mind you, the waters from Block Island to Portsmouth are teaming with ships carrying men ruthless as Blackbeard."

"I had never thought of it." Creed gazed across the blue expanse as though he expected to spot a Jolly Roger.

"*Ja*, and to tell you the truth, they may be what brings these English to their knees, not the rebel army."

"Why do you say that?"

"The English merchants love their profits more than their leaders love power. Privateers cut into profits. English merchants cut into their benefactors in parliament, who then cut into the king's authority. And so it goes."

"I am amazed, *Heer* Foch. For a grizzled Dutch seaman, you show a powerful grasp of things both mercantile and political. Now tell me about these postal bags. It would not hurt to let a bored British officer sift through them for correspondence of interest, would it?"

"They are sealed with a special mix of lead with a thin sliver of gold. An attempt to melt open the seals would be detected. My days working for the English would be over, and my life and that of my crew would be forfeit. I realize it is a tempting thing, but I cannot allow it."

"I understand. 'Twas just a notion." Creed threw the apple core out into the water, and they watched it skip across the waves before a gull swept in from nowhere and took off with it in its beak.

After several minutes of silence, Creed spoke, "Have you seen much of the Braaf women?"

Foch's brow tightened, and his face reddened again. The young man touched on a subject that tore at him. "Have you seen much Jan Braaf?"

The Braafs had helped Creed and his men during the British attack on Long Island. But it turned out that, unbeknownst to his friends and family, Jan Braaf was a British spy.

"I should not say this, *Heer* Foch, and you cannot repeat it at risk of many lives, yours included. He is long dead."

"I have always thought so. How did he die?"

"At the behest of his British masters, he tried to spy on the Continental Army. But during the sudden invasion of New York Island and the American retreat, he was captured and killed by a gang of pro-British brigands known as cowboys."

"*Verdammt!* These cowboys and skinners are worse than pirates."

"Indeed. New York and the Jerseys are full of them. They prey on each other and anyone who crosses them. The family must not learn of this, as cruel as it sounds."

"Why is that?"

"Some things I cannot reveal. Trust me."

Foch was perplexed. "Captain Lawrence, I did not get this far in life by trusting people, and I do not intend to change. However, I respect your professional advice and shall abide." Foch pointed at Creed's men, who were once again drilling amidships. "They have improved quite a bit in just a short while."

Sergeant O'Ballance stood with arms akimbo and roared ferociously at his men. One of the hapless recruits had misloaded his musket, sending the ramrod shooting across the deck. It nearly speared one of the able-bodied seamen, a grizzled-looking Dutchman named Nys, who let fly a flurry of curses in a strange mix of Dutch, English, and unsavory words picked up in ports around the world.

Creed chuckled. "Most of the lads had never held a musket. Now they are merely mis-firing them. Even veterans sometimes make that mistake. So, I see this as progress of sorts."

"Another mistake like that, and Nys will show one of your soldiers what real fighting is like," Foch growled through the pipe clenched in his teeth.

"'Tis true enough. I think I shall have to take personal charge of their training from now on."

***

Creed clambered down the ladder to the main deck, and in minutes, O'Ballance had the men formed. Creed began to put them through drills that even the inept soon mastered. By the end of the day, the men could ram home a charge, lift musket to shoulder, and fire twice in one minute.

They learned to step from line to skirmish. Most importantly, he showed them how to form pairs, so one man loaded while his partner fired or stood ready. By late afternoon, the men were exhausted. At first, O'Ballance thought these miscreants would never meet British or even Loyalist military standards. Now he thought perhaps he was wrong.

Creed stood before them. "Lads, you have made commendable progress since we put to sea. But we still have much work ahead. Master Foch informs me that we shall reach the mouth of Saint Lawrence in three days and Quebec days after. There will be little time for training when we arrive. Our company of twenty is small, but I hope to set an example that loyal Americans, properly led, make the finest soldiers on the continent."

"Let's have a huzzah for Mister Lawrence!" O'Ballance ordered.

"Huzzah! Huzzah! Long live the king!"

Bart and the men took the words in with glee. But O'Ballance thought these miscreants would never meet British or even Loyalist military standards.

Creed placed his hands behind his back. "Your Sergeant, Edgar O'Ballance, will drill you in the bayonet tomorrow. Mark him, for he is one of the finest sergeants I have served with."

O'Ballance felt a swell of pride at Creed's remarks. No officer had ever spoken well of him. This Captain Lawrence seemed so different from most of the officers he had served with. A commotion from high above broke up the drill session.

***

The ship's lookout called out frantically, "Ships off the larboard forequarter!"

"How many?" Foch called.

"Three of them, and heading right at us!"

Foch drew his telescope and scanned the horizon. Sure enough, three ships, all smaller than the *Red Hen,* were approaching from their port bow or left front, with sails pulled tight against the wind. Foch knew this meant trouble.

Creed clambered up to the quarterdeck. "What have we, Master Foch?"

Foch handed him the mariners' telescope, which was longer and more powerful than Creed's spyglass. "What do you see?"

Creed scanned back and forth. "I see ships, but they could be British on patrol. We can't be too far from Halifax."

Foch whispered, "No, Mister Creed. These are not English. They are rebel privateers, no better than pirates if you ask me. And unfortunately for both of us, we are sailing under the sanction of the British."

"Surely, we can explain...."

"It will enrage them all the more. We have little booty. But they will take the *Red Hen* and, if we are lucky, throw us in the gaol at Portsmouth or Gloucester. Oh, I know these scoundrels all too well. For I've often done the same."

"What shall we do?"

Foch shrugged. "Stay the course. They have the wind right now, but that should change if we can make it just a few hours north."

"Why not head east and hope to lose them farther into the Atlantic?"

"Usually a good tactic. However, the current and winds will work against us. You will never make it to Quebec in time."

Foch cupped his hands and bellowed, "All hands to quarters! Man the rigging and prepare to let sail!" He turned to his coxswain. "Maintain this course, but be ready to turn one quarter into the wind on my command."

The coxswain nodded. His face was tense with anticipation.

"Won't that put us on a course to be intercepted?" Creed asked.

"I wish merely to get upwind. We are a brig and will be faster with the wind fully behind us. But just in case, I have a rebel flag." Foch turned to Nys, standing nearby. "Nys! Haul down that royalist pennant and raise this...."

He handed Nys a small flag with a crude set of stars and stripes with the motto: "Freedom or Death."

Nys scrambled aft, tore off the pennant, and quickly hoisted the stars and stripes.

"Now we are rebels once more," Foch whispered to Creed.

The *Red Hen* managed to stay ahead of her pursuers for the next two hours. Foch was pleased. He was hoping the privateers would pick the wrong tack in the vast darkness of the Atlantic. If they could hold course till dark, she could disappear into the black void.

The pursuers had closed to within a mile of the *Red Hen,* and Foch knew well the next hour would determine their fate. The skies darkened quickly as heavy clouds from the west formed and rolled across the sky. The seas grew choppy, waves slapping rapidly against the bow. Then the wind started to swirl and beat against the sails.

Nys's voice filled the ship. "Captain, this storm is brewing quickly. We should take in some sail."

Foch knew he was right. "Belay that, Nys. Our pursuers are likely to do the same. We'll hold for as long as we can." He looked at Creed. "Captain Lawrence, your men must stand ready to help my *Jungs* with the lines. Do it quickly when we haul in, or we could lose the ship."

"Aye," said Creed. "Your experienced mariners should mount the topsails, and I'll have my men handle the lower sails."

Foch was impressed. "As you say, *Meen Heer.*"

Creed clambered down the ladder. "Secure firelocks and get the lads to the lines, Sergeant O'Ballance."

The sky grew darker, and the waves chopped viciously at the hull. With each chop, more foamy water poured over the gunwale and across the deck. The pursuers had closed to almost a half-mile distance, but they could barely be seen.

Foch put his hand on the coxswain's shoulder. "Steady now, *Jung.* Be ready to cut it a quarter-point larboard on my command."

The helmsman replied nervously. "The turbulence – I can barely keep her on course as it is, *Meen Heer.*"

"Just a few minutes more, a few minutes more."

One of the pursuers suddenly appeared from the darkness. For a brief moment, the skies brightened, and Foch could see that this privateer had also maintained full sail. Now it had closed to within firing distance. He took comfort in knowing they wanted to capture the *Red Hen,* not sink her.

His comfort was soon erased as a shot from the privateer, barely audible, echoed against the sea's roar. The cannonball plunged harmlessly short. *Ranging us with the vain hope that we shall heave-to.*

The skies darkened again, and thunder's crash made the cannon roar like a mere pop gun.

"Now, *Jung!* Now!" Foch said. He gripped the wheel and, together with the young boy, turned steadily larboard to get upwind of the chasers. When the course was set, he hollered to the crew, "Bring in the topsails!"

They could barely hear him over the roar of the sea and storm, but they sensed the time. As one, his sturdy mariners brought in the canvas.

The lashing wind engulfed the man high up, and a stray line wrapped around his leg, twisting him off his perch and knocking him against the mainmast. The raging wind and the ship's heaving whipped him about like a puppet. He now dangled helplessly by his ankle.

The sailor cried for help, but nobody noticed his plight in the now furious roar of the storm. A few moments later, the lines unraveled from his foot, and he dropped forty feet to the main deck, broken like a porcelain doll.

***

The Red Hen and her crew fought as cold rain and icy, churning seawater engulfed them for the next two hours. The ship bobbed uncontrollably as the helmsman tried to hold her bow steady in the wind.

The rain now blew almost horizontally into their faces and, combined with the wind, made breathing difficult. The seawater swamped the decks up to their ankles, soaking feet and stockings and making it almost impossible to stand on the heaving deck.

Creed fought to stay upright as he walked among his men, calming them and ensuring each stayed at his assigned post. Several began to panic and talked of jumping into a boat.

"Hold fast, men. Master Foch has sailed the *Red Hen* around the Cape of Storms. A squall like this will not break her." Creed could barely hear his own words.

Then suddenly, they heard a booming sound cut through the storm. "The rebels are firing on us," someone cried.

"No, that's thunder," Creed replied. "Maintain your positions. We're in the hands of Master Foch – and God." But Creed was unsure whether the privateers had not indeed stayed with them in the darkness.

Then, slowly, almost imperceptibly, the storm began to subside. The wind slowed to a steady rush of air, and the curtains of rain turned to droplets and, finally, a light mist.

"Have the men stay at their posts, Sergeant O'Ballance," Creed said.

"You couldn't pry their fingers from the lines, sir," he replied.

Then Creed saw Bart bent over the fallen sailor, trying to give him aid.

"What happened to him?" Creed asked.

"I don't know, sir. He must have fallen from the topsails. Not much I can do for him. He's broken most of his bones."

"Poor fellow. Keep him comfortable for as long as you can, Bart."

Creed returned to the quarterdeck, where he found Foch busy directing his men in repairing the damage and getting the ship back under sail.

"How bad is she?" Creed asked.

"We were lucky, Mister Lawrence. The boys got the sails in quickly, and little of the spars and rigging was damaged. We'll know better in daylight. Meanwhile, we will proceed slowly in case another storm brews up."

"My men will do what we can to assist."

"They would be better off preparing their weapons and resting, as we may yet have a fight on our hands."

Foch pointed off the starboard quarter. Twin lights faintly flickered about a mile off.

"We gained only a little more than a half-mile on her. But I think we can maintain our distance till dawn," Foch said.

"What then?" Creed asked.

"Depending on the wind, we either outrun her or fight. And since I have no cannon, we shall depend on your men to fight."

"Ironic we should both be caught leading Loyalists against rebels. The good Lord has a sense of the absurd. Well, we shall prepare to meet them unless...."

"Unless what?"

"Unless I can think of something even more absurd."

***

Dawn broke to fading gray skies and calming seas. Creed had caught a few hours' sleep in a small cabin below the quarterdeck. Creed found time to shave, wash, and change into a dry uniform. He wore the Royal Americans' scarlet and dark blue facings and carried an officer's saber.

He stepped from his cabin into the dark of the lower deck and ordered, "Sergeant O'Ballance, have the men assemble on deck." His men had spread out wherever they could find space to stretch their limbs.

"They'll be hungry, sir."

"I'm sure the cook will have a fine breakfast of water-soaked hard biscuit and some ale to wash it down."

He clambered up the narrow ladder. However, the poor mariners had alternated standing watch with fitful bits of sleep and were already at their work.

"How far off are our friends?" Creed asked when he stood on the quarterdeck.

Foch waved his pipe. "See for yourself. Only a half-mile off. She could close faster, but instead is very deliberately moving on us." Foch rubbed his wiry beard. "I can't understand why. Privateers usually pounce quickly and then scatter before the Royal Navy arrives to discipline them."

"That tells me two things, *Heer* Foch. They know the Royal Navy is not about and are waiting for the other ships."

Foch thrust an unlit pipe into his mouth and chewed on the stem. "*Ja*, but why?"

Creed scanned the ship with his spyglass. "They believe we are armed. We should do little to dissuade them of the fact."

"Meaning?"

"We turn on her and attack. Quickly, before she can get accurate fire on us."

"That is madness. I command this ship and will not put us at such risk. No, *Heer* Creed, we will outrun her."

Creed scanned to the northeast. "Maybe, *Heer* Foch, but can we outrun *them*?"

Foch turned and saw the faint trace of sails at the horizon. "*Meen Gott*, we have sailed into a nest of privateers!"

"The other option is to surrender. Perhaps we can reason with them and turn over the...."

"No...I believe you were right the first time. It's suicide, but we cannot wait for the other ships. If we can fight past this one, we can turn east and try to bear northwest once free. It will cost you a few days, but that is your problem."

Creed nodded. "Do you have any extra spars in the hold?"

S.W. O'Connell

"A few, *ja*. Why?"

"Get some black tar on them...we'll show them we have a battery of guns bigger than theirs."

Less than an hour later, the *Red Hen* had come about with sails set billowing in a favorable wind. Sailors at their posts worked their taut muscles to keep the canvas firm.

Creed's men hauled up six spars and doused them with black tar. The crew watched with anxious faces as they thrust the black spars through the gunwale on the port side.

Two of the "Royal Americans" stood patiently next to each gun."

O'Ballance and six of his men stood at attention at the brig's small forecastle. They held a musket in each hand, primed and loaded.

Then the wind died down. Now the two ships merged on a slow but inevitable course.

Foch scanned the privateer's deck with his telescope as the ships closed. "She is a lightly armed sloop. I count only two guns, and they look like small carronades."

Creed brought his spyglass to his eye. The ship seemed so close he could see the whiskers on the crew. "Aye, and six-pounders, likely loaded with grapeshot."

"Grapeshot?" Foch replied.

"Bags of balls, usually quarter-pound iron, but I'd wager they've jammed them full of musket balls."

"Meaning?"

"Meaning they need to get within fifty yards to do much damage, and then we can take cover behind the gunwales and barrels."

Creed pointed to O'Ballance and his crew. "The lads up there will wreak havoc with them first with a couple of well-aimed volleys. But I don't want to kill any Americans if we can avoid it."

"We must kill them or be killed!" Foch exclaimed.

"I have another idea, *Heer* Foch," Creed said.

"What do you propose?"

"We demand their surrender."

"Are you mad? They have real cannon to place against our mock wooden barrels."

"But they don't know that. Do you have signal flags onboard?"

"Of course, but...."

"Look! The rest of her flotilla has fallen back. They are alone for now. Hoist the signal for surrender. Then get your funnel and tell them they have one minute before our twelve pounders blast them to splinters and our Marines finish them off."

Foch, the canny sea-dog, shrugged in resignation. He gave the order, and soon four the signal flags slowly rose up the line. Minutes later, Foch cupped his hands to his mouth and bellowed Creed's demand across the 200 yards separating the ships.

The captain of the other ship observed the events. Creed kept his spyglass trained on him.

"What are you looking at?" asked Foch.

"Their captain. His decision will determine whether there is an effusion of blood or – Jesus, Mary, and Joseph...."

"What?" Foch picked up his telescope.

"The captain."

"What about him?"

"I believe I know him."

***

The captain of the rebel privateer barked orders to the crew. He knew the game was up. His ship, one of three in the little flotilla that left Marble Head a week earlier, was disadvantaged. His attempt to bluff the British ship failed.

"You are certainly not considering surrender, Captain Hazard?" The first mate implored.

Hazard nodded. "Aye. That I am. Strike the colors, Smitty. We have only six rounds left and a few old muskets and cutlasses. Their guns are larger than ours and will rake us with chain and grape. Look! They have a Marine company on board. I faced Royal Marines once before. They are killers. I won't have us blasted from the water and shot to pieces. In the end, the *Merilea* is a mere sloop."

***

Thirty minutes later, a longboat pushed through the Atlantic water with a dozen sturdy arms pulling oars in an easy cadence.

"I can't believe they struck," Bart said.

"Remember, we need to show our strength, for the show is all we have," Creed said to the young ensign.

The oarsmen grew grim as they approached the sloop. Creed sensed their anxiety.

"What if this is a trick?" Bart asked suddenly.

"Hmmm... I like your thinking, Bart. We should always plan for the worst. I have instructed Sergeant O'Ballance to fire repeated volleys at their gunners if something goes wrong. *Heer* Foch will then bring the *Red Hen* about and make a run to the east."

Bart looked stunned. "And what of us?"

Creed smiled. "We will likely spend the rest of the war in a rebel prison. In Boston, I suppose."

Creed knew Bart had seen how brutally rebel prisoners were treated in New York. He could only imagine how much worse the rebels in Boston treated British prisoners. Bart now looked dejected.

Creed felt for the young man. He reflected that his lying was a sin, just as murder was. Using people as pawns in a grand scheme seemed worse to Creed than fighting or killing men in battle.

The boat suddenly bumped up against the side of the *Merilea*, shaking Creed from his thoughts.

"Bart, grab that rope and scramble up. I will be right behind you." Creed looked at the oarsmen. "Take the boat back to the *Red Hen*. I shall be here no more than one hour. But if I do not signal a return, tell *Heer* Foch to leave us and depart quickly."

Their faces twisted in puzzlement

"No worry. I have escaped from more than one prison in my day."

Creed scrambled up the rope and barely cleared the *Merilea's* deck when they heaved hard at the oars to separate themselves from the privateer as quickly as possible.

Creed found Bart surrounded by a half dozen rebel sailors as he pulled himself over the rail. These were hardened men of scrawny stature whose worn and ill-fed looks hid a toughness that only a life at sea brings.

"Where is your captain?" Creed asked. "I have but one hour to arrange your submission before my ship commences fire."

One of the privateers spat on Bart. "Captain Hazard's below, lobsterback. Better see him quick 'cause the boys are mad as hell about this. The other two ships abandoned us, and now the captain strikes without a fight."

Creed looked about the ship. He counted little more than fifteen men. Perhaps the *Red Hen* could have withstood the paltry guns and taken her quickly. He shook his head at the desperation that brought men to privateering with such a weak vessel.

Leaving Bart topside, Creed climbed down the narrow ladder and entered the captain's cabin below the quarterdeck. It was small and cramped. However, the hatches were thrown open, and fresh sea air flowed in, bracing Creed.

He saw the captain at a small table writing his terms of surrender. A painful task, Creed knew. Under the law of the sea, privateers who sailed without letters of marque or broke earlier parole were hung as pirates.

"Top o' the mornin' to ye, Captain Hazard. Or should I say, Ezekial?"

Hazard looked up, and his eyes bulged, and his jaw dropped. "Who? Jeremiah Creed! What in God's name are you doing here? In a British uniform no less!"

Creed grinned widely. "King's Royal American Regiment, to be exact. Although I'd wager you took us for Royal Marines. Most do. Uniform's about the same."

Hazard stood up, his knees shaking and hands quivering. "Have you gone over to the lobsters then? Never would have...."

Creed motioned his hand across his mouth. "Don't say another word...you know who I am and what I do. His Excellency sent me here, unfortunately, without the lads. So, for the duration of this enterprise, I am at your service, Captain James Lawrence of the Royal Americans."

"Captain, Lawrence?"

Creed nodded and smiled. "However, you may call me James."

Hazard quickly barred the door and whispered. "So, you are on a mission? Of course, but...."

"If you have some tea handy, I'll explain. But quickly. We have less than one hour to talk about our next move."

Ezekial Hazard had been a member of the famed Gloucester Regiment, serving with heroic distinction at New York and Trenton. Sailors from Marblehead and other points along the Massachusetts and Rhode Island coast excelled at transporting the Continental Army across waterways under the most trying conditions.

They first met during the New York campaign of 1776. Hazard had volunteered for a "special mission" and commanded a longboat that took Creed back to Long Island. Along the way, the two men faced the guns of the Royal Navy and the muskets and cold steel of the Royal Marines.

"Before we do that, what brings you to privateering?"

"It's what we Marblehead men do best. And it provides a chance for great wealth while striking the enemy where it hurts most – his purse."

Hazard rang a bell on his table. A weathered tar stuck his head through the hatch.

"Danny, bring us some tea, please. But quickly, Captain Lawrence must stay on schedule."

Creed rubbed his chin. "This is the second time I have heard that today. Strike the British in their pockets and make 'em cry."

"Never mind that. What brings you to these seas?" Hazard asked.

"I can't provide details of my mission or how I arrived here, Ezekial. I must get to Canada and join the British forces assembling for a thrust south. I think you can ascertain the importance and sensitivity of this. The ship's brave captain is the only person aware of my true intentions."

"So, he's one of us?"

"Better I say no more of this. I shall write a note for you to send to His Excellency. A courier from Boston can make it to General Heath's army in upper New York in a few days' ride. Heath communicates with the main army, which should be somewhere in central Jersey."

"That's fair enough. What of the terms of my surrender?"

Hazard seemed embarrassed in asking.

"I will report that I have given you a release without condition. But no one must know of this encounter. My detachment will disappear among Burgoyne's forces."

"What of them?" Hazard motioned towards the *Red Hen*. "The skipper yonder and his crew have other interests. They are happy enough to be safe on their way."

When Danny brought in the tea, he shot Creed a dirty look. "It's tepid, captain. The cook doused the fire some time ago, expecting we'd fight these lobsters, not surrender to them."

Hazard's voice grew harsh. "Enough of that, Danny. Leave us be now."

"He doesn't seem very happy."

"My men wanted to fight the lobsters. However, I knew we had but a few rounds to your...."

"Wooden spars."

"What?"

"We tarred some wooden spars and thrust them off the bulwark to look like long guns."

Hazard smiled. "Jeremiah Creed, you are still the evil schemer...."

"Call me James," Creed said. "Nevertheless, you were wise to strike. I have trained up those Loyalists, and they make a pretty good company, if I do say so. Our muskets would have cut down your gunners. I took a gamble in demanding your surrender to avoid the effusion of good patriot blood. I thank God for your prudence."

Sounds of agitated voices came through the dry wooden planking.

Hazard glanced upward. "Near to mutiny, they are, though."

"Then let's be done with this quickly. You return to the coast, and we head north. To help your case, I've brought something to go with my note."

"What's that?"

Creed placed a small leather pouch on the table. "Seems the *Red Hen* had a contract to carry Royal Mail to Canada. I took the liberty of scanning the bags and selected a dozen more interesting pieces of correspondence. Make sure these get to Colonel Fitzgerald. You can report that you stopped the British vessel and seized the mail for its intelligence rather than the ship as a prize."

"My backers will not be pleased. They are in this for gold, not news."

"But His Excellency shall be. This is a war, not a business enterprise, Ezekial."

"Well, there you are dreadfully wrong, Jer – James. The New England states demand their mariners turn privateer. Not to face the Royal Navy but to scour the ocean from Halifax to the West Indies for British merchantmen."

"I see..."

"Do you? It started as a means of bringing the British to their knees. To deprive British merchants of their wealth so they'll squeeze their lackeys in the Parliament to pressure the king and his ministers to make peace. However, the men who ventured the capital for these privateers saw the wealth come in greater amounts than they ever dreamed. Why, one prize ship can bring in thousands, in good British pounds, not worthless continental dollars."

Creed sipped at the bitter brew and grimaced. "You need to seize a load of good India tea. Very well. A confluence of interest in a time of war is not unusual."

Hazard nodded. "Indeed. Some make fortunes while others lose fortunes."

"Or their lives," Creed replied

A commotion from above grew. They heard men screaming and swearing.

"Damn lobster! You'll not leave this ship alive," a sailor said harshly.

"Get him! And get his officer," demanded another.

"We came unarmed," Creed said to Hazard.

Hazard reached into a cabinet, pulled out two heavy naval pistols, and handed them to Creed. "They are loaded with birdshot. Tears at a mutineer's face and hands, but doesn't kill him."

Hazard grabbed his cutlass, and the two bolted up the ladder. Two privateers had pinned Bart's arms back while a large one beat him about the head and neck with a leather strap wrapped tightly around a massive fist.

"As the master of the *Merilea,* I order you to stop!" Hazard cried out.

The large sailor turned disdainfully to Hazard. "Just try an' stop me, Ezekial!"

He slammed the leather belt into Bart's stomach, bending him over in a gush of wind. Bart hung limp in the arms of the two sailors.

The large man turned and rushed at Hazard. He had a long knife in his left hand and raised it high to strike his captain. Hazard boldly stepped under the knife's cut and rammed the hilt of the cutlass into his breastbone. The resulting crack sounded more like a musket shot. He collapsed in a heap at Hazard's feet.

He turned to the crew. "I could easily have run him through. Maybe I should have. Mutiny and breaking an agreed truce are capital offenses. When we return to Boston, he'll face a maritime judge. Meanwhile, help that young man to his feet and get the ship ready to return."

"You mean we are not to be taken as prisoners?" a sailor asked.

"No," replied Hazard. "Nor will we receive parole. Captain Lawrence agreed to an unconditional release, stipulating that we return to Boston before attempting any more prizes. Generous terms under any circumstances."

The men looked at him, unconvinced.

Holding both pistols at the ready, Creed motioned at the *Red Hen*, rocking gently but menacingly in cannon range. "His Majesty needs that brig to finish its voyage. Thus, my terms. Your captain has accepted. You must accept his decision or face death, at his hands or mine."

***

Creed and Bart were aboard the *Red Hen*, heading north an hour later. He looked back to see the *Merilea* tacking against the wind.

Foch came up to him with his meerschaum pipe clenched in his teeth. "Your famed luck continues to amaze, Captain Lawrence."

Creed smiled. "Truth be told, it amazes me as well. I help it along at times with prayer and the occasional idea."

"Prayer? Don't tell me you're a man of God...."

"We are all men of God, *Heer* Foch. The question is whether we choose to believe and heed his word. I must admit that the latter is not always easy."

Foch threw back his head and laughed. "Ah, the religious sinner, eh? I've met so many of you."

Creed flashed a smile. "Perhaps you have not met enough of us."

Chapter 6

Quebec, June 1777

The *Red Hen*, sails furled tightly, arrived at Quebec City as the spring sun began to dip over the horizon. Two longboats strained against a strong current and the spring waters as they struggled towards the slip.

"The last league is always the slowest this time of year," their pilot said in a thick accent. "From April through June, the rivers and streams that feed the Great Lakes and Saint Lawrence River thaw, melting ice from a thousand miles to the west, sending floes on a long journey to the Atlantic."

"Sounds like an artillery barrage," Creed said over the roaring waters.

"The narrowing of the Saint Lawrence near Cap-Diamant and Lévis sends water and ice churning. The Indians named the area *Kébec*, an Algonquin word meaning "where the river narrows.""

The *Red Hen* did not have a full forecastle, so Creed and Foch stood at the bow and surveyed the city, one of the oldest in North America. The ramparts surrounding Quebec evinced the fortified city walls that once protected the town from marauding Iroquois warriors but now protected it from marauding Americans.

The last rays of sunlight brushed the heights of Abraham to their left, and the lower city straight ahead lay in the evening shadows. Creed had to squint to make out the steeples and chimneys of the upper town. He had not seen anything like this architecture since leaving France.

"Tonight, my men shall stay on the Red Hen for the last time. I will get the detachment off tomorrow," Creed said.

"Will you join me in a last meal on board?" Foch asked.

Creed shook his head. "I have much to do on land. Try to ascertain the army headquarters to present my 'letter' from General Howe."

"A letter from Howe?"

"A note forged on what appears to be official letterhead assigning this First Company, Royal Americans, to Burgoyne's army. 'Tisn't perfect as far as forgeries go, but the thought is new resources are welcomed without question or much scrutiny."

Foch pulled his pipe from his teeth. "The boldness, I like that."

Creed eyed him. "*Meen Heer*, nobody surpasses you in cold-calculated audacity. Somehow, I think you shall end this war a wealthy man, with friends on both sides."

"The English will never actually be my friends. However, I shall use their 'friendship' at every opportunity. I was never one for patriots and all that. Maybe it's a Dutch fashion. But this rebellion offers me a chance to hurt the British in several ways. If I can advance the cause of liberty at the expense of a king, so much the better, eh?"

Creed looked across the quay and studied the tightly packed homes along the river. The lower city would be his approach to the next part of his mission. High above it stood a massive edifice and his objective, the *Citadelle*.

***

Creed slipped off the *Red Hen* and began the steep climb up the heights to the *Citadelle*. The pilot told them that the French built the fort last century to anchor their archipelago of trading posts, which formed a chain of commerce and Christianity stretching deep into North America.

Creed marveled at how the mighty fortress dominated the waterway. While the English brought farming to their settlements in the New World, the French came for two main reasons: to establish a monopoly in the fur trade and to spread the Catholic faith to the heathen. The English built farms and towns, whereas the French set up trading posts and churches.

The sounds and smells of France engulfed Creed as he strutted by the well-appointed shops. He was nearly brought to tears by the aromas of the bread, cheeses, and pastries. Rich-smelling stews, soups, and roasting meats emanated from every building.

On an impulse, he stopped at a *boulangerie*, a bakery, to get something to ease his aching stomach. He thought it would give him a chance to exercise his command of the French language, which he had not used in a few years.

"*Bon soir, monsieur!*" came the crisp greeting. Creed noticed the dialect differed from those he had encountered in France.

"*Bon soir!*" he replied.

Creed spoke a few pleasantries and purchased two baguettes, long, thin loaves of bread. The aroma was maddening, and it took great willpower not to devour them in front of the baker.

Creed decided to glean some basic information from the baker, who informed him most of the *Anglais* and *Allemande* had gone south toward Montreal.

"You are lucky to be left here in *Belle Quebec, monsieur*. These English soldiers will face much trouble."

"Trouble? From the Americans? Their nearest army is hundreds of miles away."

"No, from the land. The land is rugged and rocky. The woods are thick and swarming with flies, mosquitoes, and other obnoxious insects. The only way to travel is by water."

"Well, then, let us hope that is what we do," Creed replied.

The cool night air braced him when he stepped into the alley. He reached the *Citadelle* as a church clock struck eight. He presented his "instructions" to an officer who seemed indifferent to his arrival.

"I shall see if the Governor will see you. He normally does not suffer unexpected visitors."

He waited almost an hour in the large chamber that served as a meeting hall, banquet hall, and courtroom. The large stone walls were covered with artwork such as he had never seen since leaving France. Long curtains of deep burgundy velvet-covered bare walls and long windows extended from the roof to the floor. The ceiling was a plain whitewash, but its heavy maple beams, embedded in it, formed a lattice pattern that seemed just right. But the four massive chandeliers are what dominated the chamber.

Each hung twenty feet from the ceiling and consisted of gold-plated metal with a dozen candelabra.

***

Sir Guy Carleton entered the room wearing just breeches and a shirt.

"So, Captain Lawrence, is it? I fail to see the urgency of an evening introduction. However, how can I be of service now that I am here?"

Creed knew Carleton would try to assess him. It was natural to be suspicious of the loss of complete command of troops within his jurisdiction to the erstwhile subordinate Burgoyne.

Creed bowed. An orderly poured each of them a glass of ruby port wine. Carleton motioned Creed to sit by the empty fireplace – one of four in the chamber. Its hearth rose almost nine feet from the floor and stretched as many across.

"I have read your papers, Captain Lawrence. May I call you James?"

"Indeed, sir. Most do."

"Well, James, being here in the frozen north keeps one isolated from the latest news – whether from Lord Germain in London or General Howe in New York. I had no idea the Royal Americans were reactivated. However, I like the idea of an American regiment that is once again truly American."

Creed shot a mischievous grin. "You mean, sir, Loyalist American, don't you?"

Carleton smiled back. "I do indeed. However, our good General Burgoyne is now mustering his new army south of Montreal. And, curiously, your papers assign your detachment to me. I suppose I could have you guard this fortress. I see no need to reinforce Johnny's little bid for glory. Command of such a venture was rightfully mine."

Creed's visage darkened as the impact of his oversight coursed through him. *I should have foreseen this.* After recruiting a force in the enemy's bosom and braving a several-hundred-mile voyage in a North Atlantic swarming with rebel privateers, he stumbled against bureaucracy.

"However, I could issue an order attaching you to General Burgoyne's forces. I think it would set a good example for all loyal Americans. You know, for them to be represented in this brilliant effort."

"I sense a trace of sarcasm in your voice, sir," Creed said.

Carleton frowned. "Johnny thinks this is a brilliant effort, as does London, apparently. What were my efforts against that rascal Arnold last year? We stopped his invasion and crushed his fleet. Only the late season and lack of resources stopped us. So, my deputy, Johnny, goes back to England to plead for reinforcements but adds himself to the brew by replacing me as commander."

Creed realized he was smack in the middle of a quarrel between competing men of power and ego. His mind raced for a way to exploit that without hindering his mission.

"I had no idea, sir. But if you assign my detachment to the invading force and my orders come from you, not Lord Germain, then in some way you share in the glory, do you not?" Creed realized he was stretching things, but was counting again on ego and malice to influence the decision in his favor.

Carleton eyed him carefully. "What glory could a small detachment bring?"

"Only time and opportunity will tell, sir."

"My God, James, you are the bold one. And I daresay you can read minds. But your report on the campaign must highlight my avid support for it if it succeeds. I shall render a report regretting the valiant effort if it fails."

"I see, sir." Creed sipped at his port.

"More importantly, James, I need a friendly set of eyes and ears to report any misstep by General Burgoyne. He may be the expedition commander, but I am still Governor-General of all Canada."

"I don't understand, sir. What sort of misstep?"

Carleton cocked his head mischievously. "I'll leave that to you. "

"A letter assigning me to the advance guard might place me just where I need to be to influence matters."

"I'll have such an order drafted. Meanwhile, I suggest you report back tomorrow with a list of supplies. Burgoyne took most with him, but we'll try to find some spare powder, ball, and victuals to get you started."

***

By the following evening, Creed and his men had reequipped and resupplied. The detachment's older muskets were replaced with muskets of recent manufacture. Creed convinced the Armorer at the *Citadelle* to issue his men the shorter version of the new land-pattern muskets. Usually carried by non-commissioned officers, the lighter firelocks would provide better handling in the heavily wooded forests of New York.

Creed now carried one himself, along with a brace of pistols and a short sword. His men also took the triangle-pattern seventeen-inch bayonet.

Carleton provided Creed with three large canoes, each manned by a crew of *coureurs des bois*, "runners of the woods." These rugged backwoodsmen were French Canadians who traveled deep into the Indian-held lands along the Great Lakes and the Mississippi to trap, trade, and hunt.

The leader was a short but powerful man with short brown whiskers named Etienne Androche. Androche greeted him with typical Gallic bonhomie. Creed assumed Carleton had selected him to keep an eye on his expedition. Besides the four *coureurs* sent to man the canoes, Androche had an Indian woman as cook. The plump woman was also what passed for his wife. He also brought a Wyandot Huron named Tsamehuhi, or Eagle, to serve as a guide and scout.

"The Jesuit fathers named Tsamehuhi, Pierre. That is what we call him. He speaks three dialects of Iroquois plus his own Wyandot and, of course, French."

"Three dialects of Iroquois?" Creed asked.

"*Oui*. Pierre was raised in a Catholic village among the Onondaga, but later spent much time among the Mohawk nation. He knows the territory between the Richelieu River and Albany better than most."

"Why are Hurons, Christian Hurons, living among the Onondaga?" Creed asked.

"From time as far back as anyone remembers, the Iroquois terrorized the Wyandot, driving those they did not kill or capture to lands west, where other tribes, allied with the Iroquois, did the same. Starvation and disease brought by us whites finished the rest. Many had to submit to the Iroquois and join their nation to survive. So it was with Pierre's people, the ones called the People of the Rock. That is why the fathers named him Pierre."

"How did he wind up in Mohawk lands?"

Androche's heavy eyelids closed for a moment, and he put a gnarled finger to his lips. "Pierre loved the daughter of a great Sachem. However, she was already married to a favored Onondaga warrior. They fought over the girl, who was fourteen. Pierre killed him but had to flee for his life. The Mohawks accepted him, and he became a renowned warrior, leading hunts and raids from Albany, through New Hampshire and points east."

Creed smiled faintly. "Always a woman, it seems. What happened to the girl? Did she join him?"

"Hah! *Mais non, monsieur*. She married the next brave who would have her. Indian women are practical that way." He nodded toward his wife. Creed could only imagine how she came to Androche's bed.

"How did Pierre come to serve you?" Creed thought he knew the answer. "Another blood feud over a lass?"

Androche's face twisted into what, for him, was a smile. "Pierre was wounded in a raid against his people, a small band of Wyandot who managed to escape the Iroquois long ago. They lived on an island upriver from Montreal, near the mouth of the great lake. He killed their chief. But the dying man uttered a phrase that Pierre had not heard since the days he was weaned from his mother. It struck him, this Wyandot death prayer. Pierre had betrayed his ancestors, and for that, he was cursed."

"What did he do?"

"He abandoned the Iroquois for whom he now holds only contempt."

"You said he was wounded? By whom? Was it serious?"

"The wound was to his heart. Not physical, you see. But wounds of the soul can be much deeper than those of the flesh. And often never heal."

Androche's words hit Creed in a way he had not expected. A flood of memories of Ireland, France, love, honor, betrayal, suffering, and death engulfed him.

"What is wrong, *monsieur*? Did I say something to disturb you?"

"No, I just remembered that I have matters to attend to before we depart tomorrow."

***

Creed carried a small Bible with dog-eared pages. It was time to turn to his instructions. Fitzgerald's instructions comprised a primitive set of codes based on Bible passages. The instructions referred him to Bible verses and specific words. The correct combination of verses and words was the message.

The second set of instructions read: *See Fr Vincennes at Egl ND d* <u>*Victoires*</u>.

The word *d Victoires* seemed ironic. *And why was it underlined? A prayer for victories? Or a prediction?* Creed burned the papers before he left the *Red Hen*. He was down to one last note, which Fitzgerald had cautioned him only to open if he had "no way of getting word of British plans and capabilities back to Washington."

Creed laughed to himself at the time. Anyone who looked at a map knew how unlikely it was to get intelligence to Washington in time to influence northern operations.

He slipped off Red Hen, strode along the Quai Saint Andre, and then doubled back through an alley until that led to the *Rue Saint Pierre*. He had shed his uniform and borrowed clothes from Foch. The evening shadows made the passages darker than the twilight. Creed ducked into several shops along the way to ensure no one was following. Finally, he found the alley that led to the *Place Royale*.

Across the square was the gray stone Gothic church, towering in the shadows of the heights and the Citadelle behind it. The original church was burned during the French and Indian War, but the new version improved on it. The spire with the cross sent a wave of religious fervor Creed had not felt since he came to "Protestant" America.

Creed loitered near a café across the small, pleasant square. The clatter of boots on the cobblestone streets came from the sturdy Quebecois hustling in and out of shops. He saw more than a few entering the church through an expansive gate of brass-trimmed oak.

Suddenly, the church bells began to toll. The distinctive clang of the bronze echoed down the alleys and seemed to soar across gabled roofs. In the distance, Creed could hear the sounds of other bells tolling. Now the entire city seemed engulfed in a rhythmic clanging in a cadence at once pleasant and annoying.

Instinctively, Creed dropped to his knees and folded his hands. Before he could recover from that reflex of an earlier day, he saw people around him dropping to their knees and bowing their heads. As one, they began to pray a distantly familiar prayer - the Angelus.

The Angelus was an ancient and sacred Catholic tradition of devotion to the Virgin Mary, usually prayed in the morning, noon, and evening to replicate the daily prayers of monastic Europe. Creed grew up praying the Angelus in Ireland and from time to time in France. But he had never thought he would hear it, nevertheless pray it, in North America.

Tears came to his eyes as he chanted in Latin along with the crowd of faithful in the square.

Angelus Domini nuntiavit Mariae...Et concepit de Spiritu Sancto

The Angel of the Lord came unto Mary... and she conceived of the Holy Spirit...

Creed was once more transfixed into another world – a world of spiritual inspiration the likes of which he had not felt since leaving the seminary as a teenager in Ireland.

Suddenly, the bells stopped, and he looked up. The locals had taken to their feet and gone about their business. Creed stood and went into the café until evening Mass ended, when he would try to find Father Vincennes.

The evening crowd had filled the café, and soon he was being jostled by an assortment of *Les Habitants,* the original French settlers of Quebec. It was dark when the Mass ended, and the devout parishioners had scattered across the *Place Royale* to their homes, shops, or farms.

Creed slipped out of the warm, smoky café and crossed the square to the building next to the church. He took off his tricorn hat and knocked on the heavy brass door knocker. An older woman dressed in black opened the door and looked at him. Her pale face showed the lines of a woman around sixty. Her white-streaked hair was piled high.

"This is not the entrance to the church, *monsieur.*" She motioned towards the church doors.

"*Merci madame,* but I have not come to pray. I must speak to Father Vincennes."

She eyed him suspiciously. "Your French is excellent, *monsieur.* You are from France?"

Creed nodded. "I have lived in Strasbourg and in Paris."

"You have a curious manner of speaking."

Creed smiled. "My uncle was Irish, *madame.* With the *Brigade Irlandais.*"

"*Les Irlandais* who serve France?"

"*Non, Les Irlandais au service de le Roi, madame.*"

She nodded as if she had heard of the famous Wild Geese, Irish soldiers who escaped British occupation of Ireland in the late 17th century to serve the Kings of France in battles from Flanders to Italy.

"Father Vincennes is serving the faithful across the river. He will not be back until ten, at the least. I suggest you come back tomorrow, *Monsieur.*"

"No, I must go away tomorrow, *madame.* I will wait in the church until he returns. It will give me time alone with Our Lord."

The woman smiled at the last remark. "An excellent idea, *monsieur.* I will inform Father Vincennes. Where will you be?"

"In the church, *madame.* In a quiet pew."

The older woman smiled knowingly.

The church bell struck eleven. Creed had waited, kneeling at a side altar near the sanctuary lamp. He prayed the rosary using the set of beads that were his only remembrance of his departed mother. He went through the Beatitudes. He prayed in Latin, then in French, and finally in English.

Creed was startled from his devotions by a firm hand on his shoulder. "I am Father Vincennes, *monsieur.* It is not usual in Quebec for someone to want to see a priest so late and so urgently. Madame Grouchy told me you were waiting here. Is someone in your family sick? Dying?"

Creed looked up. Even in the darkness of the church, he could see that Vincennes was young and vigorous. Not much older than he. Strangely, he had expected a withered, older man.

He replied in French. "No, Father, well, not in my family, and not sick or dying– yet."

"I do not understand," Vincennes replied.

"Soon, many men will be sick and die, as many have already." Creed regretted his sly comment even as he uttered it.

Vincennes ignored the remark and knelt next to him. "What are you trying to say, *monsieur*? Why are you here? Asking for me at this hour?"

"A friend gave me instructions to seek you when I arrived in Quebec."

Vincennes startled. "A friend, *monsieur*? What kind of friend?"

"A friend of liberty, from the south." Creed thought he noticed Vincennes straighten just a little at his remark.

"A friend of liberty? Or enemy of *les Anglais*?"

"Well, both," Creed answered.

"And why did this friend instruct you to seek me of all priests...of all people in Quebec?"

"I, I don't know exactly. Creed remembered that the word *Victoires* was underlined in the note. His instructions were that I should seek Father Vincennes at *Eglise Notre Dame d' Victoires*."

Vincennes nodded. "Ah, I understand now perfectly. When do you depart?"

"At mid-morning tomorrow. But how..."

The priest cut him off. "Be at the church after morning Mass. Go to that confessional." He pointed at a large structure of ornate inlaid wood that looked almost like a giant birdcage in the corner of the church. "I shall await you there with what you need. Do you understand?"

"*Oui, mon pere.*"

"Then you must not be seen in this church again. The governor has his spies, even among the clergy. I am sorry to admit."

With a rustle of his cassock, he disappeared into the dark recesses of the church.

Creed left the church more confused than ever. *What was this priest's connection to Colonel Fitzgerald and the cause?* It was evident to him that Father Vincennes was an American agent. *But how? And why?*

Creed arrived the following day before the Mass. He went to a back pew and prayed quietly after fumbling for his rosary. He had forgotten the solace he once gained from quiet reflection.

At length, the parishioners began to enter the church until it was about one-quarter full. A bell rang, and Father Vincennes appeared, surrounded by altar boys and clothed in the vestments of the Mass. He began the service, which was quiet and quick, unlike a Sunday Mass.

When it ended, Creed went to the confessional. He waited hours before hearing the door on the other side of the confessional slide open and then close. He saw the full outline of the priest through the shade that separated them. He glanced around to ensure nobody saw him and slipped in.

"Thank you for hearing my confession, Father, and on a workday too," Creed whispered in French.

"I am always ready to serve the faithful and a just cause."

"How did you come to support our cause?" Creed asked.

"It is not your cause I support as much as the cause of Canada. Suffice to say that when the *Anglais* armies came to seize Quebec, a small band of Canadian patriots never stopped their resistance. Later, those who supported the overthrow of the *Anglais* worked for your General Arnold. When he was forced to retreat, we provided him with useful information on the *Anglais*. This information enabled him to prevent Carleton from marching south last year."

Creed was astonished. So, if this priest was to be believed, General Benedict Arnold established a spy ring during his doomed invasion of Canada in 1775. And the small circle of agents, still resentful of the British conquest of Canada twenty years earlier, had helped him save the cause from the wrath of Governor Carleton's counterstroke into New York in the winter of 1776.

"So, you have information for me?" Creed asked.

"Look under your kneeler."

Creed felt under his kneeler and retrieved an oilskin pouch about the size of a small book.

"What is this? British war plans?" Creed expected some exciting revelation about General Burgoyne's intentions.

"Hardly anything as useless as the plans of the *Anglais*," Vincennes sniffed. "You should know, *monsieur*, all plans are subject to change, are they not? That is God's way with us."

The comment struck a chord with Creed. "Indeed, *mon Pere*."

"No, what I have provided you is a year's worth of sweat and study by some dedicated *Habitants*. More valuable than Burgoyne's plans, for it will provide you the key to plans he has yet to devise."

"What, what do you mean?"

"I can say no more."

"But how can...."

"I have already said enough, *monsieur*. You must go."

Creed hesitated a moment, then whispered. "*Mon Pere*, will you hear my confession? It has been over a year since I left Maryland. I have not seen a priest since."

"But of course, *monsieur*. You remember how to start?"

"I do."

Vincennes listened quietly. When Creed finished, he received absolution.

Then Vincennes cleared his throat and spoke just above a whisper, "There are others besides you. You cannot know who they are, but they each carry one of these as absolute proof of their devotion to the Church, the cause, and our small circle of patriots. I give you one as well, *monsieur*."

The priest slid the confessional screen open and drew a set of beautiful rosary beads, each bead a semi-precious stone the color of a ruby. Creed noticed that each decade had several missing. Vincennes plucked one from the end of the string and gave it to him.

"The cardinal himself once blessed these. Combined with prayer, it may keep you safe as it has the others."

"Who are the others?" Creed stammered.

"I have said too much. *Adieu, monsieur*."

The partition slid closed, and he was gone before Creed could say another word.

***

The Dunning House, New York, June 1777

Sandy Drummond's boots scraped the floor of his room at Lady Dunning's boarding house. With his hands thrust behind his back, his game knee appeared more pronounced, and he almost waddled in the effort.

His young ward, Klara Stump, sat quietly at needlework while Drummond engaged in a heated conversation with one of his best operatives, Captain Sidney Baker.

A small fire glowing in the woodstove barely warded off the late spring chill that held New York in its grip.

"Now, Sidney, the rebels control all of New Jersey except the Brunswicks and a small foothold near the Paulhus Hook. Their depredations over the winter have frustrated our regulars. This has made General Howe even more risk-averse. He has few reinforcements to make up the losses."

"I thought another five thousand troops were coming. At least that is what you told me after Trenton and Princeton."

"Yes. Our good General Burgoyne has outfoxed both William Howe and Guy Carleton. The troops milord had been counting on went to Canada."

"Canada? What on earth for?"

"To reinforce an attack from the north. Burgoyne aims to take Fort Ticonderoga and Albany and split New England from the rest of the colonies. It seems a likely strategy. The only problem is that its success will be viewed as Burgoyne's, leaving Carleton and Howe looking as unwilling lieutenants at best."

Baker rubbed the thick scar on his face. The result of an altercation with some rebel spies back in Princeton the previous year.

"Well, a quick victory is in all our interests, isn't it?"

"Not necessarily, Sidney. Oh, you could not understand. You are a merchant by profession, not a soldier. Some victories bring glory, some bring profit, and others dishonor a soldier. This has the makings of the latter for all of us here in New York."

"Not all of us, sir. Some of us just want the rebels defeated so we can return to our lives as proper Englishmen. Nothing more. Not glory. Not fame. Lord knows, not wealth. Duty to the king and back to a life of peace."

Drummond nodded. "I understand. Yes, we want an Englishman's peace for this fair land. But as soldiers, we came here for glory. I lost one chance for it when I was seconded from the 17ᵗʰ Dragoons to serve General Howe's intelligence apparatus. So now, my glory is attached to his success, or appearance of success."

"You might have attached yourself to someone more driven," Baker replied with his hand over his mouth to hide a smirk.

Drummond cocked his head, then glanced at Klara. "*Touché,* Captain Baker."

Drummond's alliance with Clinton was a card he kept close to the vest.

Klara looked up and smiled at Baker. Although she suspected some involvement of Drummond and Baker in her father's disappearance, she had warmed to her guardian and his various friends and subordinates. Of all the major's minions, she found Baker the most appealing in looks and temperament, even with his scar.

"Klara thought you clever as well, Sidney. Have you seen a lovelier young lady?"

"Never," replied Baker, looking at her with evident admiration.

"Well, bid her farewell, for she is about to be excused so we may talk of serious matters."

The rebuff annoyed Klara, but she smiled sweetly at Baker and left for her room without a word. Drummond closed the door behind her.

* * *

When Klara's footsteps reached the end of the hall, Drummond continued. "Anyway, Sidney, here is the thing. You are to take a small company of the Provincials from De Lancey's Regiment – Provincials, not a gang of rogue skinners, and probe up the Hudson."

Baker grew concerned. "My men are from New Jersey. As members of the 4ᵗʰ New Jersey Provincials, our value is knowledge of the Jerseys. The back roads and byways are useful for reconnaissance and espionage against Washington's forces. They are spread from Burlington to Bergen and west to Morristown."

Drummond glared at him. "You think I don't know that? That is why I recruited you in the first place."

Drummond softened his look and grasped Baker's shoulder. "But you are too clever and experienced to remain long, shall we say, a local?"

Praise from Drummond was rare. Baker knew something was up. Drummond unfurled a crude map of the Hudson. "You will slip through the rebel lines in a navy galley and debark near Verplanck's Point. You will proceed on foot about sixteen miles to Pollepel Island, near Beacon. The North River narrows there. We have reports the rebels have built *chevaux de frise* to block the channel."

"What in Christ's name are 'Chevoe dee freeze'?" Baker asked testily.

Drummond took a breath. "*Chevaux de frise.* I'm sorry, a French term. Fiendish iron spikes sank into the riverbed. Properly placed, they are capable of gutting our ships like fish. The Royal Navy prefers that not happen. An honest effort to breach a pathway through them is needed. An honest effort, not necessarily a success, yet."

Baker shook his head. "I don't understand."

"General Howe has instructed us to make this effort as a demonstration towards the north. If you succeed, so much the better. He retains his options. If you fail, his options may be limited but perhaps more to his liking. Do you get my drift, Sidney?"

"So, you want me to fail?"

"No, Sidney, I want you to do it. General Howe wants you to fail. This mission is his attempt to appease supporters of a northern thrust."

"And what do you think of this?" Baker felt this was a suicide mission.

"I'll be satisfied if one of us gets his wish. You shall leave tomorrow with the morning tide. A small team of British sailors will join you on the galley. They have a craft especially suited to navigating through obstacles under the enemy's nose. Their mere existence is extremely confidential, so say nothing to your men of the mission or the sailors' role."

"As you wish, sir," Baker replied. His stomach churned at the thought of leading his men on a mission of forlorn hope.

Chapter 7

Saint-Jean-sur-Richelieu, Canada, June 1777

The light breeze tickling Creed's face provided little comfort against the unseasonably warm weather. His canoe turned a bend, and he saw Saint-Jean come into view. The small farming village along the narrow Richelieu River was the assembly point for Burgoyne's army.

The force consisted of a mix of English and Scottish regulars, German mercenaries, Loyalists Provincials, Canadian adventurers, and Indians. The latter mainly were Iroquois with a smattering of warriors from other tribes anxious to share in the plunder sure to come with such a venture.

Stands of forest interspersed with small but neat farms lined the river. The town itself was small. Creed expected as much. However, it had a nice-looking stone church, and the quays seemed well-maintained.

Creed noticed one quay devoid of the usual gaggle of soldiers and stevedores. "Pull in here – *a droit.*"

The rowers deftly turned, and Creed was on the wooden quay in moments. The arrival of three more canoes made no impression.

They soon had the canoes unloaded and pulled up on shore, where they roped them together in case someone tried to steal one in the dark.

Creed gave Androche and O'Ballance instructions for making camp. The crew began the daily ritual of finding wood, preparing fires, drawing freshwater, spreading his ground cloth, and erecting a lean-to or tent.

They sat before the fires, oiling their weapons after completing those preparations.

"Is it normal for a unit to join a war like we are? Almost an afterthought?" Bart asked.

O'Ballance continued sharpening his bayonet. "There are always units coming and going. Campaigns are usually confused. You'll soon learn that all officers' work goes for nothing once a campaign starts."

"Seems odd."

"Not at all. We soldiers have to make the difference if the plan is to succeed," O'Ballance replied.

"Captain Lawrence seems pretty good at making his plans work. I'd reckon," Bart replied.

"So far. But we have a long way to go, young sir. This war has yet to begin."

"Still, I'd wager he'll see us through somehow."

O'Ballance nodded. "That's the only reason I signed up."

Bart eyed him in disbelief.

O'Ballance chortled. "Well, that and more than one debtor and angry husband on my tail."

Creed signaled for Bart to join him. "Time you learned a little about armies. Perhaps you'll meet a general or two. Something to tell your ma and the good major."

Bart cast a dismayed look. The subject of Haddix and his mother had not ceased to disturb him.

"I'm sorry," Creed said. "Let's be on our way."

They soon found the pavilions and tents arrayed on a large field.

"This looks as though it were planned for a parade," Bart observed.

"Yes, a parade now, but soon enough, a march through some of the most hostile territory in the colonies, they say."

The sights, sounds, and smells of an army camp filled the air, evoking nostalgia in Creed. He missed the Continental Army and realized suddenly he'd likely never get back to it.

Sergeants screamed orders at hapless soldiers. He saw groups of men digging, drilling, or hunched over smoky fires. A lucky few loitered with pipes plugged with sweet tobacco whose scent wafted across the camp. He noticed no sentries.

"How do we find the headquarters?" Bart asked.

"Follow the sights and sounds."

They followed the sounds until they came upon several bands playing military marches.

"Seems like a military tattoo," Creed said.

"A what?"

"A gathering of military bands. Pomp and ceremony to stir up morale."

They made their way past the bands. A line of red-coated soldiers at parade rest stood arrayed before them. Before they could skirt the formation, a burly sergeant wearing the bearskin of a grenadier stopped them.

"I'd say yer lost, sir. Where can I be directin' ye?"

Creed held his head up and glanced around the camp absent-mindedly. "I am Captain James Lawrence. Royal American Regiment. Looking for General Burgoyne's headquarters, sergeant!"

The large man rubbed his nose and nodded knowingly. "Very well then, sir. Proceed in this direction, then follow the sound of the tom-toms."

"Tom-toms?"

"Indeed, sir. It seems General Burgoyne is hosting a band of native chiefs. Not sure why we need to go to war with a bunch of savages. If you know what I mean, sir?"

Creed smiled mischievously. "Indeed, Sergeant. Next thing you know, we'll be enlisting the Irish as well."

The mark struck home, and the sergeant's eyes widened in a strange combination of annoyance and delight.

"Indeed, sir." He saluted and stormed off.

Creed chuckled. "Let's march to the sound of the tom-toms, Bart."

Soon, the two were working their way past neat rows of tents. Creed had Bart count them to estimate the number of men in Burgoyne's force.

Bart tallied the numbers as Creed called out a tent. "That makes it almost 200 tents, sir."

"Each tent sleeps ten or twelve men, Bart. There are nearly two thousand men in this camp. More importantly, I noted six regimental standards."

"Does that matter?" Bart asked.

Creed nodded. "Indeed, flags, the regimental standards, comprise the soul of each unit in an army, but most especially in the British Army. Let's see now, two thousand men under arms with six regiments. This is just one of Burgoyne's divisions. The governor told me he had over seven thousand men under arms, including Germans and Canadians."

"What of these people? Why are they allowed here?"

"They provide essential services."

Among the redcoats, swarms of sutlers, bands of French trappers, and groups of women and children went about their business with the army. They did laundry, sold or bartered goods, and provided medical care to wounded or sick soldiers. Some were the wives or sweethearts who followed the men through years of distant campaigning.

Creed laughed. "You have much to learn about armies, Bart. Burgoyne hasn't been able to do without the logistics tail required by most European armies. This might prove a problem when he enters the impenetrable American forest."

"But women with the army? Do they?"

"Indeed. Some, at least, even some who are married to soldiers or the sutlers."

Bart's eyes widened. He seemed appalled.

Along the river, several bands of Indians played some kind of game with wicker sticks and what looked like a leather ball. Creed thought the game was little different from a melee – as young braves shouted and called out, bared their chests, greased and sweaty, and collided as two or more fought for the ball.

Creed was amused. "Now what in the...."

Bart laughed. "Indians have some strange games."

Finally, they found a large silk pavilion with finely woven ropes holding the cover in place. They also found the source of the tom-toms. More than a dozen Indians sat in a circle with legs crossed, beating out a rhythm and chanting.

An aide approached. "May I help you, sir?"

Creed smiled mischievously. "Indeed. If your name is John Burgoyne."

The aide, a subaltern, turned pale. "I should say not, sir. The general is engaged in conversation with our native allies." He glanced at the drummers with disdain.

"I see. Iroquois, I presume?"

"I am not knowledgeable of tribal affiliates, sir. But if you say so."

"When will he be free to chat with the commander of his newest complement?"

"Newest complement?"

"Yes, inform the general that Captain James Lawrence has arrived with the First Company, Fourth Battalion, of the Royal American Regiment."

"The First Company? Where is the rest of the regiment?"

"Not due to arrive for some time. In the meantime, we are here to serve at his pleasure. We are at the far end of the encampment. Send for me when he is available."

Creed handed him a note explaining his late assignment to the expedition. He did not think Burgoyne would question unexpected reinforcements, however modest.

***

When they returned to the company, Creed found the camp was in good order. O'Ballance had bartered firewood and food from the sutlers and engaged a few Canadian women to cook. The smell of fresh fish grilling over a wood fire delighted him.

"Your tent is over there, sir. Thought you'd want some privacy," O'Ballance said.

The tent was in a small stand of pine trees about forty yards from the others.

Creed nodded. "You have set a fine camp, sergeant. Something tells me we'll have little chance to enjoy one as fine as this for some time."

O'Ballance nodded. "Right, sir. The ladies say supper will be ready in a few minutes, sir. Chance to wash up, eh?"

After O'Ballance left, Creed dropped his sword and belting and stripped to his waist. He took a washcloth and razor from his toilet bag and went down to the river. He found a small cove protected by light foliage. The sweet smells of spring added a strange gentleness to the spot.

He looked to the west and saw the sun dipping over the mountains. Relaxed for the first time in a long time, he shaved and washed down his upper torso. Then he heard what sounded like girlish laughter from the bushes. He dropped his blade and walked towards the sound. The bushes went still.

"Come out of there, whoever...."

A beautiful young woman emerged in an Indian-style white deerskin dress. Not more than seventeen, he thought. Her petite build was perfectly formed. Her dark hair was pleated and ran down her back to her waist. She had high cheekbones, light copper skin, dark eyes set wide apart, and what people would call a Roman nose. Beneath it was a small, plump mouth that smiled suggestively.

"Who are you?" Creed asked.

"I am Fleurette, *monsieur*. Fleurette Binoche," she replied in French,

She said it as if she expected him to know who she was. For a young girl, she had an uncanny air of self-assurance.

Creed nodded. "Well, Fleurette Binoche, do you always spy on men taking their toilette?"

She nodded as if it were the most natural thing to her. "Quite often, *monsieur*, but never with such a handsome toilette."

Creed blanched, and he could tell it was the desired reaction.

"Very well, Fleurette. But where I come from, ladies do not spy on men. But if it suits you...."

He turned and went back to his wash. The girl followed him. Picking up his cloth, she slowly wiped the excess soap and water from his face and worked the fabric down his neck, shoulders, back, and chest. Creed seemed mesmerized, and her fingers felt good. Sure, but gentle. "You should stop...."

But she continued stroking and gently whispered in his ear, "Where I come from, it is considered proper for a man to have himself cleaned by a woman."

Her breath smelled sweet. Like honeysuckle. "And just where do you come from?"

"I was born among the Canadians, but my mother was Iroquois – Seneca. My father is Serge Binoche." She spoke as if he should know her father.

"Ah, is he a *coureur de bois*?"

She smiled. "Of course, but not just anyone, no, papa is the bravest and strongest *coureur*."

They were just inches apart, and she continued to rub his shoulders.

"And who are you, *monsieur*?"

"Captain James Lawrence, Royal American Regiment."

She made a strange gesture with her tongue. "How does an *Anglais* speak French so well?"

"I had an excellent teacher."

"A woman, I will wager."

He turned and eyed her. "One or two...."

He snatched the cloth from her. "*Merci, mademoiselle.* But you need to leave now."

***

Creed and his men dug into an evening feed of grilled fish and some bread. After the long day of rowing, it went down all too quickly. A tired Creed quietly repaired to his tent. He had sent the girl away with a halfpenny for her efforts. But did not mention her visit to his companions.

Alone for the first time, he carefully opened Father Vincennes's packet. The oilskin contained an envelope with a gold-embossed cross surrounded by the words "*Ad Majorem Dei Gloriam.*" His eyes widened as he strained in the candlelight to read what he knew at once was invaluable.

Creed muttered, "For the Greater Glory of God. Sweet Jesus, Father Vincennes, you and your lads have done it!"

Creed fingered four large sheets of fine vellum parchment with exquisitely drawn maps and sketches showing routes, landmarks, and terrain features from the Ile de Noix to Albany. This vellum felt malleable and resilient to the touch so that it could be easily folded or rolled.

Creed knew at once that it took a tremendous effort to create maps as accurate and extensive as these. Years of fieldwork followed by exact measurement and marking. It was as though he had a gift from the Jesuit martyrs of North America.

He also realized that the maps could help him lead the invading British to glory – or destruction.

***

Creed made his way through the crowd of uniformed men, leather-clad woodsmen, and ornately decorated Iroquois in response to an early morning summons from

Burgoyne. The general himself stood before his pavilion. Smiling broadly, he greeted Creed with a handshake. He led him into the pavilion and motioned for him to sit at a finely appointed table laden with fresh fruit and a pair of glasses filled with vintage wine.

Burgoyne raised his glass. "Help yourself to the wine and fruit, a small appetizer. My cook is preparing roasted doves with some native corn and potato mash."

Creed picked up his glass and admired the color of the wine. "This appears to be a 1760 vintage, sir. From the Medoc?"

Burgoyne beamed. "Yes, but it is alas 1766. Not quite so fine a vintage. Your knowledge impresses."

"I am not a worldly man, sir. But then again, fine wine is not of this world."

Burgoyne laughed. "How true. How true. Now, I have read your letter with great interest, Captain Lawrence. May I call you by your Christian name?"

"Please do, sir," Creed replied. "James is fine."

"Now, James, we all know the key to victory lies in the Americans...so having your Royal Americans with us, albeit a token force, is greatly appreciated. Why the entire point of this campaign is to sever the arch-rebels of New England from the more moderate and loyal Americans in the middle colonies."

"Well put, sir. My men are not political but loyal to the king and anxious to prove it."

Burgoyne cocked his head. "How so?"

"By leading the invasion as part of your advance guard. To serve as scouts as well and probe deeply against the rebels."

"Do they have experience in such things?"

"No. But I do. I have traveled this region before and am comfortable that I can be of service in the area of reconnaissance and such." Creed was less than truthful.

Burgoyne nodded as he sipped at his wine.

Creed continued. "I have enlisted a renowned *coureur de bois* as well. Expert with the canoe and knowledgeable of the Indian ways."

Burgoyne put his glass down and placed his chin on folded fingers. "An interesting proposition. Unorthodox, but perhaps just the thing this enterprise needs. You will need some reinforcement. I shall assign you to the advance guard under Simon Fraser. Fraser has a renowned Canadian explorer who has also traveled these parts. He will be assigned to your company."

An added complication, Creed thought. "Who is this, renowned Canadian?"

"His name is Serge Binoche. I find him uncouth. Quite typical of these Canadian Frenchmen. He's practically a savage himself, so many of them are. Still, more than three hundred have joined us. Almost as many as the Americans who, thanks to your arrival, now number a bit over three hundred men."

"You have quite a few Iroquois, too, I see."

"Indeed, four hundred, or so they tell me. But who can be sure, since the savages come and go as they please."

"Then why use them at all? No troops are better than unreliable troops."

"A wise observation, James. But I need them to scout even more deeply than the advance guard. They move through these deep forests and along the waterways like birds through the air. Or so I am told."

"But can you trust their reports?"

Burgoyne thought a moment. "A good point, James. No, of course, we cannot. They'll likely tell us what we want to hear. They are in this for the blood and plunder."

"Blood and plunder?"

"A Canadian leads them. Pierre Saint Luc de Lacorne. A distasteful fellow. What does he say? '*Il faut brutaliser des affaires*'...."

"Do you think the scalp will bring the rebels to their knees?"

"Not exactly, but the threat of it will keep their militia from forming against us. The Hampshire Grants and western Massachusetts are flush with very aggressive militia units. The threat of the scalp to their women and children should keep them close to home."

Creed raised his glass. "A splendid plan, sir."

"It is, isn't it? Well, enough of this. Let's enjoy other discussions. Afterward, Lazarus Sinclair will provide you with all the details you need, James. After meeting him, I'll send you to see Simon Fraser. You will like him."

"I'm sure I will, sir," Creed replied.

Burgoyne's face widened in a grin. "Now, do you favor the theater?

***

"Are you Colonel Sinclair?" Creed pushed open the loose flap and stepped into the tent. The inside was cramped, and there was little air.

Burgoyne's Adjutant barely nodded before he launched into his plans. "I was told you were coming, Mister Lawrence. The army is poised to sail south on Lake Champlain and strike the mighty American fortress of the north – Fort Ticonderoga."

"Why, sir, the rebels boast of Ticonderoga as the Gibraltar of America," Creed replied.

"We took the actual Gibraltar from Spain, Captain Lawrence. We can take Ticonderoga from a pack of rebels. Spies and deserters have already reported the post undermanned, and in poor morale."

Creed probed him. "Would it not be wiser to avoid such a fort and bypass it?"

Sinclair shook his head. "You infantry officers need lessons in logistics, Mister Lawrence. Once taken, Ticonderoga will serve as the springboard for our second move – this time along Lake George and then down the upper North River, the Hudson, to take Albany."

Creed probed him more. "What do you feel is your greatest challenge, sir?"

Sinclair placed a finger pensively to his chin. "This is a good plan. But I am not convinced we can supply this force adequately unless we seize Albany quickly. General Burgoyne has some four thousand British and three thousand German mercenaries to feed and over a hundred cannons to transport."

"Those don't seem insurmountable, given your thorough planning, sir. Any others?"

Sinclair glanced about to make sure no one was listening. His voice grew hushed, "If our efforts are separated by too much time and space, the rebel army could muster a larger force and defeat us. And then turn on Howe."

He placed his hand on a primitive map and ran his finger from New York to Canada. Creed saw how little detail his map had, unlike his maps from Father Vincennes.

Sinclair ran his index finger along the Massachusetts border. "Rebel militia from here could cut our supply line and worse. That's another fear I have."

"So this offensive has some fragility?"

"I'm afraid so. Any delay or vacillation could prove our undoing."

"Colonel, I shall endeavor to find the fastest route to Albany. Let's hope General Howe heads north with equal speed."

Sinclair looked ruefully. "My plans can impact only our efforts. General Howe must be left to chance."

Sinclair handed Creed a piece of paper. "These are your orders. General Burgoyne wants your detachment to join Fraser and the advanced guard. He is preparing a reconnaissance in force that will muster on the Ile *aux Noix.*"

Creed's eyes widened. "And where is that, sir?"

Sinclair tapped his map. "About ten miles south of here, at the head of Lake Champlain."

Creed looked at the orders. "This states that I will have a detachment of Canadian...scouts? Is that this Serge Binoche the general mentioned?"

"Yes. Fraser will send them to you. I don't know much about them."

Creed hoped he could get Sinclair to change Burgoyne's mind about the Canadians. "Sir, I see no need for further reinforcement. A smaller reconnaissance force can move faster and attract less attention from the rebels."

Sinclair rolled his eyes dismissively. "General Burgoyne wants to make sure the Canadians are recognized for supporting this effort. Loyalists need to play a key role. He's supporting your late arrival for that reason. And since Canadians and Americans are better suited for crossing the wilderness, he's made a perfect match."

"But I...."

Sinclair began to roll up his map. "That will be all, Captain Lawrence."

***

When Creed arrived back at the camp, he called a meeting with Bart Saunders, O'Ballance, and Etienne Androche.

Androche's wife brought them warm mugs of tea. "Thank you, *madame*," said Creed as he took the cup in both hands.

She closed her eyes in reply and left without speaking.

Bart sipped his and silently listened.

"I've met with General Burgoyne and his senior officer for plans. We're attached to General Fraser's advance guard, now forming on the *Ile aux Noix.* Can you guide us there, Etienne?"

Androche grunted. "Of course, *monsieur*."

"Excellent. It's too late to depart this afternoon. Make sure our kit's packed and secured. Bring down the shelters and tents, too. The men need to be ready to depart with the morning twilight."

O'Ballance hesitated a moment, then spoke. "Sir, some of the lads were hoping to visit the Indian camp upriver. They heard the maidens are very free with their affections."

"And likely just as free with the pox. No, make sure they all stay in camp. Anyone who leaves I will treat as a deserter."

Bart looked inquisitively at Creed. "What about local women coming here, sir?" He dared not mention seeing the mixed-blood girl enter Creed's tent. Bart felt more than a pang of jealousy as he found the young woman quite beautiful, in a sultry sort of way.

"No, Mister Saunders."

Androche interrupted. "I will have my wife prepare a special meal. I purchased a quarter of fresh beef from one of the sutlers. I also obtained a small cask of wine and two dozen baguettes."

Creed smiled. "Well done, Androche."

He turned to O'Ballance, sulking about the lost opportunity to visit the Indian maidens. "Sergeant O'Ballance, make sure the men pack their kit and prepare the canoes for tomorrow. They'll all have their bellies full of good meat."

"And some good wine," Androche reminded them.

All the equipment was packed into the canoes by dusk, covered, and ready to go. The canoes themselves lay in a row along the embankment overlooking the river. The Royal Americans sat in small circles by files. Creed had organized them into three small files of six men each. Androche's men sat in a separate group, conversing heartily in a babble of French mixed with Indian dialects.

Bart remained stiff-lipped as Creed's men teased each other about the Indian women whose favors they would never enjoy. Creed's comment about the pox silenced most of the dissent brewing in that circle. Many believed that Indian pox was a hundred times worse than the white man's version. Few realized that the white man had brought the dreaded disease to the Americas.

Bart and Creed sat by the fire while Androche talked about the land ahead and some things they might encounter. Bart knew he had much to learn from these men. He planned to be like them one day.

Androche had seen much of the upper New York region. There was never any substitute for eyes on the ground.

Creed spooned a mouthful of the meat into his mouth as the bold Canadian spoke. Bart gnawed at a joint of beef.

"If the weather holds, we should make it down the waterways and reach Ticonderoga in a few days. Once the fort falls, we have a short overland portage to the headwaters of Lake George, followed by a shorter trip down the lake. Albany lies but a few days south. The Iroquois will go before us. No one can move as quickly over water or through the forests. This is their land – at least it is Mohawk land." Androche paused to sip his wine.

"No other tribes to challenge them?"

Androche smiled patronizingly. "You have much to learn, Captain Lawrence. The Iroquois rule from the mountains in the east to the lakes and rivers far to the west. When they strike, settlers and Indians scatter like deer before a pack of wolves. They kill all in their way, except the unfortunate few they capture. Those wretches suffer through hours and even days of unspeakable torture."

"You mean they scalp them?"

"Ha! Only the fortunate. Others are cut to pieces, one small shard of flesh at a time, or suffer the flames of the Iroquois fires, slowly roasting so they can watch and smell their flesh crackle and blacken. All are beaten first, usually by their women and children."

"Why would they treat their honorable opponents so bestially?"

"Who knows? It has been their way for years untold. Some rival tribes mimic their barbarity, but none exhibit the Iroquois' pure but efficient cruelty."

Creed paused a moment. "I doubt a British officer and gentleman would unleash such horrors on a people he hopes to rally to the King's cause."

Androche scooped a fistful of stew from the pot, gulped it down, and then belched. "My friend, in this land, all war is cruelty.

Bart sat silently as Creed and the trapper conversed. Shivers ran down his spine as Androche spoke. *I will never be like these men.* He wondered why he ever got himself into this misadventure. He was as loyal as the next man, but not ardently.

Androche sniggered. "I can see by his face that your young man already fears the Iroquois. That is their greatest wish."

Bart's face reddened.

"There, you are mistaken, Androche," Creed said. "During the voyage to Canada, Bart stood unarmed, surrounded by pirates equal to your savages in brutality and blood lust. He maintained his composure and performed his duty at great risk to his life. I think he can stand manfully against anything your savages can do to him. Besides, they are our allies, are they not? We are here to fight the rebels."

Androche's head shook. "In the wilderness, the lust for blood knows no allegiance, *monsieur*. One must always beware."

Bart's stomach turned with fear, and his eyes widened. He was terrified on that ship.

Creed chuckled. "Our friend is trying to scare us, Bart. The Iroquois are human, after all. And besides, you are our medicine man. They'll respect that."

"I was wracked with fear when those rebel pirates had me. I can handle my fears, sir." Even as he said it, he was not so sure.

***

When the camp turned in and the fires were damped, Creed repaired to his tent to go over the maps one more time in privacy. He made a few notes on them based on Androche's comments. The Canadian doubted the British could take Ticonderoga if the

Americans decided to defend it. Creed was not so sure, given the number and caliber of the British artillery park. Whether such guns could proceed any further was a different problem.

When he finished, Creed put away his papers and extinguished his candle. He removed his belting, boots, and coat. He stretched himself on his cot and stared at the canvas above him, pondering his situation.

His afternoon had proved productive. Burgoyne's effusive personality and natural self-confidence showed no suspicion at Creed's sudden and unexpected arrival with the Royal Americans. He noted a bit of skepticism from Colonel Lazarus Sinclair, but the colonel still provided Creed with an enthusiastic overview of the plans he had drafted.

A sudden rustling of the canvas took him from his thoughts. A figure was outside the tent.

"Is that you, Bart?" Creed reached for his pistol.

The canvas rustled again. The slender figure of Fleurette entered the tent.

Creed put down the pistol. "What brings you here, Fleurette?"

"You know very much, *monsieur.*" She dropped out of her deerskin shift and revealed herself to him.

"You are a comely young lady, but I told you once before that such a thing was impossible. I am an officer and...."

"And I am what? A half-breed? A half-squaw?" Fleurette balled her fists. Tears rolled down her cheeks.

Creed stood up and pulled up her shift, covering her shimmering skin. He wiped her tears and took her face in his hands.

"You are indeed lovely, Fleurette. But understand that as an officer and a gentleman, and for so many other reasons, this cannot be. You must find yourself a husband. Perhaps among the British soldiers?"

Fleurette hung her head in shame and anger. She looked up, and her beautiful face took on a menacing look. "Very well, *monsieur.* But you made a grave mistake in rejecting me."

Suddenly, she leaped at him like a panther and kissed him hard. Her legs entwined around his waist and gripped him tightly as she tried to press herself into him. She moaned and wailed in a language he did not understand.

Creed gripped her shoulders and then eased her away. Suddenly, she flailed at him with her fists. She grunted in anger and pounded with a fury he had never seen in a woman. But her blows, though strong, did little to stop him from pulling her off and easing her away. They struggled a moment, but Creed subdued her.

"Enough now, *mademoiselle.* Please go."

She smiled, composed as though it was all an act, and without a word, she left.

***

Fleurette slipped through the woods with the speed and instincts of a deer. In the darkness, no sentry caught sight of her.

The North Spy

Finally, she arrived back at the camp of Serge Binoche. Fleurette adjusted her shift, and her moccasins pattered toward her lean-to. A devious smile crossed her face. She felt satisfied that she had saved face. Anyone within 100 yards not asleep would believe she and Captain James Lawrence had just made passionate love.

Chapter 8

Beacon, New York

The galley seemed to glide up the North River, passing sights Sidney Baker never knew existed. His first venture up the valley showed a land both rugged yet cultivated. After passing the high palisades cliffs on the Jersey side, the terrain settled into rolling wooded hills until they passed Haverstraw, a small port on the north end of the Tappan Zee. The *Zee* was a long and wide stretch of the river that the original Dutch settlers called a *Zee* because it looked like a small sea.

Passing that, the mountains on both sides became formidable, although many had large swaths of forest missing to fill the hearths and stoves of settlers from Long Island to Albany.

Spring turned the river valley into a verdant wonderland. Between the mountains, Baker could see valleys dotted with neat-looking Dutch farms and more than a few large plantations with enormous stone houses suitable for European estates.

"How far to Verplank's Point?" Baker asked the master of the galley.

"The current is strong with the spring runoff from the melting snow in the mountains. If I time it right, we should arrive a little after midnight. That should allow you to get past any rebel patrols while still dark."

"You speak as though you have done this before," Baker said.

The master's face darkened. "Just once, and I nearly lost the ship between rebel guns and the rocks. The night's better, especially with a rising river."

"What about the rocks? I should think they'd be a greater danger in the darkness."

The master motioned towards the four navy tars busy working on a strange-looking longboat. It had shortened oars and was covered with a tarp smeared with black tar, giving it the appearance of a turtle.

Baker turned and watched them a moment. "I've met their officer. He's a young one. Barely twenty, I'd say. He was very discreet about their role here."

"Yes, Ensign Framingham. That is his way. It is a special unit—a mix of Royal Navy tars and Royal Marines. Each man is handpicked for strength, endurance, and brutality. They can all swim like porpoises, too, mind you."

"Swimmers too?"

"They will head to shore before us and mark a safe passage through the rocks," the master answered.

"Won't they catch the attention of the rebel sentries?"

The master folded his arms across his chest. "Their boat barely rises above the waterline. Once they negotiate a passage free from rocks or shoals, they'll light a lantern coated with a tincture to reduce its glare. The lantern has an opening that can adjust to focus the light beam. Unless you are between our ship and their boat, there is little chance of seeing it."

"Impressive! For whom do they work? These...."

"Scorpions. They call themselves the Scorpions. Tropical vermin that hide but then strike suddenly and with deadly swiftness. Their commander is Captain Daniel Black, and he reports directly to...."

A secret naval unit, the Scorpions were a hand-picked mix of Able-Bodied Seamen and Royal Marines. They sailed the coasts and rivers for clandestine meetings with Loyalist spies or to pick up and deliver packages at secret rendezvous points. Mainly operating in the cover of darkness, Scorpion boats moved quickly and stealthily, and because of their men's strength, speed, and prowess, they could sting like a scorpion.

The master paused. "I have said too much. The existence of these Scorpions is very confidential. So don't let on that I have spoken of this. They have friends in high places, and I command a mere galley because I do not...."

"Of course, sir, "Baker said. "You're right. Let me check my men. It may be my last chance before we touch rebel soil,"

***

A dim light from the east bank twinkled faintly across the still night waters, in the darkness visible to only those who searched for it.

Minutes later, two sleek longboats were lowered quietly into the cold water.

The first mate approached the master. "Sir, the boats and oarsmen are ready."

The master nodded and turned to Baker. "You may board the craft now, Captain Baker. I shall return here in forty-eight hours. After that, you are on your own to return to our lines. I wish I could be more accommodating, but those are my orders."

"I understand, sir. Thank you for all you have done."

The master swung his hands behind his back and thrust his chin upwards. "God be with you, captain."

The crew began rowing silently towards the shore, their oars padded to muffle their sound. Baker was amazed at the professionalism of the Royal Navy. His heart pounded in nervousness and the great pride of being part of this great enterprise known as Britain.

Baker's force comprised a dozen men from the New York Loyalists and two of his own from New Jersey. Each boat had eight oarsmen and a coxswain. Each man carried a musket and twenty ball-and-cartridge, a seventeen-inch triangular bayonet, a water bottle, and a haversack with ten pounds of specially treated gunpowder in a tight-fitting bag the shape of a sausage. Almost 150 pounds was sufficient to blow the rebel spikes from the water.

He could see the faint glow from a lantern beckoning them toward the shore. The crisp rhythm of the oars slicing the dark water drew them rapidly to the soft light from the far bank.

As the boats slid up against the embankment, two specially trained sailors emerged from the bushes and guided them up a narrow trail leading to a wooded overlook.

There, Ensign Framingham stood calmly and greeted Baker with a polite nod. "You must move quickly. The trail through the woods behind me leads to a narrow track that parallels the Albany Post Road. It is rocky and winds along a rugged ridge, but it eventually leads to your objective. We don't possess a reliable map, but one of our informers drew us a crude sketch. Take it."

"I am sure it will suffice." Baker folded the sketch into his waistcoat.

"You must reach Beacon by midnight tomorrow and strike as soon as possible. The rebels have no security there."

Baker's eyes narrowed. "Really? Why not?"

Framingham chuckled. "Too far up the river, I suppose, for the Royal Navy's reach."

"Are you certain of all this?" Baker asked.

"This enterprise has no certainties. And you must be back here in forty-eight hours if you want to return to New York by water," Framingham spoke bluntly, with little of the respect customarily shown to a more senior officer.

"Very well, go back to your boat. My men shall take it from here," Baker replied icily.

The trail that took Baker and his men north was barely more than a deer path, but it led them to Beacon by ten the next evening. Baker left his detachment in a small clearing. He climbed the hill overlooking Beacon Point, a small peninsula that juts into the river. It was a night filled with stars, and the moonlight cast a glow across the water, allowing him to see a wooden lighthouse guiding the waterway. He noticed shadows moving inside.

A half-dozen campfires suggested that at least a company was guarding the tower and the barrier along the riverbank. Baker softly cursed. Framingham told him there was no security this far up the river. He wondered what other surprises awaited them.

He returned to the men, pondering how to approach such a difficult task. He now had a feeling his British masters wanted a face-saving demonstration. But he was unsure of the consequences of failure.

"Did you see anything, sir?" the sergeant-in-charge of the Loyalists asked.

"Yes. Trouble."

"Trouble?"

"Seems there is a tower at the end of the peninsula. A line of campfires forms a shallow arc along the riverbank, protecting the tower. The unguarded point has a garrison. Probably local New York militia."

"What about those long spikes you told us about in the water?"

"Couldn't see them. The spikes are said to be on the western side of the tower anyway."

The sergeant gulped. "What do you propose to do?"

Baker hesitated a moment. He had undergone many hazardous missions, but nothing prepared him for this. *Damn Drummond and Howe!*

"I have orders to storm the tower and blow or extract the spikes. To do that, we must seize a boat. But first, we must get through the rebels."

"Through them?"

Baker hesitated again. "We'll move in file to the edge of the woods and descend to the water level. That will put us no more than ten yards from the rebel fires. We shall form a line and rush them with the bayonet. We rush to the tower and seize a boat when I signal. While your New York boys cover us, my men and I will try to take the spikes."

"Should we load our firelocks, Captain?" asked one of the New York Provincials.

"Yes, but ensure your flints are at half-cock. I don't want to risk alerting the rebels. Now let's go."

The men fought through a thick bush that snapped and spat at them. They clawed their way to the low ridge and slowly descended to the water level in a zigzag pattern.

The occasionally turned ankle sent small stones tumbling down the steep ridge. The file would halt as one and listen anxiously for a rebel alarm. None came. The rebel fires burned low now, and no one stood guard. A few small tents lay before them, but most militias slept under the stars.

"The tower watch is their only security," the sergeant whispered to Baker.

Baker nodded. "Form line, now...."

A musket shot rang out, and its crack echoed across the narrow river. One of the men had full-cocked his musket against Baker's orders. He had to move quickly, or his mission would fail before it began. They had lost surprise.

"Attack the rebels!" Baker yelled in a loud voice.

His men drove forward with weapons leveled as sleepy militiamen began to rouse from their slumber. The Loyalists plunged bayonets into the rebels, still writhing under blankets and canvas. Men screamed for quarter, but received none. A few tried to load their weapons but quickly fell under musket blows and bayonet slashes.

"Form a line, men!" A militia officer tried to rally a defense. Only a handful heeded him. The rest of the survivors ran headlong along the riverbank. With arms and legs madly pumping, they scrambled for the safety of the woods up on the ridge.

"Take them!" Baker ordered.

The New York Loyalists charged the hapless rebels, whose last stand lasted only brief moments. The line of bayonets closed on them. Many rebels jumped into the water, while some fled for the safety of the tower. Steel met steel. Baker plunged his short sword into the officer's breast. He collapsed to his knees. The attackers scattered the remaining defenders and plunged bayonets into their exposed backs.

Baker drew his blade from the dead rebel officer and surveyed the carnage. In less than five minutes, an entire company of county militia was destroyed, with more than a dozen dead or dying and the remainder scattering for safety.

"We have taken them, by God!" a Loyalist exulted.

Baker had no time to take joy in the butcher's work. "Never mind that, to the tower."

Suddenly, a scattering of musket shots peppered them from the lighthouse. One of the Loyalists fell over, clutching his leg.

I believe I'm wounded," he groaned.

His sergeant ran over to him. "Is it bad?"

"No. A piece of rock struck me." The man struggled to his feet.

"Take the tower, boys!" Baker bellowed.

The tower stood less than fifty yards away. Now panting with excitement, fear, and bloodlust, Baker's men ran out along the peninsula. In moments, they were pounding at the doors with their musket butts. Butt plates scraped against thick wood planks and heavy iron fittings. The thumping was frantic. But to no avail.

"This door is reinforced oak," someone said.

Baker had to make a decision. "Sergeant, take five sacks of powder and a match. We shall blow this tower down. Everyone else, back to the shore."

Two burly men placed the sacks around the tower, one at each corner and one at the door. A thin line of powder connected them, and a final line ran the ten yards to the water's edge.

Baker and the sergeant ducked behind a rocky shoreline, just above the lapping water. The sergeant struck his flint and lit the improvised fuse. Sparks crackled, then the line sizzled as the powder burned its way back to the tower. It seemed an eternity to Baker, but seconds later, the sacks erupted in an explosive sequence that perforated eardrums, shattered glass, and splintered wood into kindling. The tower shuddered and collapsed into a burning heap.

Several militiamen jumped before the blast at the sight of the burning powder. The explosion and fire immolated the rest.

The pop of muskets filled the air. The Loyalists began firing at the survivors, who plunged into the cold waters of the river in a desperate attempt to escape.

"Forget the rebels," Baker ordered. "We must find a boat and get to the *chevaux de frise* before rebel help arrives."

Unfortunately for Baker and his men, help had arrived. Two more companies of New York militia and one of the Continentals raced up the river road running at a revenge-maddened pace.

There were shouts from officers and sergeants. The rebels quickly scrambled up the bluffs and deployed in skirmish order. Soon, the *pop, pop, pop* of muskets began raining lead down on them.

The Loyalists raced along the peninsula to escape the hail of lead. But now, lacking any cover other than the burning remains of the tower, their situation was hopeless.

"Sir, seize a boat and try to get out on the river. The Loyalist sergeant said, "We may gain you time to blast some of the *chevaux* yet."

Baker felt guilty about leaving the command to its destruction. But his duty was to the mission first. "Very well, sergeant. God be with you!"

He called his two men, "The situation is hopeless for us here, but we yet have time to get a boat out on the river and do some damage."

They scrambled down to the water's edge. Luckily, a few small boats lay bobbing against the tide.

Let's take this one, sir," one of his men exclaimed.

The green-jacketed New York Provincials formed a line and fired a volley back at the rebels on the bluffs. But they were caught in the open. The rebels aimed toward the flash of their muzzles. Men screamed as rebel musket balls began to strike home. Cries of anguish and pain erupted along the line as they began to fall to the rebel muskets.

Baker took one last look back. Half the New York Provincials were down, but a few remained standing. Their shadows danced against the crumpled tower's dying flames, making them look like demons from hell.

Another rebel volley lit the dark bluffs, and the Loyalist sergeant fell.

Baker had seen enough. He clambered into the boat, and his men began pulling madly at the oars. The little boat skipped along the water, heading southwest towards a small island on the river.

"The rebels will have markers to warn their ships. We must find those," Baker said. "How much powder left?"

"I have two bags, sir."

"I have but one, sir."

"Damn, that tower took most of our powder. Very well. We may yet be able to...."

Suddenly, they saw a series of flashes followed by explosions to their southwest. Then came another six blasts on the far side of the small island.

"What the devil is that, sir?"

Baker paused a moment and then replied. "I have no idea. But this affair is over. Turn south. We'll find a place to beach this skiff downriver and make our way back to Verplanck's Point."

His mind raced with guilt and despair. He had failed his mission and his men.

***

Morristown, New Jersey

Captain Benjamin Tallmadge pounded onto the village green at full gallop. He pulled his horse's reins and leaped from the saddle when he reached the Ford Mansion. The dragoon officer strode into the headquarters building with his saber jingling. He found his commander-in-chief sitting among his staff, enjoying the midday meal.

"Ah, young Major Tallmadge of our Continental Dragoons has come to join us. Find Major Tallmadge a chair and get him some ale," Washington ordered.

"Thank you, sir. That is most kind." Tallmadge nodded respectfully. He had news for his commander-in-chief.

"What news from the cavalry?" asked Lieutenant Colonel Alexander Hamilton, Washington's newly appointed aide de camp.

Hamilton's bantam-like build, demeanor, and dark visage made all who met him know this was a man of uncanny intelligence, cunning, and ambition.

Still, the easy-going but no less intelligent Tallmadge deflected the comment. "As you know, Mister Hamilton, cavalry reports are strictly confidential and should not be discussed like this."

Washington beamed. "True enough. Our greatest danger isn't British bayonets but British spies. After our meal, you can prepare your report, then discuss it with me. Are the roads dried up yet?"

"Yes, sir. I made it here from Liberty Pole in a few hours."

Hamilton's eyes narrowed. He turned his gaze to Washington. "Not good news, sir. That means the British could move their heavy equipment. An offensive could begin at any time."

Washington nodded. "I had that same thought, Alexander. That is why Major Tallmadge and all the dragoons are doing double duty."

An hour later, Tallmadge was knocking on the door to Washington's study. Unsurprisingly, he found Colonel Fitzgerald sitting on a small stool with his lanky legs crossed. Washington sat erect at his desk, already engaged in correspondence.

"Take a chair, Mister Tallmadge. Colonel Fitzgerald and I are anxious for what news you bring."

One of my patrols just returned from Tappan. Heath's courier brought word of a British night assault on the lighthouse near Beacon."

Washington looked at Fitzgerald. "Is that all?"

"No, sir. General Schuyler and the New York Committee for Safety had a scheme to block the Royal Navy from supporting a thrust on Albany by blocking the river with old hulks and steel shafts."

"*Chevaux de frise*, they are called," Washington interjected.

"This could portend a move north by Howe," Fitzgerald commented dryly.

"My men, and the Jersey militia, have seen no sign yet," Tallmadge replied.

"Well, there are signs, and there are signs. Certainly, a raid so far north portends something of import. Did Heath report any casualties?"

"Yes. It's in the report. A company of local militia all but eradicated. Many slashed to death as they rose from their sleep. Horrible wounds with no quarter given. A few hid in the tower, but a blast and the resulting inferno killed them."

Washington gasped. "Naval fire?"

"No, sir. A small galley was spotted near Verplanck's Point, but it ventured no farther."

"Then the *chevaux de frise* are still intact?"

Tallmadge shook his head. "Separate explosions destroyed all but two hulks. The shafts were either bent useless or lay at the river's bottom. The channel is clear."

"Schuyler is creative. He will think of a solution," Washington said as he tapped nervously at the table.

"But in time?" Fitzgerald asked.

"Ah, it is always, in the end, about time. How soon before Howe can move his army?"

"That would depend on how many men and what direction," Fitzgerald said.

Washington looked at Tallmadge. "Mister Creed is long gone, and any report from him on Burgoyne's army will not reach us before the decision point."

Fitzgerald's chin sank to his chest. "Communicating over such a vast and inhospitable distance was always the weak point in my plan."

"Yet I approved the plan." Washington's eyes bore in on Tallmadge." So, it is up to you, Mister Tallmadge, to help mitigate things. We need to know every move they make over there."

Washington gestured east towards New York.

"But beware of their tricks," Fitzgerald said.

Tallmadge frowned. "Tricks?"

"Howe is none too clever, but he has a few bright men around him who might convince him of a way to humbug us," Fitzgerald said.

Washington placed his chin on his balled-up fists. "My main concern is guarding the approaches to Philadelphia. Despite our winter successes, losing the nation's capital would endanger morale throughout the country. Almost as much as...."

"A successful British thrust to Albany," Fitzgerald interjected.

Washington nodded and narrowed his eyes at Tallmadge. "Howe has a position on us – forcing us to look north, south, and central. Only he knows which it will be. The sooner you can advise us, the more time this army has to react."

"I understand, sir." Tallmadge saluted, turned about-face, and strutted out, his saber jingling in rhythm with his boot steps.

***

When the door closed behind Tallmadge, Washington asked Fitzgerald the question that had haunted them both. "Do you think I erred in having Lieutenant Creed use 'Mister Jons' services to reach Canada?"

"I do, sir. If Mister Jons is exposed, I have no way of receiving reports from our only agent in the city, Mister Smythe. As it is, the mission will deprive us of his services for weeks."

"Your candor is my greatest asset, Colonel Fitzgerald. Never forsake it. Now, however, I rely on you to develop a remedy for our mistake."

"Your Excellency, we both know that the best remedy is time. Assuming he succeeds in bringing young Jeremiah to Canada, Mister Jons should be back in Long Island in a few weeks."

"Time, Robert, makes prisoners of us all. We are trapped as it slowly unfolds or overwhelmed as it speeds by us with little chance to act."

Fitzgerald uncrossed his legs and leaned forward towards Washington. "That same problem presents itself to our foes, sir."

Washington looked up at him. "Our challenge, then, Robert, is to exploit that."

Chapter 9

Isle au Noix, Lake Champlain

Creed waited patiently across the table as Brigadier General Simon Fraser was absorbed with reading the orders.

When Fraser finished, he looked at Creed with a broad smile that made his egg-shaped face even more expansive. His burr would make proud anyone from his birthplace in Inverness, Scotland. "So, we have another company of Americans to join us. The Royal Americans, is it? I do like the sound of that name, Captain...."

"Lawrence, sir. James Lawrence. But you may call me James," Creed replied.

The two men sat under an open flap of Fraser's tent. They had a splendid view of the camp, which consisted of nearly 1,000 British regulars, American Loyalists, Iroquois allies, and some Canadians.

Smoke fires burned as the companies prepared one of their last hot meals and smoked beef and pork for the trail.

Fraser smiled pleasantly and drummed his fingers on his field desk. "Well, James, I would have preferred ya arrived with a few more men."

"I understand, sir. My colonel gave me leave to join this grand enterprise. If I had waited to muster more, I wouldn't have joined the column in time. Our presence has symbolism. We want to recruit more Americans and be part of a grand victory. That can only help lure active young men to our colors."

Fraser nodded pensively. "An interesting thought, although this will be no easy campaign. A force as small as yours, should I attach you to the company of marksmen or my own 24th?"

"Wherever the vanguard is—is where the Royal Americans must be. I've trained these men personally and am anxious to prove their mettle. I've got a lot of woodland experience, besides. And even General Burgoyne remains unaware I have recruited people with knowledge of this area and its back trails and waters."

"Then I should use you to counter-balance our Indian allies. General Burgoyne gave them a rousing speech, but I'm not so optimistic about their efficacy or dependability. They are hell-bent on plundering the settlers who have taken their lands."

Creed shook his head somberly. "General Burgoyne plays with fire. The natives could cause a local backlash among the locals just as we are trying to recruit them to the cause of his majesty."

Fraser nodded. "Indeed, James. I will attach your company to the Light Battalion. It has an elite company of handpicked sharpshooters. The interesting bit is that the company is coincidentally under another Fraser's command – Captain Alexander Fraser. Alex holds his commission in the 34th Regiment of Foot. He's an excellent officer."

"Fraser? Any relation, sir?"

"A distant cousin. A hero of the last war and an expert, the army's expert, on woodland fighting. You lads should get along splendidly."

"Who are these marksmen?"

"General Burgoyne had me select the two best shots from each regiment in Canada. There are but twenty of them under Alex. We call them the King's Rangers, although some call them Fraser's Rangers. They could use your talents and your men. I have also given Alex a small contingent of Iroquois, Ojibwa Indians, and some Canadian woodsmen, bringing his command to sixty."

"I am anxious to know him, sir."

"We sup tonight. You will meet him then. After we eat, the Mohawks shall perform a war dance. Alex's command leaves at dawn. The rest will follow about eight hours behind. You best make your lads ready."

***

Creed found the canoes tied in a row on the bank when he arrived at camp. Nearby, two small campfires burned with some hastily crafted bark shelters surrounding them.

He called for O'Ballance, Bart, and Androche. "We depart tomorrow. Androche, I would like you and Pierre with me in the first canoe. Sergeant O'Ballance will ride in the second and Bart the third."

"Yes, sir," O'Ballance said.

"We'll be under the command of a Captain named Fraser, who commands a company of sharpshooters. Some Indians and Canadians are also coming. Androche, I will need Rock handy to translate."

Androche spread his hands.

Creed smiled. "Send Pierre out to shoot some game – then see if your lovely woman can prepare the men one last warm meal."

"*Oui*, fresh meat before the trail," Androche replied.

When Androche left, Creed looked at Bart and O'Ballance. "The journey gets difficult now. Stay close to the men. They need firm support to get through this."

"They are brave men, sir," O'Ballance replied.

"Their courage can fail, but not their will. Only a strong will can carry a man through what lays ahead."

O'Ballance jutted his chin forward. "The boys are firm, sir. They can shoot. And they'll stand and fight."

"It is hard in the wilderness…."

Creed could tell the sergeant's skepticism in New York had blossomed into confidence.

"I spent a month in the Hudson Highlands once," Bart said softly. "The bush is thick, and every branch becomes an enemy. Going over rugged hills with no trail wears a man. Heat and flies oppress you. Logs, roots, and rocks conspire to tear shoes and snap the shin and ankle bones."

"Indeed," said Creed. "We'll be in the vanguard of the vanguard. The Company of Sharpshooters and its Indian confederates are as fast as light infantry and as strong as grenadiers. All are expert shots. We shall have much to live up to if the Royal Americans are to hold their own. And that's my goal."

As Creed prepared his uniform for the night's event, he pondered the mission deeply. Its complexity amazed him. He still had one more set of instructions to read, so his final goal remained unclear. At first, he found it strange that Washington and Fitzgerald would send him into the enemy's heart without him knowing the full details of his mission. He guessed they did so for security.

But now, Creed realized there was another reason for not revealing the full scope of the plan to him. Not having complete knowledge of his mission made it easier for him to act as a British officer. This allowed him to adopt the role of Captain James Lawrence more smoothly. Although he didn't develop empathy for the royal cause, he did become fond of his new command, which he never imagined he would. Still, this outcome improved his ability to carry out this most dangerous scheme.

***

The Beekman House, New York, June 1777

General Howe toyed with a small pair of scissors, often cutting a shard of paper from a stack on his desk. The different patterns made no sense, but he tried to piece them together like a random puzzle. So far, he had no luck, but the strange exercise took his mind off his troubles, and Howe had no shortage of problems.

Another letter from Lord Germain strongly suggested but did not demand a move to support Burgoyne up north. Without the expected reinforcements from Britain, his army would begin the coming campaign significantly smaller than the year before.

"Milord, did you hear what I said?" Drummond asked testily.

"Ah, yes. You said that the rebels in New Jersey...."

"Have grown in strength, milord. Mister Washington has been refitting his army for the summer campaign."

"Well, yes. That is to be expected, Sandy, but your role is to determine what end. Will he go north if Burgoyne reaches Albany? South, to counter a move there? Or stand fast and bide his time?"

"I would say the latter unless we influence him, milord."

"Influence him? Why, of course. But what could influence the man? The man seems to have the stoic patience of a new Fabius."

"Milord?"

"Fabius. Gaius Fabius *Cunctator*, the 'Delayer,' the Roman consul and dictator whose delaying tactics wore down Hannibal's army and prevented him from taking Rome. Did you not study the classics, Sandy?"

"Of course, milord. I had merely forgotten."

Howe eyed him skeptically. He knew that men like Drummond always felt at a disadvantage to the gentry in a class-conscious society, but never admitted it.

"Good. We have much to learn from the Greeks and Romans. As for Mister Washington, what shall we do to?"

"Perhaps we have much to learn from him, milord."

"What? What do you mean? I drove the rebels from New York and New Jersey. I defeated them in three pitched battles, captured two forts, and...."

Lieutenant Colonel Horace Stilton cleared his throat. Howe turned to him. "You have been sitting quietly, Horace. I suppose you have something to add?"

"Indeed, milord. Harlem was, at best, a draw. Meanwhile, the rebels have since countered us in two pitched battles – Trenton and Princeton."

"Washington surprised a gang of drunken Germans and made a lucky escape from destruction at Charles Cornwallis's hands," Howe replied."

"Perhaps, but he then spent the winter killing his majesty's irreplaceable soldiers."

Howe slammed his scissors on the table. "I'd say things are at a standstill."

"Precisely, milord. Burgoyne's plan is Lord Germain's and Horse Guards' gambit to break up the colonies and the stalemate with Washington."

"You agree then with marching north while Washington watches our every move? Do we risk this marvelous city for a few villages in the wilderness? Do we abandon perhaps our last chance to take the rebel capital in Philadelphia?"

"Some might say so, milord," replied Stilton.

"Would you be among them, Sir Horace? Would Henry Clinton?" Howe asked archly.

Stilton hesitated a moment. "No, milord."

"Well, perhaps we can do both. Sandy, you feel Washington will remain in place. Then perhaps we can force him to commit. If I can defeat his army in New Jersey, we can split our forces and take Philadelphia while supporting Burgoyne. But I will not subordinate two years of effort to that feckless man's ambitions."

Silence ensued. They all knew the politics that drove this strategy. But for Howe, the two were always intertwined.

"The attack on the barriers at Beacon proved successful," Howe said. "The rebels must believe this the prelude to a major thrust northward. In three days, we will reinforce our position in the Brunswicks and make a strike right at the rebel outposts in eastern Jersey. Washington will surely take the bait and try to block us. After sending him packing, we shall turn south and seize Philadelphia."

"March across Jersey? The militia will close our supply line and choke us," Stilton said.

"Perhaps by land, but not by sea." Howe smiled. "I am on intimate terms with our naval commander, you know."

Polite laughter erupted. Admiral Richard Howe was his brother.

"Sandy, you have two days to reconnoiter east and north of Brunswick. Call on every spy, informer, and 'cowboy' at your disposal. I want them to know we are coming."

"I shall give it my best, sir," Drummond replied. "Meanwhile, I have approved an article for *Rivington's Gazette*. It will tout our successful attack on Beacon as the possible prelude of things."

Howe glared intently. "Make sure that only the land attack is mentioned."

"Indeed, sir. Sidney Baker may not know it, but I will make him a Loyalist hero."

Howe slapped his knee in delight as they all laughed.

***

A weary Baker looked on as Drummond paced back and forth, seemingly wearing out the carpet in Lady Dunning's parlor, his limp giving him a slight swivel of the hips as he moved.

"Sidney, you did splendid work up there. You routed a rebel force, burned down their lighthouse, and destroyed the rebel hulks with their *chevaux de frise*."

"Splendid? I lost most of my men and didn't destroy the barriers."

"Read tomorrow's *Rivington Gazette*. It will explain everything."

"What do you mean? I was there. I led the attack. I know what I did and did not do. And I did not destroy those hulks. Rebel battery fire drove us off before we...."

"Those were not rebel batteries, Sidney. Those were Royal Navy men."

"You mean?"

"Yes. The fellows who guided you to Verplanck's Point had the additional mission of navigating north and blowing the hulks while you occupied the rebels at Beacon. It worked brilliantly."

"Do you mean our raid was a decoy for the navy?"

"I'd say the navy was a part of your command, of which, for security purposes, you had no need to know."

Baker's face darkened. "Why of all the...."

"Enough, Sidney. You were an unwitting accomplice to great success. You knew it involved skullduggery and cold brutality when you joined this enterprise. Leave it at that."

"What of the New York Provincials?"

"Casualties of war, poor wretches. I regret that as much as you. However, I rejoice that you and your men were not, for there is new work afoot. This time, closer to home. In the Jerseys."

***

Fraser's Headquarters, Isle aux Noix
A large bonfire lit the dark June night, casting shimmers of golden rays on forms and faces. Jeremiah Creed sat with General Simon Fraser and his commanders, part of a circle that included several Iroquois chiefs and a few Canadians. They gnawed on roast venison and beef slices and washed it down with beer the Canadians had brought from Montreal.

Just as they finished the last of the meal, the beat of the drums began. A group of twenty warriors and maidens slipped out of the shadows to start a ritual dance. The dancers, both male and female, had stripped to breechcloths.

Their well-toned forms shimmered in the bonfire light as they began their gyrations. The dance was a well-orchestrated ritual. The warriors stepped towards each other with war knives, waving. Creed found the battle cries bone-chilling. Each pair took turns as victor and vanquished, waving symbolic scalp locks.

Then the maidens began a chant, and the movement changed tempo. Warriors and maidens intertwined in a manner Creed understood all too well.

Occasionally, a warrior would step forth and perform a monologue that the Americans and British could not understand. But the howls and cackles of the Canadians and chiefs proved that the dance's blood-and-bawdy themes made for an entertaining mix.

Creed sat beside his new company commander, Captain Alexander Fraser. Fraser had a swagger rare among British officers. He had fought with and among the Indians since the French and Indian Wars. He spoke their languages and knew their ways better than most whites, and he displayed a knack for the wilderness that few Indians could match.

"These Indian women can be as ferocious as the warriors," Fraser said to Creed over the din.

"I gathered as much," Creed replied with a smile.

Fraser laughed. "That's not what I meant. Give them a knife, and they could gut you from your groin to your Adam's apple before you could blink twice. When they capture enemy warriors, the women prove more bloodthirsty torturers than the men."

Creed nodded. "So, I have heard, although I find it hard to believe. Some of them are quite lovely."

"Believe it, Mister Lawrence, for I have witnessed things no civilized man should witness."

"Such as?"

"Nails torn from fingers like paper from a book. Human fat bubbling from roasting flesh. Eyes gouged from sockets and swallowed whole or tossed into roaring fires. Genitals were skewered and roasted over fires or fed to their terrified owners. Beatings, stabbings, and hackings."

"Why subject a beaten enemy to such horrific tortures?"

"All for sport. Why, the women laugh harder and longer than the men. Then, when their prey is dead or dying, they take a warrior to bed."

"Well, except for the last part, it sounds like the Spanish Inquisition. Perhaps they learned a thing or two from the Jesuits."

Fraser burst into laughter. "I had never thought of it that way. But no, their ritual torture dates back hundreds of years, and many a Jesuit has been a recipient of it."

"Making the red men wiser than we think?" Creed replied archly.

Fraser guffawed and gulped his beer. "This is the one thing I miss from home, Lawrence. The Canadians have passable wine but nothing like British ale."

"They have some fine ales in the colonies," Creed replied.

"Well, then I should be trying it soon enough."

Creed used the remark to change the subject. "Do you think we can fight through this wilderness before the winter?"

Fraser put down his mug and looked at him. "That's the plan, Mister Lawrence. If it were just my company and the advance guard, I'd say we could be linking with Howe somewhere south of Albany by July, but...."

"But what?" Creed asked.

"But Burgoyne. He has taken a European army to fight an American war. Why, he even brought Germans to complicate matters."

"Colonel Sinclair told me that General Burgoyne has the best regiments of the army."

"That he does. And scores of cannons and kit that must be dragged and floated over hundreds of miles of wilderness swarming with...."

"Natives?"

"Natives indeed. Of the white variety. In these parts, especially the New Hampshire Grants, Americans are stubborn and vicious bastards. They can track and shoot, some almost as good as my marksmen."

Suddenly, one of the Indian women broke out of the group and jumped toward Creed, prancing back and forth and thrusting her hips and buttocks suggestively at him. In the semi-darkness of the bonfire, he could not at first make out her features. She stamped her foot in a ritual that needed little interpretation.

"She is beckoning you, James. I do believe you will have company tonight." Fraser elbowed Creed with a laugh.

"Not I. I'm a Christian. And my heart is with someone else."

"It's not your heart she has designs on, Mister Lawrence."

The maiden finally spun about and glared at Creed. He saw that it was Fleurette. He shook his head firmly. Her eyes widened in disbelief, and in an apparent fit of anger, she sprang back into the group and danced around the circle until she found another man to entice.

This one jumped up and joined her as the Indians in the group clapped and cheered. "Ho-ho! Ho-ho!"

The drums beat louder, and the rhythm changed. Creed sipped his beer and stared glumly at the spectacle.

Suddenly, the drums grew silent, and the reverie ended. Just as suddenly, the affable Alex Fraser turned business-like.

"We must make straightway to our camps. It will be light in a few hours. You should get some sleep since you have turned down the nubile young savage. A shame that dirty Canadian now gets to console her." Fraser pointed at a large, bear-like man with his arms around Fleurette.

"You know him?" Creed asked.

"Yes. He leads a small band of trappers attached to us, much like you. His name is Serge Binoche."

***

The next day, the small flotilla of canoes and longboats shoved off just after dawn. Men strained as they pushed their craft into the cold dark waters from the muddy shore. Grunts as men pulled hard at oars or dug paddles into the water. More than a dozen craft carried Captain Alexander Fraser's elite unit south into Lake Champlain.

Creed took in the beauty of the mountains on either side of the lake and the numerous islands and swathes of trees covering the earth. The beautiful freshwater lake was one of the largest in the northeast, surpassed in size only by the great lakes.

To his port side, in the east, the morning twilight shimmered across the water's dark surface as the last stars disappeared from sight. A light breeze skipped across the lake, making small waves that lightly brushed the prows of craft.

The company of Royal Americans was in the second group. The light birch bark canoes were speedier than the longboats and the heavier dugout canoes that the Iroquois manned, so Creed's men could ease up on the paddles and coast lest they overtake the first group. He was proud of his men. They had packed and loaded quickly in the morning darkness. When Fraser came by to give his final words, they stood tall as the most experienced regulars.

Androche and Pierre sat forward in the canoe, their expert arms guiding the craft steadily along.

After an hour, Creed broke the morning stillness. "How long till we arrive at our landing point?"

Androche whispered in Pierre's ear and nodded at the reply. He turned back to Creed. "If we traveled on our own with these fine canoes for two days, perhaps less. But with these English among us, maybe three or four."

Creed nodded. "At noon, we stop to rest and eat. Captain Fraser wants to meet. I suggest we move to the van to take advantage of our speed."

Androche shook his head. "The Iroquois chieftain demanded the lead." He pointed west. "That is Mohawk land. They know the forests and rivers better than anyone."

Creed scanned the massive mountains to the west and then glanced eastwards, where the softer hills of the Hampshire Grants slowly rose above the water.

"Perhaps we shall explore the other side," he said softly.

Androche grunted, but Pierre, who had been listening, nodded.

"Tell me more of this man...Serge Binoche," Creed said.

Androche turned and stared at Creed. "*Monsieur*, I am afraid you have crossed an evil man. He is a beast, and if he learns that his daughter went twice to your tent...."

"Who knows of that?"

"The entire camp, *monsieur*. The noise was quite loud and...."

"But not long! Do I look like some animal that would rut with a young woman and discard her in a few minutes? I'm Christian." It irked Creed that there was a time when he would have done that very thing.

Androche laughed. "A Christian? Many a Christian would gladly rut with one so young and tender."

"She advanced on me twice, Androche, once quite violently. I sent her packing. That was all."

Androche smiled patronizingly. "As you say, *monsieur*. Yet it is not me you must convince, but her father."

"You mean her lover. He took her away in an Indian ceremony that was a preface to fornication."

"As I said, *monsieur*, he is a beast."

They approached a large island covered with trees and stony promontories when the sun was directly above them. It had a long white beach of small fine stones on its northern shore.

Pierre said something to Androche in an Indian dialect.

Androche turned to Creed. "*Isle la Motte.* Our *Grande Sieur*, Samuel de Champlain, was the first European to set foot here. We will draw some fish and grill them."

Creed's mouth watered. "That would be delightful. Boil some water for tea while you are at it, Androche. I'll meet with Captain Fraser."

When they beached their canoes, Creed's party went to work building a fire and throwing out nets. In minutes, they were hauling in a fine catch of fish.

Creed walked past the beach and climbed a small promontory in time to see the Iroquois party sail past the island along its western shore.

At last, Fraser and his riflemen arrived in their longboats. They beached near Creed's men, and a short time later, Fraser and Creed sat over a couple of grilled bass and discussed the next phase.

"I saw the Indians pass by heading south," Creed said.

Fraser nodded. "They insisted on going off ahead. In truth, they are more interested in taking trophies and plunder than meaningful reconnaissance. Burgoyne may regret their presence yet. He warned them to avoid provocations, but I am afraid he drove many off to wage their brand of war."

"Well, I can help lead the way. We shall head southwest and look for rebel postings. That will free you to cover the western side."

Fraser opened a small, crudely drawn map. "An excellent suggestion, Mister Lawrence. We will meet here tomorrow at sunset. He placed his finger on another small peninsula, twenty-five miles south. I do not know the name, but the savages say it's shaped like a rabbit."

"I know it," Creed said. He had never been to Lake Champlain, but Father Vincennes's maps were much more accurate than anything the British or Americans had of the region.

"Where are the Canadians?" Creed asked.

"They went with the savages. Binoche promised to keep an eye on them. You know, rein them in if need be."

"Do you think he will?"

"Oh, he'll keep an eye on them," Fraser replied.

An hour later, they doused the fires, and Creed's party began paddling their canoes southeast toward a landing that, according to his maps, had an old fort, a relic of King William's War from the 17th century. He wondered if the fortification would even be there. Maybe the maps were a part of a scheme for him to lure the British farther, not closer, to their objective?

***

Bart and O'Ballance paddled their way south in the canoe behind Creed. They marveled at Lake Champlain and the beauty surrounding it. The pristine beauty of the deep blue lake against the pale sky contrasted with the dark mountains and bright green spring foliage. Massive flocks of birds feasted on the abundant fish that thrived in the northern paradise.

"This is a fine land, Mister Saunders. It reminds me of Ireland it does. And such a bright sky. A man could settle here."

"In this wilderness? And do what?" Bart asked.

Suddenly, the idea intrigued him. He had lived in New York City and never conceived of living anywhere else. He still had difficulty thinking of Fleurette leaving his commander's tent. Now he fantasized about settling in the wilderness with her.

"Hunt. Fish. Log trees. Why, anything is possible in a place like this if you keep your scalp."

Bart was startled at the comment, and O'Ballance broke into laughter.

They paddled along in silence, each in his thoughts. Then Bart replied, "I could settle among the Indians. The little skill I have with medicine could help them."

"You're still thinking of that half-breed girl? Forget her. She's a wild thing. If Captain Lawrence couldn't tame her, then no man can."

The young man bristled at the remark. "She's neither wild nor a savage, and it would be because of her treatment if she were."

"Mister Saunders, soldiers are supposed to take women like her, not fall in love with them."

It occurred to Bart that O'Ballance might be right. He had never felt strongly towards any woman but his mother. And when she took up with a British officer, his feelings toward her had soured.

"Never mind what I say, Mister Saunders. Follow your young heart. But you are an officer first – so let romance wait until we finish this campaign."

"You're right, sergeant. I must concentrate on my duties first. All else must wait till we beat the rebels."

"That's a good officer, now."

***

Androche and his oarsmen guided the canoes with a facility that amazed Creed and the other Americans. They reached the small peninsula where the abandoned fort lay.

"I know this place," Pierre exclaimed in French.

He spoke in a stilted dialect that harkened back to over 100 years ago. Creed learned his French while serving in the French army and could converse fluently, read, and write expertly.

"How so, Pierre?" Creed asked.

"I came here once. With an Iroquois hunting party."

"They came this far for game?"

Pierre looked down. "Yes, but game of a different kind. White men."

"Go on."

"There were farms on this side of the river then. Some whites had crossed over to the western lands to hunt and fish. This angered the Mohawks. After a council that went for days, they decided to teach the whites a lesson."

"How many did they kill?" Creed asked.

"Many, *monsieur*. There were five settlements, and the Mohawks destroyed each in turn. The lucky settlers died. They murdered the babies by smashing their heads against the walls. The others fell to knife and tomahawk."

"Were many scalps taken?"

Pierre did not answer.

"And the survivors?"

Androche looked at Pierre.

"Forced to march back to the villages on the far side of the lake. Two young men and one older man."

Androche broke in, "*Monsieur*, the natives have treated their prisoners brutally for centuries. Not just the white man. Not just the Jesuit fathers. But their people. Huron, Algonquian, Fox, Iroquois. The tribe did not matter. They would tear, cut, and roast the flesh of captives. Quite often, eat of it. Beatings by women and children. Tortures so terrible that death is more than a blessing. Most tribes along the river converted to Christianity or renounced such practices."

"But not the Iroquois?" Creed asked.

Androche shook his head. "Some Iroquois joined the Jesuits and converted, but many still have practices as brutal as their ancestors."

The canoes slid silently onto the eastern shore. Creed's men scampered into the woods to secure the area. Creed settled under a tree to check the maps. They showed several good trails and had markings that were probably settlements.

He stared intently at the maps, pondering his next move. After absorbing as much detail as he could, he folded them safely.

When all were settled in camp, he called a meeting with Bart and Androche.

"Pierre will lead the way for us. Androche, you and the rest of your party remain here until tomorrow. We'll work our way south and east for signs of rebels. If we meet with difficulty, we shall return here by dawn. If we don't return, head south along the coast. There's a cove that lies about fifteen miles from here. We'll meet there."

"The woods are difficult, *Monsieur*. Even without rebels."

"Perhaps we'll find a trail."

"Perhaps." Androche seemed unconvinced.

"Bart, have Sergeant O'Ballance call in the men. Inspect their arms and equipment. We depart within the hour."

***

The company of Royal Americans treaded quickly through the thick forest thanks to the trails on Creed's maps and the skill of Pierre. They had gone more than five miles south by late afternoon and had wended their way almost a mile inland from the lake.

The sun beat through the canopy, making the air heavy and stultifying. Creed rested the party beside a cool spring to replenish their water bottles and eat some of their rations.

Pierre slid into the woods to reconnoiter.

Creed had taken a rest under a large cypress. O'Ballance sat nearby. "The boys are holding well, sir. Except for the flies."

"They are indeed quite ghastly, but the sting is much less than a rebel bullet." Creed wiped the sweat from his brow and scratched his eyes reflexively.

"Do you suppose the rebels are nearby, sir?"

"I suppose nothing, sergeant. We're here to determine that very thing. I sent Pierre up ahead as a precaution."

Bart approached them with his medical bag slung over his shoulder. "A few of the men have horrible bites from these flies. I have applied some balm to them."

"Have you ever treated a gunshot wound, Bart?" Creed asked.

"No, but I assisted my father once when he was summoned to treat one. Fortunately, the shot went through flesh, and he merely cleaned it with alcohol and bandaged the wound."

"The bigger danger here might be ankle and foot sprains," said O'Ballance.

"Let us hope so," replied Creed. "We move out in a quarter-hour."

They had advanced several more miles through ever-thicker woods. Creed knew it would be tougher going ahead. According to the map, the trail narrowed to a path that wound through hills and valleys.

Pierre suddenly appeared from behind a large stone ahead of them. He signaled to Creed.

Creed turned to O'Ballance. "Have the men take defensive positions. I am going with Pierre. Bart, come with me."

Bart cradled his musket and slowly crept down the path behind Creed. Pierre led them about a half-mile before arriving at a clearing with a small log cabin and a few outhouses.

Pierre dropped to his knees and crawled through the high grass. Creed and Bart followed.

"Any sign of rebels nearby?" Creed whispered.

Pierre pointed to the ajar cabin door. Something was wrong.

Creed handed Bart his musket. "Cover Pierre and me. I'm going to inspect this rebel stronghold."

Creed stood, drew his pistol, grasped his short sword, and advanced with long strides toward the building. Pierre followed. Creed threw his back against the wall at the cabin, his chest heaving rapidly. An enemy trapped in a building was the most dangerous. He listened for the click of a hammer, the scrapping of a blade, or the heavy breathing of a foe ready to pounce when he stepped into the cabin's darkness.

Then they heard it. Creed looked at Pierre, who shook his head, knowing what to expect. From behind the door came the buzzing whir of countless flies.

Carefully, Pierre dropped low and peered in through the open door. His weapons at ready, Creed sprang into the cabin like a panther. In an assault on his senses, the stench of death overwhelmed him. He staggered back as if punched. Hands shaking, he hastily fumbled for a bandana to cover his mouth.

Pierre kicked the door open fully, and they entered the cabin. Swarms of tiny flies attacked their eyes. Pierre lit a torch and brandished it to scatter the cloud.

As their eyes adjusted to the dim light, they surveyed the scene. Around them lay several bodies clad in buckskins. Their blackened faces were almost unrecognizable as men. The horrific damage done by the flies and the heat left the dead with dark holes where their eyes and nostrils should have been. Each had been scalped, exposing the white of their skulls.

Creed's stomach churned with horror, but Pierre took it all in with casual patience. He held up one of the dead rebel's hands. The fingers were bloody stumps – clearly a form of torture.

"Iroquois," Pierre said matter-of-factly.

Creed signaled him out of the building, and they returned to the edge of the woods, where a nervous Bart waited for them.

"Have you seen anything, Bart?" Creed asked, still gasping for air.

"No, sir. Nothing. My God, sir! Your face has been feasted on by…."

Creed's eyes burned, and tears rolled down his cheeks. "Bart, get us some of your salve. We may need all of it…."

Pierre seemed oblivious to the stings and quietly made his way around the edge of the clearing until he completely circled it.

"Did you find a trace of the Iroquois?" Creed asked.

Pierre nodded. "Maybe twenty, maybe more. Moved south from here."

"The Iroquois were supposed to cover the western shore of the lake. What brought them here?"

"Trophies. Plunder. Liquor. Little of that on the western shore."

"Trophies? You mean scalps?" Bart asked.

"He means scalps," Creed said. "Go back and fetch the men. We must move now to make our rendezvous with Androche."

Chapter 10

Preakness, New Jersey, June 1777

Tallmadge fidgeted nervously with the reins. He was about to ride to Morristown for a meeting with Colonel Fitzgerald.

Sergeant Simon Beall suddenly called to him, "Sir, a rider from the southeast!"

The rapid pounding of hooves filled the air. A solitary horseman was galloping at a breakneck pace, sending a plume of fine brown dust spiraling up behind him.

Tallmadge squinted. "Can't make out the face. But only one man can ride like that."

"Thaddeus O'Quinn," Beall said.

"What brings him back here? I didn't expect a report for another twenty-four hours. Unless...."

Since the winter campaign ended a month earlier, enemy activity near Brunswick had almost ceased. Tallmadge had sent newly appointed Ensign Roy Harry to watch the British sentries around Brunswick, Howe's forward position in the Jerseys. Tallmadge had even considered moving his base of observation further north.

O'Quinn pulled up, his lather-soaked horse prancing nervously and kicking a cloud of dust as he circled it around his commander.

"The British!" O'Quinn sputtered excitedly. "The British are moving, sir!"

"Can you be more precise?"

"Regulars, sir. British regulars!"

"How many? In what direction?" Tallmadge shot back.

"All of them, sir. B'Jesus - the whole garrison. Or so it seems. They have barges crossing from Staten Island."

"How many barges, trooper."

"We counted over twenty-five."

Tallmadge's dark eyes evinced calm. "Very well. Where's Harry?"

"Watchin' their advanced guard, sir. Maybe a thousand B'Jesus. Some dragoons and several battalions of grenadiers and light infantry."

"Any cannons?"

"Not yet, sir. But only Jesus knows what follows."

Tallmadge turned to Beall. "Report this to His Excellency. We must send new instructions to Mister Harry. I'll carry them myself. As soon as Trooper O'Quinn gets a fresh horse, he can lead me there."

O'Quinn and Tallmadge found Harry on a slight rise at the intersection of the King's Highway leading north from Brunswick.

"What have we here, Harry?" Tallmadge asked.

"The British deployed their advance guard," Harry replied.

He left out the usual 'sir' used for superiors. Tallmadge ignored the slight. "They probably expect reinforcements."

Tallmadge crawled under a bush beside Harry and scanned the scene with his spyglass. Redcoat skirmishers stood yards apart in an arc that stretched for a mile on either side of the road. The red wings adorning their shoulders and fancy headgear marked them among the most elite of the enemy army.

"Looks like around six hundred foot and maybe fifty horse," Harry said.

"Strange, the dragoons have dismounted behind the skirmish line. They're not in a hurry," Tallmadge said.

"A small force of infantry and horse turned west, but the others certainly seem interested in heading our way."

"Hmm. This might not be much more than a ruse."

"Ruse or not, when the garrison catches up with the advance guard, we could be facing several thousand of the lobsters."

They crawled back through the brush. Tallmadge took the reins from O'Quinn and pulled himself into the saddle. "Send Karcz and O'Quinn to follow the other column. You remain here with the others."

Harry nodded. "We're not going anywhere."

"Whatever happens, don't engage these people, not even a skirmish."

Harry grimaced. "It would do the men good to take a few lobsters after so much watching and waiting."

"His Excellency will want to know whether they turn southwest toward Princeton, northeast towards Newark and the Valley, or northwest to Morristown."

Harry plucked a long blade of grass and began to chew on it. "A prisoner or two might shed light on their plans."

"I know you're anxious to make them pay amends for your ill-treatment at the Sugar House, but lobsters are best caught in season."

A few months earlier, Harry was wounded in a skirmish and fell prisoner to the British. Later, Creed, who was on a secret mission in New York, rescued him. Embarrassed by such a bold escape right under their noses, the British banned reports from the papers. Sandy Drummond issued the order.

Harry nodded reluctantly. "I do hunger for lobster, Major Tallmadge. But I understand."

Tallmadge's eyes softened. "I, too, have lost friends and relations to these people, Harry. My dear cousin died at their hands. I turned from my earlier apathy to the cause and joined it. However, I have become more cautious in my method of redress. So should you."

Tallmadge touched his brow with a gloved fist, turned his mount, and cantered off.

***

Dusk slowly descended on them. The darkness began to be broken by the sudden flare of campfires. They eventually counted over forty. The British columns had not moved. Shaking in the night's chill, they watched the British, alert for patrols and spies that might wander beyond the pickets.

The North Spy

Elias Parker and Jonathan Beall stood watch after midnight. Since joining the cause in 1776, they had spent countless hours as scouts or spies observing enemy movements. They knew from experience that the boredom dulled the senses and could lull even the most expert scout to miss a cue.

"Do you think this is a British trick, Elias?" Beall whispered.

"If it is, it's a pretty damned good one. I suspect a third of the lobster army is down there."

"So, where are the others?"

"Guarding the brothels of New York for all I know."

The evening fires began to fade by midnight. Against the darkness, they seemed indistinguishable from the stars flickering above. The night passed slowly with no activity in front of them. Parker could hear the occasional horse whinny when a fox or rabbit spooked them. But the camp remained eerily quiet. At last, the morning twilight brightened faintly, quietly bathing the field before them with its soft glow.

Parker thought he caught sight of shadows against the skyline. The rattle of drums and blare of bugles suddenly broke the morning stillness. Soon came restless cries from scores of impatient sergeants. The camp was stirring like a hornet's nest.

Harry joined them at the observation post. "What's happening?"

"Look for yourself, Harry." Parker's tone seemed jaded. He had never quite taken to Harry. He always felt the former highwayman had joined the cause for profit, not patriotism.

The British began marching onto the highway in a column of eight across. Flags were unfurling at the head of the column, and waves of crimson were forming as the army started dressing ranks. The crimson waves surged forward with white-clad legs stepping as one. A band struck up "The British Grenadier," the famed fighting song of the era.

"They are moving straight up the road. Headed to Morristown, I'll wager," Parker said.

"They want to draw His Excellency into a fight," Beall said.

Harry grinned. "Then let's hope he gives them one."

They heard shouts from behind them.

A trooper joined them. "O'Quinn has returned."

Minutes later, O'Quinn reined his horse to a halt and leaned forward in the saddle, huffing. "The other column has turned north."

Harry pulled a sketch map from his vest. "There's a back road, although it's not on many maps. This column is covering the flank of the main force."

"But how would they know of it?" asked Beall.

"Who knows? Harry said cynically. "Cowboys or Loyalists from the area. You don't think we are the only ones doing this?"

"Then we should meet them there," said Parker. He was beginning to dislike Harry even more.

Harry glared. "I have orders from Tallmadge not to engage them. We must stay here."

"That's what Lieutenant Creed would do," Beall said.

A grin crossed Parker's bronze face.

Harry flushed red. "Alright, damn it. You two come with me. If we ride quickly, we can beat them there. O'Quinn, ride back and tell Major Tallmadge the lobsters are advancing on two roads. Karcz, you and the others stay in front of the main body but let me know if they change direction."

***

A stray branch smacked the side of Sidney Baker's cheek. He peeled the branch from his face and peered down the trail, silently cursing Sandy Drummond for another impossible mission.

Although covered with secondary growth, the trail provided the British column a highway to the rebel stronghold. Baker's job was to lead the column through the overgrowth and storm one of the passes in the Watchung Hills. But as the trail grew more trying, Baker suspected he was providing the British another red herring to wave at the rebels.

"This cursed trail...." Baker huffed as sweat trickled from under his hat.

"Should I go back and fetch the first company, sir?" Lieutenant Dilley, his new subaltern, asked.

"Not just yet," Baker replied. "The rebels may have scouts up ahead. Let's flush them out first. Maybe snag a prisoner."

Baker himself had traveled to the site numerous times. He had great confidence in his nine Loyalist volunteers, all hand-picked men from New Jersey. Several hailed from these very hills and fields and knew the area well.

"So, what do we do?" Dilley always had questions.

"If I am correct, a woodsman's lodge is just ahead. Long abandoned when the first forests here got cut down. We must seize it before the rebels turn it into a blockhouse."

***

John Street Theater, New York, June 1777

Emily looked across the dimly lit playhouse. For some reason, she found the audience more interesting than the play. The play was about to enter its final act. The amateur players were British officers and a few civilians chosen to augment the cast. An avid reader, Emily preferred to let her mind interpret stories directly – without the inference of actors and directors.

She scanned the audience. The color red dominated the theater. The British officer corps, even those assigned to regiments outside the city, found every occasion to visit. Shops, cafes, and taverns seemed to brim with the scarlet coats set off by various "turnbacks," the colors adorning collars, cuffs, and trim marking each regiment. Add an abundance of white lace, brass, gold, and silver, and the city seemed awash in martial finery.

Emily ignored her escort's constantly stroking her arm with a zeal that pushed the edge for an English "gentleman." Instead, she concentrated on her new dilemma. During a routine visit to one of her favorite sites, the bluff overlooking Kip's Bay, she found a coded note. Emily did not know the identity of her espionage partner. She had several points along the island of New York's (Manhattan) coastal flats to deposit or retrieve messages.

Each routine process lasted two weeks. The latest note was unusual – it indicated no pick-up for five cycles. As the spy code-named Mister Smythe, she could not get a message to Colonel Fitzgerald for more than two months!

Emily knew she did not have that much time. During a recent tea at Lady Dunning's house, she learned General Howe had settled on a plan to satisfy London's desires and his own. London wanted his army to support the attacks from Canada. Howe wanted to seize the rebel capital in Philadelphia.

Emily had already observed British warships gathering in the upper bay. And New York was flush with officers enjoying the pleasures of city life before a tiring campaign.

The curtain dropped between acts, and a dozen ushers hurried along the walls, lighting lamps as the audience stretched, ran to the ante-room for punch, or sat and talked.

"Are you enjoying the play, my dear? You seem preoccupied."

"How can I enjoy the play, Stephen, when I worry so for my father?" Emily asked with an air of innocence.

Major Stephen Rumson was the latest among a group of British officers vying for Emily's attention, if not affection. A tall, portly man in his late thirties, he hailed from landed gentry "somewhere near York – the real York," as he often joked grandly. Emily liked him because of his rank and role as the British command's liaison to the Hessians. His thoughts gave her a valuable insight into that part of Howe's army.

Emily had quickly mastered the art of elicitation. Between Rumson's chatter about Howe's grand strategy and Klara's whisperings, she had pieced together what she believed was Howe's plan. But the challenge of getting the information to Fitzgerald had troubled her for days.

Rumson smiled patronizingly. "Your father is a soldier, dear. He volunteered to serve in the offensive against the rebels. No danger in that. You should be proud."

"I am proud of him, Stephen." She cut him off and raked his hand seductively with her long nails. It had the desired effect on Rumson.

As he looked into her eyes, she scanned the theater, noting the number of officers, regiments, and their ranks. Over the past few months, she had become quite skilled at identifying units by facing colors and other wartime symbols that armies seemed to rely on.

She returned her gaze to him and batted her lashes. "But I do miss father. And worry so much for him. He's not getting younger. I wish I could see him. It has been nearly a fortnight since he departed."

Rumson thrust out his jaw and sat ramrod in his seat. "Well then, see him, you shall. Give me a few days to arrange it, and I shall escort you to Brunswick myself."

She batted her eyes and smiled. "Thank you, Stephen. You are ever my savior. I shall never be able to show my gratitude."

Emily did miss her father, and now she could combine filial affection with her duty to her country. Rumson smiled and stroked her arm once more.

When the play ended, Rumson escorted Emily through the admiring crowd of officers. Conversations and bawdy banter turned to hushed voices and silence as they paced through the crowd. Looks of admiration, envy, and lust abounded, but Emily ignored them and smiled pleasantly.

Many of the officers crowded the bar. Others stood around the punch bowls talking with the ladies. Emily spotted Edmund Laseby, Lady Dunning, and Klara enjoying their punch with an officer she had wanted to meet for some time.

"Is that your commander, Stephen?" she asked.

"Yes, my dear. Sir Horace Stilton. This should prove amusing."

"Why that?"

"Seems both he and our good Mister Laseby are interested in Lady Dunning's affections."

"Interested? A strange term, I'd say, Stephen."

Rumson smiled. "Strange situation, my dear."

Emily eyed the two men. "Perhaps not...."

"Ah, your liaison to the Hessians has arrived. *Guten Abend,* as they say," Laseby joshed.

"*Guten Abend* to all, as they say," Rumson joshed in return. He bowed and then shifted his muscular body as if he were a curtain being drawn to present Emily.

"You all have met the lovely Miss Emily Stanley, daughter of Doctor Reginald Stanley, again of His Majesty's Forces."

Stilton bent gallantly, glanced at Lady Dunning, and took Emily's hand. Lady Dunning's handsome face and slightly arched eyes quelled his impulse to kiss it.

Laseby, however, held no such reservations. "So nice to see you, my dear. You look lovely tonight, and I take the beautiful Lady Dunning as my benchmark."

He bowed with a flourish and, taking Emily's hand, brushed it lightly with his lips.

Lady Dunning nodded ever so slightly. "Yes, dear, you look quite the beauty."

"I particularly liked how you graced through that pack of wolves," Laseby said.

"Men soon to serve their sovereign in battle are not wolves, Mister Laseby. I'd liken us to hounds, prancing, and yapping to get at the prey," Stilton said.

Lady Dunning nodded. "I should say so, Sir Horace."

Emily noticed Mister Laseby's face redden. In occupied New York, military background always seemed to trump money.

Rumson waved a hand at the now raucous gathering of redcoats in silver and lace. "I say, sir, there might be one or two wolves hiding among the hounds."

Soft laughter erupted just as a waiter arrived with another tray of punch. They sipped and made small talk to the sound of the flute in the background.

After some time, Rumson bowed to Lady Dunning and his commander. "I apologize for our rapid departure, but I must get this young lady home early. With her father gone, the mistress of the house can't be away too long. Unless it is to see him."

"Meaning?" asked Lady Dunning.

Rumson turned to Stilton. "That, with Sir Horace's permission, I shall escort Miss Stanley across to Brunswick to see her father."

"You know all civilians who cross on private business require approval in writing, and that Sandy must review each request prior?" Stilton replied.

"Yes, but I know that exceptions are made. And certainly, we have one exceptional lady."

Lady Dunning patted Stilton's arm seductively. "Yes. You must approve this, Horace. You command here, not Sandy Drummond."

"But General Howe…"

"Placed you in command of the garrison – not Sandy," Lady Dunning said.

"On Sir Henry Clinton's insistence," said Laseby. "Yet I concur. Emily, you should see your father. Who knows how long he'll be gone?"

"Or where," stated Lady Dunning.

Stilton and Laseby eyed one another and pursed their lips grimly.

***

The barge cut slowly through the still waters, which slapped rhythmically with each churn of the oars. The slow journey allowed Emily to enjoy the pleasant spring day on New York Bay.

The scent of the salt air refreshed her spirits. The quaint buildings of Richmond Towne grew more prominent as the oarsmen pulled them ever so close to Staten Island. The coastline surrounding them displayed an abundance of grassy dunes and low hills thick with verdant foliage underlined by long stretches of sandy white beaches.

The town had a mix of mostly fieldstone buildings interspersed with clapboard and brick. The shades of gray and blue with freshly painted white doors and window trim appealed to her.

"A pleasant-looking place, Stephen," she said as he helped her from the barge. She thought she felt just a tad too much fumbling with her waist.

"You have never been here before?"

"Goodness, no! Father never took me much beyond our house near the city's outskirts. I contented myself with occasional rides along the water or across the nearby farm fields. I did travel to Harlem once, but that was by wagon."

"Harlem? Well, before the battle there, I hope. We sent those rebels running back to their fortifications, you know?"

"Yes, I know. It seems every officer who lodged at our house fought in that battle. However, to your question, Stephen, I was there before that sad day."

She did not lie. But Emily could not reveal that she had departed just before the battle or had gone there to help rebel spies steal a double agent from the clutches of the advancing British army.

"It was a glorious day for us in any event."

"The death of gallant men in combat, whether rebels or our good soldiers, can never be glorious, Stephen."

They led a pair of horses down the gangway onto the quay. Emily found it surprisingly easy to convince Rumson to let her bring a horse. Her small brown mare, Pudding, seemed scarcely more than a pony, yet could sprint as fast as many larger horses and had more stamina than most. Few women of the day rode, but Emily took to it early in life, although propriety forced her to travel by coach or cart as she came of age.

"We shall ride together to Tottenville. Another barge will take us across the Raritan Bay and up the river of that name across to Brunswick. Your father is likely at the hospital near there."

"It will be so good to see him, Stephen. Will you help me up?"

"Of course, my dear." He smiled gallantly and hoisted her up as if she were a baby lamb, grasping her narrow waist.

Emily did not admit that she could have leaped into the saddle and ridden off at a gallop without him. She had learned early enough that gentlemen held women to be vulnerable creatures, and any notion that disputed that fact was considered a form of social, if not political, treason.

***

Baker led his small force along the dark, narrow trail surrounded by strangely quiet woods. He knew the woodcutter's cottage was not far up ahead. But to get there, they had to cross a small clearing about fifty yards by sixty that lay before them. Baker halted the column along the clearing's edge and placed his men into a ragged line.

"Why bother with this, captain?" one of them asked. "We haven't seen or heard anyone in an hour."

Baker held his composure. "There shouldn't be rebels this far forward, but we'll take no chances."

He looked left and right and conned the wood line across from them. Nothing stirred. "Stay in line and move quickly. Now go!"

Baker sprang forward, waving his light musket. His men followed, but the line of green jackets quickly became ragged. Suddenly, they heard the *pop* of muskets to their left, followed by the *buzz* of the leaden balls. One of Baker's men screamed and tumbled into the bushes when a shot creased his head.

***

From across the small clearing, Harry signaled, "Too high."

Beall signaled back as he and Parker reloaded. The formation of green coats was harder to see than they thought. The high grass blocked their vision.

But the second volley struck true just as the green jackets reached the far end of the clearing. Two men went down in the crossfire. The three-quarter-inch lead balls hit home with deadly effect. One had his head shattered by Beall's Jaeger rifle, one of the short hunting rifles he and Creed had taken from some Hessians on Long Island.

The rounds fired by Parker and Harry struck true, piercing one man's groin and tearing open another's armpit. Each lay in the tall grass, blood pooling in the warm sun. They cried ceaselessly, although they knew no surgeon would arrive to save them.

***

"Rebels to our flank. Turn and face them," Baker yelled hoarsely. He tried to hide his frustration and fear. Frustration that the rebels had beaten him to his objective. Fear that he would return once more from a mission with the balance of his men in the enemy's hands.

The men seemed frozen by the onslaught of lead.

"Fire at the damned rebels!" Baker shouted.

His men discharged their firelocks, spitting their lead into the wood line. Another soldier fell forward, clutching his chest.

"Reload and then affix bayonets. Quickly!" Baker ordered. He tried to sound calm but knew they were in a deadly trap. *Can I lead them out of this?*

A half dozen ramrods jangled into barrels as the Loyalists fought to hammer home their rounds. Bayonets clanged as each ring slid down the smooth barrels and locked into place, presenting the wicked seventeen-inch blade feared by most Americans, especially the militia.

"All done?"

Heads nodded.

"We shall take the woodsmen's lodge and hold it. Follow me!"

***

Harry mischievously grinned as Baker led his patrol deep into the woods. "I do believe your plan will work, Parker."

"Shouldn't we follow them and finish them off?" Beall asked.

Harry shook his head as he rammed the wadding and bullet down his musket barrel. "We aren't supposed to be here, remember? Let's find the column these boys were leading and slow them down. We might get back before Major Tallmadge finds out we've gone."

Chapter 11

Lake Champlain, New York

For several grueling hours, weary legs struggled up and down steep inclines and aching arms. Reddened faces fought through heavy foliage, thick and stinging—the trail made for a tortuous journey through woods that seemed as dark as an African jungle.

"I may have talked too soon about settling here," O'Ballance whispered to Bart.

"I think your first observations will prove correct, sergeant. This forest cannot stretch forever."

"You just want to go off with the half-breed doxie. You'd learn soon enough there is more to a woman than a warm companion on a cold night," O'Ballance said with a sly grin.

Bart reddened and ignored the barb. Captain Lawrence had gotten them into a real fix, he thought. Weeks earlier, they were all civilians, and now they were at the tip of the spear of his majesty's best military force. *How can we measure up?*

Bart squinted. The two files of Royal Americans made up the main body, and Captain Lawrence and Pierre led the van.

Suddenly, the dull *pop* of musket fire punctured the woods. The column picked up the pace. It was a mild June day, but sweat darkened the backs of their red jackets. Bart hoped the fight was not too far off. He would rather stand and fight than struggle in the steamy woods with full gear.

***

The distant sound of musket fire stopped Creed in his tracks. Ahead was a large clearing, and beyond it, smoke was rising above the trees. The sporadic *pop, pop*, now became a crescendo.

"Get the main body up quickly, Pierre!" Creed ordered. "Whoever destroyed that settlement is back at work."

Pierre disappeared into the lush vegetation.

It dawned on Creed that his enemy could be British, American, or both. His mission had him leading enemy troops in combat against his own side to defeat the enemy ultimately. How to do this, he had no idea.

Two files of tired and sweaty redcoats staggered up the trail. Creed cupped his hands around his mouth. "Spread out on either side of the trail, lads! We'll advance slowly – weapons at ready."

"Those are Mohawks up ahead, *Monsieur*," Pierre said.

"How do you know?"

"I know the sound of their powder, *Monsieur*. Let me go and see what they are doing."

"No time, Pierre. We'll advance on them now."

O'Ballance suddenly burst through the trees, puffing as he struggled with his pack. The burly sergeant was panting heavily. "I'll go with the left flank, sir. Ensign Saunders has gone over to the right."

"Very well, sergeant. But get the men moving quickly," Creed replied.

The small company of Royal Americans sprang forward with their muskets held high. Their feet raced quickly across the last fifty yards. There was no sign of the snipers, but a scene that stirred fear and revulsion lay before them.

A hamlet of six homes burned fiercely as large sheets of flame lapped at the log walls like a thirsty dog at a pond. Heavy black smoke billowed like a mushroom cloud and then drifted across the field like a scene from *Dante's Inferno*.

Terrified screams and angry cries in English, French, and Iroquois drowned out the sharp crackling of the flames. Shadowy figures ran through the smoke—a few brandished war clubs dripping blood.

"Bloody savages!" O'Ballance screamed.

"We must stop this now," Creed said.

Pierre held a hand before Creed. "Mohawk war party, *monsieur*. They will not be easily stopped. We risk a fight we may not win."

The musket fire softened and then stopped. The hamlet's defenders had fled or gone down under the knife. Creed could hear sorrowful moans and the wailing of terrified women.

The women's voices made Creed's decision. "At the slow step, march!"

The line of Royal Americans stepped through the fringe of brush that protected the wood line. They took short steps, each with his musket at high port with bayonet fixed – ready to present and fire or lower and charge on command. Creed had learned this tactic in France, and it rarely failed to scatter an enemy.

A band of Mohawks began to assemble in the smoke and ruins. He saw almost thirty warriors in full plumage and paint. They had shaved heads except for a long braid of hair encrusted in feathers and wore simple breechcloths for protection. Each warrior carried a musket, club, and long tomahawk in addition to the short scalping knives.

Will the lads be able to face such a fearsome lot?

A cloud of smoke drifted across the forty paces that now separated them. The Iroquois spread into a skirmish line while whooping, crowing, and shaking firelocks defiantly over their heads.

Creed's company stepped through the smoke, and for the first time, the Indians saw the red coats. They grew silent, and a large, brave man stepped forward and began to speak in Iroquois.

Creed signaled a halt. "What's he saying, Pierre?"

"He says his name, Solomon."

"Solomon, eh? Interesting name." Creed found the Indian adaptation of English and French names amusing. "Ask Solomon why his warriors crossed the lake."

Pierre asked and translated the reply. "His war party learned there were more white settlements to pick from on this side of the lake. So, they came here despite the words of the great leader, Johnny."

"Ask him who told them that."

Pierre posed the question.

Solomon grunted and spat his reply.

Pierre frowned. "He says the Canadians."

"What Canadians?"

Pierre asked and received a hesitant reply. "He says the ones who destroyed the farm and led them here."

"Ask him where the inhabitants of this village are."

The brave held up a bloody scalp and gestured toward the buildings in the final throws of conflagration as timbers cracked and tumbled in fiery heaps.

"They scalped all the men who did not flee and locked the women and children in the houses before burning them."

Creed's stomach turned at the news. His men began to curse and demand the order to fire.

"Stand fast, boys. Savage as they are, they're our allies," O'Ballance's voice betrayed his anger.

A mix of Canadian woodsmen and braves emerged from the burning ruins. Their arms were heavy with loot, including more than a few liquor bottles. Creed counted at least eight and recognized the leader- Serge Binoche—despite the pall of smoke enveloping them.

Binoche's heavy moccasins stomped the earth as he approached Creed with a glare. "What are you *Anglais* doing here? This is work for *les sauvages*."

Creed returned the glare with his own, fueled by anger he had not felt in a long time. "Of course it is, *monsieur*. The British Army does not scalp and kill, like *les sauvages*. Are you not aware that General Burgoyne himself has forbidden this?"

Binoche shrugged. "What concern of mine is an order from Gentleman Johnny? We are in Iroquois country now."

Several of his braves shook their heads and began waving their firelocks and tomahawks in the air while jumping and hooting. "*Ho ho! Ho ho!*"

Creed realized many understood French even if they did not speak it.

"This land is not Iroquois," Pierre called out to them. "It was once the domain of the Abenakis and Mohegan tribes. Now it is white. Go back across the great lake – those are your lands!" He pointed to the west with his musket.

The warriors began to growl. Their pride and bloodlust were at a fever pitch now. As they once preyed on the native tribes of this land, they dished out even more of the same against the upstart whites. Muskets, war hatchets, and knives shook in defiance.

Binoche smirked. "This land offers easy ground for raids. Go quickly, *monsieur*, for I cannot control my friends' need for scalps and plunder. Nor mine, for that matter. Take your English soldiers back to your general."

"These are not English soldiers, *monsieur*. They are Americans, the Royal Americans. Americans don't have the English respect for the Iroquois – only a desire to be rid of them. Don't tempt them, *monsieur*."

Binoche viewed the line of firm-jawed redcoats who stood their ground with bayonets fixed and leveled.

"But of course, you are right. We serve the same master, no?" Binoche edged closer. Several warriors inched toward Creed and Pierre.

"Now, you have violated General Burgoyne and Fraser's orders. Although Burgoyne is not one to enforce his edict, General Fraser is. If you do not abandon this side of the lake, you will answer to an authority higher than me."

Binoche spat. "Why should I answer to anyone?"

The Iroquois drew closer until there was a line of warriors between Creed, Pierre, and the company. A volley would as likely hit them as the warriors. A bayonet charge might not reach them in time to stave off the blows that would surely bring them down.

Some of the Americans began nervously edging forward. The click of cocked firelocks showed they meant business.

"Stand fast, lads, but prepare to charge on my order," O'Ballance roared. His words were meant for Binoche as much as Creed.

Creed coolly eyed Binoche. "You will answer to a court-martial. Now go find your canoes and make haste to the lake's western shore."

"You will have to carry me there, *Anglais*." Binoche twisted his wrist, held his tomahawk high over his head, and drew his knife. Fresh blood and gore stained the once gleaming metal.

"Call me many things, *monsieur*, but not *Anglais*," replied Creed.

Four of the braves pounced on Pierre and gripped his arms tightly. Another brave moved behind Creed and yanked the fusil from his hands. Creed managed to draw his short officer's sword before they could tear it from his hip. The braves began hooting and howling in anticipation of watching the close combat and their leader winning one more scalp.

Binoche began to circle right, twisting the three-foot-long Iroquois war tomahawk over his head as he closed on Creed. He would need to time his strike to avoid a tomahawk blow to the head or a knife thrust to the ribs. But Creed knew the tomahawk, although the more imposing weapon, served as a distraction for the knife, which Binoche held low.

The tomahawk came in a side-sweeping movement at Creed's left shoulder. He twisted his sword just enough to block the shaft below the blade head. Before Binoche could plunge the knife into his ribs, Creed stepped back. He shifted his balance and held the blade tip toward Binoche's throat.

"A good move, *Anglais*. But you cannot dance away from me as you did with Fleurette."

The comment surprised Creed. At that moment, Binoche lunged at him with the knifepoint. Creed dodged it at the last second. As he did, he saw the tomahawk blade coming down on him. He grabbed Binoche by the wrist. A flash of the knife under Creed's armpit would have ended the fight. But Creed slammed the flat of his sword blade into the *coureur's* face before he could strike.

Blood squirted from Binoche's mouth and nose. He wiped at his face and stumbled back in a rage.

"*Merde*! Before I finish you, you will watch me peel the skin from your   skull   and feed your living flesh to the pot."

Bart was trembling. "Sergeant - order the men forward before the savages undo Captain Lawrence."

"Stand fast, Mister Saunders," O'Ballance said.

Creed calmly stepped toward Binoche. His sword struck like a snake, snapping at the face. Binoche jerked his head reflexively, and Creed's hilt swung upward, cracking the Canadian's jaw. Binoche was lifted off his feet by the blow, and his bulky frame collapsed, senseless, into the dust.

Creed seized Binoche's tomahawk and knife. He waved them menacingly at the braves. "Take your leader across the lake, and I will not report your butchery to the great general."

Solomon spoke to his braves, waving at Binoche and then pointing west. Pierre translated. Heads bobbed in agreement as a chorus of exclamations erupted, and soon the last of the band was shuffling down the trail with Binoche straddled across brawny shoulders.

Cheers erupted from the company. "Huzzah! Huzzah!"

"Quiet now, boys. Quiet." O'Ballance ordered.

Creed calmly retrieved his fusil and sheathed his sword. "Mister Saunders, take your section and search the buildings. Sergeant O'Ballance will take the other section and make sure there are none of them lurking in the woods."

Pierre gave Creed a solemn look.

"Did they harm you, Pierre?"

"*Non, monsieur.*"

"Then why so glum?"

"Taking an Iroquois scalping party away from its rightful plunder will not go unavenged. And Binoche lost more than a fight. He lost face with his men and the Iroquois. I fear he will not wait long before trying to regain it."

Creed knew his two-sided ploy had just become three-sided.

***

Creed found Androche waiting patiently at their meeting point. His wife and one of the oarsmen had collected wood for a fire to grill fish snared while waiting for the company.

"Douse the fires. No time for hot victuals. I have decided to push farther south before we meet with Fraser."

"Androche looked shocked. "*Mon Dieu*, do we dare risk such a move?"

Creed did not answer. "Have the men board the canoes, Sergeant O'Ballance. Ensign Saunders, we leave at once."

Bart approached Creed. "Sir, I thought our orders were to meet with Captain Fraser at the appointed rendezvous."

"Indeed, Mister Saunders. But I intend to expand our range of action. The Iroquois have alerted the settlers on the east side of the lake. There are abandoned forts that I wish to reconnoiter."

"How do you know of this, sir?"

Creed paused for a way to answer. "Pierre visited them with an Iroquois raiding party many years ago. But you raise a good point. Take Androche and your section to make the rendezvous with Captain Fraser. Tell him what we saw here and alert him that the rebels are likely aware of our presence, at least on the eastern shore."

"The others?"

"Sergeant O'Ballance, his section, and Pierre will come with me."

The sun was setting over the western Adirondack Mountains, spreading its coppery red rays over what appeared to be an unending wilderness of mountaintops. The lower-lying Green Mountains clung to the last vestige of twilight to the east as shadows began to blanket the dark woods.

One of Father Vincennes's maps showed several old outposts along the lake. Creed figured they were now rebel-controlled and wanted to report on them to Fraser. It seemed to him an excellent way to justify his mission. Creed needed to build enough confidence from Fraser so he would grant him freedom of action when it mattered most.

He felt in his vest for the last two envelopes. Until he opened them, he would not know what the final leg of his mission entailed. He envisioned how he might slip away from his majesty's forces to report on what he knew.

***

They reached their destination well into the night. A small island of about five acres lay some 500 yards off the mainland. The outpost had a dock, a half-crumpled tower, and a small earth redoubt that, at best, could hold twenty-five men. Above the lake, a clear, dark sky provided a palette for the countless specks of light that shimmered across it. *Fort is a misnomer*, Creed thought.

Pierre whispered. "This place had white soldiers many years ago. The hunting parties and scalping parties avoided it. Now it has bad spirits."

"Why do you say that, Pierre?" Creed asked.

"In the last war, a large party of Algonquins and Canadians was sent by the Marquis de Montcalm to take this place. When they arrived, all the white soldiers had fled. But they left many dead. All the dead whites were found in buildings; nobody was outside."

"Smallpox or measles, no doubt," Creed said.

Pierre nodded. "The Canadians wanted to burn all the buildings, but the Algonquins fled in terror of the evil spirits, and the Canadians followed."

"The area around the fort was cleared to create fields of fire, but now it's covered in new growth," O'Ballance said.

Creed rubbed his chin. "Still, with proper attention, it could provide an outpost for the local rebel militia. Whoever controls this place could protect the land and water passage heading south along the eastern side of the lake."

O'Ballance put out sentries and set up a camp near the lake's edge. Creed sat alone and studied his map under the stars. If accurate, the second fort was a half-mile southeast.

***

Their canoes slipped from the shore and glided south in the early morning twilight. The splashing of the oars flushed a flock of ducks from the reeds along the shoreline. They circled upward and beat their wings eastwards over the haze hanging above the dark water.

Pierre sat in the bow of the lead canoe and pointed south. Behind him sat Creed and O'Ballance.

"Soldiers might still be there," O'Ballance said. "We should land away from the point."

"The settlers and the militia are long gone," Creed said.

Pierre grunted. "Iroquois might be there."

"Hadn't thought of that. Be like them, wouldn't it? Once the lust for scalps and loot is aroused, little stops them."

"*Oui, monsieur.*

"Wait, look there!" Creed pointed at a faint spiral of a smoke ring rising over the wood line some 100 yards to their front.

"It seems I was wrong, *monsieur*. Iroquois would not burn a fire in enemy territory. White soldiers are there."

It was Creed's turn to grunt. "Steer to port. We'll land north of them and make our approach on foot."

The rowers quietly applied their paddles, guiding the canoes to the lake's eastern shore. The craft thumped the shoreline in a few minutes, and the men struggled up the muddy embankment.

Creed drew his sword. "Pierre will lead. Sergeant O'Ballance, have your section follow us in single file."

O'Ballance nodded. He hoped this fort would be as empty as the last. "We'll have your back, sir."

They proceeded inland a quarter-mile, where Pierre found a deer trail. The early sunlight began to bathe the forest with pale gold. From above, they could hear birds calling one another in a morning ritual that was both reassuring and alarming.

As O'Ballance fought through bushes and low-hanging branches, he thought about the officer leading them this far down the lake. The mission made little sense from a military perspective. They were miles from the stated British objectives and could only stumble into a senseless fight.

O'Ballance knew that Captain Lawrence was different from any other British officer he had met. He thought this was Lawrence's way of showing that the Royal Americans were just as good, if not better, than their British counterparts. The British usually saw Loyalist units mainly as support forces, only fit for garrison duty. It seemed Lawrence wanted to change that view once and for all.

O'Ballance saw his captain halt up ahead. He bent low, made his way forward, and took a knee next to his commander.

Creed whispered as he checked the flint on his fusil. "Pierre went forward to reconnoiter. Let the men drink some water and get some rest. I am going forward and joining him."

O'Ballance was nervous. "What exactly is our mission here, sir?"

"To determine if this outpost poses any advantage to the rebels."

"And if it does?"

"Well, I intend to recommend another force return here to take it."

"So, we are not going to storm it ourselves?"

Creed smiled. "With ten men? I should say not. Unless…"

O'Ballance's stomach churned. "Unless what, sir?"

"Unless they give us no other choice."

***

Creed bent forward at the waist and ran up the trail. When he neared the edge of the woods, he dropped to the ground and crawled through dew-soaked grass until he was next to Pierre, sprawled under some bushes.

"I count twelve men," whispered Pierre.

Creed peered up through the bushes and canopy. The morning sun had risen, and the bright rays beat down on his face, now dribbling with sweat. "That means they could have forty or more."

Pierre grunted.

"What?"

"I remember this place. I was here with a band of Iroquois warriors and French soldiers." He closed his heavy eyelids. "I can still see the flames and hear the screams as the Iroquois lay the tomahawk into all in their reach. Few escaped."

"You were part of such things?"

Pierre opened his eyes and nodded slowly. "The braves laughed at me because I refused to join in the slaughter. A French soldier put his musket into my shoulders. I took the blows. But I would not kill."

"You may have to kill now."

"We should go, *monsieur*."

"Not yet. I want to see if they have any cannons. Cover me."

Creed slipped his fusil from his shoulder and slowly clawed through the tall grass. He paused at a small stand of trees on a slight rise. He needed to make his ploy appear like an actual survey of the rebel defenses. He reached into his vest for a sketch map on which he drew markings indicating a thrust at Fort Ticonderoga. *This should be clear enough for them.* He rolled the sketch map and jammed it into his cartouche.

Now the hard part.

Creed suddenly rose from the brush, intentionally exposing himself. Shouts came from the fort. A series of musket shots tore at leaves and kicked up dirt. Then it grew still. Creed figured he had seconds before the militia could reload.

He made a hasty sign of the cross, bounded into the open area between him and the wood line, and began to run zigzag. A second rebel volley kicked up dust around him.

A shot rang out from the wood line, followed by a second. Rebel fire turned in that direction. He saw the cloud of grey smoke where Pierre still waited.

Now's my chance! In a desperate gambit, Creed tossed his cartouche to the ground. In it, he had carefully placed the intelligence he hoped would somehow find its way to Albany.

Creed plunged into the woods. Branches scratched his face, sending blood and sweat down his cheeks. The shouts and cries of the militia drew closer. They had left the redoubt in a mad chase for him and Pierre. More musket shots snapped the leaves around him.

Then he saw it. His men were advancing to his aid. He did not want a fight between his rebel countrymen and his band of Loyalists.

Creed cupped his hands over his mouth. "Back to the canoes, now!"

The Royal Americans broke and ran towards the lake. All but O'Ballance saw the rebels storming up the trail. He primed his musket and pulled back the hammer. Drawing the stock to his shoulder, he sighted in on the lead rebel, a burly man in homespun and leather.

Before he got the shot off, Creed appeared at his side.

"Hold fire!"

"Thank Christ, sir! I was afraid they'd nicked you. Let me take one of the bastards down. A Royal American farewell."

"No time. We must join the boys before they take off."

They made it to the canoes just as the last men clambered aboard.

"Steer southwest until we are out of musket range," Creed ordered.

His words arrived just in time. Shouts and musket shots erupted from the shore. Lead balls splashed the dark water like stones. But they fell short as the canoes quickly pulled out of range.

Only then did Creed realize that Pierre had not made it back.

***

Creed and Captain Alexander Fraser sat alone in Fraser's small deerskin tent. Creed held a cup of plain black coffee. Fraser's hands cradled a large tin mug brimming with black coffee and rum.

"A fine report, James. I had feared you fell into a rebel trap or some such nefarious business. So, yer absence seems to have proven worthwhile. As for Binoche and his savages, I have little control of them."

Creed rubbed his cup with his thumbs. "What of Binoche? Why doesn't he report to you?"

Fraser smiled uncomfortably. "I suggest you visit the other Fraser – General Fraser. He can explain these things better than I. My role is to push south quickly. That's why your diversion caused me consternation."

"Well, at least you now know an important rebel outpost that could threaten the army's supply line."

"We can report all that too."

"We?"

"I shall accompany you, James. Junior officers must stick together."

Creed nodded, unsure that Fraser's company signaled support or an escort to meet some British punishment for excess zeal.

They floated north in Androche's canoe. His expert paddlers worked with speed and purpose. The sky had darkened with clouds, but Androche insisted no rain would come their way until the temperatures rose. Only then, he insisted, would the storms come.

After an hour, they reached the island where General Simon Fraser's advanced guard had camped. The canoe glided soundly to the bank. Creed and Fraser climbed out and headed up a trail. The sentry recognized the famous Captain Fraser, the general's cousin, and waved them on without a challenge.

Fraser was sitting on a tree trunk with his scarlet jacket providing a cushion. He had what looked like a map straddling his legs. "Welcome, gentlemen. I am anxious for your report on what awaits us."

"This map from headquarters will only prove useful if I come down with the flux. Guy Carlton needs to hire some gazetteers. This one was taken during the last war."

"In my experience, sir, the French often produce better maps than we," Alexander Fraser quipped.

"Ah, but then you hardly need one, eh, Alex? You and your Iroquois know every inch of this place."

"Some Iroquois do. Some do not know this place," the junior Fraser replied tersely.

"None knows it better than Pierre, and now he's gone," Creed said glumly.

"Pierre? Who the deuce is that?" Simon Fraser asked.

"A Wyandot who lived for many years with the Iroquois. Familiar with Iroquois as well as Algonkian languages and ways. Pierre knew this land better than anyone."

"Mister Lawrence's guide never returned from the rebel fort, sir," Alexander Fraser interjected. "Likely fell into rebel hands trying to hold them off. Damn shame. Rebels are known to scalp the savages, too."

With that sad introduction, the two captains rendered their report. Simon Fraser's look turned serious as he concentrated on every sentence. When they had finished, the general stood. He thrust his hands behind his back and began pacing before them in careful thought.

"Has anyone scouted Ticonderoga?"

"Just reports from the Indians, sir. I have yet to have an officer observe it," the captain replied. "Of course, the Indians are impressed with the fortress's massive presence. They saw some cannon too."

"And men? Did they count the soldiers? Guns, no matter how impressive, are useless without soldiers."

"Unfortunately, no, sir. They brought back several...."

"Several what?" The general's ebullient mood had darkened.

He glanced at Creed and cleared his throat. "Scalps, sir."

The youthful general barely controlled his temper. "Damnation and these bloody savages! I've had enough of their feckless approach to warfare."

"You might not have said that had you been with Braddock, cousin," Alexander retorted.

Silence ensued. The general's face reddened.

Alexander Fraser referred to the tragic massacre of a British column making its way through dense western forests to attack the French Fort Duquesne during the French and Indian War. He was an eyewitness to what well-led Indians could do to British regulars.

"I know little of Indians but this," Creed said. "If their heart is in an enterprise, they can be quite formidable... when they lose heart, they melt away like an ice-block in July. Sort of like the Irish."

The two Frasers burst into laughter. Creed's play on English prejudice lightened the mood again.

"By God, I like how you think, Captain Lawrence," exclaimed the general. "Alexander, we must send a reliable officer to Ticonderoga to perform a detailed reconnaissance. Maybe take a prisoner or penetrate the defenses...."

"And the Iroquois?"

"Leave them to their butchery for now. Maybe it will panic the rebels and keep the militia from mustering."

"I have an excellent officer in mind, sir."

"And who is it?"

The rugged infantry captain turned to Creed. "None other than Captain James Lawrence of the Royal American Regiment."

The general looked at him. "It is a daunting task. Can you do this, Captain Lawrence?"

"Call me James, sir. Yes, I believe I can. Given the ability to pick my men."

The general intertwined his fingers pensively. "I had hoped you would take this task up personally, Alexander, but I support your choice. This mission is a forlorn hope. It is quite likely James will come to an unpleasant end. I need your services if we are to lead this army to Albany and beyond."

***

Creed returned to the camp. He had spent two hours with Alexander Fraser going over the mission. Fraser had served near the fort during the last war and knew the defenses well enough to provide a rough description. "Ticonderoga is large. It spreads across two small peninsulas bisected by an extension of the lake. The most formidable is the northwest side of the water."

Fraser drew a twig from the fire and sketched an outline on the earth. "The rebels will fight hard for these works, for they represent their first victory over us. If you don't count Gage's muck-up of Boston."

Creed smiled. "I don't."

Fraser grunted. "Take your canoes until you are just beyond sight of the fort. Hide them well, not so much from rebels as the Iroquois. Then proceed on foot to the fort. The land is rugged and thick with woods, mind ye. But that affects the rebels as well."

Creed knew well that adverse conditions impact both sides of a struggle. The key to success was to exploit the opponent's discomfort.

He took the twig from Fraser and traced a notional path around the fort and then a line into it. "We'll do a reconnaissance and then attempt to pierce the defenses."

"And if it fails?" Fraser asked.

"If the attempt to penetrate fails, the rest of the party can at least report back on the results of our reconnaissance," Creed answered.

"A damned good idea, James! I like the way you think. By God, I should come with you."

Creed shook his head. The last thing he wanted was this crafty fighter along. "I believe the general was correct. There is every likelihood that I will not return. You shall be needed elsewhere."

"Hmmm. Very well. I suspect a certain captain wants more than his share of the credit for penetrating the rebels' stronghold. I believe whiskey is in order. Let's have a dram."

Fraser took a large hip flask of dull pewter from his haversack. He noticed Creed admiring the flask's ornate "*Fleur-de-lis*" design.

"A gift from the Iroquois, James. Got it during the last war. They say it was the prized possession of a Wyandot sachem they captured in a great raid. Was said to have been a gift to his grandfather from the great Samuel de Champlain. I'm sure the sachem prized it for the calvados contained within, eh?"

He threw the flask at Creed, who began reading the French inscription.

"The flask once belonged to the French King, Henri the 4th. It commemorates one of Champlain's first voyages. Not a precious token, but a valuable one."

"Why do you say that?"

"Well, for one thing, Henri the 4th was the last King of France that wasn't a sod."

Fraser burst into laughter. "Excellent, James. You've earned a second dram. Drink up, and then get back to your tent and sleep. God knows you'll need it."

***

Creed climbed into his shelter. The June night had turned cool. He reached for a blanket and rolled over into a fitful sleep induced by stress and alcohol. His dreams whirred through his subconscious in a moment that lasted years - or so it seemed. Visions of Ireland swirled around him and retreated just as he began to make sense of them: his family – a mother who treasured him, a father who reviled him, an indifferent brother, and priests and brothers who tried to educate him. Visions of service in France took over and suddenly dimmed.

Creed woke up soaked in sweat. He listened to the dull, unsettling beat of his heart, then gradually, other sounds started to drown out the pounding. He heard heavy breathing and rustling outside the tent. Then came low, manly groans and soft squeals. He peeked out. The tent next to him belonged to Bart. Those were his groans. As for the squeals, he knew them all too well.

Chapter 12

The Battery, New York City

Major Sandy Drummond stood tall in the saddle, his eyes squinting against a bright sun and light wind. His mare, Shoe, remained still, only occasionally swatting at flies with her dark tail. Gentle ripples lapped up against the quay just north of the Battery. The stone fort was old New Amsterdam's first line of defense but was now primarily of symbolic value.

Flush with men and equipment, sleek galleys slid from the docks and into the North River. Some steered a course for the Paulhus Hook on the Jersey side, while others plied their way south to Staten Island or beyond. But Drummond cared nothing of commerce. He was eager for Baker's return aboard one of those galleys.

The cries and grunts of the crews going through their drills relaxed him, as did the river's semi-salt air. At times, Drummond missed the routine of "regular" army work. He missed the 17th Light Dragoons and the life that allowed him to command men in an orderly way. Still, he enjoyed the cat-and-mouse games at headquarters and in the field. Sandy Drummond was getting better at running scouts and spies.

Drummond shook his hat at a mate who shuffled by. He appeared eager to slake his thirst at one of the many taverns along the water. "Any word on a captain named Baker?"

"No, sir. Nobody by that name aboard." The mate continued on his way without halting to salute or remove his hat.

Drummond would have stood the man at attention in an earlier time or had him disciplined for failing to salute a superior officer. But espionage work demanded he shed the niceties of military discipline for discretion and forbearance.

The rhythmic clatter of horse hooves interrupted Drummond's thoughts. He recognized the rider well—a sinister-looking middle-aged man with bad teeth, dressed in a slightly soiled, rumpled brown velveteen suit. His beaver hat was tilted to the side, revealing thinning, gray hair that barely held a queue.

"Nothing, sir. We've checked where he might have stopped for a pint along the water. Should we cross over and try the taverns on the Richmond side?"

"No, Sergeant Digby. I fear something has happened. His mission was clear enough. Lead the column. Find our contact and get back."

Digby swatted at a large fly that settled on his horse's neck. "Well, sir, maybe the column still needs his services."

"Blast the column! His real mission was to make contact."

"We have several contacts in the Jerseys, sir."

"I know that! He was the only one in Washington's headquarters," Drummond snapped. He immediately regretted the indiscretion. Sergeant Digby had served him long and well, but as a sergeant, he was never privy to the most intimate details of Drummond's espionage schemes.

"You never told me our spy, Golden Apple, returned to the fold, sir. When, pray tell, did that happen?" Digby had a toadying way that annoyed Drummond.

"That is of little concern now. I assigned Captain Baker the task of meeting him. General Howe's feint...." Drummond stopped himself.

"You don't mean to tell me that General Howe, our illustrious commander-in-chief, launched this attack on the rebels to...."

"Hold your voice down." Drummond slapped his gloves against Shoe's neck. The horse startled and rocked until Drummond tightened up on the reins. "Well, let's just say we had a...confluence...of interests."

Drummond squinted towards a small boat crossing the channel from Staten Island. Its small lateen sail of yellowed canvas was tight as it tacked slowly against the wind. It sailed past Drummond's position and then came about. The boom swung to the lee, and the sail billowed, sending the boat skipping towards the quay. The water breaking against its bow rippled ribbons of white foam. The sail was let loose as it grew close to the shore. The boat glided to the quay with a thump. In the cockpit sat Sidney Baker.

"Well, from your look, may I assume that you had a successful journey, Captain Baker?" Drummond asked.

Baker scrambled from the boat. "We need to discuss this more discreetly, sir."

Digby looked around to make sure nobody lay within earshot.

"Dunno, you ought to be talkin' that way to the major, sir. I knew he should have sent one of the lads or me with you. You know, to make sure the major got what he wanted."

Baker thrust out his jaw. "My boys did well on their own, sergeant."

"It's all right, Digby. We'll discuss the captain's trip over a glass of port. Meet me at Lady Dunning's after you clean up, Sidney."

Drummond yanked Shoe's head around and trotted down the lane.

***

The three men crowded around the small table in Drummond's room. The Dunning house often hosted officers and prominent civilians. Lady Dunning seemed to entertain around the clock. Drummond used it as his base because the comings and goings of so many strangers enabled him and his men to cloak their movement.

Drummond sipped at his sherry. "You certainly gave me a worry at the quay, Sidney."

"You doubted I'd return?"

Drummond nodded slowly. "Well, initial reports painted a bleak picture."

"You should know by now, sir, never to place much stock in initial reports."

"*Touché*, Sidney. I shall try to remember that. However, your mission could prove fateful to our long-term success. Now, by all means, explain what happened."

"The first part of the attack went as well as we might have hoped. We led the column forth. The usual skirmishing proved no real problem. It justified the secondary attack, which the rebels assumed was an attempt to flank them. Fortunately, they were just a small skirmish party. They held us up initially, but the rebels soon fled the area."

"Did you meet with Golden Apple?"

"Not exactly."

"What do you mean?"

"Why, he's dead, sir."

"Dead? We just received two messages from him in the code I provided him last summer."

"Don't you find it odd to go so long before he contacted you?" Baker asked.

"A little odd, yes. I tried several times to make contact with him. It took long enough. Yet the rebels have been on the run, and I assumed he had little opportunity to organize a means of communication. All I got for my efforts was a dead agent and Klara."

Drummond cursed silently. Months of anticipation, and now his one great chance to penetrate the rebel headquarters had evaporated as quickly as it appeared.

"I didn't mean to discommode you, sir. Golden Apple is dead. At least the man you recruited as Golden Apple. Before he succumbed to whatever affliction undid him, I think he succeeded in recruiting a sub-agent."

Drummond's mind raced. *Could Klara's father have succeeded after all?*

"A surgeon, the dentist, named Stumpf?"

"No, not dear Klara's father. I am afraid he is dead as well."

"How? And how do you know all this?"

Baker smiled. "We made it to our meeting point and found this. The rebels overlooked it in their haste to engage us."

Baker pulled an oilskin-wrapped sheaf of papers from his haversack. "It seems your agent recruited an agent in Washington's headquarters before he died."

"An aide de camp?"

"Better than that, sir. An engineer. With access to technical information. Locations of rebel fortifications, bridges, fording points on rivers, and most importantly, maps."

Drummond was at once surprised, perplexed, dismayed, and pleased. *What did this mean?*

The stunning message from Golden Apple had initially perplexed him. Yet, once he thought through the likely chain of events, he realized his original timeline had been overly ambitious. Valuable intelligence takes planning, time, and patience to bear fruit. But this turn of events changed everything. *Was it for the better or, the worse?*

"Did he provide his *bona fides*?" Drummond placed his sherry glass aside and grabbed at his stiff knee, hunching forward in his seat. Somehow, the ache helped focus his mind now.

"His what?"

"You know – proof of his identity." Drummond tried to remain calm.

"No," Baker said with a look of sadness.

"Good. Better we establish that in our own time. An agent too willing to put forth a name should be suspect. Do you know anything about him?"

Baker smiled. "Well, he provided that he was assigned to Washington's headquarters as a planning engineer. He mostly had surveying experience and access to maps of all kinds, primitive as they are."

"But how did he meet Golden Apple?"

Baker shook his head. "Truth be, he never mentioned him, and I didn't ask."

Drummond stroked his chin. "Hmm, perhaps he's a volunteer. A loyal Briton in the rebel midst. Anything else?"

"He included a map of the Morristown bivouac and the approaches through the Watchung Hills. They seem authentic. They also show defense works on the lower Hudson. Have a look."

Drummond reached for the map. It held several dotted goose eggs with penciled-in symbols such as a capital E turned over – trench works. He studied it in silence for a few minutes. Baker sat awkwardly, sipping at the sherry and glancing at the map.

Drummond looked up. His face showed careful anticipation. "If this is authentic, Sidney, and I repeat, if this is authentic, your little raid to the north may have had more than its desired effect."

He placed a finger on the area around Verplank's Point. "These are not in place yet. The rebels must be planning to move forces north. Since your raid, our patrols have not had any luck getting this far north – they have closed up the area between our forces. And look here. The same holds for the western side of the river, south of the West Point fortifications." His finger slid east. "And look here. There are more navigational markings between Morristown and Orange."

"Meaning?" Baker asked.

"A sign that they have plans, if not the intent, to move northeast and block our thrust up the North River."

Baker nodded. "I see. Then I should get to work on the rest of the letter."

"Yes, once you finish transcribing the letter, we can begin to vett this new 'Golden Apple.' A process, which, unfortunately, will prove difficult."

Baker reached into the oilskin wrap and pulled out a worn brass button embossed with a crude castle. "Well, then, maybe this is our beginning."

Drummond smiled. "Ah, an engineer's uniform button. A clever device to prove himself? Let us hope our new agent is indeed clever. But we shall retire the name 'Golden Apple.' Our new *nom de guerre* for him shall be 'Rook.'"

"Rook?" Baker asked.

"Why, yes, another name for the castle in chess. The symbol of the engineers. Let's drink another glass, this time a toast to Rook. Then you can get to your work."

***

The Dale House, near Brunswick, New Jersey

"This is all we have tonight, Emily. I gave the servants the night free, so we could catch up, dear." Lorie Dale crossed the dining room threshold carrying a plate of cold chicken and a small decanter of local fruit wine.

"It looks wonderful," Emily said. "You are doing quite nicely as mistress of your estate and a chef."

Lorie blushed. "I do have some help, dear. A four-hundred-acre farm requires manual labor to survive, if not thrive. With my husband off somewhere leading a detachment of the New Jersey Volunteers, I'm now learning how to run a farmstead on my own."

"You have blossomed, my dear Lorie. It has been two years since...."

"Since I left New York to become Jonah's bride? A long time to have been separated from my dearest friend. Well, I have cherished every one of your letters since. Each brings me a ray of sunshine and news of my home, all captured by your wonderful wit."

"Have you heard from Jonah lately?" Emily felt a little guilty about probing one of her oldest friends.

"I just received a letter from him. He was in the column that attacked the rebel approaches to Morristown. He asked me to send him a second pair of boots. It seems our army expends more shoe leather than bullets."

They both laughed.

After a moment of thought, Lorie continued. "You know, I had great hesitation in Jonah becoming a volunteer. But he commands one of the finest Loyalist battalions."

Emily's eyes softened. "Oh, dear Lorie, how hard it must be to have your great love place himself in harm's way for king and country."

Lorie cast her strange look, and her pale cheeks blushed faintly. "Oh, you unwed girls are so romantic in your notions of both the heart and the homeland."

Emily straightened a little. "I am almost twenty. And unwed by choice. Several gentlemen have made discreet suggestions to papa. But I always – never mind that. You surely miss your husband."

Lorie sipped her wine and cast her eyes downward. "Of course, I am his wife, after all."

"Do you think General Howe will have the rebels on the run once and for all this spring?" Emily asked innocently.

"What do I care for that? So long as neither side harms this place. I can assure you, dear, it makes one frightfully anxious to live almost squarely between two opposing armies. There are redcoat patrols, rebel patrols, and strangers passing across our fields at all hours. Threats from both sides abound, and occasionally, there are reports of cowboys or skinners about. And I, without anyone here to help or protect but servants and farm workers whose loyalties seem as divided as the country."

Lorie's pale face looked drained, and her gray eyes teared. She broke into sobs. Emily came across the table, embraced her warmly, and kissed her cheek.

Emily stroked her friend's cheek. "I understand, dear. New York was a frightful place last year, but things are slowly getting better. They will improve here, too."

Lorie dabbed her eyes. "Have you found your father yet?"

"He is supposed to meet me here tomorrow. Stephen, that is, Major Rumson, was able to contact him. We shall not have long together as his brigade needs him more than I."

Lorie twirled her glass in her hand. "Emily, dear, I had not dared to write of this in a letter, but...." She lowered her eyes and stared ruefully.

Emily grabbed her dainty chin. "But what, dear heart?"

Lorie sighed. "My feelings are quite confused about all this, ambivalent, really. I suppose I was always confused and divided. But the chasm grows each day." She lowered her head.

"You mean you are undecided as to your loyalties? Many are, and I suppose that is normal and understandable as long as you do not act against the king. Besides, your husband is a highly respected Loyalist leader."

"Well, the truth be told, I have indecision on both accounts...."

Emily startled. "Oh...oh dear...oh my poor dear. Let me embrace you."

The two young women sat quietly in each other's arms, each taking comfort in the other's quiet breathing.

Emily murmured, "No matter what you feel, you shall have my strongest support and affection."

"There is more to it, Emily," Lorie whispered. "I have a lover."

"A what? You mean?"

"Yes."

Emily pulled back and eyed her friend. "Perhaps that's to be expected. A woman alone in war. Not that I approve, mind you."

Lorie buried her head in her hands. "Worse yet – he's a rebel. Don't think too harshly of me for it. It wasn't planned. It just happened." She began to sob.

Emily tilted her head back and grasped her friend's hands. She pondered her reply carefully. "Well, so much in life turns on unplanned events. So long as your rebel lover is discreet in both accounts – his affection for you and his political sympathies."

"Emily dear, I am afraid our love has gone beyond mere affection, and his sympathies are more than political."

"Meaning?" Emily thought she knew but played at naiveté.

"Meaning, we have been quite demonstrative in our love, and he has displayed action against the crown, not just sympathy for the rebel cause."

"Is your admirer a local landholder? Has he joined a local rebel militia?"

"No, not a militiaman."

"Ah, a continental officer! Perhaps a major or a colonel."

Lorie shook her head and stared down at her lap. "He's a rebel spy, I fear. He calls himself Rip Hyde. But I am sure that is just a *nom de guerre*. He comes and goes, usually by night, and I never know when he'll appear."

Emily swallowed. She tried to hide her sorrow for her friend even as she sorted out whether this posed an opportunity or a danger.

"Oh, Lorie, my dear! How did you meet this, Rip Hyde?"

"It happened right here. Just a few weeks ago. A stranger in buckskin and black came riding through with a band of green-jacketed dragoons in pursuit. He jumped from the saddle and sent his horse down a trail leading to the river."

Emily swallowed. "How did he come to your home? Did he knock on the door and invite himself in?"

Lorie shook her head. "Not realizing he had dragoons following him, I invited him in. He said he was escaping creditors and debtor's prison. His roguish charm had me smitten from the first moment I saw him. I hid him under my bed."

"Always a signal of things to come," Emily chided.

Lorie slapped her breast playfully. "Please don't judge. When the light horse came through, they didn't stop. They just followed his horse's trace. I suppose they thought he swam the river. They never searched my boudoir."

"How did...." Emily could scarcely ask the question she so desperately wanted to ask.

Lorie blushed and hung her head. "I did not want the servants to find him. And he was so rakishly handsome. Lithe like a panther too. He spent the night with me. It was like nothing I ever imagined."

"Lorie Dale – I never expected this from you," Emily said so softly it was almost as to herself.

"I don't suppose one ever expects to take a lover," Lorie retorted.

"No, I meant hiding a rebel spy. How many times have you seen him?"

"Too many. But not enough." Her head hung in shame. "Since then, he has been back here only twice."

She placed her face in her hands, and tears rolled down her cheeks.
***

Despite the stable's inky darkness, Emily slipped the saddle onto Pudding. The horse softly groaned when she applied the harness. Emily could hear the clock in the Dale house chime twice.

"I'm sorry, Pudding. I've never done this in darkness. We'll be out of here shortly."

Emily had slept fitfully and felt a strange combination of fatigue and adrenaline. Everything she had done for the cause could be lost in this one bold gambit, as could her life and her father's career. Not knowing the exact trace of the lines between the rebels and the British had the makings of a disaster.

Although ostensibly under the protection of British forces in Brunswick, the Dale farmstead was the epicenter of the land known as the neutral ground. Much as Lorie lamented, anyone could be out there, and anyone was likely to do her no good. Still, she had calculated the risks. The rebellion's fate might well swing on what luck she had that night.

Emily pulled a cloak over her shoulders to ward off the chill of the night air. It draped down along Pudding's flanks, making her look like a Russian Cossack astride a steppe pony.

With a flick of the reins and a soft word, she and Pudding sped down the road north towards the American lines. Here, Emily's grand plan had a shortfall, for she had only a vague notion of finding the American pickets, a patrol, or a spy. As Pudding trotted along, she reluctantly admitted her plan was a bad gamble. But one she knew she had to take.

***

Benjamin Tallmadge looked down from a rock-strewn overlook with an intense and purposeful gaze. To the south lay Raritan Landing. Although unimpressive, the village, also known as The Landing, controlled a critical vantage point along the Raritan River, where it narrowed from a tidal to a free-flowing river.

One of his men, Tom Gordon, had passed through the town on the way to Brunswick and Amboy to watch British movements. Gordon, who had lived in both Amboy and Brunswick, knew the area.

With Jeremiah Creed gone, Tallmadge began to recruit line-crossers in greater numbers and sent them on short espionage missions. Although these spies lacked Creed's experience, skill, and cunning, they could be recruited and dispatched quickly. Yet only one in three had made it back alive. And their intelligence value was sketchy.

Private Jonathan Beall broke Tallmadge's reflections. "Any sign of Harry, sir?" Beall stood three yards back, holding the lines of Tallmadge's horse.

"Nothing stirring below. He should have gotten our line crosser to the Landing and arrived back by now." Tallmadge's voice showed his frustration.

"I'm sorry. I should not have spoken the man's name this close to the lines."

Recently, Colonel Fitzgerald began enforcing a strict numerical code for all agents recruited on the payroll.

Tallmadge took the reins from Beall and swung himself into the saddle. "You and Trooper Parker stay here till dawn. If he doesn't return, head to Metuchen and fetch Karcz and O'Quinn from their outpost. I'll remain in Piscataway until tomorrow night. Make sure you return by then."

"We'll get back in plenty of time, sir. Harry often falls, but he rarely fails," Parker said.

Tallmadge tightened up on the reins. "I expect Jeremiah's detachment to do its duty as he would, were he here."

He then gave a light spur to his horse and disappeared down the wooded path that led north.

***

The mare's hooves beat a measured stride.

"That's it, Pudding," Emily coaxed. "Let's keep this pace." She needed to move with a mix of caution and urgency. She had no plan to reach American lines other than to head north and hope for the best.

Pudding paced up the narrow and wooded lane. Branches whipped at her face, arms, and legs. To avoid the British, she had taken a secluded path, Lorie said her lover had used. The lane suddenly crossed an open area strewn with rocks, an endless array. Here, the route became a dark ribbon that climbed the side of a thickly wooded ridge.

She spotted a shadowy blur in the darkness that drenched the night. The faint, dull drumming of horse hooves gradually increased. In the distance, the echo of a musket shot fought its way through the trees.

Emily pulled back the reins, bringing Pudding to a sudden halt. *Were they rebels or redcoats?*

Emily looked about for an escape route. Spotting a gulley that seemed to offer a way out, she turned Pudding's head and rode. Her heart was beating fiercely, and her mouth turned dry. *They could appear at any moment.*

Emily had rehearsed a story to use if caught—she had set out to find her father and had become lost. Her story might work with British regulars. But if these were cowboys or skinners, she might end the night with men with few scruples and little opportunity to save themselves.

Two more shots rang out. Emily heard the angry cries of men and the desperate pounding of hooves.

"Where'd the bastard turn to?" a raspy voice asked.

"I don't know-damn it. It's dark as a bear's arsehole tonight."

"This will be our third chance to catch him."

The other man laughed. "Third time's a charm. We'll get him."

"Last time, he beat us to the river, and I swear – his horse is a fish."

"Pshaw! He tricked us. Sod's likely hid near that farm up ahead. We'll get him there and take our pick of the farm."

"That's Captain Dale's place. He's a Loyalist. We can't touch the place."

"Oh no? Let's fold up these green jackets. Tonight, we're skinners, not cowboys, eh?"

Oh, poor Lorie! Emily had fallen into the clutches of a gang of cowboys during the battle of New York. *The things such men are capable of!* She knew she had to do something quickly, even if it meant missing her father.

Chapter 13

Lake Champlain, New York

Creed rose from his tent in the pre-dawn darkness. He carefully packed his uniform and slipped into buckskin and homespun provided by Fraser. He looked little different from the frontier militia or Canadian *coureurs des bois*.

On his shoulder hung an old French musket instead of his light infantry fusil, and in his belt, he tucked a sleek hunting knife and tomahawk in place of his short sword. He placed a worn beaver hat on his head in a final touch.

He rubbed his face. The three days of growth would add to his appearance. He mused that if his White Knights saw him, they would think he was reprising the Root Hog Burns persona he used in New Jersey.

One of his Royal Americans stood half asleep at sentry duty. Creed approached him.

"Who goes? Is that you, Captain Lawrence?"

"Sorry for the ragged attire, Private Stedman. But I am heading into places where I need to appear a local."

The sentry seemed unsurprised at Creed's departure from regimental attire.

"Anyone about?" Creed asked.

"Just some of the savages, sir. Your man Androche went down to the canoe. And that one over there."

He motioned towards Bart Saunders's tent. "One of them, the squaw girl, made an expressive night call on Mister Saunders."

"Is she still there?"

"No. The doxie left about a half-hour ago." Stedman chuckled. "I suppose she got all she could from him for one night."

Creed was not amused. He feared Fleurette was up to something. Despite her ploys for his attention, he felt she was not the doxie she pretended to be.

Creed slipped down to the shore and joined Androche at the canoe. He had picked his two best paddlers for the journey. They sat patiently, one fore, one aft, with paddles braced across their laps.

"I wish Pierre were with us for this venture," he said.

"If he lives, he will yet join us, *Monsieur*."

"He is resourceful and strong. But I fear he fell to their bullets or their knives."

"You must trust in Pierre, *Monsieur*. There is no man, or spirit for the matter, like Pierre. He can escape a trap or a captor and move across these lands the way the angels fly from heaven to earth."

Creed felt guilty for leaving the brave man to the Americans. He remembered Fraser's comment that whites took scalps with fervor equal to that of the most savage native.

I need to focus on my mission. "Do you have the furs?"

"*Oui.* Not many, but enough for you to parlay your way past the white men."

"What makes you think I'll have only white men to contend with?"

"I did not say that, *Monsieur*," Androche replied.

***

The canoe glided swiftly across the lake, and its surface shone like glass. The two paddlers pulled expertly, each stroke making a crisp cut into the still water. The lake was dark and silent. Creed's mind raced with worry, fear, and regret. At last, he bowed his head in prayer. It might be his last chance for reflection.

Androche broke the silence. "There is your place, *Monsieur*. Ticonderoga is there."

"I see nothing but darkness," Creed said.

"You have not the eye of the Indian. Still, it is far off. We turn here, and you make your way on foot."

Creed reached for his weapons. "Give me two days. If I don't return, leave me for dead."

Despite the darkness, Creed could see the look of concern on Androche's face. *He knows well that I'll not return.*

One of the paddlers whispered something in the Huron dialect.

"What is it?" Creed asked.

"We are followed. *Allez! Tres vite!*"

The men skillfully steered toward the western shore. Paddles dug into the cold waters at a frantic pace. Morning's twilight began to bathe the lake in silver. Creed could now see the outline of a canoe no more than 100 yards behind them. Up ahead was a cove surrounded by rocky cliffs rising twenty feet above the shoreline. The morning rays revealed the outline of the massive mountains beyond.

The canoe thumped the shore, and they scrambled out. They checked their flints and powder. In silence, they dragged it into a clump of bushes.

Creed whispered to Androche, "Don't fire unless I give the word. There might be enemy patrols about."

"Or worse - Iroquois," Androche replied. "I see them, *Monsieur*."

Shadowy figures leaped from the vessel and hauled it from the water. Creed could see the shadows moving closer.

A *click, click, click* broke the silence as Androche and his men cocked the worn hammers on their old firelocks.

Then a familiar voice whispered against the darkness – Huron dialect. Androche sputtered back a trove of epithets and began rejoicing in a strange mix of Huron, Iroquois, and French.

Out of the bushes emerged a familiar figure – Pierre! Behind him stood Bart, another of Androche's men, and a slender figure that Creed recognized right away - Fleurette Binoche.

Creed jumped up and grasped Pierre in a warm embrace. He spoke in French, "Pierre! By God, you are alive. You escaped."

"The white rebels caught and bound me. Tossed me into a hut until their chief could question me. He was somewhere to the south. I heard them say."

"But how?"

"Not hard to undo the binds. With the first darkness, I was gone. A simple drift log provided my passage across the lake."

Androche approached and touched Pierre, almost as if to test whether he was alive or a ghost from the lake.

Creed laughed. "'Tis Pierre, Androche. But, Pierre, why did you follow us? And what are you doing here, Bart? More to the point, what is she doing here?"

"She wants to help, sir," Bart replied hopefully.

"Help what?" Creed was writhing in anger. Glad to see Pierre alive, he seethed that this boy and the girl interfered with his secret and deadly mission.

"Speak! Help what?"

Bart's eyes lowered. "Fleurette says you are in danger."

"I know that. But your presence here can only increase that danger. Go back at once."

"The girl insisted she come. Her father is about," Pierre said.

"Well, Fraser has many scouts out and about."

"Fraser did not send Binoche to scout this night, sir," Bart said. "He left with his party in search of you. He wants revenge. Fleurette said she went to warn you, but you turned her out. So she came to me."

Pierre pointed in a sweep at the lake and the mountains behind them. "*Alors*, his canoe is out there *sur* le *lac*, or he may await you *à la Montagne*."

Creed looked at the girl. Was she a half-breed vixen or Saint Joan?

"So, you parlay your favors while betraying your father?"

"He is not my father!" She spat like poison was trapped in her mouth. "He killed my father and then took my mother as his squaw while I was yet in her belly."

Binoche is a cur beyond imagining! Creed recalled the debauchery in the British camp. *To know both mother and daughter.* That the daughter was not of his blood provided Creed no comfort. "Where I go, no one can go. You must all wait here."

"Take Pierre, *monsieur*. Every *coureurs des bois* has a Huron guide. In this case, Wyandot," Androche said.

"I see your point. Very well. Pierre comes with me."

"Every *coureur de bois* has an Indian woman, *Monsieur*. I shall come with you," Fleurette said.

"No!" Creed's eyes narrowed. "Androche, have your men give Pierre a firelock, hatchet, and knife. We leave now."

***

Fort Ticonderoga, June 1777

The vista of Lake Champlain's deep blue against the surrounding mountains of verdant green rivaled any in North America or Europe. But Brigadier General Arthur St. Clair could only gaze across the water in morbid anticipation.

Born in Scotland but now a landholder in western Pennsylvania, St. Clair had been sent north to bolster the northern army under General Philip Schuyler. The taciturn Scot was considered one of Washington's up-and-coming generals and, although not an intimate of the Virginian, was held by him in high regard.

The faint tracings of smoke were wafting along the treetops of the Green Mountains. For days, rumors of British and Indian marauding had chilled the defenders in the beleaguered fort. Yet his attempts at reconnaissance had not provided much helpful information.

"What think you, Jeduthan? Is yonder smoke the result of battle and pillage, or merely the illusion of mist?" St. Clair asked the tall, spare man standing beside him.

"Not caused by barometric change," came the simple reply.

For weeks, Colonel Jeduthan Baldwin had worked tirelessly to turn Ticonderoga into a semblance of the grand fortress once the invincible bastion of the north. Baldwin had helped build the rebel works that hemmed the British in Boston. His innate resourcefulness became a legend in the Army.

St. Clair relied heavily on his ability to help salvage their situation. "Then see that you get this place ready quickly. I don't think we have a week before they must meet the test."

Baldwin looked down at the small bands of scrawny figures listlessly hauling wood and earth. "Not the defenses we'll lack, sir, but the men to staff them."

St. Clair nodded as he scanned the breastworks and redoubts. He had but 5,000 men, many of them sick or malnourished. Both knew he needed at least 10,000 men for a proper defense.

"I have asked for reinforcements, but Schuyler has yet to satisfy my requests, although he knows more men are needed."

"He knows?" Baldwin asked.

St. Clair nodded. "He has asked for the New England militias to assemble. But due to disputes with New York and fear for their farmsteads, they have been slow to form."

"Perhaps the Indians will galvanize them into action," Baldwin said.

"And with what would I equip them if they came? Staves? With what should I victual them? Pine cones and mud?"

"If the men of New England come, that will suffice," Baldwin said flatly.

An orderly interrupted. "Sir, the sentries have signaled in a patrol – Sergeant Heath's returned!"

"At least he's not fallen to the scalping knife, eh?" Baldwin remarked.

"Our best scout, Jeduthan. If he fails me, we fight blind."

"Well, blind perhaps, but not fully uninformed. There are only so many ways to take this place. We need the men and supplies to make the British pay."

"His Excellency always sought a second Bunker Hill. Unlike Boston, however, when the British arrive, we will pay the price."

***

St. Clair's polished shoes tapped along the stone floor of his office. He paced back and forth, rapidly spitting questions at Heath. He paused a moment and glanced out the window. His view north across the water made him tense.

"More smoke," he said, turning to Heath.

"Gettin' bad up there, general. Indians are roaming everywhere. Canadian and Loyalist bands, too. But the boats, they're the real problem."

"Boats? St. Clair's adjutant asked. "What sort of boats? How many?" The impatient officer held his quill, anxious to transcribe the report.

"I'm no sailor, sir, but they were big, and some had sails twenty feet wide. Others are just barges and longboats, but with lots of men. Maybe fifty, total."

"Fifty?" St. Clair seemed impressed.

"Well, more than twenty, that's for sure. Many more."

The adjutant waved his quill. "Where did you see these, sergeant?"

"Between the Narrows and Split Rock. Some canoes farther south. Near Chimney Point."

"That's across from Crown Point. Then they are less than twenty miles from here." St. Clair folded his hands and pondered the news.

The adjutant anticipated his general's question. "Twenty-four hours by water. Two or three days by land."

St. Clair nodded. "The question is, which shall it be?"

Heath had to try again. He desperately needed more information. "Get some rest and what food you can scrape up, sergeant. You'll need to head out again after midnight."

"Beggin' your pardon, sir. My men won't go back out there. And I don't think I could do much alone."

St. Clair's face turned the color of a fresh beet. He strode back to the window and stared at the streak of black across the water. "If you don't go out, Sergeant Heath, nothing stands between this fortress and the enemy."

***

The woods became denser as they drew away from the lake's western shore. The mighty branches that stretched above them darkened everything as though it were night. Only the occasional beam of sunlight guided them with scattered patterns of light. They encountered no wildlife. Not a deer, fox, rabbit, or bird remained. All had long since fled the probing of two armies at war.

Creed moved just behind Pierre, who seemed to create space where none existed. They followed a narrow deer path running along the western slope of the mountains. Pierre halted at a rocky crevice. Up ahead rose a high promontory Pierre called The Hill of Foxes, but the white men called it Mount Hope.

"We'll stop here and rest. How much farther do you reckon we have to go?" Creed was already pulling off his shoes and rubbing his feet. He envied the soft moccasins of his companion. His dress as a *coureur* lacked that one detail.

"We can be within musket shot before the sun is one-quarter from the horizon."

"We continue straight up this path, then?"

Pierre cocked his head. "If you listen, you can hear the rush of waters – a narrow river from the great lake to the south. No, we turn and follow the water. It travels back to the lake."

Creed spread one of Vincennes's maps on the leafy ground. "I see. There's an old French fort between Ticonderoga and us. It should provide a good place to attack the fort."

He folded the map and pulled a piece of dried venison from his pouch. Creed's tongue absorbed the smoky-salt flavor as he chewed away at the tough meat.

He ran his sleeve across his brow. Despite the forest's protective canopy, the heat was gripping. But the powerfully built Wyandot appeared unaffected by the heat. "So, tell me, Pierre, how did you let those rebels take you?"

Pierre closed his eyes and lay his head back. "The map, *Mon Capitaine.*"

Creed's eyes widened. "The what?"

"I saw you throw the map. You would not have done so unless you intended the Americans to find it. But they did not. They were interested in valuables – not paper. The papers blew into the tall grass."

"Those rebels were probably a gang of bloody skinners!" Creed whispered.

"I do not understand. Skinners?"

"Rebel thugs who roam between both armies, looting and pillaging under the guise of combat. We have our Loyalist version as well – cowboys. Sometimes the two fight each other. But mostly, they skulk like wolves in search of easy prey."

Creed did not reveal that he often posed as one or the other to transit the lines between the British and Americans.

Pierre opened his eyes and looked at Creed. "I thought the white man honors only open battle."

"A legend we white men all like to believe. In truth, we often kill quickly and quietly, not always honorably."

Pierre grunted in agreement. Or was it disgust?

"Just how did you escape these skinners?"

"They argued amongst themselves over who would take my weapons and clothing. For they intended to kill me."

"But they didn't...."

Pierre's mouth tightened and bent slightly into what Creed took for a smile.

"I told them of the papers. That the British officer I served lost his important papers in the fight, I led their leader to the papers."

"He could read?"

"He never had the chance. As he opened the papers, I seized his knife."

"So, you killed him?"

Pierre's gaze went past Creed. "I ran into the forest. Once there, an army of such men could not catch me."

"Thank God for your escape. I did intend for the rebels to find the papers. My felicitous thanks to you for seeing that they found them."

They grew silent. The forest was still except for the distant sound of water and the all-too-close buzzing of mosquitoes.

Shouts shattered the peaceful scene. Muffled by the dense forest and undergrowth, Creed couldn't tell which way they came from. But Pierre could. He pointed east and, grabbing his firelock and tomahawk, dashed off. Creed hurried into his boots and then chased after the clever Wyandot. They sped up a rocky, creek bed. Pierre moved smoothly over the slippery stones, but Creed struggled not to twist an ankle with each step.

A few minutes later, the dense wood opened into a small clearing. Pierre halted under the shade of some scrub trees. When Creed caught up, he almost choked at what he saw.

At the other side of the clearing stood Bart and Fleurette. A thick-set man with a bushy beard and two Iroquois braves had another white man pinned to a rock.

"Binoche! I don't know what they are doing here, but we must stop them before they scalp the wretch," Creed said.

Pierre leveled his musket at an Iroquois brave whose long knife waved menacingly over the prisoner.

"We can't risk a shot warning the rebel outposts." Creed grabbed for the muzzle, but he was not quick enough.

The crack of Pierre's weapon echoed across the clearing. The brave clutched his side and slumped to the rocky soil. The other brave bellowed a shrieking war cry. He rushed them with his head lowered, a knife in one hand and a musket in the other. The brave leaped over boulders and fallen timbers like an enraged stag while Pierre calmly reloaded.

But Creed flew towards the brave, who seemed larger than Pierre, as if that were possible.

Their bodies collided with a savage thud. Creed fought to regain his wind, but the brave seemed unfazed by the blow and closed quickly.

This time, he raised his musket to waist level and fired. Creed hit the ground just as the brave man fired and rolled twice before rising to his feet. The blast was deafening. A tongue of flame licked at Creed's face, and a cloud of gray gun smoke surrounded them. The lead ball whistled past him and struck a tree.

In one panther-like move, the brave dropped the musket and threw himself at Creed with the six-inch blade raised high. But Creed had anticipated the move and rolled again, pulling his knife from his belt.

The two men locked together and rolled, their blades sending sparks as each flailed or blocked in a desperate attempt to gain the advantage. The brave had extraordinary strength and skill. He quickly worked his way on top of Creed. His powerful fingers squeezed his knife hand, and the blade arced downwards toward Creed's throat.

The crack of a musket now filled the clearing. The brave's back arched, and he collapsed on top of Creed. Pierre's powerful arms yanked the dead brave off him.

Creed heaved and gasped. "Excellent shot, Pierre. The fellow nearly had me."

"I did not fire," Pierre said.

His eyes locked on Pierre's musket. *The hammer is still cocked!*

Like a demon from hell, Binoche stood grinning in the dark cloud of smoke that enveloped him. "*Merde!*" he grunted. "*Capitain* Fraser would skin me if I let one of my braves kill his officer. Besides, that is a pleasure I save for myself, eh?"

Pierre eyed him suspiciously.

Creed rose to his feet and strode toward the burly *coureur*. "Seems I owe you, Binoche. But I want some answers. What are you doing here, and what's the idea of scalping this man?"

"It is what we do, *Monsieur*. The more rebel scouts we kill, the fewer will spy on us, eh?"

Creed turned to the American and switched from French to English. "Who are you? This man says you are a spy."

"I'd say you're the spies. Come here to spy on our defenses." He glanced at the dead Iroquois. "Partnering with these damned savages will lose you lobsters this war."

Creed replied, "We would say these savages have as much right to this land — maybe more. What's more, I trade with them. Now, what's your name?"

"Heath. Some call me Sergeant Heath. Jimmy Heath. Others call me Heath."

"Well, Sergeant Heath, 'tis time you returned to your fort."

Binoche startled and spoke in French. "*Mon Dieu*! Are you mad? If you return him, he will have 100 men tracking us before we...."

Creed grabbed Binoche by the forearm and squeezed tightly, pulling him toward Bart and Fleurette.

Once out of Heath's earshot, he went on. "Listen to me, Binoche. I have a job to do for Fraser. If you do one more thing to interfere, I'll kill you myself."

"I should have shot *you*."

Creed smiled. "Yes, you should have."

"My father was only trying to help you, *Monsieur*," Fleurette said.

Her tight deerskin dress showed enough of her form and legs to disarm all but the staunchest of men.

Bart draped an arm around her narrow waist. "Sir, we came here because we thought Fleurette could assist you in your story when you tried to cross rebel lines."

Creed could scarcely control his anger. "My plan was decided, Bart. You violated my orders. This woman has taken control of your youthful energies. Where's Androche?"

Bart lowered his head. "He doesn't know we're here. Serge came to camp after you left and suggested we slip out and assist you."

"Serge, is it? So familiar are we now? I expect my officers to follow orders. The penalty for failure to do so is quite extreme."

Fleurette stomped her foot. "Bart is an officer and must learn to make his own decisions. I tell you. We were only trying to help."

Creed's eyes shifted from one to the other. *I can't trust any of them.* So perhaps breaking them up was his best defense.

"Bart, I am ordering you to take Binoche back."

"To wait with Androche?"

"No, take him back to Fraser. Tell him that he interfered with the mission. Let him decide what to do."

"And my role? I, too, am complicit." Bart spoke in a determined voice.

Creed's eyes narrowed. "Indeed, you are. But you are under my command, and I shall decide on your fate at the appropriate time. Now tell me, lad, are you willing to do your duty?"

Bart looked longingly at Fleurette. Then at Binoche.

"I will, of course, do my duty, sir. But what of Fleurette?"

Creed's eyes bored into the girl. "You have taken away my choices, Bart. She will accompany me after all."

Chapter 14

Morristown, New Jersey

The powerful bay jumper pounded across the turf of the village green. General Washington flew from the saddle and clambered into the large white house that provided his headquarters. A half dozen Life Guards snapped to attention as he strode by.

Alexander Hamilton waited at the threshold of his study, his bantam form pacing like an excited terrier. "Your Excellency, I have a report on supplies you should peruse."

"No time for that, Alexander. Where is Colonel Fitzgerald?"

Hamilton hid his annoyance. "He has not yet returned, Your Excellency."

Washington tossed his leather gloves, slid behind his desk, and motioned for Hamilton's report. "Very well, then." He glanced over it and looked up with eyes aflame.

Hamilton knew what was coming.

"Congress has seen fit to give logistics precedence to the Northern Department! Now, I am anxious as anyone to repulse a British thrust from Canada. However, the enemy's main army and its commander-in-chief sit little more than a dozen leagues from here."

Hamilton resisted the urge to correct his commander. Congress had made the correct choice, but for the wrong reason. The British thrust could cut the new nation in half, severing New England from the central states.

"Once we know Howe's intentions, sir, all will change."

Washington's eyes softened. "Yes, indeed, Alexander. If only young Creed were here. Thus, the urgency I place on Fitzgerald and Tallmadge's enterprise. I'd know Howe's objectives by now. I swear I would."

Hamilton blanched. He and Jeremiah Creed had their share of differences. The New Yorker was glad to have him lost in the wilderness of Canada.

"Indeed, Your Excellency. Lieutenant Creed was one of our most able officers." He decided to move on to another subject. "How did your inspection of the artillery go?"

Washington put down the report. "Much smoother than I had anticipated. Henry Knox does wonders with so little."

Hamilton nodded. He knew the stocky commander of the Continental Army's artillery had done terrific work preparing his equipment and recruiting and training his batteries.

"I have every confidence we can meet the British on even terms – General Knox's guns will provide the backbone our regiments need."

"Indeed, sir." Hamilton had read and written too many dispatches to be so confident. As a former artillery officer, he knew the British still outgunned them.

"Whilst I await Colonel Fitzgerald, send in the engineer officers. I wish to review our defense plans."

***

Captain Martin and Ensign Tobias spread the stiff roll of paper across the table. At Washington's direction, the two had worked for weeks surveying positions and routes for the army – one anticipating a thrust up the North River by Howe, the other a thrust southwest across the Jerseys.

"These are wonderful plans, gentlemen. The issue is execution. We don't have the supplies or manpower to establish both lines of defense."

Washington was under pressure from the Congressional Committee to shift north.

Hamilton nodded. "The question is, which should take precedence?"

They all looked at him in disbelief.

Martin ran a finger up the map's depiction of the North River. "I would favor the northern stratagem, Your Excellency," Martin said. "Howe tried the south once and failed. He rarely attempts the same approach twice."

Martin spoke with authority beyond his rank. A former surveyor, Hamilton observed that he had developed a special relationship with Washington, himself a former surveyor.

"And you, young Tobias?" Washington asked the subaltern.

"I would agree with Captain Martin, Your Excellency. The ground is more defensible in the highlands. And the Jerseys will likely result in a war of march and maneuver rather than a war of posts."

Washington beamed with delight. "Well-spoken and analyzed, Tobias. A war of posts versus a war of maneuver."

Hamilton was tired of the banter. "Sir, I humbly submit the Navy will be the key. General Howe won't separate his forces from his brother's ships. Regardless of the direction."

"True enough, Alexander. Again, the North River lends weight to a thrust northward. We have had such difficulty with the chains and reefs." Washington dipped his quill into an inkpot and made a few notes in his portfolio.

"Very well, gentlemen. I will defer my decision for now. I need Colonel Fitzgerald to shed some light on this dark issue."

***

The Dale House, near Brunswick, New Jersey

Emily kicked gently on Pudding's flanks, sending them galloping from their hiding place toward the Dale farmstead.

"What in the hell is that?" a cowboy whispered.

"The rebel spy! We have him at last! Follow me!" the leader exclaimed.

With horses whinnying and men shouting, they spurred after their quarry. At first, Pudding had the advantage over the larger horses. But soon, the older and smaller horse began to blow and lather.

"Just a bit more, Pudding. Just a bit more, dear. We are almost there," Emily coaxed the straining mare.

She could see the light burning in the barn – just as she had left it. Suddenly, Pudding's hooves caught some rocks and stumbled. The doughty little horse kept her feet, but her pace slowed to a fast walk.

Emily knew that coaxing more from her would kill the horse. "I may have to leave you, my dear." She softly patted the horse's neck. Emily decided to abandon Pudding and flee on foot through the woods.

Emily swung her legs over the saddle and was about to jump when a strong arm grabbed her around her long, narrow waist. In a quick motion, the arm swept her from the saddle onto the pommel of a large charger.

Her captor held her firmly and whispered, "Hold tight, miss. I know just how to lose those villains."

Emily knew this was the rebel spy – her friend's lover. Behind came curses and shouts as the cowboys plunged headlong into the thick woods.

She could hear their muffled voices growing shrill in exasperation.

"The traitor spy must have headed towards the Raritan again."

"I know a shortcut to the beach. Bastard must be heading there."

"Seize the horse."

"No time. It's a nag, anyway. It's the spy we want. Colonel Leslie is paying in gold."

The voices trailed off. Emily and the stranger galloped across the dark fields in silence. She realized this was not the direct route but likely an evasion route. *This man knows his business.*

It was past two when they finally trotted into the Dales' barn. Pudding had made her way there safely and seemed to be waiting for her mistress.

"I need to walk, water, and feed my horse, miss. You should gather yourself and return to the big house. May I assume the lady here is an acquaintance?"

"May I assume the same... Mister Hyde?" Emily asked a question with confidence that stunned him.

The stranger drew his pistol and looked around to ensure nobody was observing them.

"We are quite alone, I assure you. Caesar is the only servant nearby, and he is fast asleep."

"Where did you hear that name?"

"Your discretion should not end at the boudoir's threshold."

He reddened. "Not fit talk for a lady."

She smiled. "A lady should not be about at midnight either, should she?"

The stranger's mouth widened in a broad grin.

She realized how handsome and beguiling he was, how such a man might seduce her from her vows. "That would depend on the nature of her business. Now, an assignation might warrant just such a breach of etiquette."

They both hesitated at her insinuation. The stranger reminded her of Jeremiah Creed, although he was slighter in stature and wolfish in mien and stance. He carried a day's growth of beard, something Jeremiah did only out of necessity.

Finally, she said, "I must apologize, sir. I have neglected to thank the man who saved me from danger and degradation. In any case, I thank you, sir."

"You were right the first time. My name is Ripley Hyde. Most call me Rip. And you are Missus?"

"You were correct the first time. It is Miss. My name is not important. I am a friend of Lorie, that is, Missus Dale."

Emily stressed her friend's marital status. The connotation was not lost on Hyde, she noted.

Harry patted the horse. "Well, I can see that I need to care for my gallant steed and depart."

Emily saw the disappointment on his face. He would forgo a visit to Lorie under the circumstances.

Her eyes softened. "Mister Hyde, Lorie has spoken of you with great fondness and affection. Far be it from me to stand in the way, even if I disapprove. But if the green jackets ever discover...."

"Ha! Those cowboys know her husband's connections. They'd pay a high price to disturb this place."

"Even still, your comings and goings put her at grave risk, personal and moral."

Harry shrugged innocently. "We are at war, miss."

"Indeed, sir. On that account, I am going to ask you a favor."

Harry's face brightened, and his eyes wandered up and down her figure.

Is he eyeing me in approbation? He is the rogue. Now she was standing before him, her savior, with a request.

"Hopefully, one that will remain secret from Lorie," he smirked.

Emily bristled at the insinuation. But then, realizing it was only crude humor, she composed herself. "Indeed, it must stay a secret. But not just from Lorie. If you are a rebel spy, I would like you to deliver a packet."

"Did Lorie tell you I was a rebel spy? Her imagination may yet get us all a rope."

"You mean that you are not a rebel spy?"

"I mean, I would not admit it to anyone if I were." He cocked his head and smiled. "What is the request?"

"A friend asked me to deliver a package to an officer in the rebel army. I was in the attempt when the green jackets interrupted me."

"To your advantage, miss. There's no worse than them out there. The neutral ground between the two armies is more dangerous than a pitched battle. Especially at night. Most especially for a comely young lady."

She smiled sheepishly. "Then I am doubly in your debt, Mister Hyde."

"Triple debt if I deliver it. By God, you are beautiful! What was I thinking of keeping company with a married woman when the likes of you are unmarried?"

She blushed and lowered her eyes. "Will you deliver the package, sir?"

Harry rolled his eyes and nodded. "To whom, might I ask?"

"To General Washington, of course."

***

The next morning's breakfast went as if nothing had transpired the night before. Emily never let on about her foray and encounter with the mysterious spy. For her part, Lorie never mentioned a short nocturnal visit by the elusive Mister Ripley Hyde.

Emily's father arrived that afternoon, accompanied by Major Rumson. A formal dinner that night marked the occasion. After the meal, the men went to the garden to enjoy a cigar.

Lorie and Emily retired to their chambers. The two spent time talking while taking turns running combs through each other's hair. The talk did not take long to turn to matters of the heart. Emily left before breakfast to catch an early packet ship across the bay.

Lorie blew into Emily's ear, "Emily, I have a confession to make."

"What is that, dear?" Emily asked. Was her friend going to confide?

"I had a visitor last night."

Emily slowly drew her comb from Lorie's tresses. "Indeed."

"Please don't be cross. He came to me late and left early."

"Your Mister Hyde?"

"The very Rip Hyde. He rips my heart, you know."

They both giggled at the pun.

"Just your heart?"

They giggled again, then grew silent.

"Don't you love your husband anymore?" Emily asked.

"Yes, yes, I do. Well, I believe I do. However, this is different. Rip is different."

"In what way? I am curious, Lorie. How does one turn to another while locked in blissful matrimony?"

Lorie stroked Emily's long, honey-colored hair and then gently rubbed her cheek. "You have much to learn, dear. In any case, I think Major Rumson is fond of you. Are you fond of him?"

"Yes. In a certain way, you see."

Suddenly, they heard footsteps ascending the stairs and the clattering of boots jarring the wood-planked floor. They could see the shape of men's feet pacing back and forth by Emily's door through the sill. The women stayed silent as church mice. Then the feet spun about and strode down the corridor. They heard the door at the end of the hall shut.

Lorie whispered, "Major Rumson – I think he was hoping to pay you a visit, dear."

"Lorie, I do not accept such visitors. Oh, I am so sorry."

"It's quite all right. I am a married woman, dear. No maidenhead to jealously protect."

Lorie laughed at the remark, but Emily could see the regret behind the laughter.

***

Dunning House, New York

S.W. O'Connell

The dinner party was drawing to a close. From what Klara could see, many guests were bored with it. Most of General Howe's officers, the usual rakes and social climbers, declined attendance. The city itself seemed devoid of the regular soldiery.

General Clinton had received an invitation, but he, too, had failed to arrive for dinner. In fact, of the military guests, only Major Sandy Drummond and Lieutenant Colonel Horace Stilton attended. All the guests knew that the two officers had duties centered on the city and its immediate environs.

"An awful lot of transport out in the south bay this week, Colonel Stilton. I would ask what that means, but I am sure Major Drummond has sworn you to secrecy," Laseby said as he swirled his Madeira in its large goblet.

During the evening, Klara caught Edmund Laseby gazing in admiration at Lady Dunning. Klara wondered where this would go.

"I am sure he has not, Mister Laseby. His Majesty's officers are honor-bound by their commission and status as gentlemen. No other affirmations are needed to protect the crown's secrets."

"What secrets are those, Sir Horace?" Lady Dunning inquired coyly.

Laseby's jowls wobbled like jelly as he chuckled. "If he told you that now, Matilda, they wouldn't be secrets, would they?"

"It is no secret that General Howe intends to deal with the rebels once and for all," said Drummond.

Stilton glared at him. "Better we deal with them on the battlefield than through skullduggery."

The room grew still. The command had decided that too many often spoke out of turn to the locals while in their cups. It was long rumored among the officer corps that Drummond had established a security protocol and kept book on loose-lipped officers.

Drummond's face turned scarlet as his regimental coat. "I have given a leg on the field of battle, sir. But the first line of defense against the rebel is secrecy. Let them have their gossip, rumor, and innuendo to report, so long as it was ill-informed."

"The question, Sandy, as ever, is just how will Howe deal with them?" Laseby asked. He could not resist laughing at the pun, as base as it was. "Or is Howe's question not how, but who?"

Lady Dunning put her hand on Laseby's arm. "What do you mean, not by how, by who?"

"I believe the word is by whom," Stilton said tartly.

Laseby grinned. "Now it's quite simple. If the who is Washington – then Howe strikes south. If it is Burgoyne, he strikes north. So, the who leads to the how." He smugly placed his hands across his prodigious belly.

Klara smiled. "How clever, Mister Laseby."

"Yes, very clever, Edmund," Lady Dunning purred.

Klara could tell she meant it with barely a smidgen of sincerity.

Stilton leaned forward. "How is that game leg of yours, Sandy?"

Drummond bristled. "It's my knee, Sir Horace. Bones are missing, thanks to a rebel bullet. I take medicine for it, and I can get along as well as any trooper."

"Took a bullet myself, three actually, on the Monongahela," Stilton said. "But French and Indian – not rebel bullets." Stilton made it sound as if the source of the bullets mattered.

"You received your knighthood for that, didn't you, Sir Horace?" Laseby asked.

"I should say not! His majesty does not grant laurels for defeat. No, it was later. I led a forlorn hope and seized a French fortress guarding the harbor at Martinique. Strangely, I led three hundred men against over a thousand Frog regulars supported by Frog artillery, yet escaped unscathed."

"Impressive, Sir Horace. To take an entire island in a *coup de main*," Laseby said.

"True enough," said Drummond. "But getting back to the Monongahela. Were you not rescued through the gallantry of a certain young colonial officer?"

Now Stilton's face reddened. "The battle was pure chaos from the outset. Bullets zipped in a hundred directions. Humming passed us like swarms of bees. Leaves crackling and lead slapping tree limbs. Our men panicked. Could barely see a foe. Too many damned trees. Too many damned savages. Too many damned French and Indians."

"Pennsylvania is noted for its mighty forests, Sir Horace," said Klara.

Stilton glared at her. She smiled back innocently.

Drummond wet his lips. "Quite true. Klara is from Pennsylvania, Sir Horace. But if I recall correctly, we had the French outnumbered. And did you know the name of the young colonial officer who saved Sir Horace and rallied the remnants of disaster?"

"No," Klara replied innocently. She knew nothing of the war on the other side of Pennsylvania.

"None other than our current rebel band leader, Mister Washington. Fancy that he did not receive a knighthood. Oh yes, I forgot. The battle was a defeat. A disaster."

"Perhaps if the colonials received more of their due back then, we would not be facing this terrible rebellion today," said Lady Dunning.

"A Whiggish sentiment, milady," said Stilton.

"My late husband's sentiment, Sir Horace."

"Yet not entirely without merit," retorted Drummond.

"Gentlemen," Laseby said. "It's high time we leave the fair ladies and partake of some good American tobacco. I have a ship that still makes calls to Virginia. Gather your pipes and follow me." The men retreated to the study after replacing wine with brandy.

Klara and Lady Dunning finished their tea while the servants cleared the table.

"Don't let these men fool you, Klara. One can be a good citizen of the realm and an American. It is what we loyal Americans are fighting for, after all."

Klara did not reply. Her leanings toward the Loyalists were based primarily on the necessity of her situation.

***

Fort Ticonderoga

Arthur St. Clair struggled with his letter to Philip Schuyler, commander of the Northern Department, headquartered at Fort George. *Though the news is terrible, at least the message will be neatly drawn.* He carefully dipped his pen into the inkwell and made sure, steady characters, stopping to blow on the page every few words.

...And so Sir, the Situation remains unchanged from my Report of two days ago, except for increased Indian raids and the apparent progress made by the Enemy, who are expected here within days. Even my most able Scouts are refusing to leave the Bastion, as poorly armed and manned as it is. Col. Baldwin is commended for his attempts to block the Waterways and construct a Connexion between the two wings of the Fort. But Supply, Morale, and Manpower are woefully lacking. I write these words not merely to inform you but to underline the Gravity of the Situation in which you are now well versed....

The clatter of boots on the stone floor broke his concentration. The officer of the guard anxiously stood at the door of St. Clair's office. "Sir, a Canadian trapper arrived to trade goods at the fort."

"And that is of concern to me? What kind of goods?"

"That's the problem, sir. He had some blankets and trinkets, a few old furs, and a squaw."

St. Clair frowned. "Lieutenant, I have a fortress that is undermanned and undersupplied. We have much to do and little time to do it."

"Colonel Baldwin said you might want to question him as he traversed the British army. That is why he had so little to peddle, he claims. The colonel thought he might peddle information."

"Information, peddle it for what?"

"His life, sir. The Canadian can speak some English. Colonel Baldwin believes he is a British spy."

St. Clair put down his quill and shrugged. "Send him in."

***

Two Massachusetts infantrymen led the prisoner. St. Clair dismissed the guards who had posted outside his door. For a few moments, he eyed the roughhewn *coureur,* who seemed vaguely familiar despite his appearance and manner.

"You speak English?" St. Clair asked with some hesitancy.

The prisoner nodded. Jeremiah Creed had decided to unravel his story slowly to avoid hesitancy and suspicion that he knew it would engender.

The doughty Scotsman was blunt. "My chief of engineers believes that you are a spy, *Monsieur.* Are you?"

"That depends on how you define spy, sir."

St. Clair was firm but not belligerent. "I define a spy as someone gathering information on the army for the enemy while not in the enemy's uniform. Since you are not in uniform, I only question whether you are gathering information for the enemy."

Creed spread his hands. "If that is what you wish to believe, sir."

"I wish to believe the truth, *monsieur*. May we begin with your name?"

"Very well. I can tell you my name is Serge Binoche. That I have traded and trapped these lakes and those to the north since I was thirteen. That the young woman is my wife, Fleurette. I could say that my loyalty is to Quebec and the Quebecois. And to the natives whose toil and skill provide me with my livelihood. And that our journey here is made in the name of commerce and enterprise."

St. Clair eyed him cynically. "Ye could tell me that? An odd choice of words, *monsieur*, is it not?"

"Odd to an *Anglais*, perhaps."

"I'm born a Scot and am now an American!" snapped St. Clair.

Creed smiled. He had caused St. Clair to lose his temper. Now disarmed, he could accept new facts.

"This is no matter for mirth. I'm a busy man. Tell me who you are and why you are here, or you shall surely face the gallows tomorrow."

Creed replied with his normal voice and soft Irish accent, "My name is Captain James Lawrence, The Royal American Regiment."

"Coming clean now? That's more like it. And your purpose in crossing into our camp?"

"General Simon Fraser sent me here to ascertain the number and disposition of the forces defending Ticonderoga."

St. Clair's eyes widened at the revelation. "So, ye admit to this?"

Creed blinked. "I do, sir."

"Then ye are, in fact, a spy."

"I am, sir."

St. Clair rubbed his chin. "Well, I suppose there is no more to be said, is there? Other than ordering your hanging."

"I beg to differ, sir."

"On what grounds?"

"There is much more to say, sir."

"I dinna understand?"

"I have information on the British regiments, their German and Canadian hirelings. Their Indian allies. I also have some insight into how they might take this place – will take it and…."

St. Clair eyed him. "And what?"

"And save your army, sir."

St. Clair grabbed his paper and quill. "For some reason, I cannot fathom, I believe ye."

"Perhaps because I was right once before, sir."

St. Clair's eyes bulged. "What the blazes? Right about what? Where? When? Dinna try my patience anymore, lad."

"It was a cold January with the Delaware to our backs and Lord Cornwallis to our front. I suggested the army take a circuitous route to avoid destruction. 'Tis all I can say, sir." Creed was gambling that St. Clair would recall the war council at the Assenpink Creek.

St. Clair's jaw dropped. "Go on, *Monsieur* Binoche, or Captain Lawrence. I'm taking note."

An hour later, they had finished. Some eight thousand regulars with over 100 guns and ships would handily take this fortress short of Congress, sending him 10,000 more fresh and disciplined troops.

"I must say, Captain Lawrence. Your memory and insight do impress."

St. Clair stepped up to the window and threw open the shutters. He looked up at the rocky edifice of Mount Defiance. "Jeduthan has warned me to guard against the British seizing this high ground. Yet I have not the troops to defend the fort proper. We are setting defenses across the water on Mount Independence. The real truth is, I canna defend any of these."

"Why do you tell me this, sir?" Creed asked.

"Because you die tomorrow, Captain Lawrence. That gives you the powers of concentration and candor. Pity we receive these powers often when they can do us the least good."

"Then, as an officer, an American, who must die tomorrow, let me provide you one piece of advice, general."

"Take advice from a spy?"

"You have already taken information quite freely from me. Now hear this. I came to this land from Ireland only to see it rent asunder by what is by all measures a civil war. I joined the forces to end the rebellion and minimize the effusion of American blood."

"What are ye trying to say?"

"We serve the same master. The same cause."

"Who is your master, Captain Lawrence? What is your cause?"

Creed knew he had already said too much. He could not risk returning to the British camp with anyone knowing his true identity. The plan would only work if St. Clair remained convinced that he was a British spy.

"The cause of man. I'll give you this, sir. Leave this place to the British. The defenses are a shambles. I have watched them from afar and now from within. Your men are not yet fit. And you need more men. Men who can fight. I have seen the ravages of the natives in the Grants. When word gets out, your New England men will rally. And when they do, they will need an army, not a fortress, to rally to."

St. Clair reached for a bottle of whisky deep within his cupboard. He poured two tins, three fingers deep.

"Don't tell me you have a bottle from your homeland? I haven't tasted good whisky in a long time."

St. Clair smiled knowingly. "Aye, 'tis from my homeland. But not from my native Scotland." He handed Creed one of the tins. "From my new homeland – Pennsylvania. Drink up, Captain Lawrence. Sadly, 'twill be your last dram."

"I accept that with the composure demanded of my rank and station. But, if you can see to it, please spare the woman. She is not my wife but a foolish Indian girl. She cannot harm anyone."

St. Clair and Creed each took a deep swallow and sat in silence. St. Clair pondered the comments made by the strangely familiar Loyalist.

"Ya seem so familiar, Mister Lawrence," St. Clair said. "In any event, I have realized that it will likely cost my commission and reputation. But it might save the army, if not the war. What else have ye got?"

Creed drained his tin. "Just this...."

When they were done, St. Clair summoned the guards. "Wake this man at dawn to be hanged in front of the garrison."

"And his squaw, sir? Hang her, too?" The sergeant of the guard was not relishing the demise of a woman, even an Indian.

"No. She is of the fair sex and is likely to have had no real part in his base villainy. She shall be released. After the sentence is carried out."

***

The massive oak door slammed shut, and the iron bolt slid into place with a heavy clang. Creed glanced about the cell. The chamber was eight feet by eight feet with bare stone walls that felt clammy. It contained a three-legged wooden stool and a leather slop bucket. But it had light from a window almost three feet wide and one foot high. Curiously, it lacked bars. But at nine feet off the floor, the window was out of reach.

He sat there a few moments, pondering his escape. He knew the gallows would be erected on the parade field across from the barracks for the garrison to watch his execution. His only escape opportunity then was during the death march from the cell, a distance of some 100 paces.

He had to time it just right. He would not be near the western gate if he bolted too soon. Some 4,000 jeering patriots would surround him if he ran too late.

Suddenly, the door to the cell opened, and his situation grew grimmer. Into the cell walked Fleurette Binoche. The evening twilight through the window bathed her in soft rays, making her appear especially beautiful.

The guard licked his lips mischievously. "Sergeant of the guard thought you'd want to spend your last hours with your squaw. We'll be right outside, so try not to be too noisy, eh?"

Creed was flummoxed. Her presence complicated his situation. He had hoped to eliminate her as an impediment when he returned to the British camp.

"They tell me you pleaded for my life? Am I now supposed to thank you?" Fleurette spat.

"You have thanked me enough, Fleurette. I believe you have another to thank now. Save your charms for young Bart."

She rushed him and beat her fists on his chest. "I do not want a boy. I want a man."

Creed pushed her away. "That he'll be...if he lives long enough."

"That much is true. Tomorrow night, he will have warm blood to soothe me while you will be dead, *Monsieur*!"

Creed could tell she hated him for rejecting her charms. But that rejection also made him an object of her desire. Her tone was half jeer, half lament.

Creed smiled. "Is that a promise?"

For the first time, Creed saw tears come to her eyes. He suddenly felt guilty for taunting her. She could not help who she was or how she was raised, or her need to spin men in different directions. He took her gently in his arms and stroked her cheek. "I am sorry I got you into this, Fleurette. But it is all arranged. General St. Clair will release you tomorrow."

"With you dead, where will I go?" She buried her face in her hands and sobbed.

Was this an act? It did not matter. "Pierre is waiting near the old French fort, and Androche is waiting with the canoes. Go and find either of them after they hang me."

Her face rose from her palms. "Hang you? What do you mean, *Monsieur*?"

He placed his fingers to his lips. The guards were just out of earshot, and he did not want to alert them.

Chapter 15

Piscataway, New Jersey

Roy Harry was more than a day late from his mission. Sergeant Simon Beall noticed Major Tallmadge tugging anxiously at his gloves. *Not like him to be nervous.* Tallmadge had ordered Beall to assemble the troop – just over twenty of the best troopers in the Continental Army. Men who matched their resourcefulness and cunning with horsemanship and boldness. And two were expert cavalrymen fresh from the battlefields of Europe.

Beall stifled a smile of satisfaction as he slowly stepped along the line. Each trooper holding his horse by the reins and saber extended for inspection. They stood tall and erect before him with chins up and lips tight.

The burly sergeant turned and clicked his bootheels before Trooper Jan Karcz. The ex-lancer's finely sharpened blade flashed in the morning sunlight. His dark blue uniform was brushed clean as new. Helmet, buckles, buttons, boots, and spurs also gleamed and sparkled.

"An excellent turnout, Trooper Karcz. Make sure you rub just a little dirt here and there. The British sentries should see you from a mile away. But I want them to see us when it is too late for them, not us."

From the ranks, O'Quinn stifled a laugh.

Beall glared at him. "I intended irony, not mirth, Trooper O'Quinn."

Tallmadge urged his horse up to the formation. "Sergeant Beall, are all pistols loaded?"

"Checked them all myself, sir."

"Very well, we'll ride south along the ridgeline to the river. If we encounter no enemy, we'll continue to the crossroads north of Brunswick." His head tilted in a knowing nod.

Beall pivoted back to the men. "Return, sabers!"

The sabers snapped into stiff leather sheaths. A horse snorted.

"Mount!"

As one, the blue jackets turned, grasped pommels, and swung their legs over smooth leather saddles.

Horses stood motionless. A few snorted, and one neighed softly. The steeds seemed anxious for action.

Beall grabbed his pommel with the tip of his hook and painfully pulled himself into the saddle. He had become fond of Harry and was anxious to help find the wayward officer.

Beall knew Harry had a woman or two in the neutral ground. He wanted to make sure he could soften their commander's reaction. The men liked Tallmadge, who was self-effacing and highly resourceful. But they knew he tended to a strict adherence to norms.

The rhythmic thump of hooves on a dust-caked road and the soft jingle of spurs and bridles serenaded them as the troop trotted along in a column of two abreast. The day was going to be warm, Beall mused.

The early summer crops gave the farm fields around them a golden hue. The wheat and barley had already reached half a man's height. The skies were a piercing blue, and the morning sun had already begun to blister their skin. The road ahead rose and then plummeted steeply, slithering like a snake toward the river below.

The pastoral scene was misleading. Since May, his men had skirmished across these fields and forests at least four times. They were not strangers to the area.

A distant firing began with only the faintest sound of a *pop, pop, pop*.

Beall saw Tallmadge's pistol slide from its saddle holster. The entire command broke into a gallop without a word from its leader. No one needs to tell them the object of the firing was Roy Harry.

Horses snorted. Hooves began pounding furiously over the first rise and then the second. They fanned out and plunged through the wheat fields towards the river when they crested the ridgeline. The troopers now knew the fording sites and the local skinners and cowboys. Beall just hoped Roy Harry had beaten the cowboys to this one.

Ahead, a rider was struggling to get his horse up the riverbank. A troop of mounted Loyalists plunged into the river in pursuit. Their shouts and curses grew more desperate as the horses labored through the water. It was Harry! His pursuers were determined to catch their quarry, and it seemed like nothing could stop them.

Harry's horse emerged from the water but only managed a slow walk.

"Harry's horse is lame, sir! We must reach him before those scoundrels do," Beall hollered.

He saw Harry leap from the saddle and pull his horse to the ground in one motion. He flattened himself behind the animal as the cowboys peppered the wheat around him with pistol shots. The band rose from the riverbank like birds of prey and plunged into the lush field, beating the stalks with their sabers.

The zing of lead balls passed overhead. But they came closer with each shot. Harry reloaded his pistols and drew his small sword from its sheath. He tore a package from the saddlebag and tossed it far away from him.

A cowboy exclaimed, "There he is! Rebel spy just threw something away."

Harry blasted his pistol into the cowboy's throat. Two more closed in on him. But their shots flew high. Harry pulled the trigger of a second pistol, sending a lead ball into the cowboy's horse. With a high, piercing shriek, the animal collapsed into the tall wheat. But its rider managed to leap free and lunged at Harry. Blades clanged, the steel gleaming against the morning sun. The Loyalist was larger than Harry and soon had him pinned against his horse's saddle. The terrified animal snorted and kicked as the two men rolled over her.

Tallmadge raised his saber and waved it high. "Sergeant Beall, see to Harry. The rest of you follow me!"

The troop plunged into the remainder of the cowboys, who now realized their quarry had help. After just a few desultory shots, they broke like a pack of mad dogs.

Karcz ran one down and expertly pierced his shoulder blades as he often lanced Russian Cossacks and Austrian Uhlans.

O'Quinn shot one Loyalist dead from behind and faced another with his saber. Jonathan Beall and Elias Parker pursued one, who immediately dropped his sword and pistol and raised his hands. The remaining troopers rode down to the riverbank and emptied their guns into the fleeing cowboys.

Harry struggled desperately against the giant cowboy – a dark-haired, bearded man. The two recognized one another from a far-off skirmish in the wilds of New Jersey.

Beall halted his panting mount and watched them square off.

"Damn, I thought I recognized you, Roy Harry! You'll not live to see the king's justice, but you'll face mine."

"Tom Salamander? You ugly thief. Thought I'd recognized you."

"Time was, you were a thief, Harry — and a cowboy. You should have stayed on the right side, you double-dealing son of a strumpet!"

"You disparage my mother's chosen profession, Tom. For that, you'll receive no quarter!"

Beall could see that Salamander was a brute of a man who rarely had to fight because of it. But Harry's ability to resist angered him, and as they traded blades, Beall slipped from his horse and strode toward the fray.

Salamander reached for his belt and drew a small dagger. He plunged the blade into Harry's shoulder like a snake bite, sending blood oozing through his jacket.

"Ooooh… you got me, you lucky bastard!" Harry tried to move, but the pain was too great.

Salamander stood above, raising a heavy-bladed saber for a downward blow. "I'll say farewell to you, Harry, you dog! I'm going back to that house and ravish your woman before I hang her for a traitor."

Harry reached desperately for his pistol. But it clicked harmlessly.

Salamander grinned. "You already fired at me, Harry. You don't get a second shot." But his eyes widened suddenly, and his saber tumbled harmlessly into the broken wheat stalks.

A steel hook had ripped into his spine, spinning him around to face the dark eyes of Simon Beall. The burly former blacksmith plunged his sword into Salamander's gut, unleashing a gush of innards, blood, and offal erupted as Salamander collapsed.

Beall looked at the blood staining Harry's shoulder. "He almost had you, Mister Harry."

Harry managed a wry grin. "I've received deeper cuts in cheap Jersey brothels. I would have taken him, Simon. But thanks just the same."

***

Fort Ticonderoga

The midnight watch had changed. Creed knew from experience that the new guards were up all day and would use this time to sneak badly needed sleep. He felt confident enough to spring up to the window's sill above him.

Then the fun would begin, he thought. Get past the guards, across the battlements, and down the twenty-foot drop. Then, all he needed to worry about were sentries, patrols, and stray bands of Iroquois who would kill first and ask questions later. Creed had faced worse, but not for some time.

A soft bronze hand reached for him in the dark. "Are you awake, *Monsieur*? It must be past midnight. You must decide whether we make love or try to escape. And I don't care which you choose."

Fleurette thrust herself astride him as he sat with his back to the wall. She searched for his mouth in the dark but made small bites at his face and neck instead.

Creed lifted her off him. He put his hand over her mouth. "Enough of your advances. I don't plan to let them hang me. I'll take you with me if you behave. Or you can stay. They'll probably release you in the morning."

She glared at him. "What kind of man are you? Do you not enjoy the love of a woman? Do you prefer men? They have said such things about you, *Anglais*."

"Now hear me, Fleurette. I have enjoyed the love of women, as you put it. But now, I enjoy the love of only one woman. Perhaps someday you'll enjoy such love."

The watchman cried one. His voice carried little emotion, reflecting what Creed assessed as the sense of the garrison. The fort was doomed, and he was determined not to be its first victim.

A scratching sound came from the window above. But the moon had set, and Creed saw only darkness. Then more scratching came from above.

"I see you, *monsieur*. Reach for my hand," a voice from the window said.

"Pierre?" Creed breathed a sigh of relief and smiled. "What took so long?"

"They doubled the guard, *Monsieur*."

"No matter. Fleurette is here too. I will lift her to you."

"It is a long drop."

Creed turned to the girl and grabbed her chin firmly. "You must decide, Fleurette. Come with the *Anglais*, or stay with the *Americain*?"

"I will come," she replied.

Creed stepped back to get some room to jump. She lunged up and over Creed and the ledge like a cat. He launched but fell short, hit his chest below Pierre, and fell back in a heap.

"Are you alright?" Pierre asked.

Creed felt embarrassed after Fleurette displayed her litheness.

"*Oui, allez. Encore!*

With that, he tensed his arms and legs. He sprang upward in one move. This time, he managed to grab the edge of the sill. Pierre's powerful arms pulled him up and over it. They clung to the ledge and made their way to the overhang where Pierre had left a thick coil of rope.

"I will hold it and lower you each," Pierre whispered.

Soon, Creed and Fleurette were along the berm, a long rampart of earth that surrounded the base of the walls. The bastion provided a highway to freedom. The rebels had only partly finished it, and it trailed off into an open area near the northwest base of the fort.

Pierre had tied the rope off and lowered himself. It reached only halfway down, but that was enough for the athletic Wyandot to drop and land leopard-like on all fours.

When he caught his breath, he handed Creed a musket and tomahawk and picked up his own. "Follow me, *Monsieur*."

***

The clock above St. Clair's mantel struck one. The forlorn commander of Ticonderoga stirred from a fitful sleep. He had tossed and turned, thinking about everything the prisoner had told him. *Why would an English spy come here to advise the fort's defense?* His musings made for an obvious trick, thus making it less than obvious.

He walked to his window and gazed southeast across the great boom bridge stretching over narrow water to the secondary defense works at Mount Independence.

The words of the prisoner echoed in his mind. *They need an army to rally to, not a fort.*

St. Clair was with Washington when he nearly abandoned the defenses at Brooklyn and Harlem, at the fort that bore his name, and finally at Trenton. He recalled Washington's face at the war councils where each decision was made. And those decisions followed the same logic presented by the spy, Captain James Lawrence. Then it clicked. That very spy, James Lawrence, was there! He recognized the face – a member of His Excellency's special staff — but couldn't remember the name.

Was his arrival a signal from His Excellency?

St. Clair pulled on his boots in a rush. "Guard! Summon the adjutant at once. Have him meet me at the prisoner's cell."

***

Simon Fraser's Camp

Simon Fraser threw his head back in thought. Lawrence had just finished his report. His uncanny penetration of the rebel fortress was incredible. Fraser had not expected him to succeed. But once again, a bold gambit had succeeded against all odds. The question was, how to respond?

"Do you believe we can get guns up this Sugar Loaf Hill, Captain Lawrence?" He asked.

"The rebels have named it Mount Defiance, sir. But yes, I am sure you can. Pierre climbed it while I was 'indisposed.'"

They all laughed. Alexander Fraser had accompanied Creed, still assigned to his company of elite sharpshooters.

-154-

"I want your men to verify this, Alexander. One file should do it. Can your man, this Pierre, lead them, Captain Lawrence?"

"Of course, sir. I prefer to go as well."

"I have more 'strategic' work for you, James. Aha, the tea is ready. We are short on sugar, but there's plenty of rum to spice it. Let's have a mug, and I'll tell you everything."

***

Creed found his detachment some miles south of Fraser's camp. While he was gone, O'Ballance followed his instruction and kept the men busy practicing musketry drills, skirmishing, and maintaining the equipment.

"The damp heat of this continent plays hell with gun barrels and blades, sir," O'Ballance told Creed.

"True enough. One must drink clean water whenever possible, as heat also weakens the constitution. Also, it's wise to eat fruit and vegetables."

"But it's meat, especially fresh meat, that prepares a man best for battle, sir."

"Perhaps, but there are thirty days of marching for every thirty minutes of battle in an average campaign," Creed said. "Where's Ensign Saunders?"

"Ah, he is over with those Canadians again. Binoche, it seems, has ailments. He volunteered to tend them."

"Keep an eye on the lad, sergeant. He's likely but impressionable. Binoche is a scoundrel, and his daughter is a vixen. He's never known people of that sort before."

"Few of us have, sir," replied O'Ballance. "Few of us have."

"I am heading north with Androche. I'm ordered to report to General Burgoyne. I should be back tonight. Make sure the men are fed and rested. I suspect the army will soon advance."

"South? Ticonderoga, sir?"

"Of course, but after that, time will tell whether it will be by land or water."

Muscled limbs moved in rhythm, sending the birch bark canoe across the dark waters like an eel. As Androche and his men paddled, Creed took the time to admire the beauty of the deep blue water and verdant mountains.

Flocks of birds, including terns, herons, ospreys, ducks, and northern harriers, swept through the sky and danced across the water.

The canoe slid onto the shore. The main camp teamed with action. An army of 8,000 spread in detachments along the lake. Only a few regiments remained, plus the artillery train. Creed counted more than sixty guns at this place alone, many of them heavy caliber and not suited for the terrain ahead.

He found Burgoyne dressed only in a white linen shirt and breeches, dictating a letter for Lord Germain, Minister of State for North America - the man responsible for waging war against his majesty's subjects.

Creed stood awkwardly while the general finished his business.

And so, Milord, we are posed now to envelop and besiege The Gibraltar of the North. I expect rough work but know that British Arms will prevail in the end. I can only assume that General

Howe's movement north will commence while we surround Ticonderoga. The discomfort to the rebel Armies attempting to fend off actions from multiple Fronts will necessarily be depleted on all.

The orderly cleared his throat. "Captain Lawrence is here, sir."

Burgoyne turned. "Oh yes. Good day, Mister Lawrence. Fraser informs me that you have done a thorough reconnaissance around the rebel fort. Sit here. Bring Captain Lawrence a glass of port."

Creed removed his hat and sat on a field chair whose woodwork had an ornate design that would flatter the best New York or Philadelphia homes.

Mosquitoes zipped around the tent. Burgoyne snagged one that descended on his forearm, spreading a spot of blood across his skin.

"A bit early, they say, for these buggers, eh?"

"Indeed, sir. But I must correct your initial impression. I didn't just perform reconnaissance around Fort Ticonderoga."

Burgoyne's face twisted into a frown. "You didn't?" His disappointment was obvious.

"No, sir. I entered the fort under subterfuge. I observed its innermost workings. Numbers of men, equipment, and guns. That sort of thing."

"That sort of thing? Why this is fantastic!"

"The idea was General Fraser's, sir. I merely executed it."

"Ideas without execution are meaningless, are they not, Captain Lawrence?" Burgoyne paused a second to reflect on his grand idea and its execution.

Creed sipped at the deep red liquid set before him. "Please, call me James, sir."

He spent the next hour giving Burgoyne the tally of men, guns, and powder. He also sketched the new defenses the rebels had begun, especially the bridge and works at Mount Independence.

"Morale is abysmal, sir, as is supply. They don't have enough men to defend for long."

"So, a short siege, or a *coup de main*, seizing it by storm? In confidence, James, I tell you that any action that spares our men is a godsend. We are already losing valuable regulars and mercenaries to illness and fatigue. They can't be replaced."

"Exactly, sir. I spied a mountaintop that dominates the fort from the southwest. Clearing some trees, a company of good men can haul a battery up there and dominate the fort. I believe the rebels will capitulate soon after."

Creed traced a sketch of the area. "If we land here, near the old French fort at Crown Point, and march overland, a small force can discomfort the rebels from these heights."

Burgoyne brightened. "But can we do it?"

"General Fraser is sending a survey party south with my best scout. We'll know by tonight."

"You said you believed the rebels would capitulate soon after. How long can the rebels hold?"

Creed sipped again at the port. "I would leave an exact time frame for your engineers to determine, sir."

"Quite right. Regardless, in a few days or weeks, we'll bag the lot of them, by God. Then just a short march or sail to Albany, what?"

Burgoyne's aide de camp stopped taking notes. "Should we amend the letter to Lord Germain, sir?"

"No, we'll surprise him later. Send it as is. But send one to General Howe as well."

"To what effect, sir?" the aide asked hesitantly.

"Tell him to hurry north, or he'll miss his chance for glory. If we take this army and the fort and General Howe sends forces north, we might consider turning east against the blasted New Englanders. They started this damned war. It should end with our boot on their necks."

***

Creed arrived back with the advance guard to disturbing news. Bart had brought Fleurette back with him.

"Fleurette has been nothing but trouble," Creed told O'Ballance.

The sergeant nodded. "Aye. I have seen many camp followers take down many a good man. This one's a right badger. Rebuffed by one officer, she sets her claws on another. And if I might say so, sir. Ensign Saunders is not man enough to handle the likes of her."

"True enough, sergeant. But I worry more about her father. Serge Binoche is not to be trusted, which sadly extends to her too."

"Oh, she'll cause more trouble yet. I would have left her for the rebels to string up if I were you, sir."

"Often, the right thing is not the wise thing, Sergeant O'Ballance. The campaign season is still young. Keep an eye on both of them."

***

Near the Raritan River, New Jersey

The ordinarily even-tempered Tallmadge stood with hands shaking. "Your dalliance in Brunswick nearly cost us dearly, Harry. Lucky for you, these Loyalist volunteers are merely cowboys. A real unit would have likely stood its ground and sent us packing. And then finished with you."

"You have fine horsemen here, sir. And I suspect your leadership had something to do with it."

Tallmadge ignored the remark and scanned the opposite shore for possible reinforcements.

"You'd better shut up now, Ensign Harry. You're in for it enough with the captain as it is," Simon Beall whispered.

Tallmadge lowered his spyglass and snapped it shut. "Sergeant, make sure they save one of those cowboys' horses for Harry."

Beall took the hint and edged his horse across the field.

Tallmadge softened his tone. "Now, tell me, now that we are alone, what was your dalliance about?"

"Very well, sir. Some time ago, I came to know a Loyalist housewife. Her husband is away with the New Jersey Volunteers. Anyway, she hid me from these same cowboys who pursued me today. I recently began to use her farm as a place of refuge during my travels."

"Her farm or her *boudoir*, Harry? Mixing with the opposite sex, especially a married woman, can bring severe consequences in this life and the next."

Harry smiled devilishly. "My father was not a minister like yours, sir, so I never had that perspective."

Tallmadge could not restrain a smile. "Very well. Is there any more to this?"

"Why yes, sir, I almost forgot. My God!"

Harry jumped up and groaned. "Damn this wound."

He fell back on the saddle and clutched the bandage covering the knife wound.

"Sir, I met a lady."

"Married, I suppose?"

"No, an elegant young lady. The most beautiful woman I have ever seen. I rescued her from these very cowboys last night."

"What was an elegant lady doing about at night with you, Harry?"

"She was riding north to find the American lines. Said she had come from New York with a packet."

"A packet, now? A packet from whom? General Howe?"

"No, from a Mister Smythe."

"A Mister Smythe? From New York?" Tallmadge's brow furrowed.

"That's what she said."

"And to whom was she bearing this packet? General Washington?"

"How did you know, sir? That's who she said it was for."

Tallmadge startled. He had made the connection. He was aware of an American spy among the British and had heard that name used by Colonel Fitzgerald and General Washington. His men had serviced drops from a Mister Jons, but he was also aware of a Mister Smythe.

"Where's the packet?"

Harry pointed towards the field of gold. "I tossed it into the deep wheat before the cowboys closed on me. I figured they'd be searching me, dead or alive, but they'd never bother to look further than my purse and saddlebag."

Tallmadge turned his horse into the tall wheat. Ten paces out, he saw a light green felt folio about twice the size of a standard envelope. He leaned forward with his saber and lifted the packet. Tallmadge cut open the string, binding it, and gazed at the contents. It was in cipher. He closed it and called out to his men.

"Sergeant Beall! Recall the troop!"

Chapter 16

Ticonderoga, New York, July 1777

The stone walls of The Gibraltar of the North sizzled in the afternoon sun. Undeterred by the unseasonably hot weather that soaked coats and breeches in sweat, Burgoyne's legions sailed swiftly down the lake straining at oars and paddles. Bateaux and canoes thumped the lakeshore, spilling files of seasoned regulars into the densely wooded hills.

With pioneers slashing through boughs, trunks, and underbrush, stout grenadiers, gunners, and artificers strained at the heavy ropes. With each heave, the heavy brass cannon crept slowly up the mountainside. Soon, the battery of long guns rolled into position on Mount Defiance.

A group of weary, frustrated men sat around an elegantly polished maple table. St. Clair's tired eyes moved from his staff to his brigade commanders. He knew his men were ill-prepared to defend the place other than for honor. And honor was not on St. Clair's mind. Survival of the force under his command was. Now his council of war must certify a decision he had already made, a decision inferred by a British agent.

He glanced at the date in his log: July 5th. The general cleared his throat with a low gurgle and began, "Gentlemen, we are a day into our nation's second year of existence, and I canna imagine a graver situation. The adjutant informs me I have some twenty-five hundred men under arms and fewer than a thousand short-term militia. The post requires ten thousand for a proper defense. Yet the situation remains no better if we repair as planned to Mount Independence."

Colonel Pierse Long spoke, "What are you proposing then, general?"

St. Clair's white kerchief wiped the sweat from his brow. "Before I answer that, does anyone dispute that the army is in dire straits and, regardless of the character of a defense, is surely to march out under British arms?"

Men fidgeted or thumbed at papers set before them. He scanned the table for eye contact and found none. "If anyone was wondering, I have considered asking Schuyler for reinforcements, but he has none to provide and even less powder and lead."

A militia colonel with a stubble-filled chin and worn homespun replied, "So, we can expect no help from Albany."

St. Clair closed his eyes and lowered his head.

"More men are mustering in New England, General," Long said. "The depredations by the British Indian allies have stirred the people. Why in another month...."

"Colonel, we don't have another month. A day or two at most. I suspect Burgoyne already has forces moving past us to close the vise this geography has consigned us to."

"But this is The Gibraltar of the North!" General Fermoy declared. Roche de Fermoy was a French mercenary granted a commission by Congress for reasons nobody who knew him could fathom.

"Yet the Gibraltar of the North has a history of falling to its foes, doesn't it?" St. Clair replied. "A fortress is only as good as the force manning the battlements. We're too few and too ill-equipped to do anything but provide a useless gesture."

Fermoy rose to his feet and leaned across the table. "You are the commandant! What sort of talk is that from you?"

All eyes turned on St. Clair for his response to the insinuation by the French interloper.

"We served in New Jersey together, general. I believe you know of my resolve. And I resolve to save this army so it can fight another day and win."

His words won the day. The council agreed to depart that night under the greatest secrecy.

"When we leave, we'll blow Colonel Baldwin's bridge," St. Clair said.

Everyone looked at the tall, rangy colonel, who stood stone-faced.

"The engineers will fell trees. Dismantle bridges. Every pathway south must be blocked. We'll draw them east, away from the water and supply lines. We'll trade space for time."

"What then, general?"

"That depends on what Burgoyne does – and General Schuyler. We may lose him a fort, but we are preserving him an army."

St. Clair closed the session. "Remember, gentlemen, just as in Brooklyn, no one below the regimental commander must know of this movement until it commences. An army in retrograde is at its most vulnerable."

***

Back at his chambers, St. Clair began to pack his bags. An officer sat at the foot of his cot but offered no help. St. Clair turned to the officer and stood with his arms akimbo when he finished.

"'Tis done. I am ready myself. I almost wish I could stay and die here rather than face the ignominy before me to tell ye the truth."

"You may die in the trying, as might we all. So don't get too sentimental," Creed replied.

St. Clair stared at him. "I never asked. What brought you back here after shaming my guards so?"

"Duty. I was sent on a strategic mission, sir. By General Fraser himself."

"Not Burgoyne?"

"Burgoyne is too busy preparing his next gushing dispatch to Lord Germain. One would think they were lovers."

"Maybe they are," St. Clair said with a sly grin. "There are rumors about Lord Sackville."

"The barrage will begin sometime mid-morning. Fraser has forces probing around both bodies of water. If you get out tonight, most will escape the trap. Your actions must be quick."

"But you were sent here to signal them if we tried to escape."

"I'll send a signal. But one that will give you a chance to flee before they spring."

St. Clair wondered why he was even having this conversation. He had recalled this officer around Washington and that strange foppish colonel of his, Fitzgerald. Yet the man would not admit nor deny the association. But in his heart, St. Clair needed to believe somehow these actions supported a greater agenda, George Washington's. "You look different than the first time I saw you. It was at Trenton. But of course, it was dark. And a council of war was taking place. I rushed to your cell when I realized it, but ye had already escaped."

Creed threw him a wink. "I don't know what you mean, sir. I've never been to Trenton – certainly not among a pack of rebels. Although a loyal servant of his majesty, I want as little effusion of blood as possible. For that, I have played a risky game, general."

"What do you mean?"

Creed unfolded a map, the last batch Father Vincennes provided him. It showed the area from Ticonderoga to the southern rim of Lake George.

St. Clair was impressed. "Where on earth did the English get this map?"

"The English have nothing to do with this map. You must make your way along the eastern route, overland."

"But I have ordered up boats. 'Tis better if we steer down Lake George."

"For this plan to work, your army must move overland. You don't have time, in any event, to bring up all your craft. Use what you have for the sick."

"How do I know this is not a trap, Captain Lawrence?"

"Because you are already in a trap, and you know it."

"Take this road south." He placed a finger on the map. "But there is a back trail here that is not on any English maps."

St. Clair looked at Creed. "We have already decided on that route. But your trail seems better. Our objective is Castle Town."

"And the boats?"

"Supplies and the sick, mostly."

"Time is as great an enemy as our army. You must move quickly, or it might be at gunpoint the next time we meet."

St. Clair eyed the tall stranger who seemed so familiar. How could he trust him with his fate and that of his army? *Creed!* He remembered the name and the face. But his instincts told him that Lawrence was not the king's loyal servant but Washington's most secret agent.

The general breathed a sigh of relief. "Thank you… Captain Lawrence. He threw his bags over his shoulder and set off to look for an orderly.

***

When St. Clair left, Creed glanced out the window. Below, he saw little sign of the army's departure. On the lake, he saw some small American ships beginning to load. In the distance, he spied a flotilla of bateaux. *The British are closing in. They need to move as soon as it's dark. Did I do the right thing?*

Creed decided that helping save this army was more important than his mission. He was unsure at first. But when he opened Fitzgerald's final instructions, he realized saving this army would prove the key to its success. The mission in Fitzgerald's note charged him with luring Burgoyne beyond his supply base. Letting them take Ticonderoga uncontested was a risk. But it might work if the British strayed from the water chasing an army on the run.

Creed and Pierre managed to blend into the hubbub of an army preparing to march. Posing as artisans, they had roamed the fort. The few soldiers standing watch had grown used to the construction crews reinforcing walls, digging trenches, setting *abatis*, and stacking logs and boughs as barriers.

Men chattered and sipped at the last of their rum as a pair of ducks roasted over a smoky fire. They even shared a meal with some New Hampshire men from Enoch Poor's brigade. None mentioned departing, but all grumbled about the sorry state of the fort and the shortage of supplies.

"You boys don't need to stay here. Why don't you skedaddle?" a roughhewn soldier asked.

"Not done with the fort, pardner. They promised to pay us in coin when we were done," replied Creed.

The men laughed. "Good thing you boys can bag fowl because you won't be eatin' much with the worthless paper they pay us."

Everyone laughed again. Pierre silently turned the duck over the spit. The smell soon had the men licking their lips.

"Let's go to it, boys," Creed said.

Pierre pulled the fowl off the spit and passed out juicy slices of meat. Creed bit into a small piece, chewed at it, and then wiped the grease with his hand.

"You should leave while the going's good. Rumor is redcoats and Indians are all over the place," said one of the men as he sucked the crisp skin off a small wing.

"We'll take our chances, nonetheless. Now pass us here a gill of that rum," Creed said.

"They told us to draw twenty-four cartridges and five days' rations. Do you think we might be leaving?" someone asked.

"To go where? Only a handful of boats out there by the pier."

"Maybe we're attacking," one opined.

The men guffawed.

The sky had darkened by half-past nine. Creed began to see more action as shadows of men filled the fort. *Like banshees from home – dark and evil wraiths that haunted men's nocturnal affairs.* He made the sign of the cross.

Wheels began creaking, and men groaned as they strained their backs and legs to move the massive guns toward the water. Tents were coming down all around them. The shadows were soldiers carrying loads of equipment toward the water.

"The white Americans move," Pierre grunted to Creed in French.

"Maybe, but maybe not," Creed replied tersely.

"Are you going to warn the *Anglais*?" Pierre asked.

"I shall warn them when it is time, not before."

Since they met, Creed and the Wyandot had developed mutual trust and admiration, despite their cultural and linguistic differences.

Creed found in him a singular nobleness rarely found among men of any race.

After midnight, the tramp of shoes on cobblestone filled the fort. Shouts and grunts grew in number and intensity. The sounds of the army on the move were unmistakable. Yet, except for the occasional flare from a campfire, the forests surrounding the fort remained dark and silent. *The British outposts must realize something is going on.* But they would not risk a move until morning, when the guns were ready to rock the walls of the Gibraltar of the North.

***

Carts and wagons rolled along the pier, loaded with men sick from fevers, poxes, and various ailments. Some wagons carried supplies, mainly medicine. Baldwin's bridge creaked and quivered under the weight of men, animals, and machinery. Corporals fought to keep order, but men pushed and pulled in the darkness, desperately trying to escape.

When St. Clair had, at last, alerted his chief engineer and chief of artillery of his plans, they were appalled but supported them.

"Where is Fermoy's brigade?" St. Clair asked his adjutant.

"Still in disarray, sir. The general himself is drunk."

St. Clair turned dark with rage. "Someone go back and get them moving! And leave the general to his cups."

A building suddenly burst into flames with a roaring sound, illuminating the dark like a Roman candle. Golden sparks cast light that revealed the frantic activity at the base of Mount Independence. Men hurried about, some heading toward the inferno, others fleeing from it. Shouts and curses from angry sergeants pierced the night. The occasional pop of a musket added to the chaos and panic.

St. Clair looked at the building. "That's Fermoy's quarters!" It began hissing as its dry timbers collapsed, each sending a fresh plume of fire into the sky.

"Yes, but the general got out in time," his adjutant said.

"If I have my way, he'll wish he'd stayed in his inferno."

A captain rode upon a foam-flecked horse that moved nervously. St. Clair approached the horse and gently stroked its neck. "Easy there, my lad. All's well." His eyes were fixed on the rider. "Any sign of the British moving, captain?"

"No, sir."

St. Clair gazed about him. The chaos was startling, but time was of the essence. He had to get as many men out before it was too late. "Good. Prepare your company to cover the rear when we leave."

Most of his men had left by four that morning, and St. Clair was ready to depart. He summoned the captain of the rear guard.

"Where's yer horse?" St Clair asked.

"I left him with a bucket of oats and some water. He'll be of no use where we're going. I hope the British take care of him."

St Clair glanced up at the mountains thick with trees. He doubted the world held a more imposing forest. He nodded approvingly. "Aye, captain. Time to get to work with your lads."

"What are your orders, sir?"

"Tear everything apart. Slow the British as much as possible, but don't get decisively engaged. We'll rally near Skenesborough and then move to Fort George for supplies and reinforcement."

St. Clair spoke as if it were an accomplished fact. But he knew it would be a miracle if they escaped the clutches of the British – or the Iroquois.

***

The morning light barely touched the top of Vermont's eastern peaks. Creed and Pierre looked down at an empty fort. Just a few soldiers stood near Jeduthan Baldwin's bridge. One held a rope that was smoking at one end. Two others were rolling barrels onto the bridge. Suddenly, an explosion of fire and smoke burst out with a loud boom that tore through the air. Pieces of wood flew everywhere. When the smoke cleared, the 750-foot span had a large hole, but it otherwise remained standing.

Then, out of the waning darkness, a platoon of red coats rushed across the revetments and stormed the fort's main gate. A subaltern raised his short fusil above his head. On that signal, the platoon charged the bridge before the inner wall.

Creed spotted a pair of four-pound guns lingering under the archway. Their barrels pointed at the approach to the bridge.

"Those guns under the arch may discommode our friends."

Pierre grunted. Before Creed could say anything, he ran down to the battery, where the crew challenged him.

"Where you goin', red man?"

"Stay away from our guns, you savage!"

Pierre grabbed the burning wick from the lead gunner, elevated one of the barrels, and lit the touch hole. The gun belched fire and smoke, sending its payload arching high above the British, almost like a salute.

Cheers came from hundreds of excited voices as the British raced across the wooden bridge. The American gunners scattered like wheat grains in a windstorm. Simon Fraser's elite fanned out through the bastion of the north. Ticonderoga was theirs, and the only shot fired was by one of their agents.

***

A short time later, Brigadier General Simon Fraser trotted over the bridge. He found his spy, Captain Lawrence, and the Indian Pierre, gathering sundry items left behind by the retreating Americans.

Creed had done his dirty work for the British, delivering them the fortress, but now he needed to misdirect the general's efforts without drawing suspicion. Otherwise, his work was for naught.

"What are you doing, Captain Lawrence?" Fraser asked.

Creed smiled. "Call me James, sir. Pierre and I are gathering a few items for our journey south. I'm to probe as far as Albany and determine the rebels' next moves."

Fraser looked around at the piles of broken barrels and lines of powder piled high. "It looks like the rebels forgot to light these combustibles and finish stripping out this place, James."

"Indeed, they would have, sir. But we convinced the rebel officer-in-charge that we would watch the powder and blow it. Anxious to retreat with the rest of his cowardly lot, he readily agreed."

Fraser nodded. "But the bridge, the long bridge?"

"Aye, they managed to blow a barrel. Tore up about fifty feet of planks. But the pillars and piles are intact. Your fine engineers will have it operable in hours."

"Good." Fraser continued to survey his conquest. "Not much left here, is there, though?"

"No, sir, but truth be told, they hadn't much to begin with."

Fraser tipped his hat. "Very well, James. Best you get on with your mission. The rest of your band will join us in the pursuit. Any instructions for them?"

"Tell Sergeant O'Ballance to keep an eye on our subaltern."

"Anything else? Any thoughts for me?" Fraser had come to respect the doughty colonial.

"Just that the rebels headed overland on the eastern shore. I recommend the entire army pursue them as one. Crushing this army in the wilderness between here and Fort George will seal the victory for General Burgoyne."

"That's the spirit, James! Stay on the buggers till they are done. Alexander and fifty of our best marksmen are already heading towards Castle Town. You'd best get going now yourself!"

"Indeed, sir."

***

Burgoyne's Headquarters, Fort Ticonderoga

Burgoyne wasted no time dictating a letter back to London. His interest was twofold: to apprise the government of his success while pressuring Guy Carleton to expedite the supply chain from Canada.

Ticonderoga
6 July 1777

Lord Germain
His Majesty's Minister for North America

The North Spy

Sir,

We have beaten them!

I have the Honour of informing His Majesty's Minister that the Rebels under St. Clair have been forced from their dominant position at Fortress Ticonderoga. The Gibraltar of the North is once more the possession of His Majesty!

Through a Masterpiece of maneuver and the preparation of necessary Firepower, we have forced the Enemy from his Stronghold. They are now on the run. I have ordered the Army to spare no haste in pursuit and the destruction of the Enemy. To that end, Generals Fraser and von Riedesel are marching southeast to catch the rebel Rear Guard and push it in on their main body.

I expect that my next Missive will report on their success and the rebel Commander's negotiation for terms. At which point, I must decide whether to await General Howe's movement in conjunction or turn my attention towards the Colonies to my east. In either case, I believe the terms and expectations of this Campaign have been thus far vindicated.

The Army must invariably run short whether we progress south or turn east. In furtherance of the objectives, I have requested the Governor-General in Quebec expedite the supply flow such as victuals, tools, powder, etc. I would appreciate His Majesty's endorsement of this.

A full report of the action at and around Ticonderoga will follow shortly.

I remain, as always,

Your Most Humble and Ever Obedient Servant,

J. Burgoyne
Commanding General

***

Hubbardton, Hampshire Grants, July 7th, 1777

An intense summer sun had just crested the eastern mountains, but the morning sky remained dark and heavy with gun smoke—the advancing British line staggered under the fierce fire from the rebels. Men stumbled over fallen trees, thick patches of bush, and boulders. Sweat darkened their red woolen jackets.

Fraser's force had pursued the rebel rear-guard some twenty-six miles through a forest dark and broken. He pressed his men, and they were up to the task. Now they proved it. *But at what cost?* He turned to his adjutant and pointed at a prominent ridge covered with thick woods – Zion Hill. "Send the grenadiers around their left and seize that hill. Once secure, we'll await von Riedesel and press their flanks."

Fraser watched angrily as the morning ended with the rebel flank turned by the Germans and their line broken. Colonel Ebenezer Francis was struck dead on the field in one of the final withering volleys. The remaining Americans turned heel and melted into the forest to the south.

In short order, the German infantry began gathering prisoners and had some 200 rebels shuffling like scarecrows toward Ticonderoga.

As the British cleared the field of wounded, Fraser's adjutant grabbed him by the hand.

"By God, sir, we have sent them on their way, and hundreds have fallen."

Fraser knew well he had won a pyrrhic victory. "And just what is our butcher's bill?"

"Haven't tallied yet, sir, maybe two hundred. And the Germans have bagged more than that in prisoners," the adjutant said.

"And ours?"

"Maybe two hundred killed and wounded."

"Well, the rebels will replace their dead within a fortnight, yet Lord Germain will not send me one soldier to replace the fine men we have lost."

"But we have a victory, sir."

Fraser scanned the hills and fields, now strewn with corpses and the wreckage of combat. "A victory? I'd say we won a cow pasture."

Chapter 17

Burgoyne's Headquarters, Near Skenesborough, New York

His quill ran across the parchment with a flourish and a swirl. Burgoyne loved penning drama and winning at the gaming tables but loved leading men in war even more.

The door's creaking revealed Colonel Lazarus Sinclair with a sheaf of papers bound with a thick scarlet ribbon. The scarlet signified the reports were of a most sensitive matter.

Sinclair bowed slightly. "Sir, I thought it time to review our plans for the remainder of the campaign."

Burgoyne smiled weakly. "Lazarus, your presence always seems to bring my creative efforts to a halt. Very well, pour yourself some claret and have a seat."

Sinclair sat on a stiff-backed chair and untied the ribbon, placing three crisp sheets of parchment on the table. Burgoyne scarcely looked at them.

"Any news from Simon?" he asked.

"Yes, and I am told Captain Lawrence is heading south again."

"Well, he got us into Ticonderoga without the effusion of blood. Perhaps he can find a way to do the same with Albany."

Sinclair almost gagged on his wine. He put down his glass and paused to regain his composure. "Sir, if our supply situation does not improve, I recommend we conduct no further operations this year. We have already lost several precious weeks trying to chase the rebels in their wilderness."

"I know. But we almost had them at Ticonderoga. Indeed, we sent them packing. Taught them a lesson. As for supplies, I am sending Baum to seize enemy stores at Bennington. The rebels have scattered to the winds, and we shall sweep away like dry weeds whatever few militias they muster." Burgoyne sipped at his claret. "Drink up now, Lazarus."

"Sir, there is one other matter," Sinclair said.

"What is that?"

"The report General Fraser sent us from your Captain Lawrence."

"What of it?" Burgoyne personally sent Lawrence to spy on the Americans at Fort George and Fort Edward. He had returned with what appeared to be significant information about the rebels. Based on Lawrence's report, Burgoyne had reinforced his detachments and pushed his forces east to probe for reactions from New England.

"Well, even if the information proves true, weakening our main force to guard against a suspected thrust from an unknown army from New England is...."

"Is what, Lazarus?"

"Well, sir, highly speculative and fraught with risk."

"You should be the first to want to protect our supply base."

"Sir, if we do proceed this summer, this plan only succeeds if we concentrate our

-168-

efforts at Albany and combine with General Howe and Barry."

Burgoyne set down his glass. "I agree, Lazarus, but are you suggesting Captain Lawrence brought us false intelligence?"

Sinclair cocked his head. "Not necessarily, sir, but it could be inaccurate and...."

Burgoyne liked Captain Lawrence of the Royal Americans and resented the implication. "What are you suggesting we do?"

"Watch him a bit, that's all," Sinclair said softly.

"Have you spoken to Simon about this?"

"No, sir. I thought it better to hold this discreetly."

"These things are so tawdry, Lazarus. Do you have someone in mind to watch him?"

Sinclair lowered his head. "Indeed, sir. One of his men."

Burgoyne did not like where this was leading. "Alexander?"

"No. He is too forthright when not skulking about the woods like a savage. No, I have someone else in mind."

"And who is that? Burgoyne waved his hands as if to keep the affair at a distance. "Never mind. Better for now that I don't know."

"I understand perfectly, sir. The person I have in mind planted the thought of possible trickery in my head. But I have thought it through myself, and it makes sense. We have no order from Howe or Horse Guards assigning him and his command other than the paper he came with."

"Guy Carleton signed that order, although it did seem rather hurried, his late arrival and all." Burgoyne shook his head incredulously. "You think Captain Lawrence raised a detachment just to spy on us and then convinced Guy to order him here?" Burgoyne laughed. "My God, Lazarus, you give the rebels too much credit. Perhaps we should co-author a play. Your flair for drama mixed with comedy does impress."

"Do I? Anyway, I am just trying to do due diligence for this army. That is, your army, sir. If Captain Lawrence is not what he appears, we may be playing into some diabolical rebel trap to lure us away from our supply base while they build up their forces. And if he is legitimate but mistaken in his intelligence, then...."

Burgoyne felt a sudden surge of comprehension. "Disruption of our plans could be laid at his feet. Very well. I suppose it could not harm to have him observed. But don't bother me unless you have conclusive and firm proof. Meanwhile, prepare a letter to Carleton asking the basis for the Royal American detachment's presence in our army."

**

Sinclair's horse plodded down a narrow path draped in darkness. Despite his confident tone with Burgoyne, he felt ill at ease with the clandestine nature of his scheme. *Should I have trusted my informer? Too late to back out.*

He had pressured the reluctant Burgoyne, and now he had to deliver the head of Captain Lawrence, whether he was a rebel spy.

The path through the woods was narrow and twisting, lined with tall cypress, oak, and maple trees. His horse plodded along slowly. The darkness seemed to envelop his soul.

His horse snorted. Ahead was a clearing. He saw a small fire burning with shadowy figures sitting around it.

"*Bon soir, Monsieur*. You arrive late, no?"

Sinclair slipped nervously from the saddle. "I am not late, Binoche. You are merely early. Make sure you are always early for meetings with me."

"As you wish, *Monsieur*. I have brought my friend, as I promised. Allow me to introduce Ensign Saunders of *Les Américains Royale*, the so-called Royal Americans." Binoche ended the introduction in a mocking tone.

Sinclair glared at the visibly nervous ensign. "Do you know why you are here?" Saunders nodded.

"Speak to the *Monsieur Colonel*, Bart. It is the best way."

The female voice surprised Sinclair. He had not noticed her in the darkness.

"Who are you, madam?" Sinclair asked.

Binoche draped a bear-like arm around her slender shoulders. "This is my daughter, Fleurette. She entered the rebel fortress with Lawrence. She witnessed him meet with the commander."

Sinclair eyed Fleurette. Somehow, Binoche's arm about her disturbed him. "You think he provided the rebel commander information about our attack?"

"But, of course, he informed them of our great strength. That is why they fled rather than die under your guns. It is why he stopped my warriors from scalping those rebels. It is why he has that Wyandot pig as his guide. It is why he, why he…."

"Why he, what?" Sinclair blurted.

"Why does he not behave like a normal man?" Fleurette purred in a low, cold voice.

Sinclair swallowed hard. "What do you mean?"

"She means, *Monsieur*, that a man who would reject the attentions of one as beautiful as Fleurette has other things on his mind. Bart is only one of many who can attest to her charms."

Sinclair eyed them with suspicion. "This better not be the bad end of some tryst. His majesty's justice cannot be trifled with. I need proof. General Burgoyne demands proof before he will take action. This girl's musings about Captain Lawrence's actions at Ticonderoga are meaningless. I need…"

Binoche curled his lip in defiance. "What do you need, *Monsieur*?"

Sinclair took a breath. "I need Captain Lawrence *in flagrante' delecto*. Caught in the act with proof of his treachery."

Binoche balled his ham-sized fists and slammed them against his hips. "*D'accord.* That, you shall have, and more. And in reward?"

Sinclair eyed Fleurette. *She is lovely.* "Reward? You mentioned no need for a reward at our last meeting, Binoche."

"That was before you spoke to your general. Now you must deliver this man to him or face the blame for a baseless accusation, *Monsieur*. A reward for us will merely guarantee you deliver on your promise."

This foul ruffian has played me the fool.

"What do you want as a reward?"

"Exclusive rights to trade with the Indians in this region and...."

"And what?"

"For my friend Ensign Saunders, command of the Royal Americans when Lawrence is gone."

"Gone? You assume he will be convicted in a fair trial, Binoche."

"Just as you assume that he will live to face one, *Monsieur*."

Sinclair glared. "Lawrence is leaving soon. His objective is the American defenses near Albany. Follow him. See what he does and whom he meets. His twice entering the enemy camp is more than suspicious."

Chapter 18

Albany, New York, July 1777

Creed's fingers dug into the rocky precipice. The morning sun was already scorching, and the stone burned like a frying pan, stinging his elbows and knees and blistering his hands as he groped along. But the overhang, not more than two feet wide, provided a view of the American defenses around Albany.

Some 300 feet below, Creed could see thick swatches of the forest slowly open into neatly cleared fields dotted with smart, Dutch, and English-style farms stretching south and west.

To the southeast lay Albany, a Dutch settlement, until the British acquired the colony in the previous century. Albany still had its Dutch character and charm. Tightly packed but neatly arranged rows of stone houses with stepped roofs lay below him. With over 3,000 residents, the frontier town was New York's largest city north of the City of New York. The sleepy town was now the target of the most ambitious campaign of the war.

Creed could see the rows of transports along the North River docks in the southeast. Creed snapped open his spyglass and scoured the rude defense works north of the city. *Only a few sentries. These works are barely manned.* They could not withstand even the reduced British Army's onslaught. *The militia must rally, or Burgoyne will succeed, and I will be the agent of his victory.*

Turning his spyglass west, he strained to see the Mohawk River winding its way from Iroquois country through the frontier farmlands. He spotted a column of men marching west along the river. Another British, Canadian, and Indian force was supposed to push east and link with Burgoyne. *Could they be so close so soon?*

Creed carefully edged his way back along the rock.

"I must go into Albany," Creed said.

"Did you see many blue jackets, *monsieur*?" Pierre asked.

"Yes, many blue jackets. And they are preparing fortifications for big guns." It bothered him to deceive his friend. And increasingly, Pierre had become as close to a friend as he had in the north.

"Then we try to enter their camp and spy on the blue jackets just as at the great fort?"

Creed drew a breath. "I'll go alone. A Wyandot might attract suspicion. I want to count their guns."

Pierre's bronzed arms crossed his chest. "I will wait in these rocks."

"If I'm not back by dawn tomorrow, return without me. Tell Fraser I saw many blue jackets. Many guns. Here at Albany."

Pierre nodded very deliberately. "As you say, *monsieur*."

He realized Pierre saw through his ruse. Convince Burgoyne there were too many Americans around Albany for a final blow without Howe or St Leger.

***

The creek curved southeast before flowing into the North River. Following it seemed safer than risking a road with sentries or patrols. He pushed through low-hanging branches and climbed over fallen logs.

Albany surprised Creed. He expected a few rows of log hovels, but instead, he saw a charming mix of traditional brick-and-stone Dutch houses neatly arranged in rows, with flowers hanging wherever a housewife could place a box or pot.

He made his way through the midday din of traders hawking pelts and merchants seeking deals. Angular frontier farmers in homespun argued with fat burghers in the latest fashions. The newer homes were English-style wooden affairs with neat shutters and tin roofs. Pretty young girls waved fish at passers-by. Worn-looking older girls peddled something less wholesome.

Still, only the occasional militiaman gave evidence that the town was the objective of two, maybe three, armies converging on it.

A few discreet inquiries led him to General Phillip Schuyler's mansion, the headquarters of the Northern Department. Creed marveled at the large, square brick building surrounded by a spacious field enclosed by an elegant fence. He talked his way past the indifferent militiamen. Finally, the sergeant of Schuyler's guards took him to a subaltern. Creed figured he was Schuyler's orderly.

"This man says he has important information for General Schuyler, sir," the sergeant said lazily.

The short, thin subaltern sported steel-rimmed glasses that seemed to fall off his nose with each move.

He peered over the rims at Creed. "Important information? From whom?"

Creed removed his hat and wiped beads of sweat from his forehead. "From me."

The subaltern straightened his spectacles. "And just who are you?"

"That's something only the general can know. Tell him this. A friendly *coureurs des bois* from the British camp is here with news. He can meet with me and maybe save this charming town, or turn me away and meet with the lobsters in a few weeks."

The subaltern stared in disbelief.

Creed glared. "*Tell* him, *monsieur*. If you know what's good for you and your town."

"The general is only here for a day. Then he returns north to the army. The British are pressing us rather harshly."

"Then tell him quickly."

The subaltern turned on his heel and stomped into the enclosed foyer of the building.

A few minutes later, Creed stood in the general's office. The Schuylers were one of the wealthiest Dutch families in New York, controlling much of the land around Albany. Schuyler's home displayed that wealth and privilege.

The staid wooden décor of the room, imported French furnishings, and the hundreds of books crowding the shelves impressed Creed.

"Will you take a drink?" Schuyler asked. "Fine sherry, perhaps?"

Creed nodded. "Aye, sir."

Schuyler waved off the servant and poured the drinks himself. He was a dark-haired, fair-skinned bantam of a man with a strong chin and nose. "You don't sound like any of the *coureurs* I have ever met. Not Canadian, are you?"

"I can only say we were sent here by the same person." Creed sipped the sherry.

"I see. Who might that be?"

"I have probably said too much already. But hear this. Burgoyne himself sent me as a spy. Unfortunately, I was previously engaged, if you understand."

"This is absurd. You could be anyone."

"Would just anyone give you this?" Creed pulled an envelope from his pocket. His eyes scanned his last instructions from Fitzgerald.

Lure the enemy from their supply lines and give the last map to Schuyler if he still holds Albany.

He handed the note to Schuyler, who read it twice. "What does this mean? It's not even signed."

Creed chuckled. "Of course not, *monsieur*. That would be my death sentence if there weren't enough to commission it already. Does the handwriting look familiar?"

Schuyler's hands trembled. Creed could see that he had realized that George Washington wrote the note.

"Let's have another drink. Then tell me what you know, *Monsieur*."

"Captain, sir. Captain James Lawrence. But please, sir, call me James."

Creed took a pencil and marked the British locations, their regiments, and the number of guns.

"Impressive numbers. No wonder St. Clair abandoned his post."

"General St. Clair evacuated Ticonderoga at my suggestion, sir."

"By God, sir! Your actions may bring both St. Clair and me before a court-martial."

"Perhaps, sir. But now you have a few thousand more troops than if he had saved face in futile resistance at Ticonderoga. A court-martial is a small price for the survival of the north."

Schuyler's face reddened. "Don't talk to me about love of country! However, I concede your point. We have little hope based on what you tell me of the British strength. And fewer men. Many of the regiments that escaped with St. Clair have moved east – away from Burgoyne's main line of advance."

"Which is distracting and delaying Burgoyne's advance here."

"What does that mean?" Schuyler dipped a pen in an inkpot and began to write on the note.

"Sir, put down the nib, please. What transpires here must not be entered into any record, public or private. We'll begin with that note."

He plucked the note from Schuyler's hands, rolled it up, and burned it over the small candle on Schuyler's desk.

"Any connection to our mutual employer is up in smoke." Creed smiled. "As for Burgoyne's line of advance, I'll say this. I was sent north to recruit a spy among the British. I soon saw the futility– too little time or opportunity and great risk. However, I have found it relatively easy to influence Burgoyne's decisions with misleading information and other deceptions. And fortunately, I managed to get into Ticonderoga to warn General St. Clair."

"Indeed!" Schuyler threw back his head and swallowed the remainder of his sherry. "I see the advantage now, but the idea still rankles."

"The cause needs a victory more than men of high regard, sir. Besides, St. Clair and his men would be on their way to prison in Canada instead of posing a threat to Johnny's advance. At least they have lived to fight another day."

Schuyler's eyes widened, and he smiled broadly. "You are a madman, Captain Lawrence. I should not want to do business with you."

"James, sir, please. As for madness. Many would say rebelling against Britain is madness."

Schuyler's tight lips exploded in laughter. "*Touche'*! Very well, James. But I have few troops to defend this place. All of New England hates me. They favor Gates, as does Congress. So, they hold their men back."

"We shall have to change that, then, sir, won't we?"

"I fear I will be removed from this command before that's possible."

"Perhaps, but the main thing is to stop General Burgoyne. And in that endeavor, we have some cards."

"Such as?"

"The natives, for one. They are being stirred up."

"We have our own native allies, James."

"Not as many as Burgoyne and his are truly savages. The Mohawks are in this mainly for mayhem and pillage. That will rally the New Englanders to you."

Schuyler nodded in affirmation. "And many doubtful New Yorkers. John Glover just arrived at Saratoga with a brigade. His Excellency also sent a brigade. They're only a day's march south of here. He hopes to send more if need be. And we need the help. There's a British army west of Fort Stanwix, and I have only militia covering the frontier. If Burgoyne moves on us now, all is lost."

"Indeed, to my point, sir. However, I propose to help."

"You? Help? Help in what way? And just how?"

"I told you. I was sent here by Burgoyne himself. I shall report back to him that your support has already arrived."

"How will that help?"

"Knowing him, he'll slow his advance until Howe commits. I shall tell him the rumor in Albany confirms his imminent committal north. Meanwhile, I'll continue to regale him with reports of rebel stores to his east. These British generals seem to wage war with one another as with us. He'll dispatch foraging parties to collect on said victuals, and with luck, our hardy New England brethren shall be waiting for him."

Schuyler placed his finger on a town marked on Vincennes's map: Bennington. "Then this is the place we should lure him."

"Make sure you get some men there. I'll try to convince the British to do the same."

"And how shall we do that?"

Creed nodded at the table. "Pick up your nib, sir. I shall dictate how."

When he had finished taking Creed's dictation, Schuyler's face beamed. "If you want to make a lot of money after the war, you must come and work for me, James. Perhaps meet my daughter, Eliza."

"Truth be told, the only work that interests me is winning this war, sir."

Schuyler blushed. "You shame me, James. Of course, the cause is all we need to consider now. But there will come a time when our new nation will need outstanding young men of enterprise. You may well be among them."

"That is a fine sentiment, sir. And I thank you for it. Meanwhile, I shall do what I can to slow the British long enough for you to gather your forces."

***

Creed took a sip from his water bottle and wiped the sweat from his brow. He reached the edge again on schedule. "I have the information they need, Pierre. We can reach our canoe by nightfall. With luck, we'll be back by dawn."

The late afternoon sun shot rays through the canopy, casting beams that seemed to light the way for them. Pierre moved through the brush like a deer. Creed had trouble keeping up with him. Where Creed saw a wall of green, Pierre saw a path.

He suddenly froze. Creed did the same.

"What is it?" Creed whispered.

"The birds have grown silent. Someone is…"

Pierre suddenly shifted his weight and jumped on Creed, knocking him onto the roots and stones covering the hard ground.

A musket shot *cracked*, sending a lead ball *buzzing* right over them. The bullet struck the rocky precipice with a *slap* and a *zing*. A second shot cut a rock near Creed's face, slicing a chip into his cheek. He ignored the blood trickling down his face as he and Pierre scrambled behind a large tree trunk.

They swung their muskets into action and scanned the wood line for their assailants, but the dense trees hid them from sight.

Creed spoke to Pierre in French, "We must flush them out. When one fires, we'll both return our fire into the smoke. Keep your tomahawk ready, just in case."

Pierre pulled back the hammer on his musket. Two more shots buzzed through the branches, then a third.

"There's smoke to the right." Creed leveled his musket. "Fire!"

A *bang* and *whoosh* erupted. A cry came from where the thin cloud of smoke rose above the trees.

"We got one," Creed said. "Reload."

Ramrods slammed powder and ball down hot gun barrels. Hammers were quickly thumbed back with a *click* – poised to strike the pan.

S.W. O'Connell

"Hold till they fire," Creed said.

Two more shots erupted. Creed and Pierre squeezed off a return volley. Their mouths were dry from the heavy summer heat and acrid smoke. Then the forest grew silent.

Creed's mind struggled with doubt. How many more would die before he was done? *Will I have to kill an American to get through this?* A series of guttural cries broke the silence.

A brave emerged from the wood line with his musket held high in the signal for a parley.

Pierre stepped into the open with his weapon held high. An exchange in Iroquois ensued. Creed saw Pierre hand something to the brave, who quickly disappeared into the dense woods.

"Who are they, Pierre?" Creed asked.

Pierre squinted towards the wood line. "Oneidas. Friendly to the blue jackets. Sent to look for the enemy of the blue jackets. One of our shots killed their leader. They are leaving but asked that we not take his scalp."

"Strange request from a warrior."

"They are Christian converts. The priests told them scalping was a sin against God."

"What did you tell them?"

"To listen to the priests. As I had."

"What did you give him?"

"Beads - what they call the rosary. It is the one they gave me when I turned Christian."

Creed was stunned. He realized that he knew too little of this warrior guide.

"We'll get you another, Pierre. Did he tell you anything about the rebels? Did he see any red jackets?"

"He said there are just a few blue jackets in Albany and no big guns. Maybe it is a trick? Or maybe *Monsieur* was mistaken."

Creed took a swig from his water bottle. He let the warm water wet his mouth and tongue, then swallowed slowly to savor its effect. "So, which do you think it is?"

"It does not matter what I think, *Monsieur*. Whatever you report back will be the truth."

Creed realized Pierre knew Creed's observation was false yet seemed comfortable providing the British with a misleading report. He grasped Pierre's forearm and looked him in the eye. "Your faith in me is an assurance I shall not forget, Pierre. Nor is it misplaced."

"In you, I place my trust, *Monsieur*. But my faith, I place in God." Pierre picked up his weapon and pack and padded on down the trail.

They reached the canoe sooner than Creed expected. Creed removed his belting. "We'll wash in the river, eat some deer jerky, and rest until twilight. But first, let's fill our water bottles."

He stripped to the waist and began his ablutions after filling his bottle. He splashed the dust and sweat from his face, chest, and arms.

Pierre slipped from his deerskins and plunged into the waist-high water. Creed noticed scars - welts long and wide and too numerous to count. He also saw a fresh one. A neat red line cut his left shoulder. Pierre's cat-like leap saved him, but the round meant for him had slashed Pierre's shoulder.

"Pierre! You were grazed, saving me from their ambush! Let me cleanse that wound."

"Cleanse, *Monsieur*? I have had worse than this and never needed to clean them."

"As you wish." Creed had come to respect Pierre's honesty and quiet, dignified manner.

They chewed at the jerky and watched the shadows fall across the river as the western sun dipped behind the mountains. The twilight air was warm but no longer oppressive.

Creed's mind drifted as he took his last rest before they headed north. He first thought of Emily and wondered if he would ever see her again. He then thought of his men with the Continental Army and how they were doing without him. Well, he supposed, Tallmadge was a good and true leader, and even Harry had become more of a soldier as time went on.

Then he heard a *click*. Pierre had cocked his musket hammer and stood staring out at the darkening waters.

"Did you see something?" Creed whispered as he reached for his weapon.

"No."

"Hear something?"

"No, *Monsieur*. I feel something."

"What?"

"I don't know. Someone is out there."

"Could be anyone. This river is likely full of people. They could be rebels. Burgoyne's Mohawks. Maybe part of Fraser's advance guard."

"Whoever it is, knows we are here," Pierre replied. "Waiting for us."

"Maybe your Mohawk friends followed us."

"Perhaps, *Monsieur*. But I think not."

"Well, let's find out then. Get your kit."

In minutes, they were gliding across the water. The evening twilight provided just enough light for them. The sky was cloudless, and they could already see stars pushing through the grey velvet canopy stretching across the eastern sky. A stray tern sailed over them and then disappeared into the gathering darkness.

Pierre's firm hand grasped Creed's shoulder. "I see them. A longboat."

Creed squinted hard. "I don't see a thing."

Pierre thrust his powerful arm over the bow and extended a finger. "There, straight ahead."

They pushed hard at their paddles, and in a few minutes, Creed could make out the outline of a longboat. "They're heading north. Likely rebels."

Just then, the boat slowed and then quickly lurched forward."

"Bluejacket scouts would turn towards us," Pierre said.

S.W. O'Connell

"You're right. But who would be fleeing north? And in a longboat, not a canoe?"

The *crack* of a musket shot echoed across the water. Creed and his companion leaned forward and dug their paddles deep into the dark water. Before long, the canoe had closed the distance to within 100 yards of the heavier longboat.

"They're wasting powder at this range. We'll hold our fire until we can make out individual forms," Creed said.

Another shot sent a plume of fire against the darkening sky. Then another plume erupted with a *pop*.

"They're trying to scare us off," Creed said.

"Perhaps not, *Monsieur*. The boat is turning."

The oars rhythmically dipped into the lake and drew the danger closer. The longboat came about and slid towards them like a prehistoric sea monster. Soon they could make out four figures – two rowing and two at the bow with muskets ready.

"I'll fire first. Cover me as I reload." Creed aligned his barrel on the figures in the bow and squeezed the trigger. The musket *cracked*. The longboat slowed and began to veer to the port side. Then it began to circle away from them into the dark shadows to the east.

"They have lost their stomach for a fight, Pierre."

He began to reload. When he was halfway through, Pierre fired. The shot rang out across the dark water. They heard a moan from the longboat.

Creed cupped his hands around his mouth. "Surrender, or we'll cut you to pieces."

The boat did not stop. Creed squeezed off another shot. Panting with excitement, Pierre dug his paddle deep into the water, sending ripples in all directions. They heard a splash.

"Something fell into the water," Pierre said.

Creed rammed another ball into his musket and began to work his oar at Pierre's cadence.

"They have turned once more, *Monsieur*," Pierre murmured.

"Let's cut them off," Creed gasped, straining at his paddle.

The canoe seemed to skip across the waves, and soon they were no more than ten yards off the longboat's starboard stern. They could see the outline of men. Two at the oars and one standing with a musket pointed right at Creed.

Creed leveled his musket at the boat. "Come about and surrender!"

A tongue of flame spat from the muzzle, followed by a heavy *pop* echoing across the water. The *zing* of a bullet splashed the water to the port, the left, with a harmless *ping*.

An oarsman drew a pistol, but his shot missed. Creed gently squeezed the trigger, and a flash and bang erupted. He saw the shooter clutch his chest and tumble back into the boat. The canoe careened into the heavier longboat with a solid thud. The oarsman tossed his pistol, leaped over the side, and desperately flailed against the waves toward the eastern shore.

The other oarsman threw his arms over his head. "I surrender!"

They found two dead lying in the boat. Creed saw someone lurking behind the thwarts. He sprang across the gunwale onto the longboat with one smooth motion, knife and tomahawk in hand.

"Who are you?" Creed demanded of the short, plump man before him.

"I'm Ruud Steivers. These gentlemen hired me to guide them north. That's all. To the English camp. Simple transportation is what they said."

"Steivers? Dutch, are you? You've got a bit of the accent yet."

"*Ja, I am Dutch.*"

"Well, simple transportation, is it? These waters will soon be swarming with the English and their hirelings." Creed waved at the dead men. "Those two are spies. You were transporting spies, and soon you will be hanged for your simple transportation."

Steivers began to shiver.

Creed examined the dead men. They were in civilian attire, city garb, not the usual dress for the northern wilderness. Creed felt their clothes were newly bought and came from the same tailor. He turned out their inner and outer pockets but found nothing of importance. He then remembered a trick he had learned on Long Island.

"Remove their shoes, Steivers. Then their socks."

Steivers hesitated. "*Meen Heer*, shouldn't disturb the dead, *nah?* Why, their ghosts might come back to haunt...."

Creed nodded at Pierre. "I'll have my savage friend scalp you alive and feed you to the fishes."

Pierre reached menacingly for his hunting knife.

Steivers's pig-like eyes widened. He did as Creed ordered. The first body had a bloody pulp for a chest. Creed's musket ball had torn open his upper torso at close range.

With hands shaking, Steivers removed the man's shoes. He wore fine leather shoes with silver buckles.

"Nothing extraordinary, *Meen Heer.*"

"Check his mate."

A body lay sprawled across the forward bow with a gaping hole in the gullet.

"Nothing, *Meen Heer.*" Steivers could no longer fight the urge to vomit and heaved on himself.

"Never saw a dead man?"

"Please, *Meen Heer.* I am sick." He heaved again and then choked.

"Steady now. You'll need to answer some questions or join them soon. Did they wear hats?"

The two craft bobbed in the dark waters, and they drifted south.

"*Ja*, hats, where did they go?" Steivers groped in the dark until he found a pair of brimmed hats under one of the benches. "Here they are."

Steivers stretched his arms, and Creed took the hats to examine them. One had an extra lining.

He pulled a jackknife from his pocket and flicked open its heavy blade, carefully slicing the lining. His finger felt something. *An envelope!*

Creed sliced it open, revealing a letter carefully inscribed on a large silk sheet. But he could not make out the words.

"Can't read it in the dark. But this must be the message they were bringing north, poor devils."

"Poor, *Duyvels*," Steivers stammered. "Who were they?"

Creed cocked his head in disbelief. "You well know they were British officers on a secret mission."

"What are you going to do, *Meen Heer*?"

"Do? I am going to finish the mission they started. As for you, remove your clothing and swim for shore."

Steivers's eyes widened. "It's too far to shore, sir, and I can't swim!"

"But you can kick. Off with those clothes, now. Grab that oar and float back. Keep your head up and kick like – kick like the *Duyvel*!"

***

Hudson Highlands, New York, July 1777

The fine drizzle filled the air like vapor but barely cooled the heavy summer heat. General Washington tightened his oilskin against the mist. With a gentle nudge of his knees, he urged his horse up the narrow highland trail that ran along the river to West Point. Six men from his Life Guard followed about thirty yards behind.

The trail wove through soft mountains, now lush with heavy green foliage. The winding strip of blue below them looked like a ribbon adorning a cockade, its ends curving in different directions.

Colonel Robert Fitzgerald struggled to keep his horse abreast of the commander-in-chief's magnificent charger. The gangly former schoolmaster, an indifferent rider at best, stood no chance against one of the most accomplished on the continent.

"The latest dispatch from Schuyler had less panic than his previous. Still, he screams for reinforcements and supplies," Fitzgerald said.

"Don't we all," Washington quipped. His dispute with Congress and the states over the proper maintenance of the army was no secret.

"I believe Iroquois war bands ravaging the farmsteads from New York to Vermont had something to do with that, Your Excellency."

"Anything else?"

"I have reports that the Indians are gone, for the most part."

"How so?"

"Burgoyne berated them and deprived them of the plunder they wanted."

Washington turned his face upwards, letting the mist provide a refreshing spray on his face. "A report from...."

"Yes. A courier just arrived from Albany with an urgent and confidential report from the commander of the Northern Department. 'He' connected with Schuyler and provided him with insights into Burgoyne's affairs and state of mind. And since he was sent to spy on Schuyler's camp, he returned with information meant to mislead Burgoyne."

"Excellent," Washington grunted.

Fitzgerald lowered his voice. "However, the world may come to regard Arthur St. Clair, he played his role to the hilt, and our man was able to convince the British to pursue him into the hinterland."

Washington pondered the situation. Although the presence of a spy in Burgoyne's midst was only the second greatest intelligence secret of the war thus far, it was the most important one at this moment. "It is remarkable. They routed his advance guard, seized all the forts along the waterway, and are poised to strike Albany. Yet they probe eastwards, dissipating their strength, which shrinks each day. It will be Burgoyne's undoing."

"But they are still an army undefeated."

Washington reined his charger at a promontory devoid of rocks or trees. The earth and log defenses at West Point lay a few hundred feet below. "This post is vulnerable yet. It is exposed to a southern approach."

"But there is a fort just south," Fitzgerald said.

"Yes, plans are already afoot to reinforce and prop up the defenses at Fort Montgomery."

Shouts echoed up the trail. A sturdy chestnut bathed in lather cantered up, and its rider, wearing the dark blue tunic and plumed brass helmet of the continental dragoons, reined up and raised a salute.

Trooper Jan Karcz's chest heaved in excitement. "Your Excellency, I have news from Major Tallmadge. General Howe's army is gone!"

"Gone? What do you mean, gone?" Fitzgerald asked.

Washington said nothing and stared intently at the river below. *Have I been humbugged?*

"Sailed away, sir. They evacuated New Jersey, and the troops soon boarded transports that crossed Sandy Hook when the tide favored them and sailed south. Major Tallmadge told me to give you this."

Karcz handed Fitzgerald a letter.

"You may join the escort," Fitzgerald said, tearing open the paper. "So, the report from Mister Smythe was true after all. I kick myself for cautioning you against its probability. I am a scoundrel – to you and my agent."

"You are no scoundrel, Robert. It was not unreasonable to think such detailed information could be disinformation picked up by Mister Smythe. Only in hindsight do we know better."

"That also means his likely aim is Philadelphia, as Mister Smythe reported. That also means Burgoyne is now on his own."

Washington let his eyes roam the defenses below. "What if they do both?"

"Sir?"

"What if Clinton marches north as well? Reinforcing Schuyler is still necessary. I'm sending two brigades under Nixon and Glover and Dan Morgan's riflemen as well as...."

"As well as what, Your Excellency?"

"Not what, Robert, whom. Benjamin Lincoln and Benedict Arnold. New Englanders both. The New England states objected to Schuyler even before allowing St. Clair to give up Ticonderoga. They shall seek his blood now. Their presence might smooth things a bit. Salve the wound, so to speak."

"I've heard rumors Gates is arguing for command."

Washington eyed him. *Was his Intelligence Advisor keeping secrets?*

"I'm sorry. Horatio Gates is writing all his friends in Congress and the legislatures of Massachusetts, New Hampshire, and Rhode Island."

"They seem to favor him because he was a regular British officer."

"They are impressed with his credentials as a retired British officer," Fitzgerald said.

"As they were with Charles Lee, yes. There was a time when I felt as well, but no more."

"Do you have instructions for the trooper to take back to Major Tallmadge?"

"Yes. He should send his men south to the mouth of the Delaware River. Just in case they try to batter their way past the forts and seize Philadelphia in a maritime *coup d' main*. He should also send men into Delaware and Virginia."

"Virginia? I don't understand."

"Quite simple, Robert. Howe might make his way up the Chesapeake, along which we have no defenses. A landing near Baltimore or further up would require a short march north. Did not Mister Smythe report Howe would take the army to Philadelphia by a long sea voyage?"

"Yes."

Washington snapped at his reins, and his horse ambled forward. "We need to learn to trust your Mister Smythe more, don't we? You and our Mister Smythe have done well."

Chapter 19

Fort Edward, July 25th, 1777

The sun had cleared the eastern horizon when they saw the curling smoke fires and the outline of the white canvas of Burgoyne's camp. As soon as they beached their canoe, Creed opened the letter hidden in the British officer's hat. He carefully unfolded the parchment. For some reason, the British had not bothered to use code. *Disinformation?*

New York City

Major General John Burgoyne
Commander of His Majesty's Northern Department

I am pleased to inform you that General Howe has taken the bulk of his Forces to sea in a strategic Envelopment of the Rebels, whom he has humbugged into attempting to block his movement north. With fair Winds and Seas, he should have the rebel Capital by September's end and, with any luck, Mister Washington as well. He encourages your efforts wholeheartedly and has given me leave to support you in any way that I can.

The Officers bearing this letter have the authority to discuss potential Strategies for linking my Forces with yours. I must warn you that I have barely 5,000 effectives, including Hessians and Loyalists, and only a small fleet at hand.

Also, a rebel Army estimated at well over 10,000 occupies the Highlands on each side of the North River. They have chained the river near Haverstraw, although we have recently breached the Barrier. My concern now centers on the Defenses around the rebel Fortifications near West Point. Should I seize them, I may be able to pursue a Course of Action to your liking.

In sum, the challenges facing my small Force are considerable. Still, at the appropriate Time, I am sure I can move north from here and distract a portion of the Rebels now blocking your way.

My sincerest Regards and best wishes for your very excellent Endeavor.

I Remain,

Your Most Humble and Obedient Servant, etc.,

H. Clinton

Major General,
Commanding
New York Garrison

He spent some time pondering the letter's meaning and what he should do about it. He had told Pierre that their opponents that night were bluecoat spies, not British. Pierre spoke little English and read none, so in Creed's mind, the deception was complete.

They found the camp unwinding after a long day's march. Weary soldiers packed rations into kit bags and rolled up greatcoats under the impatient glare of sergeants who quickly barked out orders.

Tea and coffee were on the brew, and breakfast smells aroused Creed's senses.

"Go find Bart and the Royal Americans. I must report to General Burgoyne," Creed whispered.

Pierre nodded and slipped away. Creed worked his way through the maze of tents, searching for Burgoyne's headquarters. Intent on his meeting, he failed to notice that eyes watched him from a distance.

Creed paused by a squad of regulars busy brewing tea and re-heating porridge.

"Right crazy 'tis, expectin' a man to fight for the king on an empty belly," a private was complaining.

"Shut yer gob, Stone. You've done nothing but bellyache since we arrived here. You took George's schilling. Be a man about it," a stern-looking corporal with straw-colored hair replied.

"Can I trouble ye lads for a half mug of tea?" Creed asked.

"You look like one of them Frenchies. But you ain't no Frenchie, are ya?" Stone asked.

"Leave 'im be, Stone. You tell by his speech that he's one of us. Give him a cup."

"As you say, corporal," replied Stone. "Suppose I should give him some porridge too."

"No, he looks like he's on business, and we don't want him spending half the day in the bushes yonder!"

The men of the mess laughed.

Creed's fingers eagerly took the cup in his hands. It smelled tepid. "Much obliged, lads. A long night on watch, you know. Just some of the lovely-smelling tea, and I'll be on my way."

The mess broke into a babble of argument over the state of the invasion. Creed discreetly tossed the letter into the dwindling mess fire as they did. The stiff paper crackled and darkened as the flames engulfed it, swiftly turning the charred remains into a ball that slowly spiraled upward and dissolved in the light morning breeze.

***

An hour later, Creed was sitting across from Burgoyne. Unimpressed with the collection of motley huts available, he had his luxurious tent and pavilion raised in the small parade field inside the log and earthen fort. Burgoyne was about to have his breakfast when an orderly announced the arrival of Captain Lawrence.

"Your timing is perfect, James. Help yourself to some bacon and toast. The tea is ready, too."

"Thank you, sir. But I hoped to render my report."

"In good time. Please join us."

Burgoyne's tone seemed different to Creed.

An orderly thrust a cup into his hands, and Sinclair poured some tea. The aroma of the bacon overwhelmed him, and he forked a half dozen dripping slices onto a fine China plate. Creed handed Sinclair a letter.

"What is this?" Sinclair asked.

Creed wiped some bacon grease from his mouth and smiled. "I intercepted a rebel longboat on the river just north of Albany. Its bearers could not swim, so I relieved them of their correspondence with the promise to see it duly delivered. But since I've no idea where this General Stark is, I naturally brought it for your perusal."

Burgoyne lowered his cup. "Excellent! What does the letter say, Lazarus?"

"I'll read it to you, sir." Sinclair scanned the letter Creed had composed, and Schuyler wrote during their secret meeting in Albany.

Albany, New York

Brg. Gen. John Stark,

I am pleased to inform you that I have mustered sufficient Troops of various types for a defense north of Albany.

Our Works are impressive, and I have confidence an Enemy thrust will be easily repulsed. However, I regret that I do not have the luxury of concurrently reinforcing your Position in the Grants. I realize this leaves you little with which to defend our Stores at Bennington and our line of supply to New England, a vital and necessary component of our position in the North.

Defense of the Hampshire Grants must be left to your discretion. However, I suggest you conduct a withdrawal deep into New Hampshire if the Enemy presses you firmly.

I Remain,

P. Schuyler
Commanding General,
Northern Dept.

Burgoyne flushed with excitement. "Do you realize what this means, Lazarus?"

"Of course, I do, sir. It means that...." Sinclair turned to Creed suddenly. "Just how did you come into possession of this bit of correspondence, James?"

"I told you, sir. Fortune brought me into contact with a rebel courier boat. They put up a fight, but Pierre and I dispatched the wretches. One tried to swim off with the letter, but we fished him out of the water, retrieved his envelope, and then sent him floating."

Sinclair looked at Creed skeptically. "Quite fortuitous, it would seem, Captain Lawrence."

Burgoyne gulped his tea and slapped the cup back into its saucer. "Enough of this, Lazarus."

He took Creed's hand. "Excellent work, young man."

Burgoyne turned his gaze on Sinclair. "Simon Fraser is pushing south on the west bank of the river. But I want this Bennington scouted. James will do it." He scribbled out a short note and handed it to Creed. "These are your instructions. Be back in five days with a report."

"But my company is to move across the river with General Fraser, sir. I have been away for some time now. I really should stay with them. They need me."

"You will go where most needed, James. You may join them after we finish our work on this side of the river."

"Very well, sir." Creed saluted and left. Despite his protestation, he realized scouting Bennington was a stroke of luck. So he did not want to appear too eager. Sinclair seemed suspicious, though.

***

"Lazarus, have Baron von Riedesel come see me. I think it is time our good German friends earned their pay, don't you?"

"Sir, I am not convinced we can trust this information. Acting on it could jeopardize all my plans, the campaign," Sinclair replied. He was more suspicious of Captain James Lawrence.

"Unless you can provide some proof of perfidy, I see no reason to dismiss Captain Lawrence's information."

"I am still investigating the matter." Sinclair silently cursed. *Where the deuce is Binoche?*

Burgoyne walked to the map. "We shall thrust the rebels in Bennington and wait for word from Howe. Our regulars are busy clearing a road to move supplies and guns from the north. So, I'll use our German troops and save our lads for the final move on Albany."

Seeing a growing threat to his plan, Sinclair began to shake. "Sir, damn Barry and damn General Howe!"

The general reddened, and his brow furrowed. "What do you mean by such blunt talk?"

"Let's move on the rebels now. I have it all planned. Speed trumps caution. Schuyler has fallen back on his final line of defense. We have them on the run, and our Indian allies have scattered the militias off to aid their families."

Burgoyne shook his head. "You read the letter. He is quite fortified. No, we'll secure our flank and seize their stores for ourselves. By then, General Howe and Barry will be closing in."

"I suggest then, sir, that we keep our objective secret. I'll let it out that we are preparing to move to Manchester. Even if Lawrence proves to be loyal, we might have others who are not."

***

Bart stepped from his tent and slung his musket over his shoulder. It occurred to him that he marched off to war a cynical boy but was now an even more cynical man. He had his orders and needed to accomplish them to have his heart's desire.

Bart stood before Creed's tent. He could hear the muffled sounds of Creed talking to someone. He took a breath and flipped open the tent flap.

Creed took what looked like a map and folded it up. "Bart, what brings you here? Where's the company? You are the acting commander."

"I received orders to put Sergeant O'Ballance in charge and join you, sir."

Creed's brow furrowed. "Orders? From Alexander? General Fraser?"

"No, sir. From General Burgoyne's headquarters. Was only told I'm to accompany you on a special mission."

"Well, we could use the help carrying the canoe. We must march through some rugged country before reaching the Hoosick River."

Bart was surprised at how easily he could lie to his commander. He had come to like and respect him. Yet the thought of Fleurette drove all his reasoning. He was utterly committed to her.

When he and Binoche had finally reported to Sinclair, the colonel flew into a rage. They had confirmed the essentials of Captain Lawrence's story. They had watched him the whole way but from a distance. They saw him enter Albany and sat from a distance when he and Pierre skirmished with rebel Indians. And later, their canoe lingered in the shadows a quarter-mile off when he captured the rebel boat.

Angered at the report, Sinclair insisted he hurry and join his captain on the scout mission. He did not tell him that Binoche and a band of Mohawk would trail them.

***

They stole from camp in the inky pre-dawn. Creed and Bart shouldered the canoe while Pierre cleared the trail.

Expecting wilderness, the number of neat cottages and cabins surprised them. But the homes were abandoned, with many just blackened shells. The Grants had descended into a no man's land of rapine and murder.

They arrived at the dark waters of the Hoosick River as the sun ebbed in the west. Creed knew they had barely begun. It was time to paddle. At the junction of the Walloomsac River, their canoe slid onto the muddy shoreline. They pulled the canoe into a thick stand of bushes.

"Take your things, lad. We'll not return this way," Creed said.

"Why not, sir?" Bart asked.

"We know this approach, Bart. We'll scout a second on our return trip." Creed did not tell him that Pierre sensed strange eyes following them.

They trudged quickly along the Walloomsac, its course winding eastwards towards Bennington. They fought through thick woods with heavy underbrush that snapped with every tread.

On their left, a narrow road worked its way east across neatly plowed fields that curled over rolling hills until the ground gradually rose to a line of small hillocks rising towards the Green Mountains to the north.

As the morning wore on, the air turned heavy and breathing became difficult. The sky roared with a thunderclap stronger than a barrage of 100 cannons. Winds whipped and bent the trees. The patter of rain quickly turned into a downpour. They wrapped their weapons in oilcloth and sought shelter under a small cluster of pines near the river.

Creed pulled a piece of jerky from his haversack and passed it around. "I'd say we are close. Another mile or two, and I'll push off on my own."

"I'll come with you, sir," Bart said.

His comment surprised Creed. "You'll both stay here. Some work I do best on my own."

"But how will I ever learn to run a proper scout if I stay here?" Bart asked.

Creed spat out a piece of his jerky. "You need to learn to follow orders before you learn how to run a scout, Bart. Your eagerness is commendable. But one man can hide better than two or three. If I get into trouble, I'll fire a shot. You both head back and report to Burgoyne."

Creed opened his map and traced their approach with his finger. "They can follow our route or traverse overland, but this is a good approach to Bennington. I want to get closer and see what they have defending the place."

Bart glanced into the woods across the meadow. "Very well, sir," Bart said with obvious disappointment.

Pierre also scanned the woods. "We are under strange eyes, *monsieur*," he said in French.

"*Combien?*"

"More than three," Pierre replied.

"Prepare yourself, Pierre."

"And you, *monsieur*. Go with God."

Bart said nothing.

Creed noticed them shortly after pushing his way through the wet underbrush along the river. He moved into the thicker growth, where the small saplings and bushes, heavy with rain, guarded the bank of the Walloomsac.

He had intended to wade across before they caught him, to wait in ambush. But a *pop* and low *whoosh* broke the stillness.

Creed bent low, and his legs began to pump like pistons, turning sharply away from the river. He struggled around rocks and heavy growth, made more difficult by the steep rise away from the river.

He heard a soft *pop*, followed by a second, then the *thump* of musket balls slapping the soggy riverbank.

Two braves, imposing dark figures with shaved heads, and a single braid appeared. They came charging downhill through the undergrowth with long war axes and tomahawks raised high in one hand and muskets in the other. A series of blood-curdling yelps erupted from mouths contorted in a fury.

Creed dropped to his knee and leveled his musket, sending the three-quarter-inch ball slamming into the belly of the lead warrior. The brave stiffened at the impact and collapsed in front of Creed.

The second warrior brought his war ax down, but Creed rolled right. The ax's warhead sank harmlessly into the rain-soaked ground. The warrior dropped his musket and raised the ax with both hands, screaming in his tongue as he waved it in circles over his head.

Creed began dropping powder, ball, and paper into his barrel. He rammed home the charge and primed the pan. *Would it spark in the rain?* He saw the ax-head plummet. There was no time to fire – he threw his shoulder into the warrior's midriff, driving him back.

The brave's legs buckled, but he quickly regained his balance. His face took on a demonic look, and with eyes blazing, he doubled up his grip on the long ax handle.

Before he could wield his blade, Creed plunged his long hunting knife into the warrior's chest. The brave's strong hands gripped Creed's throat and squeezed like an iron vice. Frantic for air and his eyes bulging, Creed desperately twisted his blade. He yanked it out with a sucking sound. A plume of blood and vitals began spilling down the brave's belly. The warrior went limp, and Creed pushed his heavy, lifeless form into the deep grass.

Creed's legs wobbled as he stood gulping for air. A pair of musket balls *smacked* the wet leaves around him. A third warrior bolted from the thick bushes with a hulking, dark figure behind him – Serge Binoche.

"*Attendez*! This time, your scalp is mine, *Monsieur* Lawrence. Soon it will adorn Fleurette's tent," Binoche boasted.

Creed swung his musket to his hip and squeezed the trigger. The heavy lead ball exploded the brave's head like a melon. But another half dozen Iroquois broke from the woods howling like hungry wolves. Arms of sinew wrapped around Creed like coiling snakes, and they trussed him to a tree.

Binoche barked in their tongue. With *whoop-whoops* and bizarre gestures, they soon had a stack of wood for a fire.

"When Burgoyne learns of this, he'll have you hanged, Binoche. I'm on a mission by his order." Desperate, Creed scanned the woods and brush for signs of Pierre and Bart.

"And I am under the personal orders of Colonel Sinclair. Orders to watch you and find signs of your betrayal. Well, I have enough signs. But do not worry. I will not leave you for the *Anglais* rope. You will watch your flesh burn, and I will take your scalp when you beg for mercy. Only then will I douse the flames and leave you for the wolves."

Creed's eyes strained for a sign of his companions. "I'm not alone, Binoche. My men will be here shortly, and they will...."

"You are very much alone, *Monsieur* Lawrence. Maybe you should have accepted the eager embraces of Fleurette? Maybe you should not have stopped us at the white village."

The leafy bushes parted with a dull cracking, and Bart strode into the clearing.

"Bart!" Creed's eyes shifted as he looked for signs of Pierre. He saw none. "Where is Pierre?"

Bart did not make eye contact. Instead, he turned to Binoche and thrust a finger in his chest.

"I did not agree to this bestiality, Serge. You were to find him when he approached the rebels. How else could we prove his treachery?"

Creed's stomach sank. He cursed his stupidity. Bart's insistence on coming was not a youthful quest for adventure. He had been seduced by Fleurette to get revenge and to frame him as a rebel spy. The irony caused Creed to smile wryly. *We're both playing the double-cross game.*

Binoche kicked Creed in the side, making a hollow thud. "You find this funny, *monsieur*?"

Creed gritted his teeth and raised his chin. The Iroquois had piled brush and pieces of wood, but the storm had soaked everything, and none of the kindling would spark.

"Pierre is on his way back even as we speak to tell Burgoyne of your perfidy," Creed spat.

"No, he is not, sir. I took care of him myself when the first shot was fired." Bart looked shame-faced as he admitted to the act.

"You killed Pierre in a fight? Not possible, Bart."

"Not a fight. A simple stone to the back of the skull. He is done. Binoche and I are now the only witnesses to your treason. Don't worry, sir. I'll take good care of the Royal Americans and Fleurette."

Creed stared at his young protégé. Bart quickly looked away.

Creed realized Bart had thrown in with Binoche for possession of a woman he could never possess. She was as wild an animal of the forest. Creed almost felt sorry for him. He was out of his league.

"Bart, listen to me, lad. You're just a colonial. They'll never give you command of the Royal Americans. Some fop of a British Lord's son will take command. As for Fleurette – why she'll drop you when the next prospect comes along, or Binoche calls her back to his tent."

Bart looked at Binoche, who shrugged his shoulders. "Don't believe a dead man's desperate lies. Fleurette loves only you, eh?"

Bart turned to Creed. "That's right, Captain Lawrence. She does. As for the Americans, they'll only follow me now. Colonel Sinclair promised. But only if we could prove your treachery. He wanted proof. Now we have it. You wanted to sneak into the rebel camp alone. You, sir, are a traitor."

Creed gritted his teeth. Although they had no proof, it was true. He realized then it might be his end after all. He began to pray, "Hail Mary, full of grace...."

"*Merde!* Can't you devils make a fire?" Binoche kicked one of the warriors and snatched his powder horn from his belt. He carefully poured a pile and struck his flint.

"The Lord is with Thee...."

The powder sputtered and smoked, and slowly some of the kindling began to smoke, spark, and finally flame. But it would take some time before the fire grew strong enough to roast flesh. Some of the warriors began to cut nicks in Creed's skin and prick his flesh with the points of their knives.

"Enough of that, you dogs!" Binoche laughed. "Leave some of his meat for the fire."

"And blessed is the...."

The rattle of musket shots ended his prayer. Two of the Iroquois tumbled to the ground, groaning with fist-sized holes spewing blood from their bellies.

Shouts echoed dimly through the wet forest – American infantry. A swarm of musket balls crisscrossed the glade, *buzzing* menacingly like a swarm of angry hornets. More braves fell to their sting.

"*Merde!*" Binoche grabbed Creed by the neck. "I will not let you escape once more. I will have you this time!" He pulled his knife and raised it high. "Die quickly then, you dog Lawrence, but die!"

The dagger swept down in a long arc. But before it could slice Creed open, Bart jumped in the way. The strong arm of Binoche would not be denied a victim. The dagger

plunged into Bart's shoulder with a sickening crunch. Then two musket balls thumped into Bart's exposed side, and he slumped into the sputtering flames of the kindling.

Someone cut Creed's bonds. American militiamen now filled the clearing with cries of vengeance against the hated Iroquois. But the wily Binoche slipped through them with his few surviving braves.

***

Brigadier General John Stark sat on his colossal chestnut stallion, carefully surveying the shallow trenches and low earthen walls protecting Bennington. A runner grabbed at his stirrups, heaving and panting from a two-mile run in the summer heat.

"Sir, Captain Rife's company just chased off a band of Iroquois and a Canadian. They killed a Loyalist officer and captured another. The Indians were going to roast and scalp."

Stark tugged at his pipe. "Jim Rife's a good man. Now, just who is this man they were scalping?"

"Claims to be a Captain Lawrence, but that's all he'll say. Says he wants to talk to you, sir."

"Well, that's a strange coincidence, isn't it then? I want to talk to him too. Have him at my headquarters in an hour. I have one more position to inspect."

Stark didn't wait for a reply. He waved his pipe and spurred his horse up the road in a cloud of dust.

***

Stark sat on a hickory chair with his bare feet soaking in a tub of salted water. Creed found the sight somehow comical. But he could see the colonel was not amused.

"You are a hard man to figure, Captain Lawrence," Stark said. "Sent to warn of a British attack, but you can't, or more accurately, you won't tell us who sent you."

"'Tis hard to imagine, I know. But you can send word to General Schuyler if you want to verify my story."

"Don't need to. He sent me this. Read it."

Stark handed Creed a note. Creed's eyes raced over the words. It explained that he had an agent from "headquarters" trying to convince the British to slow their movement south by convincing them to detour to Bennington.

Creed looked up. "I hadn't intended to be Burgoyne's scout for this mission. That was purely a stroke of luck. Or misfortune. I believe his adjutant is suspicious of me. Suspicions fueled by a jealous young subaltern, a treacherous Canadian trapper, and his daughter."

Stark gazed at the trees that darkened the ridge to the west. "I find this yarn somewhat implausible."

He faced Creed. "So much so, I believe it. Question is – now what do I do?"

"Do, sir? I suggest you begin to prepare for the onslaught. Send out extra scouts. Patrol all the approaches."

Stark pursed his lips. "I know all that, Captain Lawrence. I meant, what should I do about you?"

Creed nodded as if they were talking to a stranger. "Truth be told, sir, I would keep Captain Lawrence here to help defend the town. Facing a foe in the open is more desirable than skulking between armies."

"I never thought of that. I suppose the likelihood of a lead ball in the chest more pleasurable than sneaking among the enemy as one of their own?"

"Indeed 'tis. For one thing, when you are skulking about, as you put it, everyone is the enemy. There is no peace. Certainly, no peace of mind. It tries the sanity, by God."

"I'll ask you not to swear, Captain."

"Sorry, sir."

"You were saying?" Stark absentmindedly tapped his pipe on his boot.

"The notes and instructions, the maps, all need be secreted under the eyes of the enemy. And spending weeks in the enemy's bosom is no pleasant thing. 'Tis like sleeping in a pit of vipers."

Stark nodded and pulled at his pipe. "I would think you are fairly comfortable with all this."

Creed shook his head. "Comfort is to be avoided. It is a precursor to complacency, and complacency usually leads to disaster. No, sir, being on edge is the only way to survive while in the enemy's embrace. My only consolations are the cause I serve, prayer, and the thought of a loved one."

"True enough. My family, my Creator, and our glorious cause have carried me through this war's many discomforts and dangers."

"Indeed, sir."

"Now, should I keep you here, send you back to that Dutchman Schuyler and safety, or the Englishman Burgoyne and near-certain death?"

"First, I'd like to bury poor Pierre and then return to finish my work. I only ask that you make them dearly pay when they arrive here."

Stark slid a pewter flask from his saddlebag. He pulled the stopper and took a swig. "Take some. It'll ease your pain."

Creed gulped the harsh liquor and returned the flask. "But not my loss."

"I am afraid my men found no sign of your savage friend except a stone soaked in blood."

"Then he may yet be alive?" Creed felt a surge of desperate optimism.

"No. According to Jim Rife, there was a great effusion of blood. Likely, the savages took his body for trophies. You know – scalp, fingers, maybe an ear. These devils take the knife to everything that walks, man, woman, or child. Now the dead." Stark puffed on his pipe. "You heard about poor Jane McCrea?"

Creed shook his head.

"Let's just say a few more killings as they did to her, and every man this side of Boston will muster with musket and ax. The boys are spoiling for revenge, not just on the savages but also their English masters."

Stark's voice deepened, and he darkened as he talked of the young woman brutalized by some of Burgoyne's renegade Iroquois allies.

Creed placed a balled fist to his chin. "Then I must go back and finish this work. I owe Pierre and the others that much."

Stark grabbed Creed's upper arm. "You're a good man – whoever you are. When the enemy finally comes, I'll personally shoot one of the bastards for your friend, Pierre."

"Aim well, and make sure it's a kill shot."

***

Creed saw no sign of Binoche or his warriors on his return to Fort Edward. Once at Burgoyne's headquarters, an aide de camp wasted no time bringing him before the general. Burgoyne was awash in correspondence, but waved away his secretary when he saw Creed standing at the door.

"Ah, Captain Lawrence, James. I had not expected your return so soon. Did you reach Bennington?"

Creed nodded. "Indeed, sir, but at no small cost. My guide and scout, Pierre, was killed. So was Ensign Saunders. And that Canadian swine Serge Binoche and his renegades fled. I was almost captured and just barely escaped."

"By God, sir. What happened? Wait. What were Saunders and Binoche doing there?" Burgoyne looked at the aide. "Send for Colonel Sinclair and bring us some Madeira."

A few minutes later, Sinclair strutted into the room. Burgoyne himself poured the Madeira.

"Lazarus, I want you to hear this yourself. Captain Lawrence, James, was just about to relate the horrors of his patrol."

S.W. O'Connell

Burgoyne cast an inquisitive eye at Sinclair. The two looked like schoolboys caught in the middle of a prank. "I was unaware you had dispatched an officer and Binoche to assist him. Go on, James."

Creed was spinning his version of the events. It was lie versus lie, with neither side admitting to deceit.

"Rebel militia ambushed us. That simple, sir."

"Just how many rebels ambushed you?" Sinclair asked.

"Not many, sir, but they had the advantage of surprise. Binoche's savages were not as alert as one expects from their kind."

Burgoyne nodded intently while Sinclair's lips tightened.

"But, in the end, it was my fault. I was in command. I should have regarded the flanks. About six of the natives went down under the first volley. The air was heavy with musket balls. I saw Pierre go down early – never found his body. I should have gone down or been taken prisoner but hid inside a hollow tree trunk. I lay there for what seemed like an hour while the rebels walked around me searching for loot from the dead."

Burgoyne nodded knowingly. "In the end, they are little different from the savages they revile."

"Indeed, sir," Creed replied. "But we have one stroke of luck from this affair."

"Luck?" Sinclair asked, barely concealing his anger. "What kind of luck?"

"Irish luck, I suppose."

"If you intend on trying my patience, Captain Lawrence, I must say you are succeeding," Sinclair snapped.

"Let James continue, Lazarus," Burgoyne sniffed.

Creed could tell the general enjoyed seeing his stuffy adjutant frustrated. Creed took a sip of the Madeira. "I hid in the log with the heat and moist air suffocating me. My body ached, and I fought the urge to wipe the sweat from my eyes and nose.

"A rebel officer sat on the same log in which I hid. He pulled out a water bottle and gulped furiously to slake his thirst. I cursed for the chance to jump him merely to drink his water. Then it happened."

Creed took another sip of the Madeira. It tasted less sour than before.

"Go on," Sinclair said icily.

"A runner came up. I heard him hand the officer a note saying he had new orders from the commander. After a pause, I heard the officer say, 'My God, Stark is leaving just our lone militia company to defend this place. He is taking all the other companies to join Schuyler near Stillwater."

Burgoyne leaned back and crossed a knee over the other. "Excellent. Go on."

"The runner, I believe him to be a subaltern, began to curse, but the officer cut him off. He proclaimed that no lobster would take Bennington so long as he and his hundred New Hampshire men stood watch before it. He said that after the way they had licked the Indians, the English would not dare to march on Bennington."

Burgoyne nodded, and a smile crossed his face. "Strangely, the rebel was right. He'll face no lobsters at all. I am sending some of von Riedesel's Germans to seize the place."

The news startled Creed, although his face did not show it.

"The Germans?" Creed asked.

Burgoyne smiled. "Why yes. They're stout fellows. Need some action, though, and I'll save our lads for the march into Albany."

"Yes, the Germans are very disciplined. When I mustered the Royal Americans in New York, I considered hiring a few of them to drill the men."

Just then, Simon Fraser stepped through the doorway. Burgoyne motioned towards the bottle. "Help yourself, Simon. Captain Lawrence, I'm sorry, James has been regaling us with the results of the Bennington patrol."

Fraser took a seat and poured himself a glass of the ruby liquid. "Excellent. I'm anxious to hear of it."

Sinclair grew impatient. "You have yet to tell us how you made your most fortuitous escape, Captain Lawrence."

Creed nodded. "Well, that was the simple bit of it. The rebels soon gave up their search and left. I waited a while to make sure no sentries lingered. I quietly stole my way down towards the water to look for Pierre. I soon realized he was gone."

"Gone? What do you mean, gone? No trace of his body? What about the other natives?" Sinclair's voice grew agitated.

"Oh, there were signs of a struggle."

"What signs?" Sinclair demanded.

"A blooded stone about the size of a small pumpkin. Torn bushes and footprints."

"What happened?" Fraser asked.

"Can't be sure. I suppose the rebels took off with his body."

"Likely, he was still alive, and a cowardly rebel brained him," Burgoyne opined.

Creed knew a lie could often be wrapped in the truth.

Fraser's large hand gripped Creed's. "It is never easy to lose men in combat, even savages."

Creed nodded. "Especially when one of them is a valiant comrade."

"It is heartening to see that there are some native allies who are willing to die in open combat," Burgoyne said.

Fraser scowled. "Unfortunately, sir. Not enough of them. The depredations of our native allies touch the Loyalist and the rebel."

"I heard the rebel commander say as much. Many once uncertain in sympathy have begun rallying to the rebel ranks." Creed could not reveal that he had heard it from Stark.

Fraser rose and began pacing. "Bloody problem for us. With the savages, we swell the enemy ranks out of fear and loathing. Without them, we have only Alexander's company to scout a thousand square miles of wilderness."

Burgoyne placed his chin on his fingers pensively. "Lazarus, we must summon the native chiefs to a meeting. I'll explain all this and see that they focus on the army's needs, not their own."

"I am skeptical of them myself," Sinclair said. "But if we stick to my plan, we'll have less need of their skills. We still have time to shift to the water route, sir. It will ease our logistical burden and save our men the bestial duty of cutting a turnpike through the primeval forest."

"Nonsense, I shall bring the natives to heel. We are well on our way, and I want to intimidate New England with our presence. Now, James, please continue."

"Not much else to say, sir. I beat a hasty retreat, following the river until it intersected a wide deer trail that took me northwest over the mountains."

Sinclair's eyes narrowed. "What of your subaltern, Ensign Saunders? You said he took a ball. Was he captured?"

Creed's visage darkened at the mention of Bart. "As I said, sir, he fell in the first hail of bullets, or not long after. I saw no further sign of him, but I assume the poor lad lies with the others in a shallow grave near Bennington."

Chapter 20

Chester, Pennsylvania, August 1st, 1777

Washington stretched in the saddle, straining to maintain his bearing despite a fatigue from only three hours of sleep in as many days. He watched company after company tramp south, often nodding at the scarecrow-like figures marching desperately to reach Philadelphia before the British.

"On your way, men. We'll beat Billy Howe with our feet and muskets, just as we did at Trenton. Just as we did at Princeton."

Next to him, Robert Fitzgerald sat less comfortably. The gangly officer often felt the worst part of his duties involved keeping up with the experienced Virginia hunter he served.

"Have we heard from Mister Tallmadge yet?" Washington asked.

Fitzgerald fought the urge to cough. The pounding of feet on smooth, dry roads sent a plume of dust lingering like a brown rain cloud. "Yes. Benjamin was not happy with the order but conceded your point."

"Very nice of him," Washington remarked wryly.

"Benjamin is a fine officer but very protective of his new command."

"As he should be, Robert. But a decisive Burgoyne with seven thousand effectives may pose a greater risk than a ponderous Howe with thrice that number."

"You'll need all you can muster to protect Philadelphia, Your Excellency." Fitzgerald smacked at a horsefly that settled on his nose. He noted that the various vermin of the air rarely seemed to affect the commander-in-chief, and when they did, his response was understated and barely noticeable.

"We could certainly use Dan Morgan and his riflemen. But something tells me Gates will need them more."

Fitzgerald looked aghast. "Horatio Gates?"

Washington nodded, his lower lip trembling just slightly. Fitzgerald could not tell whether to hide his displeasure or steady his teeth.

"The orders should be with Schuyler soon enough. Poor Schuyler. I did what I could to save his command. But as you well know, Gates has powerful supporters in Congress. And, of course, Arthur St. Clair will have to go too."

Fitzgerald nodded. "That, I expected, Your Excellency. Yet, his abandonment of Ticonderoga kept an army between Burgoyne and Albany. Surely the Congress realizes that?"

Washington smiled grimly. "In war, the appearance of victory or defeat can be as compelling as the reality."

Fitzgerald knew Washington's earlier modest successes against the Hessians, and the British kept the rebellion from collapsing.

"Any word from our agent, Captain Lawrence?" Washington asked slyly.

"No, Your Excellency. Nor do I expect word. I hope he has contacted Schuyler, but I made it clear in his secret instructions that he should remain evasive. The north is full of Loyalists, and the opportunities for treachery are not to be underestimated."

"Well, that's why his 'chessmen,' his White Knights, are going north with Morgan."

"North with Morgan?"

Washington raised his hat to a New Jersey Continental Line company stomping by. "Godspeed, boys!"

"God bless you, Your Excellency!" the captain leading them replied.

"Huzzah! Huzzah for General Washington," resounded a chorus of shouts up and down the column. Their uniforms were ragged and covered in dust from a long summer road march, but the men seemed in good spirits. The high-pitched notes of fifes and the rattle of drums played faintly in the distance.

"Major Tallmadge has a fine troop of men. But I thought the White Knights would help Colonel Morgan in scouting. However, you need to draft special instructions for Dan. He needs to use them to make contact with our Captain Lawrence."

Fitzgerald wiped the sweat from his brow. "I believe his efforts will yet have the strategic impact on the originally envisioned campaign."

"Let's hope he has already, Robert. Let's also hope we have the opportunity to avail ourselves of his talents in the future. You know what to write." Washington reined his horse about and put spurs to its flanks. The charger bolted up the dusty road to Philadelphia like a gunshot.

***

The charger snorted as it sped up Chestnut Street, past the red brick building where the Continental Congress had unanimously proclaimed Washington commander-in-chief two years earlier.

Just behind rode the commander-in-chief's aides-de-camp, Tench Tillman and Alexander Hamilton. Six strong Virginians of his Life Guard cantered alongside. While struggling in their dust, Fitzgerald did all he could to stay in the saddle.

At the end of a narrow lane, the horses eased to a walk in a small paddock behind a large private residence. A squad of groomsmen led by a handsome black man in a trim uniform rushed out of the stable and seized the horses by the reins.

"Take good care of him. He has borne a heavy burden very well," Washington said.

Washington clambered up the steps. A sentry snapped to attention, and an orderly held open the heavy oak door. His manservant, Billie, had already spread a modest late breakfast of bread and cheese, coffee, and rum punch on the buffet along the wall. A stack of papers awaited him on his desk.

He thumbed through the dispatches from his field commanders: Generals Sullivan, Heath, and others. Beneath them were letters from state governors and members of Congress. Washington pushed the stacks aside. His interest shifted to the Blue Notes, secret and urgent correspondence used by Washington, Fitzgerald, and Tallmadge.

He tore open a thin blue envelope and spread the paper before him. He read it twice. A *rap, rap* at the door broke his thought.

An orderly's head appeared. "Colonel Fitzgerald, sir."

The lanky Fitzgerald wobbled past the orderly. "Any news, Your Excellency?"

Washington held up the note. "Help yourself to the bread and coffee, Robert. But before you do, read this."

Fitzgerald lingered on the letter, an urgent Blue Note, his eyes drinking in every turn of phrase and nuance. He then folded it and placed it in a mahogany box on Washington's desk.

"It seems Benjamin has been busier than we," Washington said.

Fitzgerald slurped down some of the black liquid. "But this is good news, Your Excellency. And timely. With Harry and the White Knights riding northward, I feared Mister Tallmadge would have trouble keeping an eye on things. But it seems nothing could be further from the truth. And now, Mister Jons has returned from Canada. We can again receive regular correspondence from Mister Smythe. With regular couriers, we'll better know what is going on in New York than Howe will."

"Better?" Washington eyed him skeptically as he nibbled on a thick slice of brown bread.

"Well, timelier. And that might make it better."

"Indeed. Intelligence should be like this bread – oven-fresh, not stale. But the main point is that Mister Jons confirms Captain Lawrence arrived in Quebec with his Royal Americans. Truth be told, Robert, I thought perhaps we were wasting our best man needlessly."

"Ah, young Jeremiah Creed, Captain James Lawrence, has never failed you. We must trust in him, Your Excellency."

"I trust in divine Providence, Robert. In others, I have only hope. But you are right. His abilities do impress. I hope he connected with your papist friend in Quebec and provided Philip with vital intelligence on Burgoyne."

Washington walked to the open window. Below, Billie was patiently watering down his charger.

"Make sure the water is not too cool, Billie. I don't need another horse succumbing to the fevers."

"But that was not his main objective, Your Excellency," Fitzgerald said.

Washington turned back to Fitzgerald. "I know. But I sometimes wish he would be frustrated in his main task and flee south with what intelligence he gleaned. Attempting to play such a dangerous game to lure the enemy into a trap is perhaps a task no man should be asked to attempt."

Fitzgerald poured them each a generous finger of rum. "I believe the latest note from Mister Smythe was most critical intelligence."

Washington lifted his glass. "But we do not need Mister Smythe, our patriot, to risk all in such gambits."

"That's why the return of Mister Jons, our Dutch friend, is a most welcome development."

"If Mister Tallmadge can keep up contact, we should have more frequent reports. With Howe now headed south, the intentions of General Clinton become our next problem."

"Will Clinton move north to assist Burgoyne or south to assist Howe?" Fitzgerald asked rhetorically.

"Major Tallmadge must ensure our agent in New York understands our need for such intelligence. The success or failure in two theaters may hinge upon it."

***

The Dunning House, New York, August 3rd, 1777

When Klara greeted her visitor, she threw her arms around the tall, elegant woman. "Emily! I dropped my knitting and rushed to the door when I heard it was you. You have been sorely missed. And not just by me. I can't believe you coaxed your way to Brunswick. I should have liked to have gone along. I'm from New Jersey myself, as you know."

Their lips brushed, and they strolled arm in arm to the sofa.

"Where is Lady Dunning? I came to pay my father's respects. Oh, Klara, it was worth the risks I took to see him again. Even if only for a few hours."

"Lady Dunning is out riding. No tea this afternoon. So many of her usual guests have gone off with General Howe," Klara whispered.

"How many?" Emily felt guilty probing the poor girl for information, but knew that, as Sandy Drummond's ward, Klara fell beyond any suspicion. Although Drummond's position was deliberately ambiguous, she had learned through several officer contacts that the cavalry major performed special duties of a security nature for the British high command.

"You mean, how many have not gone off, don't you, dear? The garrison regiment is here, plus a few Loyalist units and some Germans."

Emily purred. "Hmmm…this means we might have to take in boarders from the ranks."

"Not really. I heard Major Drummond tell Lady Dunning that Clinton had enough soldiers to assist General Burgoyne's drive, should he be so inclined."

"Does Major Drummond believe the General is so inclined?"

"I think he is as of yet unsure. Major Drummond says General Clinton will do what suits his interests first, the army second, and his rival generals, a distant third."

Emily knew Klara was of mixed loyalty. Taken initially as insurance for her father's cooperation, Klara had become loyal to Sandy Drummond and, thus, his cause. However, she saw no problem in revealing some of the secret utterances one had picked up while living with the British spymaster in North America to her new friend. And Emily found it quite helpful.

"And what are General Clinton's interests?" Emily asked innocently.

"I don't know. Perhaps Sidney will…." Klara cut short her answer.

Emily probed her friend. "Who is Sidney? I thought I knew all the prominent British officers. Is he new to the army?"

"I shouldn't say. Major Drummond would get cross if he knew I still see him. He doesn't want me to see Sidney. He hopes to present me to a suitor of his own choice."

Emily felt she had struck at something that might prove helpful. "What regiment is your Sidney with?"

"He's not really with a regiment. Not an English regiment, at least."

"What do you mean?" Emily probed her friend gently.

"He is a New Jersey Loyalist. Like me. They call them a provincial regiment, whatever that means." Klara smiled briefly.

"Of course, dear." Emily's look softened, and she gripped her hand softly.

Klara lifted her chin. "He's a captain of the New Jersey Volunteers. A courageous and wonderful man. Major Drummond has sent him on several secret missions."

Emily chuckled. "If you know them, they could not be so secret, dear."

Klara blushed. "Maybe I've spoken too much, Emily. I could get us all into trouble."

"Nonsense, dear. How long have you known this, Sidney?"

"Baker. Sidney Baker. Not so long, as a friend. But he has been with Major Drummond since they were in Jersey. I would see him come and go from time to time. That's all until...." Klara's cheeks flushed red.

"That's alright, dear. Some moments you must hold close to your heart. Will I get to see this handsome captain?"

Klara's face brightened. "How did you know he was handsome?"

Emily's eyes softened. "Aren't all soldiers handsome?"

They both giggled as if they had just shared some profound secret. The drawing-room door opened, and a servant entered.

"Stephen, can you see if the cook can brew some tea for Miss Stanley? She awaits Lady Dunning's return, and some refreshment will make the time pass more quickly," Klara said.

"Ooh, it may be some time before Lady Dunning arrives, Miss. Can Miss Stanley spend the whole evening here?"

"What do you mean?" Klara asked.

"Ooh, Miss Klara, I believe she was meeting with someone for high tea. Did not Major Drummond tell ye?" Stephen spoke with the light sing-song lilt that betrayed his Welsh origins.

"No, she didn't. With whom?"

"Ooh, with the general, miss. I brought her a change of clothing there myself, you see."

"Very well, Stephen. Please send for the tea," Klara replied.

"As you wish, miss." Stephen grinned, bowed at the waist, and left.

"The only British general remaining in the city is General Clinton. Why wouldn't she bring me? Or tell me?"

"Perhaps she is embarrassed at her assignation with the general. Are there not others who seek her favor?"

"Well, yes, many, but...."

Emily interrupted. "I don't like that servant, Stephen. Be careful of him."

"He has some annoying manners, but he has been very polite with me. More so than others. My status here is somehow shameful."

"Nonsense, dear. Many young women are wards of powerful men. Major Drummond is kind to you and, I hope, respectful?"

Klara's face reddened, and her chin lowered. "Indeed. But controlling. Even more controlling than a father...."

"Not all fathers are controlling, dear."

When the tea arrived, Emily spent the next hour asking Klara questions. Under the guise of small talk, she learned more about the movements of the remaining British forces in New York and about the mysterious Major Drummond. She decided to mention him in her next report. It would be brief but include a few key details that might be useful to the commander-in-chief. His actions could hold the key to Clinton's intentions.

***

West Point, New York, August 12th, 1777

Baker glanced across the North River from the eastern bank, where the Catskill Mountains completely dominated the dark water. He silently cursed his luck and Sandy Drummond. He was on yet another mission far from New Jersey, thanks to Drummond.

Baker watched slender waves foam against the bow of the craft, a specially modified longboat operated by the Scorpions.

"It will be dark in another half an hour, sir. We should have cleared the damned Yankee forts and chains completely," a Royal Marine corporal whispered in his ear.

Baker wondered if the familiarity was intentional. Loyal to the crown, Baker had begun to tire of some of its servants. "How much longer till the rendezvous point, corporal?"

The Marine placed a finger on his lower lip. "Oh, about six hours, sir. We'll be there before dawn if the tide cooperates and we don't run into rebels."

"And if we do?"

"We'll try to avoid them, of course, sir."

Baker cringed at the tone of disdain. Even their enlisted men held Americans in contempt, including Loyal Americans.

The six hours seemed like six years to Baker. He marveled at how the eight men never seemed to tire as they pulled at the oars and stretched their backs in the thwarts. Their strokes were smooth and seemed effortless. The exposed upper and forearms rippled with lean muscle, and their backs cut a perfect V formed by sinew and muscle wrapped around broad shoulders and deep chests.

"Not much longer now, sir," the corporal said.

"Good news, corporal. I'm not sure I could stand much longer in your cramped boat."

"No offense, sir, Americans can't take the punishment like true Englishmen. That's why they're losing this war, ain't it?"

Baker resisted the temptation to put the man in his place. But he held his temper. His life depended on these men being in the appointed spot when he completed his mission. "Thank God for Englishmen, but men from Jersey come strong and brave."

"Indeed, sir!"

Across the ever-narrowing river expanse, the town's lights glowed like dying embers.

"That must be Albany," said Baker.

"Not a big town by any measure, is it, sir? Ever been to London?"

"Never. Keep your eyes peeled for rebel boats now."

"Pull a little faster, mates. The officer has a rendezvous to make."

Baker smiled. That was what they were told of his mission. But his real mission was to find his way north to Burgoyne's army and deliver a note, which would not make the good general very happy with Howe or Clinton.

An hour later, they touched land. A thin sliver of light streaked the tops of the trees along the shore.

"What are your orders, sir?" The corporal seemed almost bored.

Baker cast an eye eastward. "It'll be daylight soon. We'll all sleep through the day and refresh our strength."

"And then, sir?"

"Two of your Scorpions will come north with me. We'll use the river as a guide for as long as possible. But we'll need to avoid rebel patrols."

"How far north will you travel, sir?"

Baker smiled. "As far as it takes to reach General Burgoyne's column. But you have permission to make your way south if we don't return in a week."

Chapter 21

Fort Edward, New York

Sinclair heard a rattle at his door. He had taken a room in one of Fort Edward's cabins. Throwing on his night robe, he opened the door to the bloated and blackened face of Serge Binoche. Binoche looked weak but enraged, with bulging eyes and a gnarl like a mad dog.

Beside him stood Fleurette, grasping his forearm with her slender fingers. For some reason, her lithe figure and raven hair caught Sinclair's attention for the first time, or at least the first time he would admit.

"Binoche! What brings you here at this hour? And what in blazes happened out there? Lawrence is back. He led us to believe you and your band fell to the rebels." Sinclair couldn't keep his eye off the girl.

"I want my money, *monsieur,*" Binoche declared.

"Money? For what? You have yet to earn your money."

"Lawrence led us into a trap. Of this, I am sure. Many friends are dead. I tell you, he betrayed us." Binoche nearly spat his words.

Sinclair casually strode to his desk, lit a lamp, and began to make notes. He had his suspicions, of course. But he needed desperately to convince Burgoyne to secure the water route to Albany and get his dwindling army out of the wilderness.

Binoche rambled in a mix of French, English, and Indian dialect. Sinclair understood now that the rogue trapper was on to something despite his personal hatred of Lawrence.

Sinclair's suspicions of the "Royal American" had grown deeper each day the army deviated from its original course. But this reappearance of Serge Binoche clinched it.

Binoche's story had elements of truth mixed with Gallic bombast. But one thing seemed certain to Sinclair. Lawrence was not quite what he appeared to be. Moreover, Lawrence's reports had led Burgoyne to deviate from his supply line along the waters and plunge the army into the American wilderness. Now that the wilderness was doing what the rebel Army could not do. Frustrate the British offensive.

Sinclair lifted his hand. "Enough, Binoche, enough. I understand. The question is, how to proceed? You have yet to provide the proof I need to lead this man to the gibbet."

"Bah, leave it to me, *Monsieur.* The scalp of such a...."

Sinclair reddened. "No, *monsieur,* you listen to me. Gather what men you can and return here in two hours. I shall provide you with an envelope. Make sure the envelope is in his possession when you return with Lawrence. *Vous comprende, Monsieur?*"

"*Mais oui, monsieur!*" Binoche's eyes widened with a mix of disappointment and delight.

He wanted Lawrence punished. But Sinclair feared Binoche's primeval urges inclined him to the scalping knife rather than the rope.

Sinclair opened a wallet and placed five silver coins in Binoche's palm. "A small down payment for your troubles and your success, *monsieur*. In return, you will leave your lovely daughter to my protection. If something untoward befalls you, I will ensure her safe return to Canada."

Binoche gave a nod while jutting out his lower lip. "*Monsieur*, you have a bit of the *coureurs des bois* in you. I submit to your plan."

***

When Binoche returned, Sinclair was less than impressed with the group assembled. A few disgruntled Canadians and a dozen or so Iroquois were all Binoche could muster.

"You are to join Lieutenant Colonel Baum and his Germans in an attack against the rebels. Is this all you could find for your service?"

Binoche grunted. "They are anxious to show their loyalty to your king, *Monsieur*. Can you ask for more than that?"

"Very well." Sinclair peered into the darkness. "Where is the girl?"

Binoche's face darkened. "She will come of her own accord, *monsieur*. But be aware that she is in mourning for her young lover."

Sinclair stiffened. "He was not her lover. She was his bait. I suspect he is not her first love nor her last. Still, I would have preferred the young man had lived, and you had succeeded the first time. This is your last chance, Binoche. Do not fail again."

"*Monsieur*, I serve your king and his silver. But do not treat me like a fool. The forests here are immense, and one can never be free from their dangers."

"Well, make sure you bring the girl. Meanwhile, you are already half a day's march behind Baum. You must depart now and find Baum's column. When you find Lawrence, keep a close eye on him. I need proof once and for all of his treachery. This envelope will provide that proof. Do not open it. Just make sure Lawrence is brought back with it in his possession."

Binoche grabbed the soft leather pouch. His bearded jowls widened, and his bushy brow narrowed. "Such treachery. *Eh bien*. At last, *monsieur*, we can agree on something – *Revanche!*"

***

Bennington, Hampshire Grants, August 15th, 1777

The post-storm stillness broke with the *crack* of muskets cutting the thick summer air. The volleys dragged on, and what was to be a quick foray collided with a wall of lead.

Lieutenant Colonel Friedrich Baum cursed silently. Though a professional, Baum had little combat experience and was unprepared for the rugged land he fought in and the tough people he fought. He had divided his force against what was supposed to be a demoralized militia. Now, stopped in its tracks at the Walloomsac River, his attack had lost its advantages – surprise, discipline, firepower, and maneuver. The rebels, it turns out, outnumbered them and were now out-fighting his men. Baum's narrow eyes and dark face displayed his anger and frustration.

"*Wo ist der Fraser?*" He shouted to an aide as another staccato volley ripped through the woods, sending branches cracking and leaves snapping.

The captain shrugged. *"Irgendwo im Wald!"*

Somewhere in the woods, Alexander Fraser's company of elite sharpshooters had spread like jackrabbits along the flank and disappeared among the woods and thick brush along the river.

"Wo ist der Lawrence?" This guide, Captain James Lawrence, had led the expedition on Burgoyne's orders and over the objections of Colonel Lazarus Sinclair. Now Baum thought he knew why!

A small pack of his soldiers loped past him in search of a place free of the sting of rebel bullets. They wore the blue coats with yellow turnbacks of the elite dismounted dragoons. Tightly-wound black gaiters had replaced the heavy boots of mounted dragoons.

"Halt!" Captain Schroeder, Baum's senior company commander, ordered. "We must stop *die Rebellen*, here."

A sergeant railed at the dragoons. They halted and drew long draughts from their water bottles. Then they followed him back to the trenches.

Baum's column arrived the day before, and while his band of Iroquois and Canadians ravaged the countryside, his men prepared defenses. A report to Burgoyne seeking more men and explaining that the situation was not what had once been believed remained unanswered.

"That *Schwein* Lawrence! He is the cause of this," said Baum's aide, a lieutenant from Brunswick, named Glich. "We should have known the people here were all rebel traitors."

"This is my fault. I trusted his report, as did Burgoyne and Fraser. Still, we can hold steady until Breymann arrives."

"Then a counter-stroke?" Schroeder asked.

Baum nodded. "But first, we must hold this redoubt. The Iroquois must secure our flank until Breymann pushes through the woods. He should be but a few hours behind."

Baum had no way of knowing Breymann had encamped for the day and could not arrive in time to help his command.

A volley of musket fire suddenly sprayed just over their heads, and, contrary to tradition, training, and inclination, both officers ducked.

His jaw stiff with determination, Friedrich Baum rose to his feet and pointed his saber toward the rebel fire. "The Iroquois must have fled. Why else would we receive rebel fire from there? Move a platoon to the south. Then bring up the cannon and quickly before they overrun us."

"We are already low on ammunition," said Glich.

"Then bring up the last caisson. No sense saving powder now."

Glich ran off in search of the caisson.

Another rebel volley ripped through them, and a musket ball sliced like a hot knife through Baum's side and spun him to the ground. A panting Schroeder ran to help.

Baum's teeth chattered as shock began to control his muscles. "Forget me. They are between Breymann and us. Form a line at the gap, now!"

The captain signaled a nearby sergeant to help the commander and set off.

Glich returned after placing the two guns and began barking orders, "Get him behind the redoubt, give him water, and cover the wound. *Schnell!*"

A file of dragoons led by a stout sergeant struggled through the thick mud in their heavy, knee-high cavalry boots.

When Baum was behind the log and earth wall, the sergeant forced a large swallow of fiery liquor, *Kirschwasser*, between Baum's cracked lips. The sharp, sweet taste of the alcohol seemed to revive Baum. He sat up with his back straining against the logs. The *boom-boom* of the two guns began to spit iron balls into the smoke cloud that hung across the field.

Baum stammered, "You must be my eyes, sergeant. Let me know if the rebels break through. Any sign of Breymann?"

The sergeant peered over the parapet.

"*Was ist da?* What do you see?" Baum asked between shallow breaths.

"*Viel Rauch.* Lot's of smoke. Rebels moving like locusts. Our boys in skirmish line are holding the outer line of defense. They are aiming well despite the smoke. Many rebels are falling, but they keep swarming across the field. We need more men, sir."

Glich staggered up and flung himself next to Baum. "We cannot hold, *Mein Herr*. The *Jungs* have only a handful of cartridges. The guns had fewer than a dozen rounds. If Breymann doesn't arrive soon, we must withdraw, or it is over."

Baum winced in pain and licked his parched lips. "There is no retreating before rebels. If we cannot hold, then have those who can draw sabers and attack. We charge downhill and cut a path through the enemy."

Even as he said it, Baum knew it was pure bravado. So did Glich.

"As you command, *Herr Oberstleutnant!*"

***

Alexander Fraser sensed the worst. His sharpshooters had entered the woods confident they would make short work of the rebels. But instead of a quick skirmish and pursuit, his men ran into a swarm of sturdy men. He would be even less at ease if he knew their leader was John Stark. The two fought in Roger's Rangers during the French and Indian War. Now they faced off in a struggle for the northland.

A lieutenant in a stained red jacket scrambled through the brush and flung himself next to Fraser. "There must be over a thousand of them, sir. We lost almost a dozen of our best lads in the first volley. The Indians have fled as well."

Fraser nodded. "Is your fusil loaded?"

The lieutenant did not answer.

"Blast it, Peter! No wonder the rebels are besting us. We've forgotten the basics: fire, reload, then move."

The officer began to tear a cartridge.

"Have you seen Captain Lawrence?" Fraser asked as he peered through the bush. His fusil cracked as he squeezed off a shot at a rebel.

"Not since the rebels struck us. He might have gone down in one of their volleys. We'd never find him in these woods – they're damned thick."

"We're the cream of the army, Peter. We do our best work in thick woods!"

"Not when rebels outnumber us ten to one, sir."

A chorus of cheers and shouts combined with a crescendo of fire from their flank convinced Fraser to get his men moving. His elite light infantry was not meant to be squandered in a stand-up fight.

He rammed home his charge. "All right, Peter, rally the lads and follow me. We'll cross the Walloomsac and follow the creek north to cover Baum's flank. Let's go. At the quick!"

But deadly streams of rebel bullets tore into the marksmen, and soon the men from the Grants broke through. Fraser's elite unit was cut in two, and the handful who escaped death or capture at the hands of Stark's hardened men melted into the forests to save themselves.

***

A canopy of smoke clouded Creed's view from the rocky ridgeline a couple of hundred yards north of the redoubt. Creed scanned the ridgeline with his spyglass. He saw the last of the braves scattering from their position on Baum's flank. To the south, a thickening cloud of gun smoke rose from the riverbank where Fraser's command was in the last throes of its desperate fight.

He adjusted his spyglass. Creed saw the Germans jockey a pair of light guns and a small ammunition caisson into position near the redoubt. A handful of gunners stripped to their shirts and began sighting the barrels towards the rebels.

Deep columns of angry men began to converge on the redoubt like ants on an anthill. They were all anxious to pay the enemy back for their invasion of the Grants and avenge the depredations of the Indians. The rebels wore only homespun brown and gray but were well-armed and experienced sharpshooters and knew the land.

Creed thought he saw Stark leading several companies directly towards the guns. The Germans could manage to bang out only a few shots in response to the cloud of musket balls from the Americans. *They haven't enough munitions to hold.*

A swarm of cheering Americans rushed from the tree line and soon blended with the Germans. Musket barrels *clanged* against the heavy cavalry sabers. A sudden flash made Creed blink. A resounding *boom* followed, and the ammunition wagon erupted in a massive explosion. Shards of metal, splinters of wood, and chunks of flesh, both animal and human, tumbled through the air.

The carnage and mayhem went suddenly still. The explosion's shock sent men on both sides dropping to the ground, covering their ears, or running for safety.

Moments later, Creed heard Stark's powerful voice.

"Up, boys! Get them now before they run off on us!"

A series of "Huzzahs" erupted from hundreds of men throughout the woods and fields.

Creed snapped the spyglass shut. His work at Bennington was done. He needed to get back to Fort Edward, collect his maps and papers, and work his way south before the British could react to his role in their disaster.

A few hours later, he crossed a ravine and made his way along a narrow ridge near a place called Van Schaick's Mill.

"Halt!" A British voice came from his right.

He turned to see two redcoats brandishing the long, sturdy New Land Musket with wicked 17-inch-long blades.

"State your business or receive our fire," one of them ordered.

"I am Captain James Lawrence of the Royal American Regiment, seconded to Captain Fraser's scouts," Creed replied. "The rebels are attacking the entire column near Bennington. I am bringing a request for reinforcements from Colonel Baum."

A tall, elegant-looking figure with a deep scarlet coat and black facings stepped from the trees and offered a hand. "My name is George, sir. Lieutenant George Beatty of the Queen's Loyal Rangers."

"Captain James Lawrence. Royal American Regiment. I have come to expedite relief before it is too late."

"Glad to have another good, loyal American unit in the army, sir. However, Colonel Baum has already requested reinforcements, and General Burgoyne has dispatched Colonel Breymann's relief column in response. My detachment is guiding that relief column forward. But you say you were with Captain Fraser. I know Alexander Fraser. Where is he?" The officer's voice displayed a caution that bordered on suspicion.

Creed assumed his most charming smile. "If you know Alexander Fraser, then you know he is killing rebels, even as we speak."

Beatty immediately relaxed. "Indeed, sir. I wish we too were there and not leading this pack of Germans."

"I know nothing of an earlier message to Burgoyne, George, but I assure you the situation near Bennington is grave. You must move the column now. I can lead them."

"Unfortunately, our good Colonel Breymann has the column taking up defenses for the day."

"Here? Now?" Creed asked.

Beatty shrugged. "His men saw some Iroquois on the run from here. That may have influenced his decision."

"Who comprises the column?"

"Mostly Brunswick Grenadiers. Big fellows in dark blue coats and leather breeches. Plus a few platoons of light infantry. We're here to guide the column and question stragglers or deserters along the way."

"Brunswick Grenadiers? How many?"

"A battalion. Over five hundred, I'd say."

"Well, if we march them now, there might be time."

"Sorry, sir. You know the Germans. They are organized but stubborn and dogmatic. Breymann has ordered them to prepare defenses. I'm afraid today the men will do their work with the shovel, not the bayonet."

"Well, if he doesn't march to Baum's aid now, he'll need those shovels to bury their comrades. Can you point me towards his headquarters? I feel obligated to report to him in any case."

"Very well, then, sir."

An hour later, Creed had bypassed Breymann's primitive breastworks of log and earth berms. *Stark will make quick work of these.* He suddenly had a sense of being followed. Creed glanced back along the deer trail once or twice. *Did Beatty grow suspicious? Did Breymann receive word of him?* It was possible that small bands of Iroquois still roamed the area searching for quick plunder.

Two warriors sprang from the bushes like a pair of wolves, yelping savagely and brandishing muskets and tomahawks.

Creed crouched and squeezed off a round, sending a hot lead slug into the belly of one. The brave's eyes widened in shock, and his chest darkened as blood pumped in all directions. He sprawled backward onto the moss-covered rocks.

The second brave was on him, swinging his long musket like a club. Creed quickly stepped in, ramming his fusil's butt into the brave's rib cage with a sickening crack. Still, the brave grabbed Creed's weapon.

Several hands pulled him from his assailant as a burly figure with a beard ran a musket butt into his stomach. Creed fell on his hands and knees, breathless and in pain. A large moccasin thudded against his ribs and sent him rolling along the mossy ground. Creed managed to move into the bushes. He crawled through the brush, trying to find a way past them. He reached for his tomahawk, but it had fallen in the struggle.

"Here he is!" a voice cried in French.

Musket butts whipped through the bushes around him until one sent him thudding onto the soft, muddy ground. Creed suddenly felt a sharp crack to his head and slumped face down into the soft earth. He last recalled a vague feeling of hands jerking him roughly by the ankles.

Chapter 22

Stillwater, New York, August 20th, 1777

The Hoosick River's narrow waters rushed by in a frothy torrent that sliced through rocky hills on its way to join the North River to the west. Baker cursed himself for not taking the Scorpions' longboat farther north. After days of struggling through the rugged hills, he found no sign of the British advanced guard.

"How much longer, sir?" a small but powerfully built sailor named Silas Milford asked.

"Too long, I fear." Baker regretted the words. It would do him no good to dampen the men's spirits. He had learned that the Scorpions were fearless and determined men, but even the most elite warriors needed hope.

"We'll march with you to Canada if that's what it takes, sir. Besides, I hear the Frenchie lasses there are a marvel," said a Royal Marine named Harvey Robson.

Baker chuckled. "We haven't enough shoe leather for that, Robson. No, we'll...."

A figure in dark blue suddenly emerged from the treeline on the north bank of the Hoosick. The figure waded through the near chest-high water, fighting the current as he grabbed and pulled at his uniform. He held his musket high over his head. Behind him, two more men entered the water and also began struggling against the current.

"Rebel infantry," Baker whispered. "We'll take them when they emerge. We need to capture one and learn where Burgoyne's army is."

Robson and Milford exchanged glances. They primed their short, navy blunderbusses and, with a click, activated the releases on the spring-bayonets attached to each. The result was a formidable combination of firepower and cold steel, perfect for close-quarters combat. They slipped partway down the slope into an ambush position. They struck when the last rebels, soaked and heavy from the water, slogged by.

Milford's blunderbuss exploded into the face of the lead man, bursting his head like a hammer smashing a melon, and sending his torso rolling back into the river.

The third rebel turned to run, but Robson stepped out of the thicket, plunged the twenty-inch steel blade into his side, and pureed his innards with a flick of his wrist. He yanked the bayonet free, and the man slipped into the muddy soil and died.

Robson and Milford closed on the middleman, who raised his arms high in surrender. His eyes widened in terror.

"*Ich gebe auf!*" he choked in German, then in English, "I yield!"

Blast! Baker realized they had not ambushed a rebel patrol but German allies.

He cupped his hands and bellowed, "Don't harm him! They're Germans!"

His feet pumped madly down the slope to reach the German before Robson or Milford. "Do you speak English?" Baker asked the frightened soldier.

"*Ja*, some English," the German replied.

"Who are you? What is your unit?"

"*Brunschweiger Dragoner.* Brunswick Dragoons, *Mein Herr.* My name is Hoffman. *Unteroffizier* Gert Hoffman."

"Brunswick? Ah, the king's German friends. Where is the rest of your regiment? Are you on patrol?"

The dragoon lowered his eyes in shame. "We have no more, sir. Rebels killed or captured most of us near Bennington. We saw our commander, Colonel Baum, dying of his wounds. So, we ran south, where the rebels would not think to search for us. We are the only men in our platoon to escape. We were…"

"Deserters! You are heading south towards the rebels. You're deserters, aren't you?" Hoffman hung his head. "*Ja.*"

"Well, you are in our hands now," Baker said.

Hoffman's face brightened. "So, you are rebels, *na*? *Gut so.* We want no more of this war. Few Loyalists have rallied to Burgoyne, and the natives have all fled. Many of my *Landser,* too. The English here are *fertig,* finished."

"Well, that's just it. We're not rebels, Corporal Hoffman. We're British subjects."

"British? But…."

"You are our prisoner charged with desertion from his majesty's forces. Unless you tell me what you know about the location of General Burgoyne's army, you'll hang from that tree."

Hoffman gazed at the weathered white oak tree nearby and swallowed.

It took Baker longer than he expected to finish his questioning. The German had about exhausted his limited English vocabulary, and in any event, corporals of the Brunswick dragoons were not privy to the grand plans of the army.

Baker learned Burgoyne was low on supplies and had exhausted his men with useless forays against rebels, real and perceived. He also knew Burgoyne's army was a two-day march from them at Fort Edward, but the area to the north swarmed with rebel militia units. The promised barge ride to Albany had turned into a nightmare of forced marches through steamy bug-infested forests that wore down the spirit as much as the body.

When Baker finished his questioning, Milford slipped his boarding knife from his belt and brandished a rope. "Shall we hang him now, sir?"

"As distasteful as it is, we have no choice. Make it quick – a long rope with a thick knot works best."

Milford smiled. "A snap and crack, not a stretch, eh sir?"

As Hoffman watched silently, the rope was knotted and strung over a sturdy limb stretching over the ravine.

"We'll give a push, and he'll drop ten feet and be done, sir. Quite simple. Bring the Dutchman here, Harvey," Milford said.

Flight was hopeless. But Hoffman's desperate eyes searched for a way out, but Robson's blunderbuss was primed and loaded. Hoffman suddenly turned and made a desperate swing at Robson. A long arm and a ham-like fist reached over the short barrel and smashed a blow to Robson's jaw, stunning him. Robson jerked back and reflexively pulled the trigger.

The weapon unleashed a powerful explosion of smoke, fire, and lead, but the heavy-caliber ball struck a nearby sapling with a loud crack.

The dragoon launched himself forward, bent at the waist and arms and legs pumping like a bellows. He sped along the edge of the ravine. However, the blast had singed his eyes, and he ran blindly through the woods with bushes and branches tearing at his face, neck, and hands.

A sudden *pop, pop, pop* erupted from along the river. Bullets *hummed* around them, slapping tree leaves and cracking branches. A well-aimed ball slammed into Hoffman, rolling him into the wet underbrush as he clutched his side.

Another volley tore through the foliage, and Milford fell bleeding with the rope still coiled around his shoulder.

"Rebels. We must move back!" Baker ordered.

"I'm a dead man, sir. Take off with Harvey. I'll hold the bastards off as long as I breathe." Milford panted while his hands clutched frantically at his belly.

Bubbles of blood were oozing from the Scorpion's stomach. He faced a slow, painful, and sure death.

"Take this." Baker handed him a pistol.

Milford nodded and placed it next to his blunderbuss. "Thank you, sir. Can I have a sip of water before you go?"

Baker shook his head. "Will make it worse, I am afraid. Try some rum."

Baker pulled a small flask from his bag and poured a long swallow into the tough marine's mouth. He turned back into the woods to join Robson just as a militia squad scrambled up the riverbank. More musket blasts, now mixed with a babble of shouts and screams, filled the air.

He found Robson calm but anxious for action. "The musket shots are getting closer. The place is swarming with rebels, sir. Where's Milford?"

"Done for. A rebel ball got him in the belly. He'll try to keep them at bay so we can escape. We'll head south, then southwest, and try to get back to the boat before it leaves."

A series of musket shots cut leaves and smacked the tree trunks and rocks behind them.

"Halt, or the next volley will be our last!" a rebel officer shouted across a narrow clearing.

"Damn! They're south of us now – we're surrounded," Baker said.

"I'm not being taken alive by damned rebels, sir." Robson stepped out from behind the cover of a small pine tree and fired his blunderbuss across the clearing. The heavy ball and large charge boomed like a small cannon and echoed along the river.

"Come get us if you can, you damned rebel traitors." He began reloading – powder, ball, patch, and ram home.

Baker saw a demonic glint in his eye. He had never met Englishmen as zealous, courageous, or brutal as these Scorpions.

A line of men in a mix of brown, white, and black farm clothing emerged from the meadow's edge. They brandished old muskets, tomahawks, and hunting knives. Their officer carried a large saber, holding it close to his side. They didn't cheer or yell. Instead, they came at them in eerie silence.

Baker squeezed the trigger. A rebel kicked back and fell with a loud moan. Robson calmly reloaded as the line drew closer, twenty yards, then ten. Robson stepped out and pointed his weapon at the lead man, who aimed his musket at Robson with a sure eye.

The rebel was tall, gaunt, and crazed-looking, like Robson. The firelocks discharged at the same time. A terrific roar and swirl of smoke enveloped the two in a cloud. The advancing rebels entered the cloud. Baker reached for his pistol, but he had left it with Milford.

Several pairs of strong arms had secured him and slammed him to the ground in seconds.

"They're not in uniform, sir. Tory spies!"

A quick series of musket blows to the chest and stomach sent bolts of agonizing pain coursing through Baker's body. He struggled vainly for air. His eyes bulged, and his vision blurred. He tried to reach for the packet that contained the letter for Burgoyne. With his mind swimming, he fought to focus on getting rid of the letter before the rebels found it.

A farmer slammed his musket into Baker and roughly seized the packet. "What have we here?"

The officer grabbed the letter, tore the packet open, and scanned the contents. Two of his men threw a rope over a nearby tree limb and ran a noose around Baker's neck. Amid shouts and hoots of "Tory spy," they began to hoist up his limp body. The rope dug into his flesh and began to tighten around his windpipe. Baker stood stiffly, almost indifferently, until three men tugged and slowly lifted his body off the ground.

Sidney Baker's eyes turned to a teary glaze. He swore silently in the frustration that his service to the king had ended in a God-forsaken backwater that both sides would soon forget.

***

Kip's Bay, New York
As the *Red Hen* pulled into Kip's Bay, Foch gazed southward into the darkness. Star-like twinkles from the buildings dotting the East River's wooded shore provided him a view of the New York Island shoreline.

His voyage north with the mysterious "Captain Lawrence" had been worth the risk. Although transporting the detachment of Royal Americans to Canada had yielded him no revenue, his return trip made up for it in profits. With all available ships commandeered for military supplies, a fine brig like his Red Hen was in high demand among Canadian fur trappers. He bought over 500 pounds of quality pelts: fox, bear, martin, and beaver. The profits would be substantial when he traded them in New York. British shippers heading for Europe would pay well. Cornelius Foch was most pleased when he could combine his revenge against the English with a good business deal.

"Why do we anchor here, captain?" Foch's first mate, Tom Willets, asked.

"I prefer to arrive at Brooklyn in the morning. The bay provides a good shelter for the night, eh Tom?"

Tom shot him a confused look.

Foch laughed and puffed at his meerschaum pipe. "We'll sail down to the city tomorrow. Meanwhile, the boys can rest and have a drink. They earned it, *Na*?"

Tom, a lanky Dutch seaman who never lacked a pipe in his mouth, nodded. "*Ja*, but less than an hour, and we are home, captain."

"But we are here, Tom. And it's dark. When you lower anchor, break out some *Genever*. We will all have a drink, then rest."

Tom shrugged. "As you wish."

"You know, there are a few interesting taverns not far from here. After such a journey, the boys deserve some pleasure. I believe Coos Dederick has a small place not too far from this very harbor," Foch said.

"Thought you didn't favor Dederick," Tom said.

"He is a right bastard's bastard. But my dislikes should not stand in the way of the crew's pleasure. And like him or not, I still must have business dealings with him, *na*?"

But Foch did not plan to rest long. He had chosen this particular place for a reason. He had been gone many weeks, and now it was time to begin his other work – retrieving messages destined for the hands of Colonel Fitzgerald and the eyes of his master. Foch had no idea who left the packets he recovered for the lanky American colonel, but little mattered. The English were his enemy, and America his new home, which was enough for him.

Most of the *Red Hen's* crew had finished their work, downed a few Genever shots, and trotted off for the taverns waiting in the tiny hamlet nearby. Foch and Tom had remained on board, along with six unlucky sailors.

Foch slipped on deck just before midnight. A sailor named Niklas stood watch on the foredeck, listening to the water gently lapping against the ship. An occasional scurrying sound broke the tempo – rats prowling for food.

"Quiet enough up here, Niklas?" Foch asked.

The sailor nodded, the glow from his pipe arcing slightly against the black of night.

"Niklas, I'm going ashore to stretch my legs. When I return in an hour, we'll share a plug."

Another glowing arc brought a terse reply, "Aye, captain. You always have the better tobacco. Enjoy your stretch. The lads are at Coos' place and warming up the wenches for you!"

Foch smiled. Niklas assumed his skipper had given in to a long voyage without carnal pleasure and at last decided on a discreet visit to one of the taverns.

He swung his legs over the gunwale. "You are an old sea dog, Niklas."

Foch's footsteps barely made a sound as he tread north along the coast. The lane, an offshoot of the Post Road, just a quarter-mile to the west, ran along the wooded hills and cliffs that hugged the riverbank. The occasional glow from a cottage lit the lane. But the woods thickened and enveloped him in complete darkness after a quarter-mile. He dared not risk a lantern or torch, so his pace slowed, and the next quarter-mile took him longer than usual. Finally, he reached the large outcropping of white rock – the first landmark.

Foch slipped into the woods and followed a narrow path that snaked along the rocks to a small clearing. He could hear the water breaking along the stony sand. Even in the darkness, Foch could make out the shape of the three large boulders. He reached them in a few more steps, sliding into the crevice between the two facing south.

Safe among the rocks, he reached about and lifted a large flat stone. He found what he was looking for in a neatly cut hole – an oilskin pouch sealed tight. He quickly replaced the stone and returned the way he came.

An hour later, he was aboard the *Red Hen*, enjoying a smoke with Niklas. Not long after, they heard muffled voices and the tramping sound of a band of men growing closer.

"Ah, the lads are returning," Niklas said.

"Too early for that, I'd say," Foch replied.

They could make out the shadows of a half-dozen men carrying firelocks and cudgels out of the darkness.

"Who goes there?" Niklas challenged.

"His majesty's night watch. What ship is this?"

"The *Red Hen*, out of Brooklyn, returning from Canada. Cornelius Foch, Master, and Proprietor," Foch answered.

"We thought we saw someone moving about the cove north of here. Followed the trail this way. Have you seen anything suspicious?"

"I have been at sea for over twenty years. I've seen many suspicious things," Foch said smugly.

"Don't trifle with me, sir, or I'll arrest you. Just answer my question."

"Then the answer is no. We have been enjoying our pipes for some time and have seen nothing but the rats that inhabit your island."

Niklas laughed at his master's remark.

"You trifle with me, sir. Very well, what is the nature of your cargo?" The leader gestured to his men, who began to load their firelocks.

"Are you a customs inspector too? I have legitimate cargo with all the papers signed by the customs house at Quebec."

Foch realized he faced a shakedown by brigands posing as Loyalist irregulars.

Foch whispered to Niklas, "These are cowboys – rogues searching for bribes or plunder. Fetch Tom, and bring up what arms you can find."

Foch stalled for time. "What is your authority?"

He drew a pistol and waved it menacingly. "I have all the authority I need. Now stand back. We intend to board and inspect."

Tom and Niklas arrived back with a pair of blunderbuss firelocks and cutlasses.

Foch took one of the cutlasses and pointed it. "I'll allow you to board, sir. But your men must remain where they are. If not, there shall be blood."

"I'll ignore that threat for now," said the leader, who stuck the pistol into his belt and clambered up the gangway.

"Show me your letter of authority, and I'll show you my customs papers from Quebec," Foch said in a low voice.

The man drew his pistol, cocked it, and pointed it at Foch. "My authority comes from Coos Dederick! If you know of him, you'll do well to reach into your coffers and pay a small tax."

"Do you wish to die for the likes of Coos Dederick? As soon as your hammer strikes, my mate's blunderbuss will explode your head like a ripe melon," Foch spat.

"Prepare to storm the ship," the leader cried to his men.

A cutlass poked his ribs. Niklas suddenly appeared at his side.

"Oh, oh, stand fast," he stammered.

His men halted, and Foch could hear mumbling.

"When the rest of my men return, you will be outnumbered and surrounded," Foch called out. "I suggest you all go on now. We'll see no harm comes to your leader."

Niklas's strong hand wrested the pistol from the cowboy. The group shuffled off into the darkness. Foch knew cowboys were in it for easy pickings. A real fight was rarely part of their plan.

"I will report this," the leader said.

"To whom? Coos? He'll beat you to a pulp for failing."

"Not to Coos. To Cunningham. The provost. We saw movement out there, and whatever had to come by here. If you know Cunningham, you know he's hung men for less."

Foch stared at him. "And I have fed men to the sharks for less."

The man swallowed. He suddenly seemed to lose his bravado. "Of course, sir, I'm likely mistaken. Might have been some deer, maybe some savages?"

"Likely a smuggler," Foch replied slyly.

Foch took the man's pistol from Niklas and motioned for him and Tom to leave the deck. "This is quite a fancy pistol. French-made, isn't it? Just where did you get it?"

The man looked across the water. "From a bugger who lies over there."

Foch frowned. "The prison hulks? Looks like a fine officer's pistol – a rebel officer. Did you take it in battle?"

The cowboy lowered his eyes.

"I didn't think so."

"Well, I fancy it. I'll buy it from you for ten guineas."

The cowboy's eyes widened. "That's a king's ransom. Is this a jest?"

"No jest. The blunderbuss has grown heavy. I need a fine pistol in keeping with my station as the master of this ship. However, we must keep our transaction in the strictest confidence."

Both recognized what this was – a bribe.

"Your offer is gratefully accepted, sir."

Later, Foch escorted the cowboy to the quay and handed him a small leather bag containing ten silver coins.

"This is more than an offer. I am sure you'll share the proceeds with your men and Coos," Foch said sarcastically. Neither Cunningham nor Coos Dederick would know of the night's work.

The next day the *Red Hen* made a gentle cruise down the river. As they neared Brooklyn, the wind shifted, and a terrible stench choked at the crew. Some still had hangovers from the night's revels, and the stench made them bend over the bulwark in search of relief. A quarter-mile to the port, a dozen or more ships rocked slowly in the tide. Devoid of masts and sails, they rotted away at anchor with a cargo that rotted no less quickly.

"The prison hulks are a blight on this fair land, sir. They say those who don't starve will die of fever or the flux," Tom remarked.

"Well, all war is a blight, Tom. The English seem to have the upper hand. If this is how they wish to deal with rebels, that's their business, right? What does it matter to us?"

Even as he said the words, Foch's stomach turned at the thought of several thousand men slowly wasting away. He hid his sympathies from his men. It was how he protected himself and them from the authorities.

***

Emily ran a needle through a bright salmon-colored outfit, one of her favorites. She tore it the previous night while visiting one of the East River coves where she deposited her special packages.

Nancy slowly opened the parlor doors. "Miss Stump is here to see you, Miss Em."

Emily kept on with her stitching. "Please send her in, Nancy. I must finish this line."

Nancy smiled. "Yes'm."

Moments later, Klara Stump clicked across the room, beaming brightly. "Oh, Emily, I am so happy you asked me to go on one of your excursions. I am so tired of the Dunning House. Pleasant as it is, I sometimes feel I am a prisoner there."

Emily arched her eyes. It had often occurred to her that Klara's status as Drummond's ward was little more than a form of imprisonment.

While genuinely fond of Klara, Emily had determined to use her place at the Drummond House to develop new sources of information. She had already uncovered Drummond's unique role as spymaster for the British command. Now, Howe's departure meant Drummond would serve Clinton.

But the idea of drawing Klara out on her various excursions was a bold stroke that could provide her with some semblance of protection. If anything suspicious developed, having the ward of one of New York's most powerful officers was no small benefit.

She finished the last stitch, tied a tight knot, and cut the strand. "There, done. Good as new. Let me change, and we can be off. There is a farmhouse that sells the most delightful peaches. Lady Dunning does enjoy peach pie?"

"Oh yes. Major Drummond as well."

"And your nice Captain Baker?"

"I never asked. He is gone some time in any event. Major Drummond could not, or would not, allow as to his return."

"Went south to join Howe's army?" Emily was fishing.

"I don't know. But for some reason, I believe he was going north again."

"Again?"

"Yes. I overheard him speaking with Major Drummond. He was not very pleased with things at the time. The war is wearing on him, I'm afraid."

"As it is on us all, dear."

Emily threw her arms around her and ran up to her room to change for the long ride ahead.

Chapter 23

Fort Edward, September 10th, 1777

The sounds overwhelmed Creed – faint, familiar, strange, and loud sounds. He felt as though he were locked in a tin drum. In a dream-like state, he closed his eyes and rolled over. Pain creased his side, shocking him awake. He flipped himself over and sat up.

"Bastard's awake, Steve."

"Give him a musket to the noggin', Fred. He deserves another don't he? Rebel spoy!"

"Better not. The colonel wants to talk to him. Better let him know this one's up."

The door to the cell opened shortly after, and a familiar figure stepped across the threshold.

"Colonel Sinclair? What happened? Where am I?" Creed's head was woozy, and he felt the grip of nausea.

"Back at Fort Edward, Mister Lawrence. They brought you in quite bruised, although the surgeon says nothing is broken. You are most fortunate."

Sinclair took a pewter flask from his pocket and offered it to Creed.

"Take a few swigs of this brandy, among General Burgoyne's best. It will help dull the pain. Your eye and lips are healing nicely."

"How long have I been out? I vaguely recall being ambushed on my way back from Bennington. I was trying to report on the battle, which, I fear, went badly." Creed was beginning to make sense of what had happened and sought to cover his tracks.

"Badly is an understatement, Captain Lawrence. Baum is dead, and his column is annihilated. Our relief column fared little better. Rebels are rallying against us. Savages abandoning us. Our chances of seizing Albany this season are all but ruined. My plans all but ruined. And somehow, I find you at the center of all this."

Creed blanched. "I assure you, sir, when I get out of the hospital, I will...."

"Hospital? You think you are in the hospital?" Sinclair laughed. "It should be apparent, Captain Lawrence, that you are in the gaol–in jail."

Creed rose unsteadily and staggered to the window. He saw only the iron rods barring exit from the place.

"I'm confused. Does the gaol double as the army's surgery, sir?"

"Not at all. You are his majesty's prisoner and will face a military tribunal at length."

"Prisoner? A tribunal? Don't you mean court-martial?"

Sinclair thrust a finger into Creed's chest. "Court-martial is reserved for his majesty's officers. We are quite certain you fail to qualify on that account."

"Sir, I am an officer in the Royal American Regiment. I arrived with the advanced detachment...."

"So you did. And you managed to convince Governor Carleton to dispatch you, and caused our impulsive commander to place you in a position to execute this scheme to cause our army the most harm. Very convenient, James Lawrence, if that is your name."

"Colonel Sinclair, I assure you my loyalty is unquestioned, and my efforts have been intended to bring victory to General Burgoyne."

"We have a different opinion, which will be read to all at your tribunal. You face it in four days."

"What is the charge, sir?" Creed knew well what the charge would be.

"Leading our forces into a death trap, spying for the rebels, and masquerading as an officer of his majesty."

Creed maintained a calm bearing. "This is all circumstantial conjecture, sir. I am the scapegoat for your campaign's failure. Do you not recall that I led the way to Ticonderoga?"

"Ah yes, Ticonderoga. Well, the rebels could not have held that place very long, and you know it. They did their cause more service by abandoning it and luring the good General Burgoyne into the wilderness. God, I warned him not to deviate from my plan. But he did. Somehow, I believe you had a hand in that."

"The rebels held me prisoner at Ticonderoga, sir. I escaped their justice."

"Yes, well, a lovely young lady has given testimony that tells a different tale. She says you schemed with the rebels all along. And that you staged your miracle escape by the hand of your savage friend, who, by our good fortune, perished on one of your devious excursions. I have statements from Serge Binoche, two of his men, and your Sergeant O'Ballance. He is also charged in your plot. Unfortunately, your man Androche has absconded. But your plot is uncovered nevertheless."

"Sir, I believe Alexander Fraser and General Simon Fraser will vouch for my conduct during the advance of this army. I served under them, after all." Creed gazed out the cell window and saw a narrow courtyard with a wooden portcullis. He also saw a scaffold under construction.

"There is no obligation to call defense witnesses during a tribunal like this, Mister Lawrence. Besides, those fine gentlemen are already engaged. The body of the army is crossing to the west bank of the river and moving south, at long last, and no thanks to you, you scoundrel."

Sinclair bounded to the door. He turned suddenly and tossed the flask at Creed.

"Savor each drop, Mister Lawrence. Or better yet, save it for the hour of your execution."

The jailer pulled open the heavy oak door. When Sinclair stepped out, he slammed it shut with a loud bang and echo that lent a certain finality to Creed's situation.

***

The guards led Creed into a small room just above the gaol. The air was heavy and moist, and the heat barely tolerable. Three officers sat at a makeshift table of freshly cut pine planks with a slightly sweet aroma.

The officer in the center was Colonel Lazarus Sinclair, who wore his scarlet tunic with regimental turnbacks of dark yellow and a powdered wig. A silver chest plate, a *gorget*, hung from his neck. He held a stack of papers that he thumbed through nervously.

Creed did not recognize the other two officers Sinclair identified as a major of Quartermaster named Brown and a Loyalist colonel named Colmes.

O'Ballance had already sat before the tribunal. Despite his denial of any wrongdoing and a lack of evidence, the tribunal had just sentenced him to hang. He had every reason to hate Creed, known to him as Captain Lawrence. But as they led him past Creed, he held his head up and nodded faintly at the man who, by all accounts, had caused his demise.

"The defendant will rise," Sinclair said when O'Ballance was gone.

Sinclair gave a lengthy preamble about the proceedings. Then he read the charges: high treason, spying for the rebels, and misrepresenting his status. Sinclair would lay out the tribunal's case based on statements from unnamed "witnesses" about the accused's treachery. He mumbled something about the results of the unfortunate campaign into the Hampshire Grants and the lack of specific notification from Horse Guards that the Royal Americans were being sent north.

Sinclair droned on about the various charges, occasionally stopping to wipe his spectacles or make a note to himself. Sometimes one of the other officers would whisper something to him, and he would whisper back in an almost schoolboy-like conspiracy.

Finally, he put down his papers, folded his white hands neatly before him, and smiled at Creed. "Does the accused have anything to say before we pass judgment?"

Creed rose and pointed his finger at Sinclair. "Don't I get to challenge the evidence? And where are your witnesses? You didn't even name them in your statement of charges. And don't I have the right to call witnesses on my behalf?"

Sinclair smiled patronizingly. "Mister Lawrence, this is no trial. It is a tribunal. Justice is swift and unencumbered in a tribunal."

"Sinclair's justice is swift, in any event," Colonel Colmes said with a chuckle.

Peals of laughter filled the room.

Sinclair smiled knowingly. "You were found leaving a great battle after leading the army's advance guard into a rebel trap. You have punished loyal savages in the conduct of just retribution against rebel settlers. You have witnesses who ascertain your loyalty to the rebel cause and your consultation with rebel officers."

Sinclair glanced at Serge Binoche and Fleurette, who sat along the backbench.

"Are they my accusers, Colonel?"

"I shan't name your accusers, but there are many."

"How many?"

"Enough to buy you the rope, Mister Lawrence. Your efforts have cost this army precious weeks, thousands of casualties, the loss of native allies and Loyalist recruits, and its honor. You have deceived the royal governor, our esteemed commander, and some of our best officers. But you didn't fool me. And now I have been vindicated!"

The soliloquy seemed to exhaust Sinclair, who acted as though the tribunal relieved a heavy burden from him. Creed wondered if they had found his maps. Father Vincennes's network would be at significant risk if that were the case. Perhaps they were already being used to march on Albany. Yet, Sinclair would mention that and ask him more about their origin. He had burned his "secret instructions" before heading for Bennington, but the maps were invaluable.

"How are you vindicated, sir?"

Sinclair rose and shook an envelope, then intoned deeply. "Have you any final words?"

Creed looked at Binoche. The trapper smiled smugly, satisfied that he had achieved his revenge on a sworn enemy. Fleurette, however, showed a look of ambivalence, almost bordering on sorrow. He thought he saw tears in her eyes. But she seemed different. The fiery woman who had tried to seduce him more than once and then turned on him when he hesitated now appeared to show another side. She was clearly the source of their knowledge about his actions at Ticonderoga – one of the "unnamed" witnesses against him.

Creed nodded, then raised his chin and looked at the three men before him. "Only this: if this is the king's justice, then the rebels' cause is easily explained and justified. Yet, I hold that this is not the king's justice but rather a ploy to appease the critics of a failed campaign."

Sinclair glared at him. "The tribunal will take that as an admission of guilt. Not that I needed one. This envelope contains a letter from Governor Carleton. He sheepishly admitted being duped by you, an impostor."

"Impostor?" Creed grew nervous.

"The Governor informs us that the *real* Captain James Lawrence just arrived in Quebec. He has given testimony to your treachery. You are proven a fraud and a spy!"

The news, the one fear that gnawed at him throughout the mission, had arrived. And it knocked the wind out of Creed. *Damn the luck! I'm truly hoist on my own petard.* He raised his hands in protest. He knew the game was over, but he tried to deflect the charges.

"That officer is the impostor," Creed stammered desperately. "He is a rebel agent sent to disrupt the campaign!"

An evil grin crossed Sinclair's face. "Even if I thought that to be true, I'd hang you and explain the mistake later." He slammed the envelope on the table. "The prisoner is sentenced to be hanged by the neck. Sentence to be carried out upon approval of General Burgoyne. Take the prisoner away!"

"But…" As Creed shuffled from the room, he glanced over at Fleurette. She had her head in her hands and was softly weeping. Somehow, he felt sorry for her. Roughly treated by her stepfather, she had been raised with little empathy and much brutality. But now, strangely, she seemed genuinely remorseful and vulnerable.

***

"Will they hang us together or one after the other, sir?" O'Ballance asked.

It was not wholly a rhetorical question as they knew that the construction of two gibbets might delay their combined deaths, albeit for only a bit.

"I am sure they want the full effect of two American traitors swinging in tandem, don't you think?" Creed replied.

Prisoners were fed once a day at three in the afternoon. The repast was surprisingly good, a joint of roast venison with roasted ears of corn and a half-pint of rum each. They had just finished what was likely their last meal.

"What will become of the lads, sir?" O'Ballance asked.

"Likely, they'll be split up as replacements for the dwindling ranks of Loyalists up here."

"Was it all a game then, sir? Accusing me falsely? And to what end?"

"I'm as innocent as you, sergeant," Creed replied. Silence ensued. Creed felt a surge of guilt wash over him. He had done all those things. But of course, to him, they were duty. *One person's duty is another's crime.* This was the tawdry world he signed up for so long ago.

"I'm sorry you became the target of their anger, Sergeant. You are a good man and a good soldier. You don't deserve to be subjected to a baseless charge for your association with me. I suppose they would hang Bart along with us if the lad hadn't fallen."

"I don't believe so, sir," O'Ballance said.

"What do you mean?"

"I believe Mister Saunders was seduced by the half-savage woman, Fleurette, and she was one of our secret accusers."

"That would mean Binoche and Sinclair had colluded well before Bennington and that...."

"What makes you so sure?"

O'Ballance lowered his head. "Just little things I observed, sir. Nothing firm. Nothing is ever firm, it seems."

"Nothing? That's no basis for suspicion. You must have seen or overheard something. Think, sergeant."

Creed entered the discussion as much to pass the time as to solve the mystery. But regardless of Binoche's actions, their fate was sealed.

O'Ballance stood up and stared out the window. "I overheard the wench and Ensign Saunders while in the throes shagging. I realize my actions were prurient. However, it struck me odd that in the midst of things, Colonel Sinclair's name came up - as did yours."

"In what sense?"

"A sense of conspiracy - their tones grew hushed, and then I heard only whispers until, finally, the ensign moaning. Likely some savage perversion she pleasured him with." O'Ballance seemed lustful as he recounted the story.

"She is quite a sensual creature," Creed mused.

"I am aware you rejected her, sir. That is why I know she coaxed the young ensign into her web."

"How do you know?"

O'Ballance grinned sheepishly. "I like to walk the camp at night, sir. Check on things. Sergeant's duty. You know that."

"Sergeant, did you examine my kit on your nocturnal junkets?" Creed asked impulsively. He worried about the maps.

"Do I look like a man who would rifle his officer's kit?" O'Ballance asked indignantly. Creed did not answer.

"You were gone a long time, sir. I had to ensure the savages or one of the men hadn't taken anything."

"Did they?" Creed asked.

"Not that I could tell," he said softly.

"Did you find my maps?"

O'Ballance nodded. "I did. But I left them. Figured they were his majesty's property."

"But they were in French," Creed said.

A sly grin crossed O'Ballance's face. "Don't read French, do I sir?"

"But Binoche does. If you found them, he may have turned them over to Sinclair. That's the only reason they could have suspected me."

O'Ballance eyed him warily. "So, you *are* a rebel agent then, sir?"

"What do you think, sergeant?"

"I think you are the finest officer I've served. That's what I think. If you have rebel sympathies, well, many of us do."

"Are you a rebel?"

"Well, maybe not an outright rebel, sir, but I am a Whig."

"A Whiggish sergeant joins the Royal Americans?"

"I must say, I wouldn't join another regiment. I liked the idea of fighting under the banner of America while taking the king's shilling."

That explained why O'Ballance did not turn him in and why he accepted his fate.

"Look here, sir. Look at this. Someone has loosened these two bars."

Creed went to the window. "You're right. But it would still take some tool to remove them."

He scanned the courtyard. The scaffolding was nearly complete. Tomorrow at dawn, they would die there. But he noticed that there were no redcoats standing watch. A few slovenly-looking soldiers in faded green surcoats stood guard – *Loyalist militia.*

"Sergeant, those aren't lobsters guarding this gaol. Sinclair did say the army had begun its final move on Albany. Why, our tribunal officers were a quartermaster and a Loyalist. Not regulars. Not regular infantry, at any rate."

"What do you have in mind, sir?"

"Well, if we could get these iron bars loose, we'd have weapons. I don't know about you, but I'd rather go down fighting than meekly stretch my neck for the hangman."

O'Ballance smiled for the first time in a while. "By God, sir. It's worth a try. The Royal Americans won't go down without a fight!"

It was after midnight. The two condemned men had fashioned a cutting tool from the metal frame of the single bed in the corner, and since nightfall, each had taken turns twisting and chipping at the cement that held the bars. No one had noticed them, almost no one. For some time, a pair of eyes had watched them. Around one in the morning, they heard a shuffling sound.

Then they heard a voice, a female voice, from behind the door. "*Monsieur, monsieur.*"

"Fleurette?" Creed whispered. "What are you doing here?"

"I love you, *monsieur*. I know you can never love someone like me. But still, I must help you escape. I cannot bear to see you die. It is all my fault, *Monsieur*. My anger and pride. I stirred up my father. That did not take much. He is very jealous and hates the *Bostonais*, the Americans. And has no love of the *Anglais* as well. To think I seduced poor Bart. Now he lies dead. All my fault."

Fleurette appeared sincere, but Creed grew suspicious. "You risked coming into this place for my love? Do you expect me to believe that?"

"My father has all but sold me to that *Anglais* colonel. I am no man's property. Not even my father has the right to use me in such a manner."

"Where is your father?" Creed was still suspicious.

"Drinking with his friends. He celebrates your death."

"How did you get through the guards?" Creed asked.

"There is only one guard, and He likes squaws." She looked at him as though she dropped a few shillings into the guard's hands. In his day, Creed had known many high and low-born women but never one who seemed to give of herself so casually.

Still, Creed's heart softened. "He'll never have another as comely, Fleurette. What we need is a chisel or a long piece of steel. We have scraped at these bars for hours...."

"I have something better, *Monsieur*." Fleurette smiled and pulled a set of keys from inside her skirt. "The guard fell asleep, so I took them."

She unlocked the inner door, then the outer. "I know a safe way. There is a back alley. Nobody will see us."

O'Ballance looked up at the gallows as they crossed the narrow courtyard. "It would have been a long drop."

They cleared the archway when a flame was seen moving along the alley.

O'Ballance whispered, "A patrol, sir. Looks like only two, and they move quite casually."

"They don't expect to encounter anyone at this late hour, and I see no reason to disappoint," Creed said.

"They circle the building, *Monsieur*. They never even check with the guard. Follow me."

She led them down a passageway between the outer wall of the fortification and the town. They watched the flame pass by and disappear behind the wall.

"A good thing General Burgoyne has ordered almost every man south," O'Ballance said.

"It will take only a few to end this night for us. Be vigilant." Creed's eyes searched for any sign of more patrols or sentries.

"I saw a small boat on the river, *Monsieur*. We might reach it and pass by the *Anglais* army while it is still dark."

"We?" Creed asked.

"*Mais oui*! I cannot remain here after this. There are Americans who like squaws too. I will find one."

He clasped her small brown hand. "No need for that, Fleurette. You can find honest work with the army. And many soldiers would vie for your hand, not just your pleasures."

In the dark, he did not see her blush.

They reached the water just before three. As Fleurette said, a small canoe was on the creek's bank, only about twenty feet across.

"This is the river?" O'Ballance asked.

"It runs a mile and empties into the great river that flows to the American lands south of here," Fleurette replied.

Creed glanced at the sky and thought he saw a faint glow to the east.

"If we paddle quickly and remain quiet, we might make it past Burgoyne's army before dawn. If my calculations are correct, General Schuyler's pickets should be no more than twelve miles south of them."

O'Ballance pushed the canoe halfway over the bank, its prow dangling a few feet above the fast-moving water.

"No paddles here, sir."

Creed turned to Fleurette. "Did you see if this canoe had paddles?"

She just looked at him. Even in the dark, he could see her face twist into a look of hate.

The voice of Serge Binoche hissed from the trees like a snake, "I see you are still meeting my daughter in the night, *monsieur*. That is something I plan to end once and for all."

Before Creed could think, a dozen rough hands were on him, pulling him from the riverbank while kicking and beating him. He flailed with his fists, and several men went down to his blows until someone threw a rope over his head and bound his arms to his torso.

"Go, Sergeant. Go now! We're betrayed!"

Instead of going, O'Ballance lunged at the closest brave with the cutting tool taken from the gaol. He plunged the blunt end into the warrior's stomach, cracking bone and crushing vitals, but the brave was quick with the knife and plunged it into O'Ballance's side.

O'Ballance staggered back with a moan. Two of the Iroquois struck at him with war clubs. The first blow broke O'Ballance's left arm with a loud crack.

Now enraged, O'Ballance went at them with his metal shaft in hand. He swung sluggishly but methodically, first right, then left. As one brave reeled back in pain, another would rush up and replace him. By the time O'Ballance had beaten off three assailants, a young brave had leaped on his back and plunged his hunting knife into the sergeant's chest, back, and neck. But O'Ballance cast him off, sending the youth tumbling.

The sergeant staggered in slow circles, weak on his legs from trauma, shock, and blood loss. The warriors stopped the attack to watch his death dance. They began a frightening combination of cheering and jeering until Binoche stepped from the dark, grabbed O'Ballance by the hair, and ran his knife through his scalp. A cry of victory went up from the braves as Binoche waved the bloody scalp in the air, then tauntingly thrust it into his victim's face. O'Ballance's eyes narrowed in scorn before falling to his knees and tumbling face forward on the wet grass.

Binoche turned to Creed. "He was too weak to cry for mercy, but I shall make certain you remain strong enough to feel much pain before returning you to the *Anglais* for hanging."

Creed crumbled to the soggy ground when Binoche's large foot struck his stomach. Another kick caught Creed's jaw. Fortunately, Binoche's blow glanced off the side of his chin in the darkness. Several arms lifted him from the soft earth and carried him along a path that followed the creek upstream about 100 yards. They had prepared a pole sunk into the ground in a clearing for him. With whoops and cries in the pigeon mix of Iroquois, Huron, and French, they twisted thick ropes around his body and bound him to the pole.

Binoche cried in French, "I will not let the *Anglais* rob Serge Binoche of his revenge! No one robs Serge Binoche. No one deprives him of his due or his pleasure. No one!"

His bearded face rubbed against Creed. "So, my daughter is not good enough for you? *Bien*, then watch her love a dozen men and then spit in your face. Before I take the knife to you."

Binoche looked into the starry sky and pounded his chest. "My justice, before the English king's!"

His men gyrated and danced in a frenzy – all acclaiming the victory of their leader. They bowed to no king, chief, or Englishman. They had no morals, followed no law, and had no love for anything but themselves. They were renegades who knew only the wilderness in which they lived and thrived.

Binoche pulled out a large, wicked-looking scalping knife and waved it over his head. Creed, hunched forward against his bonds, looked up. He saw Binoche dance a strange dance in a tight circle with his daughter. Fleurette undulated and responded to his every move. Then Binoche grabbed a bottle from one of his men and threw his head back. Creed could smell the rum dripping down his black, hairy jowls from six feet.

Binoche began to laugh. "*Monsieur*, we will yet deliver you to the gallows from which you had thought you escaped. But I will wave your scalp in victory while I watch you hang."

He staggered towards Creed with a grin and poked at Creed with the point of the knife, but it was clear his hatred would only sate itself with Creed's bloody scalp.

Fleurette emerged from the darkness and scratched Creed's face. The blood dribbled down his chin, and he turned his head the other way. She stroked the blood and then licked it from her fingers.

"I will enjoy myself with these men, but that will mean nothing next to the joy of seeing my father swinging your scalp in his hand," she purred like a feral cat.

Ritual-like, an orgy of hate-filled lust exploded before Creed's eyes. They formed a semi-circle before Creed as Fleurette joined them in a chain. Creed could only see shadows of their forms writhing in a dance-like rhythm in the darkness, while others yelped and howled.

Creed tried desperately to loosen the bonds as they performed but to no avail. Soon, they would take his scalp and then return the "escaped" prisoner to Sinclair and claim some reward to boot. At last, they finished their ritual, and everything grew strangely quiet.

Fleurette slipped from the group and spoke softly. "There is still one left. Will he not show his love for me?"

The group exploded again into howls and began a dance around Fleurette as she approached Binoche with the ritual knife.

Creed averted his eyes. *What perverse act is next?* Then, from the corner of his eye, he saw a knife clenched in a massive dark fist. The blade cut swiftly, and Creed's bonds dropped to the ground.

"Can you run, *Monsieur*?" Pierre whispered.

"I think so," Creed replied weakly.

"Pierre? Are you a ghost? Or am I, too, dead?"

"We are both alive, *Monsieur*, but your friend the sergeant is dead, and we may join him. Move quickly! Friends wait with a canoe."

Creed realized this was no dream. "Let's go!"

They slipped into the dark wood line and sprinted along a deer trail that snaked south towards the river. They had gotten no more than 100 yards when a cry went up from the group. Binoche's drunken voice was cursing them all and beckoning a thousand demons on their families. "*Allez, vous chiens!*"

Creed's wobbly legs pumped harder.

Pierre plunged into the woods, hunched forward with a tomahawk in one hand and a long musket in the other. Branches slapped at their faces, and the soft ground turned almost sponge-like when they approached the creek.

Creed could make out the shaded form of Etienne Androche and two Huron companions sitting in a long canoe! Pierre grabbed the stern to hold the craft steady as Creed jumped in. A pair of musket balls hummed through the dark branches hanging over their heads.

"Push off quickly, Pierre," Androche said.

But Pierre stopped and swung the musket to his shoulder. Two of the faster Iroquois plunged out of the darkness, brandishing their muskets. Pierre's shot exploded the chest of one, who tumbled back into the ferns. The second kept coming at Pierre, waving his musket like a club. Pierre charged him, deflected the musket with his own, then twisted around and plunged his tomahawk into the man's exposed side. Blood spurted, and the man fell back with the blade still buried in his torso. Pierre sprang into the canoe and pushed off as the other Iroquois began arriving amid howls and curses.

"Quickly, *monsieur*. Take a paddle. We must hurry," Androche urged.

Creed reached into the canoe's bottom, where he found a paddle and plunged it into the cold water. They all began rowing in frantic unison. The canoe picked up speed as it twisted through the low hills leading to the North River. They could hear Binoche's men trying to close on them.

"This creek twists its way west and south. They might still reach us before we reach the river," Androche said.

Several musket blasts erupted to their right as if on cue, sending lead buzzing past them. With a horrific *whoop*, one of Binoche's braves plunged into the creek ahead of them and swam toward the canoe. A second plunged.

"They are trying to delay us while the others come up. Keep paddling till they reach us," Creed said.

The rowing invigorated Creed, and the depredations of the past few days began to fade. He was back in command.

The first brave slowed himself to allow his partner to catch up, and then they swam in tandem towards them.

"Steer directly at them, Etienne. When they try to avoid our prow, use your paddle on them," Creed said.

Androche brandished a tomahawk. "These are not the first Iroquois to try to take my canoe, *monsieur*."

The canoe swirled through the creek, which began roiling as the rushing, plunging waters grew louder.

"Rapids around the bend! That's why they are trying to stop us here," Creed said.

Suddenly, the long, bronzed arms grabbed at the canoe. One brave pulled himself over the side with one hand and plunged a dagger at Creed. But he was ready and ran the end of his paddle into his chest. The brave seemed unharmed and thrust the knife at Creed's forearm. Before his blade could strike, a blow from Androche's tomahawk sent the attacker toppling into the water with a mix of gray and red fluid squirting from his skull.

Creed turned to thank him and saw the second brave sink his knife into Androche, who slumped over with widened eyes locked on Creed. Pierre's arm shot out, and his dagger flew past Creed, striking Androche's attacker squarely in the chest. Creed pushed his body over the side, and they continued around the bend.

"The falls," Creed announced. "I'll hold Androche. You try to keep the canoe pointing downriver."

As Pierre and his companions struggled with the canoe, Creed wrapped his arms around Androche's bleeding body. *Stay with us, Androche.*

The canoe began to pitch and roll as it darted through swirling waters, frothing and spraying in all directions. Despite the summer heat, the water chilled to the bone. The current grew in strength. At any moment, they would be dashed against the rocks.

The river now began to roar like a thunderstorm. The canoe plunged forward into the darkness and seemed to hang for a second, then tumbled nose-first down a twelve-foot drop and struck the roiling waters with a flopping sound. It continued a few more seconds and plunged a second time, rolling and yawing from side to side. The canoe pitched back and forth with a fierceness that nearly shook the men loose.

Suddenly, everything turned still. Yet, although waterlogged, the canoe careened downstream towards the North River.

Chapter 24

Batten Kill, New York, September 13ᵗʰ, 1777

The long, dark column slithered down the road like a prehistoric serpent – over 5,000 men counting von Riedesel's Germans. Marching two abreast, each company saluted the commander-in-chief as it crossed the long wooden bridge over the North River before turning south towards Saratoga. Sinclair sat nervously watching, hoping there was still time for his plan to succeed.

The morning sun glinted off gleaming buttons, buckles, and silver *gorgets*. Leather, cleaned and brushed, stood out sharply against the mix of red, white, and blue uniforms. Flags and pennants snapped crisply against the breeze. Wheels creaked as gun after gun and caisson after caisson wheeled across the wooden plank bridge.

John Burgoyne took it in with unbridled satisfaction. "Look at them, gentlemen! The lads are simply spoiling for the fight despite hardship and depredation, ungodly weather, disloyal native allies, and rebel chicanery."

An aide de camp nodded. "Indeed, sir, and they are aching for *revanche'*. I almost pity the rebels."

Several staff officers shifted their field of vision to ensure their commander did not see their reaction to the comment, for, as all knew, the army had reached dire straits. Yes, the men, when competently led, still made a powerful and dominating force to face. But most realized this was the last roll of the dice. They had outrun their supply chain, and failure to reach Albany could result in destruction.

Sinclair struggled to keep his horse still. "All drama aside, sir, if we stick to my plan, we shall prevail despite past frustrations."

"Indeed, Lazarus," Burgoyne sniffed. "Any word from Captain Fraser?"

Sinclair's face darkened. "No. He assured me his riflemen would run 'Lawrence' to ground. But no sign of him."

"And the rebel army? Any sign of them?"

"No, sir. Pity, the savages have all but left us. That wastrel Binoche and his handful are almost all we have left, and we now know of his unreliability." Sinclair had to hide Binoche's part in Creed's escape to protect his role in the affair.

"Where is he now, Lazarus?"

"Attached to General Fraser, sir. The western flank, wilderness and all, would better suit that lot."

"Good thinking, Lazarus. And the girl? I understand he has quite a becoming half-breed daughter."

Sinclair swallowed. "With my baggage, sir. For her protection, of course. And it ensures Binoche's reliable performance in the upcoming battle."

Burgoyne eyed him briefly and guffawed, "Why, Lazarus, aren't you the old lecher! You can't fool me. I wager that you had your eye on the fetching little strumpet all the time. Very cunning sending her father off into the wilderness."

"I only want what is best for the army, sir."

"Well, in that case, see that she is sent to my pavilion tonight. She'll be safer there."

The other staff laughed at Burgoyne's humor. Many felt his *bon vivant* reputation added to the army's *elan*. Few realized that beneath his rakish demeanor dwelt a cunning and creative mind. For Burgoyne wanted, needed, desperately to succeed. And this, Sinclair hoped to exploit.

Almost out of supply and nearly cut off from his base hundreds of miles to the rear, only he and Burgoyne knew there would be no help from Howe. With Barry Saint Leger's small force repulsed at Fort Stanwix, he and his reduced force were now on their own, with rebels closing in from three sides.

Burgoyne motioned for Sinclair to ride with him. When some distance from the staff, he spoke, "I should have listened to you back at Richelieu, Lazarus. This diversion by our young captain may have cost me this campaign. The letter from Clinton leaves little choice. Howe has headed south and aims to take the rebel capital while I lure rebel forces north. I have been played the fool, I'm afraid. Better to have lost my wife's fortune at the gambling tables."

"You have already, sir." Sinclair retorted, still smarting from the rebuke over the wench.

"Indeed, Lazarus. You are right. And yet I recovered from that to command this great endeavor. But Howe has thoroughly humbugged me."

"As did Lord Germain, sir, with his ambivalent directions to Howe," Sinclair said. He needed to stoke Burgoyne's resentment, which would make him rely more on his adjutant.

"Yes, that gave him all the leeway needed to lead me into thinking I could count on his support."

Sinclair grimaced. "While intending to use his army to lure Washington north so he could make a move on the rebel capital."

"We are the cape to Howe, the matador, I'm afraid."

"As Barry was ours...."

"Howe, the ponderous commander, had gotten his way. We must now take Albany at all costs, Lazarus. *Alea iacta est.*"

"I know that better than anyone, sir. Even if Howe had come north, our men would begin to lack victuals and supplies in weeks. I have done all I can to move supplements south."

Burgoyne grasped Sinclair's upper arm. "You are a good officer, Lazarus."

"Thank you, sir."

"Join me with von Riedesel and his lovely wife for dinner tonight."

Sinclair beamed. "I would be delighted, sir."

"And Lazarus...."

"Sir?"

"You'll get the wench back as soon as we take Albany." Laughing at his wit, Burgoyne spurred his horse down the road and clambered across the bridge.

Waving his hat when he reached the other side, he spurred south, crying, "Albany, Lazarus!"

***

The canoe spilled into the North River just as the rising sun broke over the horizon. Trees and bushes along the river glistened with the freshness of the morning dew. The water shimmered in the early sunlight, and an azure skyline completed the scene.

Creed enjoyed none of it. His focus was on moving south as fast as possible. The Batten Kill creek dumped them into the North River. When they turned south, Creed's stomach cramped at the sight ahead. Directly ahead, a wooden bridge spanned the river. Armed men in brilliant red coats stood on either side, clutching muskets primed and ready. To their left, the road leading to the riverbank was crammed with red-clad troops forming for the long day's march.

Creed knew they had seconds to act. "*Anglais* up ahead, Pierre, steer tight left into this cove. Quickly!"

Pierre spoke a few words, and the two Hurons shifted their paddles, guiding the canoe gently into the cove and under a canopy of bushes.

"We have no firelocks that work and few tomahawks," Creed said. "How is Etienne?"

"He is with God, *Monsieur*," Pierre said.

Creed made a sign of the cross, as did Pierre.

"Are you Catholic?" Creed asked.

Pierre nodded. "The Jesuits brought me into the Society. I hoped to serve my people someday. But that dream is gone."

"You are a Jesuit but did not take Holy Orders?"

"I killed a man." Pierre hung his head. "A Mohawk."

"I knew that, but that was long ago, and ...."

"No, *monsieur*. After my Holy Orders."

"What? What happened?"

"What does it matter? The Mohawk is dead. I can never be a priest again. So now, I serve one."

"Who?"

Pierre pulled a ruby-colored bead from his shirt.

Creed startled. "Father Vincennes! So, you are part of his company of patriots?"

"We are few now who serve him. The war has taken some—sickness and apathy, others."

"So, Father Vincennes! Speaking of whom – do you have more maps?"

Pierre motioned to a leather valise.

"Likely soaked and ruined."

The North Spy

"Perhaps not, *monsieur*. You must take them and go quickly. The *Anglais* are just stirring. If you move quickly, they will not catch you. We will go north on foot."

"But poor Androche."

Pierre rummaged through Androche's pockets and removed another ruby-colored bead. "He took an oath as well. Along with the maps are Androche's notes."

"His notes?"

"In French, *monsieur*. During the trip south, he wrote the numbers of the *Anglais* regiments. He noted their leaders. The *Anglais* take no notice of a vagabond *coureur* and his squaw walking through their encampments."

Pierre and his companions gently carried Androche's limp form from the canoe. "We will carry him north and bury him with his people."

"His woman?" Creed asked.

"She has gone north already, *Monsieur*. Our task was to see you safely past the *Anglais*. Unfortunately, this is all we can do."

"You did enough. Pierre, I can't believe you are alive. I returned to look for you and found only blood. Later, Bart said he had killed you."

"I was struck in the head by your officer. Fortunately, Androche and his men were nearby. They saved me."

"So, they...."

"*Oui*, monsieur."

"I should have known better about Bart. He was under the spell of Binoche's daughter."

"The power of a woman is often impossible to resist. But it is all in the past. Take this."

He handed Creed one of their tomahawks. Creed took the weapon by the hilt and grabbed Pierre by the arm. "I am forever in your debt, Pierre. A debt I can never repay."

"One does not do this for pay, *monsieur*. In the end, we both serve the same master." He stared at Creed with piercing dark eyes that bore into his very being.

"What do you mean by that?"

"I have already said too much, *monsieur*. Go now, before the *Anglais* are up in numbers." He turned to the others. "*Allez! A Nord.*"

They lifted Androche on their backs, and their worn and waterlogged moccasins slowly tread up the narrow path into the dark forest.

***

Creed's feet slogged through the black mud until his canoe slid into the still waters of the cove. He quickly slipped into the steady current of the North River. He took several bold strokes and let the current quietly carry him downstream. The paddle steered him around the dark moss-coated rocks and hanging tree limbs.

He saw another obstacle ahead – a bridge spanning just feet above the water. The air was filled with the skirl of bagpipes and the piping of flutes, a mix of martial music to rouse the troops for their early-morning march.

He saw no sentries. But he caught the sounds of sergeants and corporals urging men across the creaky wooden span.

"Keep movin', you beggars!"

"Your betters are across, and General Johnny awaits ye! "

"Come on now! Get a move on!"

Music and shouting, plus the *click-clack* of hobnails on the wooden planks, gave Creed the chance to risk the paddle. Thanks to the music, his powerful strokes could not be heard over the din of the column. He began to dig into the black water.

The canoe glided downstream, and he quickly closed on the bridge. *Faster now. I've got to slip past before they notice me.*

The tree limbs and thick green brush along the bank screened him from the casual viewer while the early morning mist spread a shroud across the water.

He paddled rapidly as the canoe glided toward the bridge in a burst of speed. *Keep it going, lad.* He slid under the creaking bridge. He dug his paddle. *Ten yards... twenty... thirty.... The mist began to thin and lift. Fifty yards.*

He then spied a sentry on the west bank, 150 yards south of the bridge. His dark blue coat marked him as a German, one of von Riedesel's men. He stood motionless on a rocky overhang, looking southward.

The sentry had an easy shot at him. And even if he missed, there was no telling how many other sentries or patrols would come running after the blast. He steered the canoe to the west, directly towards the sentry, and waved. Creed's German was rusty, but he hoped to get within range for a desperate gambit with the tomahawk if it failed.

"*Achtung!*" Creed called out softly. "*Wo ist* Fraser? *Chef der Aufklarungs Truppen. Ich habe eine wichtige Meldung.*"

"*Weiss ich nicht. Hier is die Stutzpunkt.*"

He bluffed him into thinking he had a message for Fraser. Creed nodded and waved his paddle downriver, indicating he would sail past the sentry point.

"*Ich gehe voran,*" Creed shouted. "I'm going ahead."

His nerves gave him a boost of energy. He dug the paddle into the water. Another 200 yards would get him free of the forward line of the British.

He reached a sharp bend in the river, but a cold, wet sensation began to seep into his breeches. The rough and tumble of the journey had finally taken its toll on the canoe's birch hide. He placed the packet with Androche's notes inside his shirt and tucked the tomahawk into his belt.

The canoe inched lower into the river. *I've got but seconds.* Creed pointed the vessel toward the bank as the water began rising over his ankles. Moments later, it settled in waist-high water at the bottom of the river. Exhausted, he began to slog through the thick muck to the riverbank.

He stumbled over tree roots and bushes, pulled his way arm over arm up the steep embankment, and collapsed. His body ached from exertion and the blows he had taken from Binoche and his men.

Creed shrugged off the fatigue and forced himself to his feet to get his bearings.

"Halt in the king's name!" A smartly dressed officer in the garb of a Canadian Royalist pointed a sword at him.

A patrol! Creed bolted through the trees, dodging branches and bushes and clambering over the gray rocks that seemed to be everywhere.

Shouts in French came from behind him. From his right, he heard the pop, pop of muskets. He pumped his legs madly, leaping rocks and logs like a gazelle. He suddenly burst into an open area over 100 yards across and long. The far end of the clearing had a thick stand of trees with a steep rise of the ground leading to a wooded ridgeline running west.

Creed stopped gasping for breath as he scanned the edge of the woods for signs of the Canadians. Nothing – then he saw the glint of metal along the upper reaches of the ridge. He cursed himself for getting cut off. He heard the rustling of branches behind him. The Canadians would be on him soon. Bending forward, he began a steady trot across the open.

Muskets crackled from the wood line behind him. Lead balls pinged the ground just twenty feet behind him.

"Form skirmish line!" An officer called out in French. Behind him were a score of men in hunting clothes. The officer wore a dark green jacket and black leggings. The Canadians skirted forward like rabbits, stopping only to take shots, then dropping behind to reload. Then they would rush forward and rejoin the skirmish line.

Their shots peppered the trees around him. And they were getting closer.

Creed saw a draw up ahead to his right. He ran for it. But the Canadians quickly formed a "V" and scampered effortlessly in pursuit.

General Burgoyne must desperately need a prisoner! Creed felt the head of the tomahawk with his right hand. He was determined not to be taken alive again. He would make the Canadians kill him first and take as many with him as possible.

By the time he reached the draw, he was panting from exhaustion and the morning heat. The draw rose quickly up the steep ridge. *Never make it.*

"*Attendez!* Halt in the king's name before we shoot you dead, *monsieur!*" the officer ordered.

The crack of musket balls tore into a tree on his right. *Warning shots!* They were thirty yards behind and gaining on him. *They want me alive.* With lungs burning and legs numb, it would soon be time to stand and fight. *But where? How?*

The trail suddenly bent sharply left and steepened. Creed began the forlorn scramble up the draw.

A new torrent of fire erupted, sending lead humming through the trees, cracking rocks, and slapping at branches and leaves. Creed dropped to a knee and drew the tomahawk. He tossed Androche's papers deep into the bushes.

Like a Bezerker of old, he summoned ferocity and rage to draw upon his last measure of strength. The firing increased in tempo. He knew he would be running straight back into a sheet of hot lead that would melt right through him. He made the sign of the cross – no time for a final Hail Mary.

Creed launched himself back down the trail at a run. He turned right at the sharp switchback and began waving the tomahawk.

"God save Ireland! God save America!" he shouted.

When he turned for his final charge, dense gun smoke blanketed the trail – the black powder seemed to envelop everything. His eyes teared, and his throat choked in the mix of morning heat with thick smoke. Tomahawk raised, he pushed forward blindly through the smoke and the Canadians.

Suddenly, a strong arm grabbed him and pulled the tomahawk from his hand. Another pair of arms gripped his shoulders and spun him about while a third held him fast.

"Whoa, now, pilgrim! Don't think you want to greet your friends. Most of 'em are dead anyway." The voice had a flat New England sound.

"Who are you?" Creed asked.

"Captain Ebenezer Utley, New Hampshire Militia. We just sent those lobster-loving Canadians running back to Quebec. Who are you?"

Before he could reply, a large horse appeared through the smoke. The horse snorted, shuffling its feet, almost as if it expected its rider to take off in different directions.

"What have we here?" the rider asked.

"This man was running from the Canadians. They seemed to be sporting with him cause none of their balls struck home. We decided to impress them with some Yankee firepower," Utley replied.

Creed rose and met the officer with a steady gaze. He was not tall in the saddle. His skin looked swarthy, but his close-set eyes, nose, and chin had a piercing effect. He exuded nervous energy like a hawk anxious to launch after its prey.

"Who are you?" the officer demanded.

"Lieutenant Jeremiah Creed, late of the Second Continental Light Dragoons."

The officer frowned. "This army has no dragoons."

"But General Washington's does. I'm here on his instructions."

The officer looked skeptically at him. "Washington? Up here? What instruction is that?"

Creed pointed towards the trees. "Have someone search those woods. I threw a packet there, expecting my greeting those Canadians was my last earthly event. There's information that could prove useful to General Schuyler."

"Hah! Schuyler's gone. Relieved of command. Gates now has the honors, sad to say." He turned to Utley. "Fetch his packet and bring him with it to headquarters."

"Yes, sir," Utley replied with a surprisingly crisp salute.

General Benedict Arnold twisted his horse in a tight circle and cantered south.

Chapter 25

Bemis Heights, September 15th, 1777

Creed wiped the last of the soap from his chin. Someone had found him a spare cotton shirt, leather breeches, and moccasins, which he donned after tying his hair back in a tight queue.

The stone-faced corporal led Creed from the tent and down a trail to a large log and mortar farmhouse that served as headquarters for General Horatio Gates, newly appointed commander of the Department of the North.

Minutes later, Creed stood before the general, who sat at a small pine desk covered with papers. A lieutenant colonel dressed in the dark blue uniform of the Pennsylvania Continental Line stood next to Gates. Unctuous, almost swarthy in appearance, he looked familiar to Creed.

Gates was a former regular British officer who settled in Virginia after the French and Indian War. He had many influential connections in Congress and was widely regarded as a rival to Washington. But he had never led large-scale forces in combat.

He had a shock of gray hair tied loosely, and his coat hung neatly on the back of his chair. Large, nickel-framed glasses were perched on his nose. He hardly looked up from the papers spread before him.

"I am finishing reviewing the documents you captured, sir. They are barely legible – almost a pigeon scrawl and in some version of French. Some of the information I find interesting. I believe we can surmise the approximate strength of Burgoyne's force. The proximate number of cannons. The names of some regiments. But the questions I need you to answer are simple. Where are they at this moment, and when will they attack?" Gates's gaze slowly turned up at Creed. "Can you answer that, sir?"

"Burgoyne will attack as soon as he can fix your positions. His native allies have deserted him except for a few renegades and their Canadian friends. He is reduced to one small company of sharpshooters for his scouting."

"Just one?" the colonel asked.

The voice sounded familiar.

"Yes. But under the command of an experienced and talented officer named Alexander Fraser."

"I know him from the last war," Gates said.

"Alexander is a fine officer, leading hand-picked men, but they're not Indians. Burgoyne's options will be limited if you have chosen your defensive position wisely."

"When in blazes will he attack us?" Gates demanded.

"Soon. A few days at most. He has exhausted his supplies. He can't retreat. And if he does not take Albany within the fortnight, they shall begin to starve."

Gates nodded with a mild show of satisfaction.

"How many men?" asked the colonel standing by him.

"Maybe seven thousand left, but they are all quite good. The gravity of their situation is widely known amongst them, and many are discomforted by it."

"So, they'll fight?" Gates asked.

"Oh, they shall indeed. These men are professionals who do want to best us."

Gates looked at the officer next to him. "What do you think, James?"

The officer looked at Creed. "Based on Mister Creed's assessment, our chances are good. We dig in and let him break himself on us."

Creed could not place the face or the voice. Yet they seemed so familiar.

"General Arnold thinks you are a British provocateur sent to fill us with false information, which would mean most, if not everything, you have presented has a nefarious purpose. Arnold is a brilliant officer but impetuous in judgment and quick to anger."

"On the other hand, Lieutenant Colonel Wilkinson claims to have known a Lieutenant Jeremiah Creed. In New Jersey, of all places."

Creed looked closely at the officer standing before him. And then it hit him. Wilkinson, then a captain, was Major General Charles Lee's aide. They met near Basking Ridge, and their exchange was less than cordial.

Wilkinson eyed Creed and then looked at Gates. "I knew a Lieutenant Jeremiah Creed who was a 'specially assigned officer' of General Washington. This might be him. So much has passed since then. My memory cannot vouch with complete and unreserved certainty that this is the same man."

Creed was flabbergasted. He had always held this man in high suspicion, unsure of what, but now that officer was failing to vouch for him. *Because I know he abandoned his general, Charles Lee, to the British.*

Gates crossed his plump hands on his desk and leaned forward. "I must use due diligence in these matters. Therefore, I will send a discreet inquiry to General Washington. That will take some time."

An orderly opened the door, revealing a large, broad-shouldered man filling the doorway. He entered the room and stood arms akimbo, with giant, ham-like fists on his hips. He wore the weathered hunting smock favored by American light infantry. The officer's sword hung casually at his side, with a rifle and powder horn slung across his back. His large, weathered face could not hide his powerful nose and steely eyes, which seemed to take in everything at once.

"Good of you to come, Dan. I wanted you to speak with our 'prisoner' directly," Gates said. The interruption seemed to miff him, but, like so many in the army, he had too much fear and respect for Colonel Daniel Morgan to risk his ire.

"I heard from Arnold that you had a rebel spy in tow. Wanted to chat with him before you strung him up," Morgan replied with a large grin.

"Did General Arnold provide his name?" Wilkinson asked.

"No, no, he didn't. Said the man claimed to be on a mission for General Washington. Arnold doesn't believe it, but I do."

Gates removed his glasses. "What reasons have you to believe this man's claim?"

"I've got a letter."

"From Washington?" Gates asked.

"No, from a colonel named Fitzgerald, but signed for His Excellency. It was sealed with orders to open it upon my arrival up north. Guess I'm up north, huh?"

"And how did you receive this letter?"

Morgan crossed his arms. "His Excellency sent me three of this officer's men to help here. They had it. Their mission was to be on the lookout for him if he got through British lines. Guess Arnold helped with that one, though. He wasn't too happy when I advised he may have rescued our spy, not bagged a British one."

"Sir, as I look at this gentleman, my memory refreshes. I believe this is the very man I knew in New Jersey," Wilkinson said.

"Are you certain?" Gates asked.

"Yes, sir. General Arnold accused this man wrongfully," Wilkinson said.

Gates' face lit up. "Of course, he did. He is often impetuous. We might have hanged an innocent man on account of Arnold."

"Not just innocent, general. But a man who risked his life for the cause on a mission nobody else could attempt," Morgan said roughly.

"Indeed, Dan. He may return to Washington's camp if he can find it," Gates replied jocularly.

Morgan shook his head, and his face reddened.

"I think Colonel Morgan has other ideas, don't you, sir?" Wilkinson said.

"Damned right, I do! I need men like him and his boys. And he knows these woods. We've got a better chance of figuring out what Burgoyne's likely to pull on us with him. Besides, from what I hear, he's a pretty good scrapper when he's not spying."

Gates stood up. "Very well. Tell Arnold he is released to your command with full rank."

Morgan grinned. "By golly, I knew you'd see it my way, general."

***

Creed and Morgan tramped along a wagon track that led west to Morgan's encampment. He took in the pungent aroma of the campfires. To his right, Creed saw the trappings of a military camp. Not the neat white tentage of Burgoyne's army, but a mix of worn-looking canvas and weathered leather of different sizes. Soldiers stripped to shirt sleeves, strained, weary arms and legs, hauling carts and wagons.

A half-furlong north along a stretch of earth and logs marked the primitive defenses at the northern extreme of the camp.

"This must stretch a mile across," Creed marveled.

Morgan spat a piece of tobacco. "Keeps them farm boys and city soldiers busy, I guess. Like camping in a giant box, if ya ask me. We don't put much stock in that nonsense in my outfit. The boys stay on the move, looking for the lobsters, not sitting behind a pile of logs waiting for him."

"Still, sir, the design of these works is quite good. European-like. I wonder who the chief engineer is."

"Some fella named Koskeeyooska. Polish, they say. Not sure I like the idea of all these foreigners coming here and being made officers overnight."

"Kosciuszko? Colonel Kosciusko?"

"That's right. You know him?"

"No, sir, just of him. They say he prepared the defense works at Ticonderoga. Who are those men up ahead?" Creed asked.

"Why, that's General Dearborn's men. Continental Light Infantry, they call 'em. Good men, if I do say so, almost as good as my riflemen."

Morgan bent over and slapped his thigh as he laughed out loud.

***

The aroma of bacon stirred Creed from his first real sleep in many days. He stretched his arms and legs to fight the chill of the early autumn morning.

"How long have I been sleeping?"

"'Bout twelve hours, sir. It's almost nine," Thomas Jeffries replied.

He flipped the four strips of bacon with a sharp-pointed stick. Thomas, Elias Parker, and Jonathan Beall had ridden north with Morgan. They were sent, ostensibly, to scout for the elite corps of riflemen, but Tallmadge had given them a more important mission: find Creed. But his Irish luck brought him to them.

Creed stood up and stretched the muscles in his arms and legs. "Tis a lovely mornin' to be a patriot, isn't it, Thomas? Hungry as I am, I must enjoy some of that lovely-smelling stuff."

"It's all for you, Lieutenant. We ate hours ago."

"Where are the other lads?" Creed was beside himself when Morgan introduced him to his men. After the tense moments behind British lines, this was like a dream. He still had trouble believing it.

"Fishing."

"Fishing? You jest."

"No, sir. Fish fry for dinner. Fish all but jump into your arms up here. Colonel Morgan's orders. It seems we may be busy after dark."

"I see. And where is the good general? He nearly killed me with his damned Pennsylvania moonshine. The British spirits were much kinder to the palate and the head. Any tea by chance?"

"No, sir. Just black coffee," Thomas replied.

"Yankee tea, eh? Very well."

An hour later, Creed inspected his gear. When they came north, his men had packed his weaponry, clothes, and a money box.

Most of what he valued in this world lay before him: his men, his horse, Finn, his weapons, and his mother's inheritance. Yet the one he held most dearly was living in the enemy's bosom hundreds of miles away.

He thought of Emily constantly, and although their separation was a struggle, the fact that he could never write her was worse. Then guilt struck as Creed realized he was not alone in his isolation. Thomas had no family. Beall and Parker had not seen their loved ones in over a year. And he knew much of the army would never see the faces of their loved ones again.

Creed smeared the last drop of oil on his rifle and sword-bayonet and casually slung the weapons over his shoulder. Morgan had provided him a hunting shirt of worn deerskin. He looked more like a rifleman than a Continental Line Dragoon.

A tall, rangy rifleman in a dun-colored hunting shirt approached. "You, Lieutenant Creed?"

"At your service."

"I'm Tom Guthrie. Colonel Morgan appointed me your sergeant."

"'Tis considerate of the colonel. But my unit is small, and my men have little need of a sergeant. Why, they have little need for me, for that matter."

"I'm the best-damned shot in the corps, Lieutenant. That's why he sent me."

"You were the best shot, maybe. Till Lieutenant Creed got here," Thomas boasted.

"Why, you little...."

Creed put a finger to Guthrie's lips. "Now, now hear this, laddie. We'll have nothing of that sort spoken around here. If you're under my command, you'll follow my rules and orders. And rule one is that each of my White Knights is a brother in arms, regardless of his look, language, or belief."

"It's just...."

"Just what? Be sure to choose your words carefully, now."

Guthrie's eyes lowered. "Nothing. You're right. Please accept my apology."

"I need no apology – just obedience. Apologize to him."

Guthrie reddened. "I'll not...."

"Thomas is more of a soldier than you. He's just seventeen and has already felled more lobsters than you'll see in this war."

"I've got four notches on my rifle stock. Two taken at Trenton and two at Princeton. All officers," Guthrie boasted.

"Most impressive, Sergeant. But Thomas Jeffries would have no musket stock if I allowed him such braggadocio."

Guthrie regarded Thomas and nodded. "Accept my apology, soldier."

"Accepted, sergeant," Thomas replied.

"Now, let's see who the best shot is," Creed said.

Guthrie's mouth tightened. "What?"

"Let's have a friendly match. Just to see where we stand," Creed said. "You're not afraid of losing, are ye?"

Guthrie's chin rose, and his chest puffed like a rooster. "Wasn't a man in Wyoming Valley who could outshoot me before the war. Ain't nobody can do it here, neither."

"Never heard of this Wyoming. Where is it?" Creed asked.

"Pennsylvania. We have plenty of reason to be good shots. Plenty of Indians sniffing around."

"So, you're an Indian fighter?"

"Not exactly."

"Well, when it comes to fighting Indians, 'tis better to be exact. But we shall take our shots at the fish fry and let Colonel Morgan judge."

The fish fry was the talk of the camp. Morgan had sent fifty men to the North River with nets and hooks, and they returned with a bountiful harvest: mostly herring, shad, and bass. By three in the afternoon, the day's catch was grilling over open fires with ears of corn. They washed the food down with black coffee. A few men snuck in a pint of pine beer or a half cup of raw whiskey or moonshine.

The men gathered in an open field, where Morgan addressed the group after they had eaten. "Now, boys, we have a new officer, and he's said to be a better shot than Sergeant Guthrie."

Boos and *whoops* erupted. Morgan raised his hands in supplication. "Now settle down, boys. We're gonna have a little shootin' match."

Chapter 26

The Swords House, Saratoga, New York, September 18th, 1777

The rumble of wagons reverberated throughout the British camp. Lazarus Sinclair rubbed his hands together in anticipation. The supply wagons arrived from a village several miles north of them. They would likely be the last.

Sinclair glanced south. Some three miles away, the Americans waited on Bemis Heights. Burgoyne established headquarters at the house of a Loyalist, Thomas Swords, who rented a neat fifty-acre farmstead along the river that prospered in leather tanning.

Swords' wife Mary maintained the place after her husband was arrested for refusing to renounce the king. Now, she gladly opened her home to the British commander, who had come to crush the rebellion and save them from the depredations of the Whigs.

While the army prepared itself for the onslaught against the Americans, Burgoyne kept Captain Alexander Fraser's company busy scouting the rebels. Fraser's men and the few Indians and Canadians remaining with Burgoyne were frustrated in their attempts to find a weak point in the American defenses. And Sinclair knew with good reason: there was none.

Deserters reported that a Polish engineer named Kosciusko had built an impressive array of works stretching from the river to the rugged, thickly wooded mountains just a few miles to the west. Sinclair learned that Gate's deployment was well balanced, and his numbers grew each day while Burgoyne's dwindled.

Sinclair stepped back into the house and entered a room filled with colorful uniforms glinting with silver and gold braid. The aroma of tobacco hung over the room. Burgoyne had summoned his staff to his headquarters for a final discussion of his plan. Generals Fraser, Hamilton, and von Riedesel crowded around a table.

"I am glad you deigned to be with us, Lazarus," Burgoyne sniffed.

Cringing at the barb, Sinclair spread a rough sketch of the area across the long maple table – they lacked anything that would today be called a map.

"You've been out there. What does the land hold for us, Simon?" Burgoyne asked.

"A largely wooded plateau rises from the river south of us. Two large ravines running east-west between us and the rebel camp cut right across the plateau, sir."

"And just how large a camp?" Burgoyne asked.

"Considerable, sir. It runs along that entire ridge behind well-placed fortifications a few miles from here," Fraser said.

"We don't have enough cannons to lay a proper siege, and we have even less time," Sinclair said.

"Time?"

"I just watched the last supply wagons roll in from Saratoga."

"And the guns?"

"We had to fortify the rebel forts we seized. The others are taking longer to move. So we have but a few batteries in hand.

Burgoyne's ebullient manner suddenly drained from him, and his face darkened. "Who do we have to blame for that, Lazarus?"

Sinclair glared at his commander. The general seemed to forget Sinclair's earlier warnings as the army moved south.

"Our rear posts must be maintained, sir. And this is hardly ground for heavy artillery," Sinclair replied calmly.

Sinclair's relationship with Burgoyne had cooled. He had received an official reprimand for allowing the rebel spy Lawrence to escape at the hands of the rogue Canadian, Binoche. Binoche was put before a tribunal, but instead of prison or a firing squad, he was condemned to lead a forlorn hope against the Americans to open up the attack.

Burgoyne turned to Fraser. "Just how strong are the rebels along the river approach, Simon?"

"Quite strong, sir," said Fraser. "Behind their defenses sits a pontoon bridge. My men have observed supplies and troops coming over that bridge. It appears well defended."

"Have we received any word on the rebel center and right flank?"

"My men have scouted as far as the second ravine, called the Mill Creek. Between it and the larger ravine to the north is a place called Freeman's Farm. Some fields around provide cleared areas suitable for deployment. Shame the rebels decided not to defend it, as it can be easily taken."

"Why not take it then?" Sinclair said.

They all looked at him, and the room erupted in a babble of insults. Burgoyne raised his hand to silence them. "Go on, Lazarus."

"Make it our objective. Take it. From there, send forces through the woods and come in on the rebel left. What lies here, General Fraser?"

Sinclair pointed to a spot to the left front of the rebel defenses.

"High ground, thick with woods," Fraser said.

Sinclair tapped the map. "Then take that, and drive the rebels to the river. We demonstrate on their left to draw reinforcements and thin their lines. Then you pounce."

Burgoyne smiled. "By Jove, Lazarus, it might just work. We'll place some light field guns in the center to ensure it. While our guns pound them from the front, we'll...."

"Be advised, sir, that the land is hilly, as rugged as anywhere," Fraser said. "Our forces will necessarily move along narrow approaches."

Sinclair could not believe his ears. *It's as though he is talking him out of this.*

Burgoyne drummed his fingers pensively on the table. "What has become of that scoundrel Binoche?"

"Awaiting punishment with his pack of curs, sir. Our tribunal found them guilty of freeing the traitor Lawrence in an attempt to take the king's justice upon themselves," Sinclair said. He was proud of how he covered his role in the affair.

Burgoyne slapped Fraser on the chest playfully. "I suggest putting his band at the far end of your attack."

"Is it prudent to trust such a man one more time?" Fraser asked.

"Your men are expert shots. Use Binoche and his pack to flush out the rebels. Feel free to shoot them down if they fail to please you. I find it a dramatic fit for this campaign. The savages have betrayed me. So let us say one of their ilk must redeem the lot."

How can I ensure I don't attack before the other columns are ready?" Fraser asked.

"By the time you are around their flank, the other columns should be up," Sinclair replied.

Burgoyne waved his palm. "I'll move some light guns up with Hamilton. He is leading the center column directly at Freeman's Farm. Once there, we shall fire three shots to signal the attack."

Burgoyne turned to von Riedesel. "Baron, your Germans will proceed directly south to seize the pontoon bridge."

Von Riedesel puffed his chest. "*Ja*, we'll drive the rebels into the river."

Burgoyne's face brightened. Nobody mentioned that his plan was a repeat of what Sinclair had just proposed.

"When do we go?" Hamilton asked.

"At first light," Burgoyne replied.

He turned to Sinclair. "Lazarus will prepare the necessary orders. Meanwhile, let's have a bottle of claret."

When the wine was poured, they toasted the king, the plan, and the army.

Burgoyne raised his glass high. "A final toast, gentlemen. To our comely and generous hostess, Missus Swords."

"Here, here!" The officers clinked their glasses in unison.

"Seriously, gentlemen, this lovely woman has graciously offered her house, indeed her room, to our hospitality. Had we more Loyal Americans like the Swords, our work would be much simpler and pleasant."

They all murmured their agreement. But a few wondered if Burgoyne's comments hinted at more than gracious thanks for using her dwelling.

"Gentlemen, you are dismissed to attend to your commands. Lazarus, can you have orders to them in time?"

"Of course, sir," Sinclair replied tersely.

"It is all settled then. And Lazarus…"

"Sir?"

"You may have Binoche's wench back."

"So, our comely hostess beguiles you more than the Indian girl?" Hamilton asked.

"Indeed, but Mary Swords is no strumpet, nor will she play my mistress. No, the savage girl bites like one of these damned American copperheads and scratches like a hen in a fit."

Laughter erupted as the officers reached for their hats and took their leave.

***

John Freeman's Farm, September 19ᵗʰ, 1777

The morning fog cloaked the land with a chill that you could almost touch. They had found a tall maple tree and built a small platform to observe the front edge of the British camp. Jonathan Beall had the dawn watch.

Creed was growing frustrated at the inactivity. For the past two days, his men near Freeman's Farm had manned an observation post in a thick stand of woods at a road junction between the Great Ravine and Mill Creek. They were one of a series of outposts ordered by Arnold, who also chafed at the inactivity.

The modest farm dominated the only patch of open land in the area. Ripened wheat that almost rubbed a man's chest filled the fields. This season, the harvest at Freeman's farm would be of a different kind.

Sergeant Guthrie and his small file of six riflemen had joined Creed's White Knights. They had watched the British cook fires, dig trenches, post sentries, and stand in unending formations for two days.

But this morning, something was different. The morning fires were absent, and the sentries fewer than usual. They also caught a glimmer of sunlight on metal in the tree line a half-mile off.

"I see something now, Lieutenant," Beall called down.

Creed cupped his hands. "Light infantry?"

"Maybe. Skirmishers, for sure. No, wait. There's a column moving about a half-mile west of us. Heading right towards the farm."

"I can see them from down here now, Lieutenant," Parker hollered. "Looks like a battalion, at least. With at least one cannon, make that two, no three. They're man-hauling them."

"That means they plan to put them in battery soon," Creed said.

They watched the head of Hamilton's column closing on its first objective.

"I see something to the north of the ravine now. Too much fog, but looks like a column moving due west," Beall said.

Creed looked at Guthrie. "This means a major attack, sergeant. A road north of the ravine turns south about a mile west of us. I believe they're planning to turn our left flank."

Guthrie spat a piece of tobacco. "What do we do?"

"Find Colonel Morgan. Tell him if he pushes his men into those woods, he can slow them down and give General Arnold time to plan a countermove. But he must move quickly. I reckon our good General Fraser himself is leading that column. Fraser will strike quickly. We have little time to waste."

Guthrie shook his head. "With all respect, sir, I'd like to stay. I'm the best shot in the army. I'm needed here with my boys to kill lobsters. Send Parker back."

Creed rubbed his chin. "You're right. Elias, go back and find Colonel Morgan. Tell him to act quickly!"

"Right away, Lieutenant!" Parker took off at a run. Their horses and equipment were back at camp under Thomas's care.

"Jonathan, cover our front with the riflemen. If you see anything in range, you have my permission to fire. Sergeant Guthrie and I are going forward to the Great Ravine. We may get a few shots in when the column turns south."

When they reached the western end of the ravine, Creed realized he had miscalculated. The enemy column had moved faster than he thought. "It's Alexander Fraser's company."

The redcoats were already scrambling south when Creed's men spotted them. Creed and his small party were in danger of being cut off.

"I know these men and what they are capable of. We'll have bloody work this day," Creed said to Guthrie as they watched the British marksmen.

"How do you know them?"

"Simple, I once was one of them."

"What?"

"'Tis no time for stories. Here is what we'll do...."

***

Serge Binoche crept through the dark woods with the instinct and stealth of a lynx. Ancient trees reaching sixty or more feet combined with younger growth, saplings, and brush gave this northern forest the feel of a jungle. Random rays broke the darkness, beaming a soft light through the heavy canopy of green. The quiet was broken only by the occasional buzz of a mosquito or the rustling of the underbrush.

Binoche's companions, a few Iroquois, and Canadian *coureurs* followed their master on what he assured them was their last work for the *Anglais*. A small band of desperadoes was all that remained of the once-mighty force of Indians led by the famed Canadian Luc de La Corne.

Binoche had one last chance to redeem himself in the eyes of his British masters. With Luc gone, he was the most experienced of the coureurs left with Burgoyne. Binoche felt he was once more in a position to win glory despite his failure. But Binoche did not seek recognition, only gold and *revanche* – sweet revenge.

A trapper named Jean-Paul Tremblay whispered in Binoche's ear, engulfing Binoche with the smell of fouled onions and rotten peppers. "*Mon Dieu*, the *Anglais* are stubborn fools. They should be sitting nicely at Ticonderoga instead of pursuing these mad Americans. They should let their cannons and the walls of our fortress break the backs of these dogs. These men place too much trust in their bayonets."

"*Oui*, but it is their way, Jean-Paul. They joke that the bayonet is too painful to sit on. And what's more, there's no booty to gain sitting on one's ass, right? So they may be right. Now run on ahead. I give you the honor of leading us."

"*Merde!*" Jean-Paul whistled and pushed his way through the thickets and secondary growth. Instead of a lynx, a wild boar now led the pack.

***

Morgan's Headquarters
Parker stuck his head under Morgan's tent.

The colonel quickly pulled on his boots. "What brings you here, soldier? Wait, I think I know."

Morgan intently listened as Parker revealed what they saw and then decided on his actions. "Arnold is with Gates right now. Parker, you get one of the horses and ride to Gates. Tell him the lobsters are coming in on us from Freeman's Farm. We need to beat 'em there."

"Yes, sir."

Parker leaped into the saddle, and his mount's powerful hooves began pounding down the wagon trail. The horse raced madly, upturning tents and sending soldiers diving for cover. He bulled past the sentries and orderlies when he found Gates' hut. There, Arnold and Gates were in a heated discussion. His large frame filled the doorway.

"What is the meaning of this?" Gates asked the aides who scrambled in Parker's wake.

Parker's powerful arms barred their passage. "Sir, Colonel Morgan sent me to advise you that the British are on the move."

Gates peered over the spectacles on his nose. "Are you certain?"

"Of course, he's certain," Arnold snapped. "Where are they?"

"A column is marching towards Freeman's farm, but Lieutenant Creed believes a larger one is heading west of it."

"We must assemble the regiments and attack them now," Arnold said.

Gates shook his head. "We have good works built here. Let Burgoyne try to bludgeon his way through them and lose his army in the attempt."

"You can't be serious!" Arnold exclaimed. "We need to take the initiative and strike them."

Gates chuckled. "And give up the advantages of prepared works?"

"Burgoyne will haul up his guns and blast a breach in your defenses," Arnold said. "Then his regulars will pour in with their bayonets lowered. Our men are better fighters in the woods and fields. We must take advantage of that,"

The hum of murmurs filled the room.

But Gates remained firm. "British regulars against our men in the open? You are mad, Arnold! This might be a subterfuge. In any case, the situation we face remains unclear. I believe Burgoyne wants to draw us from behind these ramparts. We now outnumber him and have plenty of cannons. A solid defense is called for."

Arnold bristled. He began to pace back and forth, his face becoming a deep red and his arms gesticulating wildly with each step. "You heard what the soldier just said. The larger column is moving west. A two-pronged move might be his plan. They could pour artillery into the camp if they took the high ground to our west. Worse, he could push his infantry around us. Our rear is undefended. You, at least, must allow me to lead a strong reconnaissance to determine his intentions."

Gates blanched. He removed his spectacles and rubbed the bridge of his nose as he gathered his thoughts. It seemed clear to Parker that he did not like Arnold. But Arnold, unlike Gates, had held several successful field commands.

Gates sucked in a deep breath and exhaled. "Very well, Arnold. You may take Morgan and Dearborn. But the rest of the brigades will man these works."

"Fair enough, general."

When Arnold and Parker galloped up to Morgan's camp, his men stood with rifles ready for action.

"Show us the way, private," Arnold barked.

Parker spurred his horse and led them forward. One thousand of the finest riflemen in the world fanned out into the woods ahead of them, supported by Dearborn's 200-plus light infantry. They began the trek towards the farm where they had been assured lobsters would be ripe for the picking.

"Just wondering why Granny Gates gave you this command," Parker heard Morgan whisper to Arnold.

Arnold smiled grimly. "Simple. If he sat behind the defense works and didn't win, the loss would be on his shoulders. But letting a peddler from Connecticut lead a force forward, he profits regardless of the result."

"How do you figure that?" Morgan asked.

"If I succeed, Gates can still claim the victory as his. If I lose, I suffer the blame."

"You're willing to risk all this for him? A loss will mean your career?"

"I don't plan to lose. I have the best fighting force with a commander who knows how to fight in the woods."

The confidence sent a chill through Parker. It reminded him of another officer.

***

The steamy fog had begun to rise slowly, and the sun's warming rays were driving out the morning chill. The crisp dawn would soon turn into a hot midday.

"The enemy columns are moving slowly," Creed whispered to Guthrie. "But I'd wager Fraser's lads are already sniffing at our flanks."

"What do we do?" Guthrie asked.

"Why, we shall find them, of course. Jonathan, you'll remain here and apprise the colonel when he arrives."

"You think he'll get here in time, Lieutenant?" Beall asked.

Guthrie spat a piece of tobacco. "He'll get here, alright. He'd never miss a chance to shoot lobsters."

"Just save him some redcoats to shoot, Jonathan," Creed said with a wink.

Along with Guthrie and his rifleman, Creed plunged into the thick woods to the west. Grim-faced, the men moved cautiously through a dark forest lit only by stray beams of sunlight that occasionally broke through the treetops. They pushed through undergrowth that seemed to hold them in its grips. Finally, they found a deer path that snaked westward.

After what seemed an eternity, they stumbled on another deer trail and followed it north. They halted at a small clearing while Guthrie slipped forward and scouted the area. He returned, panting with beads of sweat running down his face. He took a knee beside Creed. "Folks have been through here already, Mister Creed."

"Indians?"

"Maybe. But not too many just yet. Scouting party, most likely." Guthrie spat another piece of tobacco.

"How are you loaded?" Creed asked.

"These rifles take just a ball at a time. No ball-and-buck, I'm afraid. But we seldom miss 'em, once we see 'em."

Creed nodded. "Mine as well. But unlike you lads, I can mount a blade."

Creed drew his sword-bayonet and affixed it to the lock on the bottom end of his Jaeger rifle.

"We'll trust in these, sir." Guthrie put a hand on his tomahawk and hunting knife.

"Your men good with them?"

"Don't know for sure. Never had to use 'em except in practice. These rifles have a way of keeping folks from getting too close."

Creed nodded. "We'll sit here a while. Either the scouting party will return, or we'll catch the main column. Either way, we'll get the jump on them, move in a circle around them, and fire in pairs. One man shoots while the other is loading. With lead stinging them constantly, their numbers will be of little help."

"We could use a little more room to range 'em. I've fought regulars in woods before, though, and we should put the fear of God in them," Guthrie said.

Creed shook his head. "If I'm not mistaken, these are Fraser's men. Pick of the army. We'll have to move quickly, then fall back and find the rest of the lads."

***

Treading silently as rabbits, the grim-faced men in tattered red jackets and dark leggings came down the deer path. It was just after midday, but no one would know as the heavy-laden treetops masked all but the faintest light.

Alexander Fraser's sharpshooters had a special mission. His orders from General Simon Fraser had pushed him west to cover the right of the central column and find a way around the flank of the Americans. If possible, find a way to the rebel rear. The few Indians still under Binoche now had the task of solving that particular problem.

Fraser had misgivings about these men. They had failed in the past and even facilitated the traitor Lawrence's escape.

Lawrence! Fraser still bristled at his name. He had befriended the eccentric "Royal American," never suspecting he was a rebel agent. The fact that Lawrence had duped everyone from Guy Carleton to Johnny Burgoyne to the astute Simon Fraser made the pill no less bitter. The impostor Lawrence had escaped the hangman. He was likely now laughing at them from a tavern in Albany.

The sudden crack of rifle fire up ahead broke the eerie silence and stopped Fraser in his tracks. His men had found the rebels!

Fraser called on one of his aides, a young subaltern. "Run back and inform the general we found the rebels."

Curses erupted from his men as they frantically tried to return fire at an enemy they could not see.

The North Spy

"I think they have found us, captain," the subaltern replied.

Fraser looked up through a break in the canopy and saw narrow light beams spreading across the leaves and boughs above him.

"Just around midday, I'd say. We have lots of fighting ahead. Go quickly!"

***

Creed had let Fraser's advance file cross the deer path, then opened fire on the second. Well-aimed shots stunned the second file. A shiver of guilt coursed through him. Although his enemies, he had marched with them. More than half tumbled into the undergrowth while the rest scampered back through the bushes.

"On me, gentlemen!" Creed leaped across the deer path to their front and sprinted, bent over, through the woods.

Guthrie and his men followed.

Creed raised his arm, and the group took a knee and began loading. "Catch a breath. Sip at your water bottles, lads. We're fighting the heat and the British," Creed glanced up. "'Tis midday, and the heat will soon suffocate, even under those boughs above us."

"What now?" Guthrie asked.

"We cut off their first file. They're expecting us to fall on them, so we won't. The files behind them are likely preparing to attack the position we just vacated. They'll have light infantry covering their flank."

"Then they should be coming right through here," Guthrie said.

"Indeed. We need to take them with blades, then strike a counterattack from behind. Understand?"

They all gave knowing nods.

"Very well, lads."

"But what then?" Guthrie asked. "We ain't never fought an enemy up close like this."

A grim smile crossed Creed's lip. "That depends."

Guthrie squinted. "On what?"

"On whether there is a then."

"And if there is?"

Creed could see he was flustered. He needed to instill confidence. "We'll circle south, finish the advanced file, and then make our way back."

"The boys are up to it," Guthrie said.

They soon spied the flank guard. Three light infantrymen struggled with the tangle of underbrush with fusils at high port. Creed's men sprang on them like leopards when they were within reach. Four riflemen bounded from the thick bushes and tore into them with tomahawks and knives. Screams, curses, and groans erupted. Without firing a shot, they had destroyed the flank guard.

"Form skirmish line of twos and advance on my pace, tree by tree," Creed ordered crisply.

They formed up. Quickly, the pairs bounded from tree to tree until they were no more than ten yards from the deer path. Ahead, they could make out an occasional redcoat as the British formed to retake their former position. But now, they were behind the enemy.

Creed set his sights on an officer and prayed for forgiveness as he squeezed the trigger. His Jaeger rifle *cracked*, and the officer fell, a dark stain spreading across his back. Guthrie's men began to squeeze off shots. They worked in pairs, one reloading while the other found a target and fired.

The British were in disarray. Most of the light infantry went down, bleeding their last. The few who could respond fired wildly into the dense trees. But then, the undergrowth shook, and the soft ground felt the pound of boots. The rest of Fraser's company was rushing to the sounds of combat. Rifle fire began to sting the trees around Creed's men.

A British voice rose above the fire. "They have sharpshooters to our right! Sergeant Barnaby, take ten men and move around them."

Creed recognized the voice as Alexander Fraser's. He realized he needed to clear out the advance file or be trapped on the wrong side of the deer path. The British fire tempo increased as Fraser sent more men forward. Lead balls slapped tree trunks and branches or whistled through leaves.

"They're on to us, lads. Follow me!" Creed angled west for thirty yards, then south fifty yards. The men soon caught up with him.

Creed was breathing heavily and drenched in sweat. "We should be thirty yards west of the north-south deer path."

Guthrie spat a piece of tobacco. "Reload and sip your water, boys. Don't guzzle it."

The men obliged. Sweat trickled down their powder-blackened brows and stained their hunting shirts black.

Creed gave his last instructions as they sipped, "This is an elite unit we face. We have them in chaos, but it will not last long."

"What'll we do?" Guthrie asked. "The boys are tired and heated."

"So are the redcoats," Creed said. "We'll form a wide Vee and push east. If the advanced file is there, we'll blast our way through. But we must keep moving. Stay in pairs. Anyone separated – try to make your way back to our camp."

They formed up in three pairs, with Creed in the lead. He started pushing through the heavy undergrowth. They moved more slowly than he would have liked. The heat had sapped their energy.

As Creed predicted, the advanced British file held the ground ahead. The file waited patiently, fusils at the ready, for the relief they expected shortly. Fraser's tactic left the main body with the task of pushing through to them.

One of Guthrie's men at the apex of the V fired first. His shot struck true, and a redcoat fell forward before he could respond. The remainder formed a line facing Creed's men, each using a tree or rock for cover. The riflemen came on, bounding from tree to tree and only exposing themselves for fleeting seconds.

But at five yards, there was no more cover. The woods erupted into a deadly storm of lead. The British began to fall, clutching frantically at wounds they knew would never heal.

"Push through them, lads," Creed ordered.

Then one of the Americans took a bullet in the chest and fell dead. His mate grabbed his rifle and continued with the group. In a moment that seemed like an hour, they had fought through the British. The remnants of Fraser's advanced file lay dead or wounded in the thick brush behind them.

Two of the Americans stopped to catch their breath. Creed spotted them. "Just another quarter mile through this jungle, lads. You can make it."

Guthrie came up behind them. "You sons a bitches get your asses up right now! You know what Morgan will do to you if he hears about this?"

The men sprang to life at the thought of big Dan Morgan's wrath. As scattered shots erupted in the distance behind them, Creed and his party moved steadily east toward the American lines.

***

Serge Binoche cursed at the first *crack* of a rifle. Somehow, he thought he'd find a way to satisfy his British masters without getting caught in combat. Or at least get into an action where he did not hold all the cards.

"*Merde*, they are behind us!" he said to Tremblay.

"How could that be?" Tremblay replied. "We came from there. We saw nothing."

"The rebels know this land," Binoche said. "They know the deer paths and hunting trails. I wish we had Tsongas now. He was the only one of our Iroquois to have hunted these parts,"

"Lawrence made sure Tsongas would never walk these paths again," Tremblay said.

Binoche's eyes blazed. "I hope on the sacred blood he died in those rapids."

"What do we do?" Tremblay was pragmatic, if unimaginative.

"First, we wait—no gain for us to die for the *Anglais*. Then we position ourselves to take advantage of the situation. If the *Anglais* win, we want to arrive in time to share the victory."

"And if they lose?" Tremblay asked.

Binoche shrugged. "Then, we gather loot from red-jackets' bodies instead of blue, *ne pas*?"

They both shook with laughter.

Binoche led his band towards the firing and then turned east. They moved slowly, careful not to get too close to the fighting until it reached its conclusion. By the time they crossed over Mill Creek, the firing had died. Then, they saw them.

"*Soldats!*" An excited *coureur* signaled with his hands, relaying the message to Binoche. Instinctively, two of his Iroquois circled east to intercept the head of the advancing men.

"*Vestes rouges?*" Binoche asked. He soon learned that they were not red coats.

***

One of Guthrie's men stumbled into an Iroquois brave, who thrust a wicked scalping knife just under the rifleman's breastbone. He twisted it upwards and pulled it, dripping blood from the American's chest. But before the sturdy Pennsylvania woodsman collapsed, he discharged his long rifle into the belly of his killer. Both fell in a tangle of blood, foam, and undergrowth.

At the dull *crack* of the rifle, Guthrie scrambled forward. A second, Iroquois leaped from behind a thick tree trunk and raised his musket. A shot rang out, and the brave fell back, his weapon tumbling into the thick bushes.

Creed quickly reloaded and then joined Guthrie. "How bad is he, Sergeant?"

"Gone. Damned savage gutted him good. Willy was a good rifleman. He got a kill-shot off with his dying breath. Morgan will like that."

"Gather his rifle and powder. We must keep moving."

Two Canadians opened fire. But their shots were erratic, zinging leaves high above. Guthrie's men began to spray lead in return. Shadows moved from bush to tree and tree to rock as the men tried to gain the advantage – the first was to see the enemy. The thick forest was engulfed in the acrid smell of smoke that stung eyes and choked throats.

***

Binoche slinked into position behind trees and low shrubs. His band was down to Tremblay, two *coureurs*, and a handful of Iroquois.

"Jean-Paul, one push and these fleas will run from us. At them now!"

Tremblay grabbed the remaining *coureurs*, and they rapidly ran from tree to tree towards the cloud of heavy smoke.

He was frantically jamming home a new round into his rifle. He saw a rifleman kneeling behind a log. The rifleman looked up just as Tremblay swung his musket butt, slamming his face with a savage crack. His neck snapped, and the rifleman collapsed lifeless over the log.

"Take his valuables and then follow me," Tremblay said.

The two *coureurs* needed little goading to engage in plunder. They searched the dead man's pockets, grabbing a gold chain and some coins, leaving his pack, powder horn, and rifle. Finished with their debouching, they headed into the smoke-filled brush where Tremblay had disappeared. They had stepped into a semi-dark hell of heat, gun smoke, and death.

***

The first *coureurs* into the brush stumbled over something. The lead Canadian struggled to his feet and cocked his musket. "Tremblay!"

Creed stepped from the smoke, raised his blood-coated rifle with its sword-bayonet, and plunged the blade into the Canadian's chest. The second *coureur* fired a round that caught Creed in the side. Searing pain, like a score of wasp stings, rippled across his ribs. Creed staggered, then steadied himself when the *coureur* lunged at him with his scalping knife.

The crack of a rifle shot dropped the Canadian, sending the other *coureurs* diving into the brush before he got within arm's reach of Creed.

Guthrie ran to Creed. "Did he get you?"

"Yes. But it's only a scratch. See to your other lads. Get out of this hell."

"Okay, but I'm coming right back." Guthrie disappeared into the leaf-laden branches.

Creed steadied himself and then pulled up his hunting shirt. He felt some blood, but no major organ or artery seemed affected.

"A scratch, *monsieur*, merely a scratch. My men have orders to save your filthy hide for me."

Creed turned and saw Binoche standing beside an Iroquois brave.

"You have killed many of my men, it seems. Most of the Indians have fled. But no matter, I shall finally get my *revanche*. That is all that matters in the end, no? Not this war, not Fleurette, not even *Anglais* gold."

The Iroquois stepped forward and grabbed Creed's weapons before he could react. His head felt woozy, and shock was setting in.

Binoche drew his scalping knife and moved forward deliberately. He walked slowly, relishing each step as if it brought him nearer to a delicious pleasure he had long considered lost.

"*Victoire* is mine, *Monsieur* Lawrence. We have stopped your attack. I will yet get *Anglais* gold for your scalp. And Fleurette? Well, the *Anglais* colonel can have her. Besides, she'll soon tire of him and run away to find her papa, no?"

Binoche laughed and took his final step towards Creed, his powerful fingers grabbing him just as he began to swoon. Binoche now held him in his powerful grip.

"See, he faints like a housewife at my sight!" Binoche exclaimed.

He raised the scalping knife. But Creed had feigned the swoon to lure Binoche. He lashed out with a desperate kick that caught Binoche by surprise. Creed struck at Binoche with his fist, but the powerful coureurs wrapped his arms around Creed in a death grip. But the coureurs tightened his grip and shook him like a doll. He slammed Creed against the dark trunk of an oak tree.

Creed moaned in agony when his wound struck the oak's rough bark. Fighting through excruciating pain and struggling to stay alert, he jammed his thumb into Binoche's eye, digging and gouging with a ferocity driven by desperation.

Binoche merely squirmed at the discomfort. "I need but one eye to kill you, Lawrence."

Binoche slammed his prey against the oak with a mighty shove that sent Creed onto the tree's thick roots. An Iroquois handed Binoche Creed's rifle.

Binoche fondled it tauntingly. "A fine weapon, *Monsieur*. I will kill many Americans with it. Just for you. Each one will be my revenge for your memory."

Binoche removed the sword bayonet and grasped its hilt with his bear-like paw. "But first, I will scalp you with your blade. Then I will cut out your manhood and feed it to you. You shall enjoy your last meal!"

Binoche and the Iroquois laughed. But their laughter was cut short by a burst of gunfire at close range. The brave fell to the leafy ground, pierced by a bullet to the neck.

A ball struck Binoche in the side. The burly Canadian's eyes widened in fear mixed with hate. He took a step and, raising the sword over his head, turned to Creed.

A *crack*, *crack* sent two more bullets into his heavy torso. His eyes fluttered while his face twisted into a demonic frown. The blade tumbled onto the soft earth. "*Merde!*" He spun about, and then the large body of Serge Binoche collapsed with a solid thud.

Guthrie and his men stepped through the smoke filling the clearing.

"Make sure they're dead, boys. Use the knife," Guthrie grunted.

He ran to Creed and felt his neck. "Lieutenant Creed's alive. We need to get him back. One of you, grab his weapons. The other can help me move him. Quick now, before more of the lobsters get here."

One of the riflemen called out. "The Indian is dead, but the big Canadian is still breathing."

"Now, what would Morgan say if we left him alive?" Guthrie asked. "Take his scalp."

A desperate voice, followed by a shrill scream, pierced Creed's dulling senses as he vainly fought to stay conscious.

"*Non! Non! Noooo....*"

Chapter 27

Bemis Heights, September 21st, 1777

Creed quickly covered his eyes and sat up abruptly. The mid-morning light's rays seemed blinding. He slowly moved his hands, letting his pupils adjust. Then he ran his hands down his sides. He felt bandages and carefully probed them with his fingers. A sharp pain wracked his side, and he abruptly fell back onto the cot, exhausted from the effort.

"Please ask for help next time you want to examine yourself, sir," Parker said. The former seaman had some medical skills and often stepped into the surgeon's role.

"Elias? Is that you?" Creed squinted up into Parker's face.

"Yes, sir."

"What happened? Where am I? Where are the rest of the lads?"

"You took a ball during the skirmish in the forest, sir. Seared your ribs good, but no permanent damage. Problem now is, you're feverish. We have to watch that. As you know, it's the infection that....."

"Kills more than the wound. Where are the other patients?"

"This isn't the hospital, sir. Colonel Morgan had you moved to his hut. He is once more enjoying sleeping under the stars, or so he says."

"He didn't need to do that on my account."

"The doctors wanted to start bleeding you the first night. He nearly broke one of them in two."

"Colonel Morgan has a temper and the means to reinforce it." Creed chuckled, sending searing pain stabbing at his ribs.

"I know. So I volunteered to look after you – and keep the surgeons at bay."

"Thank you, Elias. Where are the others? Have the British attacked yet?" Creed's mind was slow at putting the pieces together with the fever.

"Sir, they moved on us two days ago. Your skirmish in the woods turned their advanced guard back and gave General Arnold time to rally a force in response."

"Arnold?"

"Yes, sir. He had Colonel Morgan and a general whose name I can't recall. I led Morgan back to our position by the farm. He got his men into the woods, and we stopped the first British column in its tracks. They tried all their tricks. Artillery: the riflemen shot them from their guns. Formation volley: the boys picked them apart, starting with the officers."

Creed's lips tightened.

Parker smiled. "Sorry, sir. I think that was one of your old tricks."

Creed smiled wanly and then exhaled. "Go on. What happened then?"

"Well, the riflemen chased the British through the woods. But just then, General Arnold brought up another unit to help stop a British counterattack. The riflemen rallied."

"How many lobsters?" Creed asked.

"The British had about four regiments and a battery at the farm. Plus, lots more infantry in the woods to the west. The riflemen and light infantry spent the whole afternoon shooting at the British. They fired back too. But we had the better of it, I'd say. I think I saw some of their generals in the middle of it. Never saw that from them before."

"Any of them hit?" Creed asked.

"Not that I can tell," Parker said. "But plenty of officers went down, sorry."

"Sometimes that's the sorry lot of officers, Elias." Creed felt a burning on his side, and it ached as he spoke. But it was worth the pain. The sound of victory was melodious.

"General Arnold was in a rage and stormed back to headquarters for reinforcements. We never saw him again. I heard later that General Gates ordered another continental brigade forward. But for some reason, he wouldn't let General Arnold go forward. Now, why would he do that? We had the lobsters."

Creed startled. "Arnold kept from the field of battle? Did Morgan know?"

"They don't tell us privates much about those things, sir. All I know is Sergeant Guthrie came up and told us what happened to you. A column of Germans hit the line from the east about that time. They began their usual drill. They lined up in rows. Artillery is shooting along the front. About that time, we got the order to pull back."

"When was that?"

"Around dusk. I can't figure out those turkey calls, but Guthrie knew. Jonathan and I were perplexed at the retreat order, sir. We saw scores of the enemy go down. More than at Haarlem, Trenton, or Princeton."

The door suddenly flew open, and the large frame of Morgan filled the entrance. He strutted into the room with Guthrie in tow.

"How is your lieutenant doing?" Morgan asked.

"Better, sir. But he's with the fever. I need to get him some broth," Parker said.

"We'll watch him," Guthrie said.

Morgan bent over Creed. "Good thing for Burgoyne you got hit, or you might have whipped the whole English army for us, by God!"

Creed stared up at him. "Your Sergeant Guthrie saved me twice, so the laurels go to him."

"He's your Sergeant Guthrie now, and I got his report. You're to be commended. If Gates would allow it."

"Allow it?"

"You know I don't like Arnold much," Morgan said. "Nobody does. But Gates confined him to the camp when he went back for help. Gates sent help – Ebeneezer Learned's boys. But without Arnold to lead 'em up, they came slow. We might have whipped them outright at the farm if they'd joined the fray before those damned Germans. Instead, we had to withdraw."

"Why would he?" Creed asked.

"Stubbornness, caution, jealousy. Gates has political dreams. Wants no competition. That son of a bitch adjutant of his, Wilkinson, ain't no better. He came up just to make a show. God knows what report he'll make on this."

"Wilkinson? He's not to be trusted. Wanted me to report on you and General Arnold."

Morgan's broad face and thick neck reddened. "Report? Report what?"

"That's what I said," Creed replied. "To report on your comings and goings. I refused. But, sir, what of our situation? Are we to withdraw?"

"Heck, no. That's the one thing about Gates. He likes our defenses. Besides, our little expedition stopped a British assault on the works. We think they lost over one thousand men. More than half of them killed. Burgoyne is sitting tight and digging in at the farm. Guess he's waiting for Howe or Clinton to save his butt. Our boys are keeping an eye on them, though. You never know if they'll try another sneak attack."

"And what of Binoche? He thrashed me well. Did he escape?"

Morgan and Guthrie glanced at each other.

Guthrie leaned forward. "He was fixing to scalp you, Lieutenant. But by luck, we got back there before he could."

Morgan broke in. "Thanks to Guthrie, he and his savage friends will do no more scalping, by God."

"Thank you, sergeant." Creed raised his hand, but the pain forced him to lower it.

Parker arrived with a steaming bowl of broth.

"Rest easy, Mister Creed," Morgan said. "You need to take some of this soup Parker fixed and get more sleep. Soup and sleep fix most anything."

***

Freeman's Farm, October 1st, 1777

The powerful charger plodded slowly across the soggy field. Burgoyne patiently urged it along the British lines. General Simon Fraser and Colonel Lazarus Sinclair rode with him. He was in no hurry. Inspecting the fortifications required a careful, unhurried eye. Since Morgan and Arnold checked their attack, his men had been swinging picks and shovels.

He had Riedesel's Germans entrench along a half-mile stretch west of the river. To ensure rebel riflemen could not enfilade his men from the flanks, he ordered ramparts and *abatis* built south of Freeman's farm. Hundreds of hammers and shovels hacked out a line of secondary works north and west of the farm to complete the effort.

Burgoyne waved at a crew of soldiers in shirt sleeves, lazily dumping soil into a tall wicker basket. "The men seem to take to this. Keeps them busy as well."

"I suspect they'd rather be charging the rebels than burrowing like so many moles, sir," Fraser said.

"What proper soldier wouldn't? Still, there is a certain purpose in their work."

"These defense works would be better near Fort Edward, sir," Sinclair said. "Or at Ticonderoga. The days are cooling fast, and the nights even faster. Supply is dwindling as well."

Burgoyne tugged a leather glove from his hand and playfully slapped his saddle. "Always the pessimist, Lazarus. We thrashed them here once without these works. If we lure them here, we shall defeat them in detail. Don't you think so, Simon?"

Fraser hesitated. "Truth be told, sir, it is we who were thrashed. Our men are in good spirits, but each day takes a toll on them. Their riflemen snipe at us from dawn to dusk."

A rifle *cracked* in the distance, then another. An exposed soldier dropped his shovel and collapsed into a water-logged trench.

"Rebel sniper!" roared a sergeant.

A score of British muskets responded, raking the tree line with gusto.

"The lads are quite ebullient in their response, are they not?" Burgoyne quipped. He had to place a good face on things.

"They're wasting precious powder. Just as the rebels intend," Fraser replied. "As I was saying, their snipers are taking a toll on our strength and the men's morale. The few Indians and Canadians left will not venture forth."

"Yes, of course, Simon. Lazarus, make sure you inform the regiments. We'll match them shot for shot, but no more over-exuberance." Burgoyne responded tactfully. Fraser was the army's pride, and everyone except Fraser knew it.

Burgoyne pointed north and then to the east. "Have they probed our flanks in the past two days?"

"No. But they can observe everything we do from those treetops, and with those rifles and the quality of their marksmanship, we are wont to get any work done in daylight," Fraser said.

Burgoyne turned to Sinclair. "Any idea of their strength, Lazarus?"

"Our pickets have seen some movement by their pontoon bridge. And rebel militias are aggressively probing our posts to the north. Some are in danger of falling. I must say, a withdrawal until next spring is in order."

"Simon?" Burgoyne instinctively trusted Fraser's judgment.

"Unless we can force Gates from this position, he is bound to wait until we are too weak to resist. Whether now or next spring is not material."

Burgoyne twisted his glove in his hand. "Had the man who called himself Lawrence not proven a rebel spy, I would have sent him in search of Howe or Clinton's column. We have no savages left and few worthy Tories or Canadians to send."

"What of Alexander?" Sinclair asked.

"No. I need him with me," Fraser said. "And he took many losses."

"Have you heard anything from your Canadian brute?" Burgoyne asked.

Fraser blanched. "Binoche? Well, yes, Alexander's men came upon him in the woods after the rebels withdrew. He was shot dead, and his throat and scalp cut."

Burgoyne's eyes turned to Sinclair. "I never saw that report."

"I didn't think it would do the army's morale good to expose that the men we hired as throat cutters were themselves skewered," Sinclair replied.

"Excellent point, Lazarus. By the way, are you enjoying Binoche's vixen?"

Sinclair's face reddened. Burgoyne knew he was a man of strange and introverted passions but did not share them with the world, unlike his peers. He laughed at Sinclair's discomfort.

Ignoring the banter, Fraser conned the distant tree line with a spyglass. "Rebels appear to be in every other tree. They can observe our every move now, sir."

Burgoyne slapped his glove on his saddle once more. This time, not playfully. "By God, I'd give a month's pay in silver if we had a patrol or an agent who could enter their lines and render us knowledge of their dispositions to rival their knowledge of ours."

Fraser appeared chided. "Sir, I have sent six of my best men through their lines. None has returned. Alexander's company is now reduced to fewer than two-score. I need every good soldier for the coming fray."

Burgoyne's voice softened. "I know that, Simon. It is no reflection on you or your men. They are soldiers, after all. Spying behind enemy lines under false pretenses requires a person of questionable character. Thank God our army has precious few such men. Such activity is more suited to one of the savages, say, a Canadian like Binoche or a colonial like Lawrence."

"Sir! A month of your pay in silver, sir? Are you serious about that?" Sinclair asked.

Burgoyne grabbed the spyglass from Fraser and began to scan the treetops. "Of course, Lazarus. I don't suppose you will coax von Riedesel into sending one of his jackboots? They are fine fellows on the field of honor, but are quite useless in affairs such

as this."

"Allow me to attend to the details, sir."

***

The canvas tent flap ruffled. Sinclair struck flint to a small candle, throwing a pale light across the face of the young woman lying on his cot. He stood over her and caressed her cheek and her long, dark hair. But each stroke grew more intense until he was tugging, not stroking, and finally pulling, not dragging.

"Sit up, my dear. We have much to discuss. I have found a way for you to earn your keep."

She winced. "Have I not earned my keep, *Monsieur*? Your general thought so."

Sinclair resisted the urge to slap the young beauty. "Really? Then why did he give you back to me? God knows you haven't earned it with me."

He knew her thoughts and passions lay somewhere else. It darkened his feelings until he had determined to get rid of her. Now, the military situation allowed him to use her to his advantage before packing her off.

"The general has a task for you, my dear."

She sat bolt upright and shot him a puzzled frown. "Johnny? He wants me back?"

The blanket dropped, displaying enough of her charms to Sinclair. *She is toying with me.*

"Cover yourself, Fleurette. I have no time for your games. Nor do you."

"What do you mean?"

"Johnny doesn't want you back. He wants you to take a little journey south and meet some men."

"South? What men?"

"It doesn't matter what men, so long as they are part of the rebel army."

"There are men enough right here, *Monsieur*, are there not?" Her fingers softly stroked his face.

He pushed them away. "Enough! You will find a canoe—paddle down the river. Talk yourself into their camp. I think you have some experience there. Learn what you can of their plans."

"Plans?"

"Learn of their numbers and their weapons. Find out if they have any word on General Howe or Clinton."

"Who?"

"There may yet be an army marching north to join us. Find out whether the rebels know of its location. Then find a way back here."

"Impossible, *Monsieur*. Your army has cost me my father and his friends. The rebel militia will have their way with me and discard me like trash. They have no silver. Now you want to cast me to certain death at the hands of the rebels who killed him?"

Sinclair realized this would be a more difficult persuasion than he thought.

He caressed her arm and cheek and then took her hands in his. "You know how much you mean to me, my dear. I need you, as does General Johnny. The entire army needs you. I cannot bring back your father, but I can help you find a suitable man to marry. We have many fine young sergeants and a few subalterns who admire you."

"No. I wish to go north and live among my people."

Sinclair startled. It never occurred to him that she would not prefer to be the wife or mistress of an Englishman.

"Indeed. If that is your wish, suffer me this one favor, and I'll see that you go north and do so with a purse full of silver."

"Silver?" Her dark eyes widened. "How much silver?"

"A fortnight's pay for a colonel. That's what Johnny promised, Fleurette. In coin. That's just over ten pounds sterling. You would have a dowry to find a suitable husband with whom you could buy a small farm near Quebec, a tavern, or just live in great comfort for a long time. Think of it."

Sinclair's mouth twisted into a sly grin. She probably had never seen more than a shilling at a time in all her days. She had no idea that Burgoyne had promised a whole month's pay, but he decided to take a share for his troubles.

"When do I get my silver?"

"When you return, of course."

"No. I need silver in advance, or I won't leave." She lowered her eyes demurely. "I risk my life, *monsieur*."

Sinclair studied her a moment. Her beauty was beguiling yet deceiving, for she had more cunning than her father. She was a she-wolf disguised as a fawn.

He waved a small leather sack in her face. "I'll give you a handful of shillings. That will be enough to bribe the occasional rebel. The rest upon your return."

"*Merci, monsieur!*" She threw her arms about his neck and kissed him fiercely.

He shoved her away. "Make sure you return with information useful to General Johnny. We need to know where Clinton is. We need to know the state of rebel supply, rebel morale, and rebel numbers. Where are they weakest, where are they strongest."

"*Mais oui, monsieur.* I will bring you and General Johnny the information you need."

She snatched the purse from his hands and pulled the worn leather strings to open it and check its contents. "Fifteen shillings. *Bien.*"

Sinclair pinched her chin tightly. "Hear me, Fleurette. Fail us, and you'll lose the balance of your money. Betray us, and I'll send Alexander Fraser's entire company to hunt you down."

***

The militiaman at the far end of the pontoon bridge observed, looking for signs of movement in the woods. John Abbot enjoyed sentry duty. It helped him escape the constant swinging of a pick or lifting a shovel. Gates had the whole army working ten hours a day. They all joked about digging a second Great Ravine. "Gates's Ravine," they called it.

Abbot longed to be back on his small farm in the Grants. He missed his wife and son. Like most of the men from the Grants, Abbott worried that the Indians would arrive while he was gone with the county militia. He feared that he would return to find his wife, another Jane McCrae.

Abbot turned his gaze west and waved at his mate, Tim Stiles. Stiles was also a farmer but was glad to drop the hoe and harness to add some adventure and maybe gain a fresh perspective on life.

A faint splashing sound broke the quiet. *A frog leaping into the water?* Another splash rippled the water, this time stronger. He signaled to Stiles. The moon glowed brightly, and its light reflected off the river, illuminating everything.

Tim's shoes make a loud *click-clack* over the planking.

"What is it, John?" Stiles asked.

"Thought I heard someone paddling," Abbot said. "Listen."

Stiles turned his head. "I don't hear...."

Something smacked the water.

Abbot grabbed Tim's arm. "I see something."

"Where?"

"Look at the bend...."

"Got it, now, John." Stiles swung his musket from his shoulder and pulled back the hammer to half cock.

Abbot did the same. "It's my post – I'll challenge. What's the watchword tonight?"

"Excelsior, I think."

"What's that mean?"

"Don't know, John. Just say it. Whoever's there is already in pistol range."

"Halt. Present the challenge." Abbott spoke with an authority that hid his frayed nerves.

The paddling stopped, but they caught sight of a shadow fifteen paces off.

"Present the challenge, or I'll shoot!" Silence ensued. Abbott hesitated. He had never fired his weapon other than the one practice round allowed after it was issued.

"Do it, John!" Stiles exhorted.

Abbot thumbed the hammer to full cock and pulled the trigger, spewing a tongue of flame. The shot's explosion shattered the quiet on the river. A cloud of acrid smoke choked them for just a moment. During that time, the shadow moved closer, and the paddling became distinct.

"You missed! And now it's closer. Could be a redcoat attack," Stiles said. "Reload while I challenge again."

Abbot began the loading sequence, fumbling nervously in the dark. The clatter of shoes on the planking meant the corporal of the guard was coming.

"Halt and present the challenge, or I'll shoot!" Stiles spoke loudly.

"Do not shoot, *Monsieur*. I am unarmed."

Abbot grabbed Stiles's musket. "Tim, that's a woman's voice. Hold your shot."

***

Creed winced as he turned onto the cot to flex his muscles. The sharp sting in his side had dulled to a numb ache. He slept as much as he could. When he was awake, he thought about the mission. Guilt overwhelmed him when he recalled the men he recruited and then betrayed. He marveled at the dedication of Father Vincennes, Pierre, and Androche. He mourned the loss of the heroic Sergeant O'Ballance. He wondered how Benjamin Tallmadge and the rest of the troop were doing. He considered how Fitzgerald and His Excellency were managing their efforts to contain Howe.

But Creed thought most of all about Emily. He pictured her face the last time she saw him. He regretted that only his special missions brought him close to her, and that his proximity could put her in danger. Still, he decided that somehow, he would write to her – anonymously, of course. He would pour out his heart to her as an anonymous admirer. He was confident she would realize it was him. But he wondered if the British would suspect.

A hand shook him. "Lieutenant Creed, need to wake up. I have some coffee for you."

Creed sat up. Sweat had soaked his skin, undergarments, and bedding.

"Thomas! What time is it? What have I said?"

"You were sleeping, Lieutenant. You mumbled a lot in your sleep. Mostly about Miss Emily. Say, your clothes are wet."

"So they are. 'Tis a strange way to take ablutions. I feel better now, though. Stronger."

Thomas handed him a tin cup. "Try this coffee. I have a hunk of bread to go with it. Cornbread."

Creed sipped the coffee. "This isn't the usual Yankee mud."

"Dutch coffee, they told me. I traded for it with a militiaman from Albany."

Creed munched on the bread. "I need to get into something dry."

"Jonathan found a washerwoman to do your clothes. You have a fresh set of breeches, stockings, and a shirt. We had her pound the grime out of your hunting smock too."

Creed was tightening his breeches and shirt when the door swung open, and a tall, broad-shouldered figure entered.

"Private Parker. A sight for sore eyes ye are," Creed said.

"Sir, Colonel Wilkinson wants to see you if you are up to it. Says they caught a spy from the enemy camp. An Indian woman. He thinks you might know something about her."

"Tell him I'll be right there," Creed said. *What could he be up to?*

"Should I have Thomas saddle Finn?"

"No. Don't think I could climb a saddle right now. Besides, the walking will do me a world of good."

***

Wilkinson's log hut served as his lodgings and his office. It was a simple twelve-by-twelve affair of roughhewn timbers and a poorly thatched roof. Creed wondered if a good tent might offer better protection from the elements.

Wilkinson greeted him with a wry smile. "I see your wound is healing nicely, Mister Creed."

Creed nodded carefully. Each knew there was a time when either would have preferred to see the other's demise.

"As good as can be expected, sir. Seems my Irish luck has held. Another quarter-inch, and you'd be talking to my headstone."

Wilkinson gave an oily grin. "Luck, indeed. A strange confluence of events has us working on a common cause now. I hope your luck holds until this campaign is finished."

Creed stifled the distaste for Wilkinson that had suddenly rekindled. "I was told you captured an Indian girl."

"She claims to be Canadian French as well, but she's a savage, all the same. She has brought us information on the British, but I am not so sure. Line crossers are rarely to be trusted."

"His Excellency uses them to some effect. General Lee to lesser effect." Creed could not resist the barb at Wilkinson's former commander.

Wilkinson's face darkened. "Indeed, Mister Creed. Well, unlike others, General Gates requires verification. The woman implies great weakness and indecision in Burgoyne's camp. The general is not so confident."

"And you, Colonel?"

"I'll reserve judgment until you talk with her, Mister Creed. You lived among them. You can confirm her claim or not."

An orderly led Creed to the shed they were using to house the prisoner. A guard let Creed in and locked the door behind him.

Even in the dim light, Creed knew right away it was Fleurette. She looked more beautiful than ever and a little less savage, if not less dangerous. He wondered if she knew of her father's death.

"*Monsieur* Lawrence! You live?" Her voice displayed genuine surprise.

"I do. No thanks to you, Fleurette. You betrayed me to your father and cost a good man's life. Perhaps I should say, two good men. Both Sergeant O'Ballance and Androche are gone thanks to your betrayal."

Fleurette's finely chiseled features softened. She buried her face in her hands and sobbed softly.

"What charade is this, Fleurette?"

"*Monsieur*, I am so sorry that these men died. Sergeant O'Ballance was a good man, and Androche....."

"What of Androche?"

"He was... my father!" She began to sob deeply and loudly.

"Your father? What nonsense are you spinning now, Fleurette? Androche would have said something. Would have stopped your step-father Binoche from....." Her deliberate lies astonished Creed, even after all she had done.

"I know you do not believe this. But it is true, nevertheless. Binoche took my mother from him soon after I was born. I was not raised by my mother but by Androche. It was only recently that I came to the company of Binoche."

She spoke softly, but did she speak truthfully?

"How did you go from Androche to Binoche? I can't believe Androche would allow it. Especially the behavior before his eyes."

"Oh, he detested it but also encouraged it, *monsieur*."

"Why would Androche allow that? He hated Binoche more than...."

"I, too, detested every moment with Binoche and his pack of pigs. I detested having to throw myself at him. He made me try to seduce you. He also made me seduce poor, foolish Bart. Insisted that I place myself before the *Anglais* officers. Binoche despoils everything he touches."

"If what you say is true, why would Androche send you to him?"

She looked up at him with large, dark eyes. "We serve a higher master, *monsieur*. A higher cause."

"What cause? Whom do you serve?" Creed was both confused and suspicious.

"Even now, even here, I cannot say."

"How do you expect me to believe any of this, Fleurette? I must know everything. Many men have died because of your charades. The time to tell the truth is now!" Creed grabbed her chin and cast his eyes deeply into hers. "Who sent you?"

Fleurette's eyes welled up again. "The same one who sent you, *monsieur*. See my proof, but I can say no more."

She reached into a small pouch hanging from her dress and opened it, carefully removing its contents – a single ruby-red rosary bead!

Creed's mouth was agape. "Sweet Jesus! I should have known. How well you played the strumpet. How stupid I was. How well you deceived me."

He had hardly been more surprised in his life. Fleurette, as well as her Pierre and Androche, were agents of Father Vincennes. Creed felt for his bead but then realized he had lost it in the rapids of the Battenkill Creek.

"I needed to deceive everyone, *Monsieur*. Otherwise, Binoche or the *Anglais* would become suspicious. Instead, they sent me to spy on the Americans."

"But why lead O'Ballance and me into a trap?"

"Binoche forced me to do it. But he did not know that I had hidden the canoe ready for your escape. And I warned my father and Pierre to come."

"My God, Pierre! So, the three of you knew who and what I was?"

She lowered her head. "As I said, we all serve the same master."

"But how?"

"When my mother abandoned us to be with Binoche, my father sent me to be raised by the sisters in a convent near Quebec. Pierre was in a nearby seminary. That is how we came to work for…."

Creed interrupted her. "I understand now. Say no more."

His mind wrestled with how this unimpressive-looking French Jesuit could be a master spy with a network that seemed to blanket everything from Albany to Trois-Rivieres. There was somehow a connection between him and Fitzgerald.

"What do we do now, *Monsieur*?" She began to tremble. "I have played the savage, the whore, the slave, and more. My father is dead, and now I have no place to go."

Creed held her gently. "Quiet now, Fleurette. That's all over. I'll tell Gates that your information is accurate. He'll grant you a pass that will take you to Canada."

"They took my shillings."

"What shillings?"

"Colonel Sinclair gave me a pouch full of shillings as part payment for this work. Your soldiers took the money, and their officer took it from them. I planned to use that to pay my way home."

"I'll get you more than enough to get you home, Fleurette. Once this is over."

***

Gates removed his spectacles and rubbed his eyes when Creed finished his report. Thanks to Fleurette, they now knew the actual state of the British.

"This must not become widespread knowledge, Mister Creed. Arnold is itching for an attack. This would be all the ammunition he needs to launch one. Although I generally distrust savages, I believe that the information she provided is correct. She must be spirited from this camp as soon as possible."

Gates's last comment caught Creed by surprise. "I, I don't understand, sir. Spirited where?"

"A flotilla of longboats heads south to pick up supplies the day after tomorrow. She'll be remanded to the officer in charge. He'll find a farmstead that needs a good servant. Or maybe one of the friendly Indians will take her for a squaw. I really don't care."

Creed fought to control his anger. "I promised her passage back to Canada."

"Promises to savages are null and void," Wilkinson said. He had put down the quill he used to make the meeting notes. "If I were you, I'd enjoy her charms for a few nights. Then bid her a fond farewell."

Gates and Wilkinson broke into ribald laughter.

"I'll do no such thing, sir," Creed replied.

Gates shot a look at Wilkinson. "Well, then maybe you should entertain her, James."

"The thought excites me, sir. But perhaps Mister Creed is right. A promise from an American officer must be honored. I believe she should be released to Mister Creed's custody until we decide on the best way for her to go north."

Gates looked askance. "Seriously?"

"Trust me, sir." Wilkinson smiled.

"I always do, James."

Chapter 28

When they arrived at Morgan's camp at the west end of Bemis Heights, Creed's men built Fleurette a small lean-to out of pine needles and a blanket. After a long sleep, she awoke to an ear of roasted corn and a slab of deer meat prepared by Jonathan.

"Sorry we have no milk, but Mister Creed allowed us to brew you some of his precious tea, miss," Jonathan said.

She ignored his comment and devoured it ravenously.

"Where is your Captain Lawrence? I mean, Mister Creed?" She had trouble not thinking of him as Captain Lawrence.

"With Colonel Morgan. At headquarters. He'll be back by dark, I hope. Thomas and Elias are with Sergeant Guthrie, checking on things."

Fleurette did not ask any more questions. She only wanted to get back to the convent with her father gone. She was tired of being around soldiers. Tired of these *Bostonais*. To her, all English speakers were *Anglais* or *Bostonais*.

The trappers, the Iroquois, and the English treated her worse than they would treat property. Fleurette longed for the company of the sisters. She decided to rejoin them and spend her life praying for forgiveness for grave sin – even if it was for a noble cause.

She fingered her ruby bead and thought of Father Vincennes and the cause he served. The cause to which he had brought her. Fleurette was done with the world of men and war. She did not regret her actions or what they had cost her. But now, she needed to return to a world of peace, prayer, and reflection.

***

Guthrie returned with the rest of the squad. "Where's the savage wench?"

"Resting. I fed her what we had. She seems very nice. What do you think Lieutenant Creed will do with her?" Jonathan asked.

"No telling with him. I know what I'd do with her before I skinned her. Savages are all the same."

Jonathan glanced at Parker, but his face remained impassive at the slur. Parker was part Indian, yet just about the best man Jonathan knew. During the French and Indian War, the Maryland frontier was ravaged by French war parties.

"Can't say folks in Frederick don't feel the same. But I reckon once they settle down, they can be tolerable neighbors. In any case, Miss Fleurette seems nice."

"Rubbish and bull! Keep an eye on that vixen, or she'll sell her wares to the boys if she doesn't flat-out rob us and skedaddles."

Parker approached Guthrie and crossed his arms menacingly. Yet his voice was calm and matter-of-fact. "I know your family fought the Indians. But I'm living proof that they are just as settled as whites. My Indian grandmother raised me. Don't think I turned out too savage – unless a man gives me a reason."

Guthrie's eyes averted Parker's. "Well, maybe so. Maybe they can be settled and such. But you're the first case I've seen."

Parker nodded. "You just keep looking, Sergeant Guthrie. There's more of us out there."

***

Creed and Morgan sat at the table across from Gates and Wilkinson. Wilkinson just finished explaining the general's plans. Creed sensed trouble.

"You see. The general is convinced his plan is best," Wilkinson purred like a wily old tomcat. "Wait for Burgoyne's next gambit. Defeat him from behind the works we have erected."

"Are there other plans, general?" Morgan asked. "And why isn't Arnold joining us?"

Gates' pale face flushed. "Arnold is insubordinate! A firebrand who refuses to follow orders. He is under house arrest until I get him out of here."

"But you haven't answered my first question. What other plans are there?"

"No plans, precisely," Wilkinson interjected. "Just ideas,"

Morgan's face turned red, and his hands balled into angry fists. "No plans? Just ideas? Just what the blazes is goin' on?"

Creed feared Morgan would give Gates ground to take his command as well.

"We have received correspondence from General Washington asking for the return of your corps to his army," Gates said softly. "But he left the decision with me. I naturally have declined, respectfully, of course."

"Of course!" Morgan's large hand slammed the table with a thud that sounded like a cannon shot. "But I can't sit here forever behind your 'works', taking potshots at lobsters all season. We need action."

"Now, you are sounding like Arnold," Gates said icily.

A chill went through Creed.

"Arnold and I have our differences. But we see eye to eye on one thing. We're here to fight the British. Not watch them set up house for the winter. Do you understand, General? I aim to fight them!"

"I do understand. And I would gladly fight Burgoyne again, but on my terms."

"What do you mean, your terms?" Morgan's teeth were grinding.

"Quite simple, sir," Wilkinson said. "We lure Burgoyne out of his present defenses. To attack us. We cut his men down from behind our works. Like Breed's Hill."

"Fair enough. But how do we lure the redcoats out to waltz back into our sights?"

Wilkinson and Gates looked at Creed. His stomach dropped at the thought of what they might propose.

"That is where Lieutenant Creed comes in. He will lure them out," Wilkinson said with eyes shifting back and forth.

Morgan exploded. "How in damnation is he supposed to do that?"

Gates waved his spectacles at Creed. "He has lived among them as has his woman. Between them, they should find a way. Until then, I need your corps here. If we don't settle things soon, you may spend the winter in Stillwater."

Creed looked at Morgan. He needed to calm him. "Very well. I'll figure something out, sir."

"We'll talk to Arnold first. I'm still under his command," Morgan said.

Gates shook his head. "No longer. Arnold is without command here."

"Listen to me," Morgan retorted. "Arnold took Ticonderoga, and he took Quebec. I want his take on this before I send this officer on another mission that will end in his needless death."

Wilkinson looked at Creed. "Colonel Morgan, this officer has an uncanny way of cheating death. He'll see it through."

Creed nodded with a wry smile. "It seems I have no choice. My Irish luck will have to see me through, then."

***

Squads of soldiers were swinging picks and shovels as they rode to Arnold's quarters. Creed smiled to himself. *Gates is indeed preparing for a long defense.*

"A-hah! I see the word of my arrest has not made its way through the army. Arnold exclaimed when Morgan threw open the tent flap. "If you have come for orders, you'll get none from me, Dan Morgan. Granny Gates relieved me. Then he coaxed me from departing to plead my case with Washington."

"Gates places no stock in Washington's orders," Morgan replied.

Arnold nodded. "I'm afraid this small victory presented to him by our efforts has made him flush with arrogance. No telling what chicanery he is up to."

"No telling," said Morgan.

"What is this officer doing here? I am still not so sure we should trust him."

"You can trust him. I trust him," Morgan spoke with an authority that took control of Arnold's suspicions.

"Well, perhaps you are right. Why the visit, then?"

"Gates wants Mister Creed and an Indian wench to return to the British camp and lure them out. Says he'll only fight them from behind these works."

"Bloody granny! Typical. Caution is too often the coward's mask. Just how do you plan to lure them out?"

"I'm not so sure yet. If we can figure out how to get Mister Creed there, I figure he might just trick them," Morgan said.

Arnold's face beamed like a lighthouse. "Yes! A ruse *de Guerre*. I'll draw up a fictitious order. Burgoyne doesn't know I am out of command. See if Kosciusko can provide a draft of the defense plans. I'll modify them to display weakness on our left. I'll write a fake request for troops, pleading we are dangerously weakened on the flank. It could work!"

Creed was amazed at how rapidly Arnold's mind worked.

Morgan shook his head. "Now, just how are we getting this to the lobsters? By post? We still have to figure out how to get Jeremiah behind their lines without getting hanged."

"Quite simple. You'll send the Indian wench back to their camp with the documents. They'll show sketches of our defenses and expose our weaknesses. They'll also indicate

Howe is not coming north. We have reinforcements marching to make us even stronger in a few weeks. That should goad even Burgoyne."

Creed grew anxious. "Sir, I can't place Fleurette in any more danger." He looked hard at Arnold. "She has served the cause under extreme circumstances, sacrificing more than her life at our behest."

Arnold chuckled. "More than her life?"

"Indeed, sir. Her father, her home among the cloisters, her virtue. All but her soul."

Arnold's face twisted into a knot. "Don't talk to me of Indian women and virtue. And what makes you so certain she did not come here intending to spy for the British after all?"

"This, sir." Creed pulled her ruby rosary bead from his pocket. "The signal of loyalty from a certain Jesuit whom we shall not risk naming. This priest provided me with the resources to delay and divert Burgoyne's march. By the pluck and courage of our troops, a victory was added at Bennington. I think you know this priest, as you have once made common cause with him."

Arnold stared blankly for a moment. "I did more than make common cause with him, Mister Creed. I recruited him. Common cause with the papists. Anything for the cause, eh? But that was long ago. Yet, he cannot have eluded the British this long."

"That he has. He expanded his network and managed to get word to His Excellency."

"How?" Arnold asked.

"I don't know, sir. Nor do I want to know. But I can attest Burgoyne would be shaking hands with Billy Howe about now if he hadn't helped our cause."

Arnold flashed a rare smile. "It's good to know my efforts at Quebec had some positive legacy on this war."

"'Tis indeed, sir." Creed felt a bit of relief.

"Very well," said Arnold. "Morgan, you and Creed must determine how to get the false papers into Burgoyne's hands. I'll prepare them. They'll be ready by noon tomorrow."

By the time Creed and Morgan arrived, they had formulated a simple plan. Cross the river and head north. They'd go beyond that point and cross over. Guthrie and the men would remain on the east bank. Creed would cross over with Parker.

***

They stole out of camp just before dusk the following evening. The autumn twilight cast a peaceful glow on the North River, and the pontoon bridge swayed gently to the rhythm of the cold waters below. They were on a deliberate mission to break that peace. And the agent of that disturbance was Fleurette – the little flower.

Creed marveled at her courage, her poise, and her grace. The young woman he once scorned as a wanton firebrand turned out to be a woman of dedication and courage. Now she agreed to take on the role one last time and enter the enemy's lair. Creed felt guilty at his ready acceptance of her sacrifice. He was using her, yet both agreed there was no other way.

He wondered whether Gates was right to wait patiently for the British to decide on attack or defense. *Or were Morgan and Arnold right?* Force their hand. Deceive them into a course they would not usually choose. Feed off their desperate plight. Strike this invader from the *north*.

Creed stealthily slipped past the eager soldiers and joined Guthrie. They had reached a point where they could see the British campfires struggling against the October chill. "That promontory is a British observation post. We need to get about a quarter-mile further to cross with safety."

"What if the lobsters have sentries on this side?" Guthrie asked. "We can't afford to fire. It'll warn the enemy."

"More likely, we'd encounter our lads. The New England militia is pestering the British posts from here to Ticonderoga. I'm afraid 'tis trigger-happy Yankees we need to fear."

Parker saw the shadow first. The form of a man kneeling with what looked like a musket pointed across the river. He tugged at Guthrie's arm and made a sign towards the figure. Guthrie tapped Creed's shoulder.

Creed nodded. "I see it."

Parker drew his long fishing knife.

Guthrie's tomahawk slipped from his belt. "I'm right behind you. Keep low."

They crawled through the scratchy underbrush and clambered around several large rocks, slowly moving towards the overlook.

Creed did not tell Parker their quarry could be an American. He did not want him to hesitate and risk a shot being fired by a skittish sentry – from either side.

A shaky voice broke the night, "Who's there? Who's there?"

The sentry's voice was aimed at them. Parker crept closer with Guthrie just behind. Creed watched them move ten yards, then five. For someone who hated Indians, the Pennsylvanian sure moved like one.

The figure suddenly leveled his musket. "Who...."

Parker sprang at him like a bobcat and plunged the knife into his chest while smothering his mouth with a large hand. A gurgle and choking sound ended the affair. Parker lowered the body gently to the ground so his weapon and kit wouldn't rattle and alert anyone else.

"Is he dead?" Guthrie asked.

Parker stood panting over the corpse. "He's no British regular. He's American militia. Just a farm boy."

Creed stepped past Guthrie and placed his hand on Parker's shoulder. "'Twas but a lad, yes. But equally dangerous to us if he had sounded an alarm, Elias. You did your duty, no more."

"He's not alone. We need to move quickly, or we'll be fighting our boys," Guthrie whispered.

Two of Guthrie's men emerged from the bushes with a birch canoe, straining their shoulders. In a smooth motion, they slipped it into the dark water.

Creed, Fleurette, and Parker climbed aboard and took to the thwarts. Creed and Parker grasped a pair of paddles. Creed nodded, and the two began to dig into the water. Cautious strokes carried them slowly across the river. Each stroke sent tingles down their spines. In the still of the gathering night, the slightest swirl of the waters might alarm both armies.

The canoe made a soft thud against the riverbank, and Parker jumped out. Creed and Fleurette followed. They dragged the canoe into the woods above the water.

Creed took her chin in his hand. "'Tis the place, Fleurette. Are you sure you want to do this?"

"*Oui monsieur, oui,*" she whispered.

"I can still figure another way to get these papers in their hands," Creed said. "I can sneak into the camp and find a place where a sentry will surely discover it. They'll think it is another blunder by the incompetent rebels. I have used their hubris to good effect before, you know."

He held her gently as if his touch would change her mind. It did not. It seemed to strengthen her resolve.

"I have been there before. Besides, the *Anglais* expect me to get back to them with the information. No, this is the best way. I will be safe enough for a while. As soon as they attack, I will steal away."

"We can wait for you then," Creed said.

"No. Colonel Sinclair will be sure to guard me until my information proves itself. It might be days before I can leave. Your army will need you." She stroked his stubble-flecked chin. "Please, for my sake, go. Let me do this. For my father."

They kissed gently, he warmly, but she more warmly, almost passionately.

Creed gently pushed her back. "Very well, Fleurette. I will pray for your safe return to Quebec."

She flashed a grateful smile. "*Merci, Monsieur.* When I return to the sisters, I pray for you daily. Take this as proof."

Fleurette reached into her pouch and removed the rosary bead. She kissed it and placed it in Creed's palm, her small hands gently touching his.

"I go now!" She said suddenly, grabbing the small canvas bag with the plans craftily doctored by Benedict Arnold. Before Creed could say anything, her lithe figure slipped into the dark woods.

Creed stood as precious minutes ticked away. He vainly hoped she would return, perhaps after losing her way. He knew she would never lose her nerve.

Parker's voice broke from the darkness. "Sir, I think we should go. The boys across the river may encounter more militias."

"Of course, Elias. Let's be quick." Creed glanced into the inky woods and scrambled down the bank to the canoe.

The craft skimmed across the water. They approached the eastern side in minutes when a series of flashes caught their eyes. The dull crack of musket fire followed.

"That's our militia!" Creed said. "Steer south!" They guided the canoe not more than ten yards when the musket balls began slapping the water they had just occupied.

"Faster!" Creed said.

Parker needed no order and began digging his paddle into the dark water, propelling the light craft rapidly. They heard more fire. But this time, the sharper crack of rifles.

"Guthrie is returning fire, hoping to draw their sights from us," Creed said.

"I hope he succeeds, sir!"

The canoe suddenly crashed into the dark bank. The impact split the prow open like a banana skin, suddenly rushing cold, muddy water around their ankles. Creed and Parker stumbled out onto the rocky shore. A strong arm pulled them each up and over the steep embankment.

"We thought you'd never return," Jonathan said. "Sergeant Guthrie is drawing the militia to the east. He said he'd meet us at the junction."

"He's firing at our men?"

"No, he said he'd fire over their heads."

"Very well. Let's be off then."

They reached the intersection of the hunting trails a quarter of an hour later. Something was wrong. Creed sensed it.

A British voice came from the shadows. "Who goes?"

"A friend," Creed replied. "Captain Lawrence, Royal Americans."

"Step forward then, Captain Lawrence."

"Cover me," Creed whispered.

Creed stepped into the junction. A man rose from the brush. He was tall and lean. Clean-shaven. He wore the uniform of a British light infantryman.

"I know your name, captain. I'm Sergeant Reynolds. Royal North-British Fusiliers. We thought you were dead. But now you are my prisoner. You shan't beat the gallows twice, Captain Lawrence. Up lads!"

Six grim-looking men in faded crimson coats, muddied white leggings, and torn black caps emerged with their fusils ready.

"Captain Fraser sent my file across when we heard the musket fire. Looks like the damned rebels stumbled into each other in the dark. Saves us the work, eh? But I'll likely get a nice bounty for bringing you in, sir. Now, be the nice gentleman and put down that firelock."

Creed nodded, then suddenly dropped to a knee and swung his rifle into action. At eight yards, the round fired true, and the ball tore through Reynolds, who keeled over and staggered twice before sprawling into the grass.

Creed immediately dropped and rolled to his left into the tall grass. Musket shots banged out a drum roll, and muzzles flashed against the darkness as Reynolds' men exchanged shots with Parker and Beall.

Creed's men had the edge on the light infantrymen, who had left the cover of the trees. One fell immediately.

Jonathan's shot grazed his target's shoulder, and the light infantryman calmly pulled back the hammer to full-cock and steadied his aim. Another rifle shot rang out, then another. Two more fusiliers fell writhing in the leafy soil.

The last two tried to run back towards the river and the boat waiting for them. Guthrie emerged from the dark underbrush and led his men in hot pursuit. They caught the unlucky fusiliers as they piled into a waiting boat.

One of the fusiliers saw Guthrie's men clear the bank. He raised his light musket and fired. The shot struck the belly of one of Guthrie's men, Lew Emerson. He fell to his knees, staring as blood oozed from the gut shot he knew would kill him.

"I'm hit!" he moaned, staggered, then slid to the ground, trying desperately to plug the hole with his fingers.

Impassively, Guthrie's men unleashed a hail of fire at the boat. Their balls struck with deadly accuracy. The Americans carefully reloaded and sent a second volley. They saw the body of one move, then slump to the bottom of the boat. The other lay twisted over the rudder, sending the vessel circling as the current carried it downriver.

***

The Hudson Highlands, October 7th, 1777
The last company of grenadiers formed ranks to the rattling of a single drum. General Clinton watched impassively as the redcoats presented arms in a snap, snap, snap precision that brought a swallow to the throats of the few Loyalists watching.

Clinton steadied his horse and spoke to the officer sitting next to him. "I know you cannot ride too long, Sandy. A galley about ten miles downriver will take you back."

Drummond's face reddened. He did not like allusions to his stiff knee, his "indisposition," as he often called it. But he was not unwise about it either. "Thank you, sir. With General Howe down south, it is more important than ever that I keep a close watch on the rebels around New York."

"My thought precisely," Clinton said.

"Shame though, isn't it, sir?"

"What's that, Sandy?" Clinton asked.

"Well, it's just that, after humbugging the rebels at Stony Point and breaking their lock on the highlands, we stop here and now retreat."

Clinton paused. "Is that what they are saying, Sandy?"

Drummond nodded. "And I wager they'll say the same in New York and perhaps at Horse Guards."

"Now see here, General Howe put us all in this fix. I completed the task that should have been his with less than one-quarter of the forces. Burgoyne should have pressed on. With less than two thousand effectives in hand, I cannot hold Kingston. Nor march any farther north."

Drummond cocked his head. "I understand, sir. My intelligence report will confirm the woods north of here are full of rebel infantry. So, your actions cannot seem imprudent
just...."

"Ineffective? Is that the implication? We took a half score of rebel strongholds with just a few thousand men. We broke their chain barriers and reclaimed a hundred miles of the river for his majesty."

Drummond suppressed a smile. If Clinton was trying to avoid sounding defensive, it was not working. "I know that, sir. Your key officers know that. The men know that. Push any further, and we risk the City of New York itself. No, you have made the drive north that General Howe abdicated. With the changing seasons upon us and a supply line so long. Perhaps General Burgoyne will fall back on his as well, and we can have a go at them in the spring."

"You don't think Howe will take Philadelphia and force the rebels to sue for peace?"

Drummond shook his head. "I don't know, sir. He may have by now. I produce intelligence, but I cannot divine the future."

"Burgoyne now knows his actions must not count on any conjunction with me. I have given him the diversion he wanted. The rest is up to him."

"General Howe would not have said it any better, sir."

"You best start down the river now. I'll ride with the rear guard from Kingston and see you within the fortnight. Good day to you, Sandy."

"Good day, sir." Drummond turned Shoe down the post road.

***

Swords House, October 8th, 1777

Burgoyne stared at the papers before him. "How did our dear girl get her lovely hands on these, Lazarus?"

"You know she has a facility for drawing men out. In this case, I believe it was an engineer officer. A Polish officer named Kosciusko," Sinclair said.

Burgoyne chuckled. "Indeed. It seems the rebel hirelings have their vices, too. Now, if I am to understand this, they suffered greater than we on the engagement of the 19th."

"Morale is weak, she says. But help is coming soon. Another five thousand men are expected, along with supplies. They plan to swell their ranks and finish us in the spring." Sinclair said.

Burgoyne nodded. "I must admit, our friends down south have disappointed. Howe has left us to our own devices."

"Not entirely. We still have Clinton," Simon Fraser said.

"Indeed," Burgoyne sniffed.

"If they are as weak as this spy says, I think we retreat across the Batten Kill, now. Wait for supplies," von Riedesel said.

Fraser nodded. "Staying here further is folly."

"Sir, their defenses have a distinct weakness in the center," Sinclair said. "The rebels have shored up their left along the high ground and their right along the river. I believe an all-out attack there will snap them in two."

"That's easy for you to say!" Fraser snapped. "My men are the best in the army. They have given their all and will continue to do so. Yet even they see the futility in this."

"They are professionals," Sinclair said.

"What do you think, Acland?" Burgoyne asked.

"I am not so sanguine," Major John Acland replied. "But the men will fight. The question is, to what aim?"

Fraser's voice tightened, "General von Riedesel is right. We should pull back and resupply. Colonel Sinclair's proposition is well taken, but he is, after all, a staff officer, not a fighting man."

Sinclair's face reddened. He could not publicly state that he had counseled Burgoyne against his distractions and cautioned him on the supply situation.

"The situation is grave, sir. I agree. But the men deserve one last chance to regain their honor on the field."

"Damn you and your honor!" Fraser said. "Another word, and I'll call you out!"

"Enough, gentlemen!" Burgoyne stood and slapped his hand on the map before him. "Lazarus has long urged caution and a return north to tighten our supply line until the spring. But even he sees the opportunity that has fallen into our lap. The decision is mine alone. We will move tomorrow."

Von Riedesel's face brightened. "To Batten Kill?"

"No, on the rebels. But since we have not vetted the information the savage girl brought to us, we'll make it a reconnaissance in force. If the center proves weak, I'll order a full attack on the rebels."

Fraser blanched. "And if the information proves faulty?"

"We'll see. I'll lead the column myself. Fraser will accompany, of course. And I'll bring along some of my staff. You are quite right, Simon." Burgoyne looked at Sinclair. "Staff officers need the occasional blooding."

Sinclair's mouth tightened. Perhaps his support of the advance was hasty. Maybe he should have continued to urge retreat, despite Burgoyne's insistence.

He fingered his *gorget* nervously. "Sir, I believe my place is at the headquarters. Reports will come in. And I have matters of supply to attend."

Burgoyne threw up his hand. "Enough! It is all decided. Now, gentlemen, I believe we have time for a glass of claret."

Chapter 29

Bemis Heights, October 7th, 1777

Creed spread his hands as he finished his report. "I believe we were successful. But British actions will be the test of it."

Morgan seemed skeptical. "I lost a good man bringing that woman back to her British friends. Not sure all these shenanigans were worth losing a good rifleman."

"A poor militia lad died as well, sir," Creed observed.

Arnold sat with a quill in hand, jotting down notes. "We knew the gambit was not without difficulty. But it will be worth it if they believe her and the false papers."

"What are you writing?" Morgan asked.

"My observations on the fray in September. For Congress. That Gates humbugged me out of my glory," Arnold said with a frown.

"Seems you best think about how to explain jumping into the next fracas," Morgan said.

"What do you mean?"

"I just spoke with Gates. The man has a real potato head. You are out of any chance at command when we face the lobsters. That is, *if* we face the lobsters," Morgan said sourly.

Arnold cast a mischievous look. "Don't mind him. The senior officer *in loco,* dear Morgan, is always in command."

A knock at the door from an orderly interrupted the discussion. "Sir, a messenger arrived summoning you and Lieutenant Creed to General Gates's headquarters."

Morgan hesitated, then nodded. "Alright. Tell him I'll be there soon enough."

Creed gauged the two men. He felt the energy they exuded.

"What do you think he wants now?" Morgan asked Arnold.

"What do *you* think he wants?" Arnold replied cagily.

"Probably wants my men to start planting flowers to gussy up his defenses," Morgan said.

"Plant some hemlock! Just what they need to scare off Burgoyne!" Arnold threw back his head in laughter.

"Should I tell him about the false plans?" Morgan asked huskily.

Arnold rubbed his chin. "Yes. But don't reveal the author. He might suffer apoplexy. On reconsideration, go ahead and tell him." Arnold broke into laughter.

***

Creed and Morgan sat at a weathered plank table with a map stretched before them.

Gates paced opposite them, waving his spectacles. "Kosciusko's men drafted this. As the season progresses, we will be sending your men on patrols to fill in the many blank areas. I am thinking about a major offensive by the militias to seize various posts in the spring while we tie Burgoyne down right here."

"Seems it'd be better to go right at em, general," Morgan replied.

Wilkinson pushed back his greasy dark hair. "Sir, General Gates did not commission these fine defenses only to abandon them."

"But if the British attack, sir?" Creed interjected.

"Well, that is another matter. But we'll face them behind stout works this time," Gates said.

Wilkinson turned on Creed. "We are told you brought the Indian woman back to the British. An action like that should not have been attempted without General Gates's express permission. After all, he is the commander-in-chief."

Morgan turned red. "Excuse me, Wilkinson. Last I knew, General Washington was the commander-in-chief. Did I miss a bulletin from Congress?"

An uncomfortable silence filled the room.

"She is true to our cause, sir," Creed said. "We concocted a set of false plans. Now we must wait to see if they take the bait."

Gates twisted his face into a frown. "Can we trust her not to play us with the British, Mister Creed?"

"Ah, as for her trust, sir. You must trust *me* on that account," he replied.

Wilkinson eyed him. "We have no choice now, do we, Mister Creed?"

"Aye, sir. You do not."

***

Mill Creek, October 7th, 1777

The late morning chill receded as the sun's gentle rays brushed the fields and woods along the Mill Creek with a comforting warmth. Soon, the afternoon sun would bring a soaking kind of sweat to men on both sides of the ravine.

Creed's spyglass scanned the line of trees along the creek, leaves now golden and speckled with red. He yawned. He and his men had little sleep since returning Fleurette to the British camp.

They lay in a skirmish line 200 yards from the British defense works.

"What do you notice, Sergeant Guthrie?" Creed asked.

"Lobsters are sleeping late. I see no sentinels. Lazy curs."

"In garrison perhaps, but in the field, the British regular is not lazy, Sergeant Guthrie. He is well-trained, sometimes cruel, often greedy, and always brave, but his sergeant makes sure he is not lazy. No, look closely."

Creed handed Guthrie the spyglass. The tough rifleman scanned the wall of earth and logs that stretched across the wheat field.

"The flag! The flag's gone!" Guthrie gasped. "It's flown from the day the first log went in place there. Now it's gone. But look!"

Ahead glinted the bayonets and buttons of the light infantry under Colonel Balcarres – part of Simon Fraser's right wing.

"Aye," Creed said. "Those are light infantry. They skirmish without their colors."

"But if they have taken it down, they are either preparing to retreat...."

"Or attack," Creed said with finality. He wondered if the plan had worked on them and how they received Fleurette. Perhaps they suspected her and forced a confession, and now this was a ploy to cover a retreat to better lines of defense.

He heard shouts to his left. Parker and Beall bolted like deer from their positions, each bent forward at the waist and zigzagging, just as he had trained them.

"What are the lads after, sergeant?" Creed said.

"I think they saw something or someone."

Creed raised his spyglass again. "'Tis a soldier. They have him! Looks like he gave it up without resisting. My Irish luck. We bag a deserter just when we need one."

Guthrie spat a piece of black tobacco. "Can't trust no deserter, sir. Any man who'd leave his unit high and dry before a battle is plain scum."

"Your frontier sense of justice impedes wartime, Sergeant. Men have many reasons for serving a cause and even more for abandoning one. And not always for dishonorable reasons. In this case, 'tis likely about starvation, maltreatment or lack of faith."

"Faith? You sound like a preacher now."

"Oh, I'm no preacher. Bit of a priest in me, yes, but no preacher."

Parker and Beall approached with the soldier in tow. He had unkempt hair, a small frame, and an ashen face with hollow eyes.

"We found you a present, sir," Parker declared proudly. "Meet Private Jones from the 24th Regiment of Foot."

"Top of the morning to ya, Private Jones, is it?" Creed grinned knowingly. Many professional soldiers, especially those fleeing justice, enlisted under assumed names.

"Yes, sir," Jones replied, rubbing his eyes.

"The 24th is a fine regiment. What causes you to leave it at this particular time and place?"

"Food, sir. Not much of it left in camp. So, they are going to make us fight for it. But I think the attack is doomed. Most do, but they are desperate for victuals, as am I. I just decided to avoid the fight and ask for mine as a prisoner on parole."

The man's word did not come easily. Creed knew he was ashamed of what he was in the eyes of his captors and his former comrades.

"Tell us how they plan to take our food, then," Creed said in a comforting voice.

"Reconnaissance-in-force, Gentleman Johnny calls it. Some reconnaissance force – over a thousand, they say. Our regiment and light infantry under General Fraser, the Germans, Brunswickers under an officer named von Specht, and the grenadiers under Major Acland." Jones's eyes widened. "They're all coming!"

"And just when are they coming, Private Jones?"

"Why, now, sir. The columns are formed, just beyond the ridge there."

"Very well. Private Beall, take Private Jones back to the camp. Find Thomas. He'll get him to the provost. Then come right back."

"Yes, sir," Beall said. He slipped his long sword bayonet to his short hunting rifle and pointed south. "Let's go, on the quick."

Creed looked at Parker. "You heard his report. Take word back to headquarters."

***

Less than an hour later, Wilkinson's horse was pounding through the heavy grass and bushes. His horse pranced in a tight circle as he spoke to Creed in a huff, "What seems to be the problem?"

"The British are on the move. I believe they've taken the bait. They're attacking."

"Attacking? Where? When?" Wilkinson's face flushed dark and grew menacing.

"The attack has begun. See now. Their columns are just emerging." Creed pointed to the north and west, just three hundred yards distant. The morning sun's rays picked up the brass of buttons – the brilliant glint of bayonets.

"Give me that glass!" Wilkinson grabbed the spyglass from Creed and scanned the wood line. "By God, you are right. There must be thousands of them."

"I'd reckon on hundreds, sir. For now."

"Well, Creed, my plan worked. It worked. General Gates shall have his Bunker Hill. I must go back to prepare the defenses." Wilkinson threw the spyglass at Creed and spurred off.

"What now, sir?" Guthrie asked.

Creed did not answer right away. He conned the mass of scarlet growing in the distance.

"They have formed three columns. Look there - bluecoats on the flank. The Germans have joined in. Maybe a thousand or so. In the center, several officers on horseback. Can't be sure, but I believe Simon Fraser is one, and wait! Gentleman Johnny himself is there."

Guthrie spat another chaw. "A full-scale attack."

"'Tisn't a full-scale attack – yet. But with Johnny himself, who knows what will develop? Go back and find Colonel Morgan. Tell him they can have a real turkey shoot if he gets his lads up here quickly."

Morgan's horse cantered up the trail and halted by Creed. Despite his size, Morgan sprang from the saddle. "That poltroon Wilkinson said the whole damn lobster army was on the march, so Granny is holding the men behind the works."

"So your men aren't coming, sir?"

Morgan grinned mischievously. "Didn't say that! They're a-comin'. When your message got to me, I convinced the old cow to let me slow down the attack. Where are those lobster bastards?"

"Look across the field. I thought they'd roll over us by now. But the gentleman is with them. I saw him halt the column to let foragers scythe up the wheat in the field ahead of us. By Jesus, they must be starvin'."

Morgan shook his head. "Gates released Enoch Poor's Brigade and mine. He'll come right through here with his men. Should be about fifteen minutes. Tell him to strike at the lobsters to our front and squash 'em. I'll move my boys further west and strike the right flank of their attack."

"Those are Simon Fraser's lads out there on the British right," Creed warned. "General Poor will run into the grenadiers. They have already formed a line of battle."

"We whipped 'em before...we can do it again." Morgan pulled out a flask of corn whisky, took a swig, and offered some to Creed. "Here you go, boy. Cut the last of the mornin' chill with some of this."

Creed shook his head. "Thank you, sir, but it is already past noon. The sun is warming things, and the gunpowder will finish it."

A runner tugged at Morgan's buckskin sleeve. "General Gates agreed to release Learned's Brigade. He wants to know where to attack."

Morgan studied the columns forming in the distance. Several companies of his riflemen trotted by, heading to the high wooded ground west of them.

"Well, I got their right flank, and Enoch's got the grenadiers on their left. Guess that leaves the center for Learned. Let's all meet on the high ground behind Freeman's Farm."

The runner turned on his heels without saluting and sprinted back towards the defense works.

Morgan glanced towards Guthrie and placed a large hand on Creed's shoulder. "You help guide Poor and Learned in the right direction, Lieutenant Creed. Then join me. Something tells me I'm gonna need your rifles."

Chapter 30

General Benedict Arnold paced back and forth in a lather, his heavy boots pounding the floor planks and spurs jingling with each angry step. "This attack is our chance, damn it! Give me command of the regiments, and I'll drive an iron fist into Burgoyne's nose and send him reeling back to Quebec."

"Likely with the same results you last had there," Gates sniffed. He needed to keep the hot-headed Arnold in his place, yet a small part of him feared Arnold was right. *What to do?*

"I'll ignore that insult for now. Look, both Lincoln and I have gone forward. If you commit enough troops now, you'll win this thing outright instead of sitting here waiting for Burgoyne's next move."

General Benjamin Lincoln nodded. "Arnold's right. The British might turn our flank and roll up our works if reinforcements aren't committed."

Gates adjusted his spectacles. "Morgan and Dearborn can push around their flank and slow their advance."

"I'm afraid the situation calls for something more," Lincoln said calmly. A farmer, who led the men from Massachusetts, Lincoln was known for having a level head.

"Very well, Enoch Poor's brigade will go forward, and Learned will move into reserve," Gates said reluctantly. He did not want to earn Lincoln's displeasure. His ambitions required sufficient support among the senior officers in the north. And just maybe they were right.

Arnold stared into Gates with dark, steely eyes. "The line needs more reinforcing. Otherwise, you risk defeat, despite your numbers. Give me the word, and I'll go."

"I say this for the last time, General Arnold. You have no command in this army. I do not need your services, and you certainly have no business here."

Arnold stormed out with balled fists and a clenched jaw.

***

Simon Fraser scanned the patches of woods and fields that lay south of Freeman's Farm. The foraging party had just finished scything the wheat, and acres of stubble lay before them.

He saw columns slowly limping along on his left and lifted a gloved hand. "Form for battle, lads."

The light infantry, superbly equipped with the short version of the New Land Musket, hefty tomahawks dangling from their belts, and razor-sharp bayonets shining, silently formed.

Hundreds of yards on the left, the powerfully built grenadiers under Major John Dyke Acland formed a smaller column of some 200. Between them, in the center, marched von Riedesel's hand-picked column of Brunswickers under von Specht.

Although the sight of powerful formations of crack veterans in scarlet and blue inspired him, Fraser still felt Burgoyne's ploy was doomed.

Captain Alexander Fraser rode up, his horse already frothing with the heat. His cousin looked tired and nervous. "We have cleared the woods on the far right, sir. Their pickets have fallen back."

The thought of his cousin's sharpshooters in full array brought the general's confidence back. These were troops who could fight in the Americas as intended. "Excellent, Alexander. The rest of the advance guard shall be up shortly."

Alexander Fraser pursed his lips and made a faint grimace.

"What is it, Alexander?"

"Sir, I do not see what this foray will accomplish. The whole attack couldn't be more than two thousand men. Not enough to take the rebel works."

"Actually, we are less than two thousand. The council of war hesitated on whether we should retreat, hold or attack. This is the compromise. We are to explore the situation, and General Burgoyne plays his hand accordingly. It's as if this was one of his damn card games, and we are his cards. In this case, I'm afraid we are the face cards."

"Well, the lads are up for it," Alexander Fraser replied. "After all this skulking about and ducking rebel sharpshooters."

The general grinned. "I know how they feel. However, the question is, are the rebels up to it? Alexander, regardless of this day's outcome, I want you to know you have the right approach to this war. Fight the rebels using their tactics. Take advantage of the land, the weather, and the populace. I plan on writing directly to Lord Germain. An army of men like yours is what's needed."

Alexander cocked his head in disagreement. "It takes years to make men as good as mine, sir. Anyone can join the light infantry or grenadiers. But these men are special."

The general smiled. "They are indeed but...."

A pair of cannons suddenly roared, belching sheets of flame and clouds of smoke. Then, the British columns shuffled and spread out into attack mode.

"That's the signal! Here we go, Alexander. Best get back to the men, eh? We'll talk of this at length at dinner." He did not say what he thought. They might dine that night, but they would likely not celebrate.

"Aye, sir," the captain replied.

***

A few hundred yards to the southeast, Sinclair was becoming nervous. He heard the *crack, crack, crack* of rifled musket fire slowly fill the air. He could see Simon Fraser's men dodging to and fro to his right front as they exchanged long-range fire with the rebels. The damned rebels constantly tried to extend around the far-right flank. *They fight like the savages they hate*, he thought.

Other columns of rebels began forming. Sinclair heard a slow but steady *pop* and *crack* as the light infantry and grenadiers exchanged desultory volleys with the enemy.

"This may prove difficult, sir," Sinclair said to his commander.

"Patience, Lazarus. You are a planner, not a fighter. These things take time to unfold. I am comfortable, thus far."

"Sir, they are massing for an attack. General Fraser might be cut off if they pierce our center and take Balcarres's redoubt. Without his men, we are lost in these woods."

"I have no fear on that account. Simon's men will prevail. Look at our lads now."

They watched a brigade of Americans push forward against the redoubt's outer works only to fall back as a company of regulars poured fire into their flanks.

"Discipline triumphs over zeal, Lazarus."

Sinclair saw something else. "They are pouring fire into Fraser's men on the right. They continue pressing hard against our center despite the volley fire raking their flank. We should consider redeploying behind the great ravine and defend at the Grand Redoubt."

"What? We have them in the open, Lazarus, where our lads excel. I shall go forward now. Stay back here. It should prove safe enough for a staff officer." Burgoyne put spurs to his charger and rode across the field, waving his sword in an outburst of martial bravado Sinclair had not seen in a long time.

A line of British infantry had just fallen back, and Burgoyne had to rein back himself to avoid capture by a regiment of Poor's Brigade. Then, two British cannons belched smoke and fire, unleashing a pair of steel balls into the American flank. Stunned by the enfilade, men scrambled back like rabbits.

"That's the way to do it!" Burgoyne exulted.

But more rebels could be seen – formless blue, brown, and gray columns edging forward. Burgoyne galloped back.

"What is your plan, sir?" Sinclair asked.

"I am afraid we need some way to change our luck, Lazarus." He pulled a large gold watch from his waistcoat and checked the time. "Past three pm."

Sinclair looked at his commander's face and saw neither despair nor desperation but something more nuanced. *He has only a few hours of light left to turn his reconnaissance into victory. But even he must realize now that the advantage is with the rebels.*

***

Creed slowly squeezed the trigger. The hammer struck the pan, sending sparks and igniting the powder with a flash and puff of smoke. His round struck true. A burly British sergeant grabbed his hip and fell, twisting to his right.

Still, the grenadiers stomped across the field, halting only to pour careful volleys into the advancing mass of Americans.

Guthrie's men guided the brigades of Poor and Learned into position. Once there, the Yankee regiments did not need help finding the columns of red and blue coats stretched before them. Creed had followed Morgan's instructions.

Anxious orders of officers and sergeants were barely heard over the *whine* of musket balls and the *boom* of the iron shot. Companies of nervous men rushed forward and then fell back as the battle along the front ebbed and flowed.

Parker came up beside Creed. He was breathing heavily, and beads of sweat drenched his face. "Sir, I gave the report."

"Good. Now let's go find Colonel Morgan. We've tarried here long enough. Tell Sergeant Guthrie to gather his lads. Have you seen Private Beall?"

Beall's smiling face suddenly appeared, equally perspiring in the growing heat. "Delivered my charge, sir. Am I too late to bag some lobsters?"

"You're just in time."

They skirted behind the American lines and turned north along a shallow ravine. The woods on their left were thick with American riflemen. Only a handful of British were there – Alexander Fraser's company and a few Canadians and Loyalists. The rest of Simon Fraser's column struggled to hold the right of the British line. American riflemen peppered them with steady fire. Slowly, their numbers dwindled as clumps of red moved back to avoid the leaden deluge.

Creed halted his men at a knoll that gave them a vantage point to snipe at the British. *Fraser's men!* Creed sprawled along the side of the mound. He scanned the front with his glass.

Guthrie threw himself down next to him. "What have we got?"

"The smoke obscures much, but the redcoats still stand tall when it drifts," Creed said.

"Well, we should do something to change that, sir."

"Aye, I'm going to inform Colonel Morgan of our presence. Place the rest of the lads in an arc along the front of this knoll. From here, we can support the Morgan's Rifles or Learned's men."

The taciturn Guthrie chortled. "They're only a little over a hundred yards from us. We'll fire those lobsters up, alright. I guarantee that."

Creed grimaced. "Choose your shots wisely, Sergeant Guthrie."

Guthrie rushed off to set the men in pairs, ensuring each team had a good line of sight on the British.

To the right stood lines of continental infantry mixed with New York, New Hampshire, and Massachusetts militia. From their left came the shrill crackle of rifle fire – both sides launched a torrent of lead that took its toll on American, Briton, and Teuton alike. The once crisp volleys had degenerated into a choppy mix of independent fire that popped like Chinese fireworks against the steady volleys from the British.

***

Creed found Morgan trying to coax a swarm of riflemen through heavy woods.

When he saw Creed, Morgan stopped to take a long swig from his water bottle. He then wiped his sweat and powder-streaked face and rubbed his neck with a dirty red bandana.

Creed shot him a quizzical look.

Morgan grinned. "It's water this time. I see you got Poor and Learned in place. I told the boys to look for the officers now. We are running low on ball and powder and won't get any more till sundown. How goes it over there?"

Creed threw his head back and took a swig from his bottle. "Tolerably, I believe, sir. The firing on the right flank is intense, but Poor's brigade is gaining ground. His lads have driven Acland's grenadiers back. The enemy's left flank has all but collapsed. Losses on both sides looked frightful from where we sat."

"So long as we drive the enemy back, it's worth the blood. We need to break their lines before dark, or this stalemate will result in Gates putting us on defense." Morgan wiped his mouth with the back of his hand. "Maybe permanently."

The roar of voices echoed from somewhere to the south.

"What's that?" Morgan asked.

Creed scrambled through the bushes and snapped open his spyglass. A figure on a light-brown horse was galloping along the line and rallying Learned's brigade.

"I believe it's General Arnold! He's riding towards the lobster lines in a lather. Looks like several of General Learned's regiments have joined in."

"Good! Damned good!" Morgan exclaimed. He cupped his hands and shouted, "Let's get more rifles up and support General Arnold! Rifles up!"

Creed slammed his spyglass shut. "B'Jesus! That's one of my lads with him. And the general is riding my horse! He took Finn!"

"That's Arnold for ya. He'd take your woman if you'd let go of her hand. But don't worry - he'll give 'em hell!"

"I don't care so much for that. So long as he gives me back my horse."

Arnold galloped at the head of a swarm of angry and excited men. He charged straight up the slope where a solid line of bluecoats waited - von Specht's Brunswickers.

Exhausted gunners strained already aching muscles. Slowly, their cannons edged up the slope and into position. Soon, the ridge was aflame with musket balls and round shot. The air began to fill with heavy smoke and the screams of men reacting to the hoarse voices of desperate officers.

Bodies toppled in large numbers – muskets at twenty yards were lethal. The *clang* of bayonets and sabers and the frantic beating of drums joined in a symphony of death. The heat and gunpowder choked men's throats. Fear and confusion added to the brew.

Determined to stop the rebels, the large-framed Germans in dark blue coats and miters of gleaming brass stood their ground, fired patiently, and thrust bayonets desperately.

Arnold's men wavered, but they had taken a toll on the Germans, and now the columns to their right began to buckle as another wave of desperate rebels threw themselves at them. Assaulted from the front and their flank in danger, the Brunswickers threw firelocks to their broad shoulders and slowly stepped back. They were disciplined, platoons halting to unleash crisp volleys by turn. But they were giving up the field.

***

To the west, Morgan's and Dearborn's infantry leaped over rocks and pushed through dense foliage, advancing tree to tree against the British right flank column. The British began to break up into isolated platoons and squads as they fell back under the onslaught.

"Get back to your men, Mister Creed. Keep the fire up so they can't get between our boys and the continentals." Morgan bounded into the woods, hollering and bird-calling to urge his men forward.

Creed bent forward and pumped his feet as he raced between the two armies – the most direct route to his men some 200 yards distant. Musket balls flew overhead, pinging off rocks or smacking tree limbs from both directions.

***

General Simon Fraser saw the danger to the British line. Ignoring the din and confusion, he turned to a subaltern. "Freddie! Ride and find Captain Fraser. Tell him his men must anchor the line, or we are lost."

"Sir!" the subaltern swung effortlessly into the saddle. Fraser watched him canter off, his horse's legs moving in unison with its rider sitting tall in the saddle. The thought occurred to Fraser that he made a splendid target.

At that moment, a rifle cracked. The shot struck the subaltern, who reared his horse wildly and then tumbled from the saddle.

"Damn! They got Freddie!" Fraser exclaimed.

Two squads of redcoats limped past the downed officer. Not one stopped to offer help.

Fraser saw his regiment, the 24th Foot, disintegrating before him. *Action is needed to avoid a rout.* Fraser stood in his stirrups, and his saber flashed in the sunlight. "Hold the line, lads! We must hold the line!"

He twisted his gray charger about and spurred along the field where three platoons were trying to disengage from the sting of rebel lead. One platoon stiffened at the sight of their general. A sergeant barked orders, and they formed a solid skirmish line that began peppering the oncoming rebels with a taste of their own medicine.

Fraser grew excited at the sight. His men would soon show their mettle. "That's the way, lads! The 24th shall hold the rebels!"

The other two platoons looked back at the swarm of rebels flooding the field and began to run from them. Some dropped their muskets to hasten the retreat. Men stumbled and jostled to get away from the deadly lead. The 24th Foot was starting to collapse against the American onslaught.

Fraser galloped before a band of fleeing men, thrusting his saber high. "Rally, lads! We'll soon have them on the run."

A musket ball creased his charger's harness. The startled horse let out a snort. Another ball zipped by, just behind the horse's ears. But Fraser focused on his men and ignored the danger. "Hold the line, my fine fellows!"

"Sir, they are ranging you, sir. Please dismount or go to the rear and out of their sniper's line of sight."

Fraser turned to see Freddie. The young officer was bleeding, and his face was whiter than a sheet. But he had managed to remount his horse. Fraser took it as a good sign.

"Nonsense, Freddie. If a rebel ball couldn't take you, one won't take me, either. My place is here with the 24th…."

A third bullet swatted Fraser square in the belly with a sickening sound.

***

Creed watched grimly as the British subaltern took a well-aimed round. He made the sign of the cross. Despite years of soldiering, watching brave men maimed, wounded, or killed disturbed him. "Whose shot was that?"

"Mine, sir," Jonathan Beall replied.

Creed nodded. It was his duty to encourage his men. "Keep the heat on them, lads. Colonel Morgan is trying to clear their sharpshooters from the woods."

A cry from Sergeant Guthrie followed the crack of another rifle. "We got the son of a bitch! We got the damned lobster general!"

Creed looked up to see a mounted officer in a scarlet coat slouch forward on his horse and drop his saber. *A gut shot – most likely mortal.*

A sinking feeling gripped Creed. He raised his glass to get a better look. As he feared, the fallen warrior was General Simon Fraser. He watched, panic-stricken, as officers grabbed his bridle and led Fraser from the field. Creed slipped the glass into his belt and made the sign of the cross.

"Are you alright, Lieutenant?" Guthrie asked.

"The most honorable of our foes has just fallen, Sergeant Guthrie."

"Sir?"

"You have shot their best general, Sergeant Guthrie! Shot their best man, a good man. I knew him."

The battle's toll and pain from his wounds began to grip Creed. His hands began to shake, and his head grew woozy from the acrid stench of smoke. He was in command and had to remain calm. As calm as one could be in the smoke-filled Hades around him.

"Even their good men have to die if we're gonna win this war," Guthrie said. "Besides, I didn't shoot him. One of my boys did."

Creed began to recover. "Who?"

"Tim Murphy. He climbed that tree for a better shot. "Come on down, Tim. You did good!"

Creed's jaw tightened. "Yes. He did his duty. 'Tis God's will. Who knows who will be next?"

Guthrie shrugged and checked his flint. "We gotta kill the enemy quickly and efficiently. Can't do that if ya have remorse."

"You're right, Sergeant. Let's get the lads moving forward and support the attack."

***

Arnold's first wave began to falter. Exhausted, many threw themselves to the ground. Some chugged frantic swallows from their water bottles. Not a few slugged down their last draughts of rum.

Still, the British recoiled from its ferocity, and soon sergeants and officers were ordering their men back all along the line. In squads and platoons, they streamed back to the safety of their defense works at the Balcarres redoubt. At Breymann's Redoubt to the northwest, a few hundred stalwart German grenadiers stolidly awaited their turn. Creed eyed both entrenchments. He decided these would decide the day.

Creed and his men watched Arnold lead several assaults on the earthworks. Arnold spurred Finn recklessly to and fro, whooping and cursing. The Americans now sensed a chance for victory.

Through clouds of gun smoke, the glint of gunmetal and streaks of flame revealed the steady and desperate defenders who unleashed volley after volley.

Creed watched in pride and dismay as his horse Finn leaped over defender and attacker alike. Arnold's blood-lust was in full display as he led units as small as a platoon forward, only to be driven back. At Arnold's side was Thomas Jeffries, himself a master horseman. In the first attack, Thomas had fired his two pistols, but Creed saw him wielding his long leather lash with tremendous effect whenever an enemy soldier threatened Arnold.

"Good lad, Thomas," Creed whispered. "Keep them away from Finn."

Most who watched the attack probably thought Thomas was protecting the general, but Creed knew better.

"Seems General Arnold will break the British this time," Parker said to Creed.

"No, Elias," Creed replied. "Those lads will not give up that redoubt. He'll need another tactic."

"Maybe Colonel Morgan will find him one," Jonathan Beall said. "Look there!" Beall pointed to the northwest, where all hell was breaking loose under a dark fog of smoke.

***

Arnold desperately scanned the battlefield, searching for an opportunity. Then he spied the opening on his left. *We've got to break the British now.*

Morgan's men were pursuing Fraser's shattered command. Those redcoats who could move were now streaming into the Breymann Redoubt. The excited men in hunting shirts moved from tree to tree, rock to rock, and bush to bush with whoops and shouts. And they recklessly ignored the sheets of lead poured at them by the grim grenadiers defending the earthworks.

He turned to Thomas. "Look to the northwest, boy. Some of Learned's companies are marching on the Breymann Redoubt. Its rear is unguarded and just ripe for the picking. Ride to Colonel Morgan and tell him to keep the pressure on their front while I slip in from behind. Go now!"

Thomas dug his spurs, and his horse flew across the open field. The buzz of musket balls filled the air around him. His horse sailed over dead and dying figures in red, blue, and brown coats. Busted cannon chassis, limbers, stray logs, and stone walls did not impede his skillful riding.

Arnold spotted a new formation of Massachusetts men. He stood in his stirrups and pointed his saber at the earth, stone, and timber pile. "Look, boys! Morgan's men command their front. We have a clear path to their rear. Follow me!"

Arnold's frenzy did not abate until he spurred Finn into the defense works. He wheeled Finn about and galloped between the redoubts to join the attack despite heavy musket and cannon fire. Arnold's daring emboldened Learned's men. They charged right in with whoops and hollers like men possessed, ignoring the lead that filled the air around them from two sides. The German and British defenders faced a hopeless fight with the enemy to their rear.

Curses in English, French, and German competed with the crack of musket fire, the explosion of cannon, and the whine of lead that flew in all directions. Desperate men on both sides stabbed and blocked repeatedly. Muskets parried savage bayonet thrusts. Musket butt strokes slammed crushed bones. Wicked blades tore into exposed bodies.

The sweltering heat of a warm autumn day clung to them, staining heavy wool uniforms on both sides. Men stood legs apart, eyeing each other in a deadly game of cat and mouse. Each knew that hand-to-hand combat must ultimately decide the day.

Arnold thrust his saber towards a mass of blue, the stiff-jawed German grenadiers. "Come on, boys! One more charge and they are ours!"

The grenadiers blasted a desperate volley that caught the battle-maddened general in the crossfire. He spurred forward in a frenzy but soon cursed his quarry. A burning pain seared through his bad leg – a bullet! Round after round *buzzed* in all directions like a swarm of angry hornets. Despite the pain in his leg, he dug spurs into Finn, who leaped over a pack of defenders.

With a *thud, thud*, a pair of musket balls struck Finn. The horse gave a sickening shriek and fell in a heap, pinning Arnold to the ground. Arnold screamed in agony at the burning in his leg and the crushing weight of his mount. He lay helpless, cursing his plight and his bad luck. Arnold felt faint and was about to fade when several strong arms dragged him from under the noble horse.

"We have your assassin, sir. I'll give him the bayonet," a New Englander shouted as a hapless German crouched with his hands uplifted.

"No. He did his duty. Treat him accordingly." Arnold grimaced as a makeshift litter carried him and his crushed leg to the camp and its hospital.

***

Arnold was gone. But Morgan, Learned, Poor, and others maintained the pressure. Creed rushed towards the redoubt, his legs pumping harder than ever. He watched a band of Americans carrying a limp form.

"It's General Arnold!" Beall exclaimed.

Creed grabbed Arnold's arm. "Sir, how goes the battle?"

Arnold's face was pale, and he looked weak. But he managed a nod. "Still time to kill some of them. But hurry."

"And Finn? Where's my horse?"

Arnold lowered his eyes. The men rushed him back over the corpse-strewn field.

"Check your flints and load buck and ball, lads. This is for keeps."

Creed was the first of his band on the redoubt. He ignored the *zing* of bullets and took a steady bead on a giant figure in dark blue. He recognized the miter of a tall grenadier sergeant. Creed sent a slug into the grenadier's chest with a flick of his finger. He grimly fumbled for another cartridge.

His men sent round after round of lead into the dark mass of defenders from either side. Despite the smoke and chaos, they managed to strike only the enemy. *These are good lads*, Creed thought. He was unsure whether he meant his men or their quarry.

The Americans reached a frenzy stoked by the scent of victory, but the Germans resisted with Teutonic determination. The struggle for the redoubt continued with a fury, with no one asking for quarter. The bloodlust on both sides was not yet sated.

But nature eventually decided the outcome. Creed felt the slow chill of the gathering October darkness descend on the once-hot field.

"Sir, I'm low on powder and ball. And I can't see much beyond fifty yards," Parker said.

"Me neither," Beall chimed.

Creed looked over at Guthrie. The rangy sergeant and his riflemen had stopped. As one, the men gazed across a field quickly dimming before their eyes. The *pop* of musket and *crack* of rifle had stilled. The sounds of men moaning, choking on blood or bile, and crying for their mothers or wives began to fill the air.

The steady tread of a horse broke the quiet. From the shadows, they saw Thomas pull up and halt. "Sir, Colonel Morgan, and Dearborn put out the word to stand to."

"The British still hold the heights," Creed said as he gazed across the dark field."

"I heard Colonel Morgan tell some of the men that we'd get 'em at first light," Thomas replied.

Creed nodded. "I reckon those heights can stay British for one more night."

Chapter 31

The Great Redoubt, October 8th, 1777

The scene seemed eerily beautiful to Burgoyne. The dull glow of an autumn sunset turned to shadows. Rebel cannon balls passed over them now and again, occasionally spraying rock and debris. But the cannonade was more annoying than anything else. For, despite the presence of the rebel army, the British had to bid farewell to their finest officer.

Once so cocky and cheerful, the British commander stood grief-stricken as a file of Fraser's men discharged their muskets in a farewell salute to their noble leader.

An Anglican minister in a dark frock coat thumbed quickly through the Book of Common Prayer. With a gravelly voice, he rattled off the rite for the dead. Pipers doled a mournful tune as the body of Brigadier General Simon Fraser was slowly lowered into a makeshift grave. Tears flooded the eyes of all present, all but Lazarus Sinclair.

Sinclair broke the silence when the ceremony ended, "A day's rest has done the men some good, sir. I have sent orders to move north under cover of darkness. We'll leave our fires burning to fool their pickets."

Burgoyne did not hear nor care what his adjutant said. "What is the final toll, Lazarus?"

"Nothing is final, sir, as many of the wounded will be dead within a fortnight. But thus far, the rebel response to our 'reconnaissance' has taken over five hundred of our men. I fear the actual number will be much greater. Not the least of whom we have just laid to rest."

Burgoyne lowered his head. "We'll regroup north of the Fishkill. Once the men have rested and refitted, I'll decide our next move."

"Perhaps there will yet be succor from the south," Sinclair said.

"Perhaps," Burgoyne said ruefully. He did not believe it. "But we both know better."

John Burgoyne was sure he had rolled his dice for the last time. Still, there was always one last ray of hope.

"I'll send out scouts, sir. Perhaps a courier has stolen past the rebel lines in the confusion of this reconnaissance," Sinclair offered.

Burgoyne drew a breath, and his eyes narrowed. "The girl, Lazarus. Our charming Fleurette. Her information proved false. I fear we marched into a well-planned trap."

Could they hang a woman? Could I, Gentleman Johnny, hang a woman? Still, because he had sent her south, any repercussions had to point towards him. "My God, I might have to hang a woman."

"I think not, sir," Sinclair replied nervously. His mind raced for a way out. Fleurette was his idea, after all.

"You don't? Why not?" Burgoyne's voice had a curious inflection.

"No, sir. You, that is, we, weren't duped by a savage girl. Her information was *generally* correct, and your foray *would* have succeeded as you planned, except the crazed

Americans left their defenses in an impromptu attack. It was merely bad luck and ill timing."

Burgoyne's face brightened. "By Mars, I believe you are correct, Lazarus. The gods did not favor us this day. But another day will come."

"Indeed, sir."

***

Creed and his men fell asleep on their arms, completely exhausted, on the battlefield. Most of the Americans did as well. There was no rejoicing, only exhaustion. The moans of the wounded and dying gave the night a ghoulish feel as scavengers began to strip the fallen of their worldly possessions.

The autumn light broke early, casting an almost pleasant hue over the dismal field. Creed huddled over a small fire with Thomas, who shared the sad news of Finn. Creed nodded. But he felt a fierce sense of loss. Finn had been with him from when he first arrived in America.

"I tried to stop the general, but he threatened to have me sent south," Thomas sobbed.

"'Tis not your fault, Thomas. I know you would have given your life for Finn. He was a fine horse. I'll never find the likes of him. Bred in Maryland, you know."

Thomas sobbed again. "I just knew something bad was going to happen. I wished that general had died, not Finn."

"As much as I am devastated by losing my beloved Finn, you should not say such things. I hear that he's seriously wounded and may well yet die. And what's more, his actions may have won the day for us. We can thank Finn for much of it. Finn's noble power carried General Arnold through the enemy's ranks."

Thomas rubbed his tears. "That's right! Finn's the one who won the battle. No other horse could have gotten General Arnold through all that."

Despite his words, Creed felt a sickening in his stomach. "He did indeed, Thomas. With the help of you and a few others. He did indeed."

Suddenly, the field erupted with thousands of deep-throated shouts of huzzah. The British had abandoned the area.

***

Creed and his men stood their watch from a lonely outpost near Freeman's farm for the next few days. But nothing moved there by day or night. Occasionally, Guthrie would take a few men and quietly creep toward the British lines. But Creed forbade sniping. "Only fire in self-defense. Too many others are willing to do the butchering." He knew Guthrie resented it. Guthrie lived to shoot.

As they lay quietly at the outpost, a rider galloped up. "I'm looking for Lieutenant Creed."

"I'm he," Creed said.

"You're needed at headquarters."

Creed threw on his hunting shirt and buckskins and grabbed his sword. "Get your kit ready, lads. It usually means we'll be on the move when I'm summoned."

The door to the American commander's office slammed behind Creed. Gates and Morgan were in another heated conversation. Wilkinson sat on a wooden chair, watching the two go at it.

"I'm leaving as soon as I can, damn it," Morgan exclaimed. "My job's done here."

"You'll leave when I order it," Gates said.

"Sir, General Burgoyne has offered terms. We need your men until his sword is given," Wilkinson said.

"He's hemmed and hawed since the retreat. He's stalling 'til help comes. I'm tired of the trickery. Either we attack them and finish the job, or I'm leaving."

Gates shook his head. "No one wants this over more than I. The last thing I want is a continuance of this campaign. It could risk squandering my victory."

Morgan's eyes bulged from his massive head. "*Your* victory?"

Gates ignored him. "Clinton, after taking Fort Montgomery and nearly splitting the Hudson defenses, has returned to the City of New York. But who knows whether he'll return north?"

"John Stark's militias have cut most of Burgoyne's supply line north at Battenkill. We should attack him," Morgan said.

"What are you doing here?" Wilkinson asked when he saw Creed at the door.

"Ah, Mister Creed. How good of you to come," Gates said jocularly.

"Jeremiah is under my command. I requested him," Morgan said.

Wilkinson's swarthy face darkened.

"Go on," Gates said placidly.

Morgan crossed his brawny arms in defiance. "I intend to send Mister Creed to the British camp to demand terms. While there, he'll check their strength. We need to press them now. I don't like this stalling."

Wilkinson protested, "I have had several exchanges with the British and...."

"I don't give a damn. My corps of riflemen leaves tomorrow if we don't send him now," Morgan bellowed.

Gates blanched and then smiled mischievously. "Very well, Colonel Morgan. Why not?" He furrowed his brow and glanced at his adjutant. "James, prepare another letter with our terms. If Burgoyne stalls, Mister Creed will inform him of Colonel Morgan's intent."

***

The Schuyler Mansion, Saratoga, New York, October 17th, 1777

Burgoyne's army had recoiled like a snake after the repulse of the reconnaissance in force. For days, tired men tended wounds, repaired shattered muskets, and mended torn uniforms while their commander struggled with his next move. Burgoyne sat in Philip Schuyler's bedroom. The scorched paneling still had an acrid stench. The darkness of the place was magnified by the rain splashing incessantly against the tin roof like a drumroll.

"I should not have torched this place before heading for Albany, Lazarus. Why, a tent would be more comfortable and drier," Burgoyne said.

The North Spy

"Yes, punishing this rebel landholder was impractical," Sinclair said. He had advised against it, but that was now forgotten.

Burgoyne leaned back in his chair and laced his fingers behind his head. He gazed at the weak fire sputtering in the hearth. "Von Riedesel still counsels pulling back. But with the rebels now at Batten Kill, my chess game with Gates has come to an end. I was hoping to delay until a way out could be found. But now…"

"The girl is gone," Sinclair said suddenly, hoping Burgoyne would ignore him.

"The girl? What girl?" Burgoyne snapped.

"Fleurette is gone."

"I thought you had her under lock and key, so to speak."

"I had her manacles removed. They chafed."

"They chafed? Did they chafe her or you?"

Sinclair hung his head. "When the patrol caught her returning north, I assumed she was being truthful about escaping from the scoundrel Lawrence. This is all his doing."

"What matter is it now? Some savage will take her as his squaw. That was to be her ultimate fate anyway?

Sinclair reddened. He had wanted her almost as much as he wanted to kill Lawrence.

"Don't tell me you cared for her, Lazarus?" Burgoyne chuckled.

Sinclair hung his head like a schoolboy. "She played the vixen with seeming gusto, but I'd hear her whimpering at night and…."

"And what?" Burgoyne asked.

"Praying in French. My wife died last year, sir. I thought once the rebellion was quashed and these people had been taught their lesson, I might settle somewhere here. The colonies will need good British citizens."

Burgoyne's face widened in a grin. "My God, man! All this time, I thought you were a cold-hearted clerk, but you are more romantic than I am. I like it! Perhaps I'll write a play about it."

A knock on the door interrupted the discussion.

An aide peered in. "Sorry to disturb you, sir, but an officer representing the rebel commander Gates is here."

Burgoyne and Sinclair jumped to their feet in surprise when the tall frame of Creed filled the doorway in the hunting smock and leathers of an American rifleman.

"You!" Sinclair bristled.

"Sir, I am Lieutenant Jeremiah Creed, here to offer final terms from Major General Gates, commander of the Northern Department."

"You? You are no envoy! You are the *faux* James Lawrence, the rebel spy!" Sinclair gasped.

"That's enough, Lazarus. Whether this man is James Lawrence or this Jeremiah Creed is no longer of interest," Burgoyne said calmly. "Come share a glass of claret, Mister Creed, is it?"

Creed waved a paper at the general. "I have come to receive your final signature on this convention. The terms are quite generous—honors of war if I do say so, sir. Return to England. Until then, you and your men are guests in America, at our expense. I tried to convince General Gates not to offer you such generous terms, but he insisted."

"And the wounded, of whom there are all too many? How do I know they won't fall to the tomahawks of your militia or the savages?" Burgoyne asked.

Sinclair could tell he was hiding the excitement he felt at the scheme – a convention relieved him of signing a surrender treaty, saving his reputation in London.

"I can assure you neither General Gates nor Colonel Morgan will allow that. Our men rallied in no small part because of the tomahawk. We would not use it now in reprisal," Creed said.

While the general and Creed bantered over a document that was *fait accompli*, Sinclair's face twisted into a grimace of fury, envy, and anger. Finally, he burst uncontrollably, his voice ending in something close to a screech, "This man is a traitor and the cause of our misfortune. The rebels' escape at Ticonderoga, our deviation from our base of supplies, our delay in the woods, our loss of supplies, our defeat at Bennington, and now our final disgrace. He is the cause of my plan's failure! He must face the king's justice."

"Whatever I have done, I have done as a patriotic American. I am a traitor to no cause. No country," Creed said.

"Enough of that, Lazarus! Regardless of his treachery, this officer represents the army that now encircles our position. We owe him all due protocol. I'll sign the convention, now, if you please."

Creed handed the document to Burgoyne. An orderly fetched writing material, and after a cursory read of the paper, he scrawled a signature across the bottom. Creed carefully folded the document and placed it in an oilskin pouch.

Sinclair's voice quivered, "We return to England in disgrace, sir."

"No, Lazarus, we return with honor. Unlike the Hessians at Trenton, I signed a convention, not a surrender. Horse Guards, Lord Germain, and his Majesty will surely understand."

Creed stood coolly. "All I know is that five thousand of your regulars will stack arms by sundown. Do you understand, sir?"

Burgoyne's lip had a slight tremor. "Of course, Mister Creed. I'm a gentleman of his word."

"Very well, sir. General Gates will accept your arms in four hours."

***

The wind blew in a steady breeze across the river's high ground. The rain had tapered off, but everything seemed wet and cold. Creed shivered, watching from a knoll on the river's west bank. His men were there to observe the British departure across the plank bridge and take the road to Boston, where they would await transport to England. Instead, he would have had his men participate in the scene below.

Several hundred rough-clad men with long rifles formed a rigid square around the soggy field. Weapons loaded and primed, they had orders to shoot if any of the enemy broke the protocol. However, the British failed to oblige. And Burgoyne had already ridden off with most of his staff. As usual, he left Colonel Lazarus Sinclair to attend the unpleasant details of the "convention."

A New York Continental regiment stood rigidly while its small band played "Yankee Doodle." Musket after musket was slammed into the mud by angry men in scarlet and blue. One by one, the regimental colors, the heart and soul of each unit, were piled in a heap. As Sinclair watched, he mused that the Americans would need more than this victory to win their freedom.

As each regiment surrendered its colors, Sinclair checked its name: Specht, Riedesel, Recht, Hesse-Hanau, and Breymann for the Germans; the 20th, 22nd, 24th, 9th, 62nd regiments for the British. With each tally, his stomach tightened. The final total was seven generals, over 5,700 men, 27 guns, and thousands of small arms, powder, and ball.

But the "convention" came with a much larger price – honor. The British Army had never suffered such ignominy in 100 years of fighting on the continent and across the globe. *Much worse than Braddock's travesty.*

Sinclair raised his hand in a half-hearted salute that a brawny American officer in a hunting outfit returned with gusto. Sinclair turned wordlessly, climbed on his horse, and slowly rode towards the bridge – the last member of the broken army to cross.

He glanced up at a knoll along the river edge as he neared it. He saw several figures in buckskin staring down at him. But one caught his attention. *Lawrence!*

An explosion of feelings overpowered him – his detailed war plans, foiled at every turn by the spy, James Lawrence. And worse, once caught, that spy had eluded the king's justice through chicanery. *Why, that contemptible spy is gloating!*

Sinclair was sure he gloated not just over the army's defeat but also over Fleurette. He, an accomplished senior officer of the British Army, could never admit that a savage girl loathed his company, cause, or touch. Somehow, this spy was responsible for her loss.

Sinclair's face shifted from a twisted frown to a sly smile. This was the opportunity he had planned for, and he had volunteered to oversee the "convention." High time to finish what was denied him in the forests to the north.

Sinclair slowed his horse as he passed Creed. Nodding, he lifted his hat as if to salute. His gaze shifted to a small wood where six hand-picked British marksmen waited for his command. "Now!"

***

A ray of sunlight broke through the gray clouds overhead for a brief moment but long enough to expose the glint of gunmetal.

"Ambush!" someone exclaimed.

From a patch of woods, fifty yards off, a series of musket shots *cracked*. The sting of lead splattered the rocks and trees along the knoll in a rhythm of destruction.

One struck a rifleman in the armpit, slicing upward into his neck. He fell, wide-eyed, into the thick, wet bushes.

A half-dozen American rifles spit back an angry return fire.

Jonathan Beall stepped from the brush to take a well-aimed shot. A tall, wiry figure in a red tunic and light infantry bonnet reached over a rock. His musket belched a lead ball that struck Jonathan.

Creed squeezed off a round, cutting through the marksman's bonnet. The light infantryman's head snapped back, and he dropped behind the rock.

The ensuing crossfire sent deadly lead balls flying in all directions in a mix of dull *pops*, sharp *cracks*, humming lead, and the *snap* and *crack* of shots that cut through wood and chipped rocks. The firing suddenly stopped, and the air grew still. Smoke began spiraling upward and drifting over the river.

Parker ran to Jonathan. "Where are you struck?"

Jonathan's face was ashen. "My thigh."

Parker cut open his leggings with his fisherman's knife and examined the wound.

"This will take a pint," he said definitively.

Jonathan stammered. "A pint of blood?"

Parker smiled. "No, a pint of rum. Half to cleanse the flesh wound and the other half to drink."

Creed and Thomas climbed through the brush.

"How's Jonathan?" Creed asked.

"You can ask me directly, sir. I'm not dead. Truth is, I've had worse dog bites back home."

***

Sinclair watched the eruption of gunfire anxiously. When it stopped, it was clear that his luck had failed him again. *A half dozen handpicked men, trained marksmen, should have killed the traitor-spy and his minions with the first volley.* He cursed it.

Sinclair saw Creed rush to the comfort of one of his downed soldiers. Although just ten paces from his horse, Creed failed to notice him. Sinclair slowly drew his pistol from the saddle holster, a Scottish regimental pistol, simple and lethal at fifteen paces. Red-faced and hands quaking, the adjutant pulled back the hammer and, using both hands, steadied his aim right on the center of the traitor's back. *You may now die, Mister Lawrence or Mister Creed, as you please. By either name, you die a traitor to the crown.*

***

A shot exploded, breaking the stillness, and a puff of smoke wafted over the knoll. A bullet struck Sinclair's chest, and he slumped forward. With a terrifying shriek, his horse bolted. Frantic hooves clattered across the plank bridge where Sinclair's body toppled and plunged into the cold embrace of the dark waters below.

A figure rose from the knoll, sliding a ramrod into his rifle as he stepped forward.

"Got the sonofabitch lobster, Lieutenant Creed," Guthrie called out. "And my boys got the rest of 'em red-jackets,"

Morgan galloped up with a platoon of riflemen panting to keep up with him. "Secure the area, boys. Check the lobsters and flush out any others."

Morgan slid from his horse. "What happened, Mister Creed?"

"'Twas an ambush, sir. Some of Alexander Fraser's lads and the last of the Royal Americans. My own lads. Set upon me by your good Colonel Sinclair."

"Why in the hell would he do this?"

"He recognized me when I took the terms to Burgoyne. As Captain James Lawrence of the Royal Americans, I had disrupted his invasion plans. For that, he had tried to have his henchmen kill me on more than one occasion. I suppose he decided to take his last opportunity in person."

Morgan slowly shook his head. "He must have hated you much. Nearly suicide trying something like that within gunshot of the Rifle Corps."

Creed nodded. "He was a desperate man indeed, sir. Greatly frustrated in all aspects of his privileged life. His invasion plan would have succeeded, though."

"You changed that, Lieutenant Creed. The army and the nation owe you a debt."

"They owe me no debt, sir. I did my duty in pursuit of a cause that I freely embrace and which, when successful, will grant me a homeland and freedom."

"Still, the risks you took on and off the battlefield."

Creed raised his hand. "No, sir. Your Rifle Corps, the continentals under Learned and Poor, the militias at Bennington – they all risked much to quash this threat. But...."

Creed hesitated. He did not want to reveal matters of the utmost secrecy. He thought of Father Vincennes, waging a silent war against his British masters and his church hierarchy, and of Pierre and his band – Androche, Fleurette, and others. They knew nothing of the Declaration of Independence or any other political screeds that brought the colonies into the struggle for freedom. Yet they risked hardships, depredation, and death to support him for reasons he did not quite understand.

"But what?" Morgan asked.

"Let me just say... others have sacrificed silently and resolutely for our cause. Yet if successful, our cause yields them no gain."

Morgan's mighty hand slapped Creed on the back. "I don't understand you, Mister Creed. But I suppose, in the end, your Irish luck brought this about."

A wry smile broke across Creed's face. "'Tis better for all that you don't understand, Colonel. Indeed, let's chalk this up to my Irish luck."

Epilogue

Lady Dunning's House, New York, October 29th, 1777

Emily worked steadily at her needle. Just one more line, and she would be finished with the quilt. As the Indian summer faded into oblivion, she and Klara took to meeting like this. It gave Klara the company of someone her age and Emily a chance to glean tidbits involving Drummond, Loyalist politics, and the state of the British occupation.

"I think we are facing an early winter, Emily. The ground is frozen solid with a thick frost, which I have never seen back home in New Jersey," Klara said.

"The poor soldiers will suffer much, I am afraid." Emily put down her quilt, fighting the tears forming in her eyes. *Jeremiah has gone north. How much colder will he be? If he still lives.*

Klara's eyes sparkled as she peered over her quilt. "The only soldier I care about is Captain Baker."

"You should care about the men on both sides," Emily replied, "but Captain Baker was someone special to you."

Klara lowered her eyes. "Major Drummond is taking me to the dinner at Mister Laseby's house tonight. Are you coming, Emily? Please say you will. The talk of the men is tedious."

"No. I did receive an invite, but with my father gone to Philadelphia, I have to watch the house. Besides, I have no escort."

Klara giggled. "Only because you don't want one with Stephen off to join General Howe's army in Philadelphia. Many an officer would love to have you grace his arm."

Emily's face reddened. "I think not."

Lady Dunning looked up from her needlework. "Celebrating the occupation of Philadelphia is a necessarily joyous occasion, ladies. But I understand Emily's situation. It is always better, my dear, to keep men guessing as to your true affections. It makes them more amenable."

"Amenable to what?" Klara asked.

"Nothing," Emily said. "Very well, I'll go. But only for a bit. I'll catch up on the latest gossip, of course."

Lady Dunning beamed with delight. "Splendid! I am sure there will be news of the war. According to Sandy, our success at Germantown has the rebels on the run. Soon things will be back to normal. Why, you'll be able to visit your dear friend Lorie Dale once more."

Emily's heart and mind drifted. *They are all ignoring the terrible news from the north.* She could not. *Terrible battles were fought, and many men were killed or wounded. Could Jeremiah be among them?* Her mind sought further insight into the British reaction to the surrender. Her heart yearned for information of a different kind.

***

General Clinton's Headquarters, New York

A grand fireplace dominated the main room of the mansion. The damp wood caused the flames to sputter and smoke, occasionally sending a crackle or a hiss across the room.

The floor's long planks squeaked with each tread of Sandy Drummond's boots as he paced before the fireplace. Though he limped with each step, he kept his hands behind his back and stared at the oak flooring.

Clinton glanced up from the crude map spread across the large oak table. "My letter to General Howe and Horse Guards is done. Would you care to read it?"

"No, sir. I know what it will say. With the small force at your disposal, you made every effort to drive north and relieve the rebel pressure on General Burgoyne. You took a mighty rebel fort on the North River by storm, but Burgoyne's lack of progress made your position untenable, thus hastening the retrograde to your base of operations in the city."

"My God, Sandy! I couldn't have said it any better. Of course, we tried every way to get word to Burgoyne."

"I know full well we tried to inform him, sir. We lost several good men in the attempt. Some of the Scorpions as well and...."

"And what?" Clinton demanded impatiently.

"Not what, sir, whom," Drummond replied. "And that would be Captain Sidney Baker. My best officer."

Clinton rolled his eyes. "Baker? An American?"

"We can only win this war if we have the Americans with us."

Clinton eyed him skeptically. "So I have heard you say. But so far, the Loyalists have failed to deliver, right?"

"They fight and die as we Britons do, sir." Baker had not returned from his desperate journey. Drummond was tired of the high command's disdain for the value the Loyal Americans brought to the crown.

"So you say! I say Loyalists did not deliver the rebel capital to General Howe. The Royal
Navy and British regulars did. And the Loyalists seem to have been nowhere in sight up north. I recall Burgoyne's boast that they would rally to his army as it marched south. Quite the opposite has happened, I'm afraid."

Drummond stopped, swallowed hard, and rested his chin pensively on a balled-up fist. "Well, that's the truth for ye. But here, it's different. They do rally. Some of the Provincial regiments fought well at Brandywine. The rebels have moved their capital to Baltimore."

"Thanks to British arms, Sandy," Clinton said archly.

Drummond shrugged it off. "Yet, an entire British army has capitulated. Despite seizing Philadelphia, the war will likely be a long one. More reason to court the Americans."

Clinton shook his head. "Use them, yes. Court them, never. Besides, Washington is hiding in the Jersey hills. This winter will starve what's left of his miserable pack. They'll come begging to surrender by winter's end."

"We thought that last winter, sir," Drummond retorted.

The door opened, and a subaltern entered. "Sir, an officer outside asks to see Major Drummond."

Clinton waved his hand dismissively. "Tell him to come back later. Major Drummond and I have not finished."

"Wait! Who is it?" Drummond asked.

"He says his name is Captain Baker, sir."

Drummond glanced at Clinton. "Send him in at once!"

The subaltern ushered Baker in while an orderly brought a bottle of brandy and three glasses. Drummond could not believe his eyes. Baker had lost twenty pounds from his once sturdy frame. His hair was long, with streaks of gray, and his eyes were red and sunken.

"Where have ye been, Sidney? What happened? The report said you and the Scorpion escort never returned. We thought ye captured or dead."

Baker sipped at the brandy. "That's exactly what happened, sir. Rebels ambushed us while we tried to cross one of the many creeks. It was rugged country like nothing I've ever seen. It happened quickly. We fought gamely, but they had us."

"Your men?" Clinton asked impatiently.

"Dead, sir."

"But you escaped?" Clinton asked.

"I tried to escape, but they seized me. I was tied and hanged by the neck from a tree."

"I don't believe you," Clinton said.

"Then believe this, general." Baker unwound the heavy serge muffler enveloping his neck. Drummond and Clinton averted their eyes.

"My God, Sidney! How did you survive that?" Drummond asked.

The gash was over an inch wide. The skin was rubbed raw and had scaled over but had healed into a dried-out scar of black and grayish color.

"I didn't, at least in their minds. They choked me good and thought me dead. But they failed to break my neck. Somehow, the spinning kept me alive. Then I heard a musket shot. I blacked out after that. When I awoke, an Indian was caring for me. He had cut me down. Salved the ripped flesh, you see. He had shot the rebel leader, and they broke and ran. Guess they thought more Scorpions had joined the fray." He paused with a rueful look. "Suppose, in a way, the Scorpions saved me."

"Who was this Indian?" Drummond asked.

"I don't know who he was or what he was doing there. He got me to a house near Saratoga. Owned by the Swords family. After a few days' rest, one of their sons helped guide me back down to the city."

"Why did it take you so long?" Clinton asked.

"The Hudson was crawling with rebels, so we had to keep to the back roads and trails. At one point, a band of those damned skinners almost got us near Poughkeepsie."

Drummond poured him more brandy, which he sipped slowly.

"God, it burns. But I need it." Baker took another sip and put down his glass. "I'm sorry I did not get the message to General Burgoyne."

"Burgoyne's army was destroyed," Clinton said flatly.

Drummond cut him off. "It was my mistake to waste your talents in the north, Sidney. For that bit of arrogance, you have paid a bitter price. Burgoyne *has* capitulated. But General Howe has taken Philadelphia, and there is plenty of mopping up in West Jersey."

Baker looked at him with dull eyes. "So, I still have your confidence, sir?"

"Of course, Sidney. Your knowledge of the Jerseys and Pennsylvania will prove invaluable yet. And there is the matter of Rook. We must find out if he is still with Washington and then find a way to contact him. But first, you must rest. The armies will soon go into winter quarters and all that. By spring, you should have recuperated enough to raise a band of Jersey Loyalists and get back in the game, eh?"

Baker nodded weakly. "Thank you, sir."

***

Washington's Camp, White Marsh, Pennsylvania, October 30th, 1777

Colonel Robert Fitzgerald stood patiently at the doorway with Major Benjamin Tallmadge hovering behind him.

Washington looked up from his correspondence. "To what do I owe this visit, gentlemen?" He motioned them to come in and close the door.

"I have a report from Mister Scovel, sir," Fitzgerald said. "When I told him of Mister Tallmadge's suspicions, I had no idea he'd get back to me within days."

"And?"

"His men are on it. Our friend is under discreet surveillance."

"Anything to report?"

"Nothing. And that's suspicious in itself. It's as though he knows they are watching."

Washington was concerned. One of Tallmadge's patrols had found some engineering sketches left behind in the retreat from Brandywine. They included defense plans for the fort on Mudd Island and two others on the Delaware River outside Philadelphia. "Keep watching. There is always time to question him. I prefer to catch him *In flagrante delicto*."

"Indeed, sir."

"What else?"

"Mister Tallmadge has another report on the cabal, sir."

Fitzgerald held an envelope, a "Blue Note."

He handed it to Washington, who scanned the note twice before burning it over a candle. He watched silently as the flame enveloped the heavy velum and crisped it into dust. The contents disturbed him.

Who is his source?" Washington finally asked.

Tallmadge replied. "He does not say, Your Excellency. But I received a letter from one of your allies in Baltimore."

"Gates sent Lieutenant Colonel Wilkinson to report the surrender of Burgoyne's army, although he has called it a 'convention,' rather than surrender," Fitzgerald said. "I suspect he is the source."

Washington put down his pencil. "A convention? What does that mean?"

"It means we must feed the British until they can board ships to England. They are our guests rather than our prisoners," Fitzgerald said.

Washington's face darkened, and his eyes narrowed. He struggled to remain calm in the face of perfidy. "Whoever heard of such a thing? General Gates did not receive permission from me to make such an offer."

"I don't think he views himself as subordinate to Your Excellency any longer. The proclamation to Congress behind your back is proof enough. But another report on this cabal...."

"Insubordinate officers cannot be tolerated." Washington's knuckles whitened as he balled his fists. "How many members of this cabal have we identified?"

"Just three, but they are fairly senior and all, like General Gates, have friends," Fitzgerald replied.

Washington nodded. He needed to take action. But also remain circumspect. "See me tomorrow with Mister Scovel. I want his men in the provosts to guard for signs of this spreading to lower ranks. God knows the pitiful supply situation will give men enough cause to mutiny. Without faith in their officers, all is lost."

"Morgan is heading south, though."

"That is good news," Washington said.

"And Gates's ploy has angered as many in Congress as it has pleased," Fitzgerald said.

"Well, I don't begrudge his victory, only his ambition. My main concern is this army's well-being. We have a powerful foe before us. Our capital is occupied. I need the army behind me to stop Howe in the spring."

He fumbled for a pencil and scribbled out a note, handing it to Tallmadge. "Get this to Mister Jons."

"May I ask what it is, sir?"

"My intelligence needs from New York. Regardless of our capital's loss, New York is still the big prize in this war and the British and Tory seat of power. We must never lose sight of that fact. You will also need to get someone into Philadelphia."

"It shall be done, sir. I'll use Roy Harry. He has proven most resourceful, despite his flaws. When Mister Creed returns, we'll...."

"Jeremiah Creed? Is he with Colonel Morgan?" Washington smiled for the first time in a long time.

"I meant to tell you that straight off, Your Excellency. I apologize."

Washington rose from his desk and smiled broadly. "Cabal or no cabal, Lieutenant Creed and Morgan are indispensable for the type of war we face."

Things were bleak. But Washington felt suddenly at ease. "Come, gentlemen. Let us share a glass of wine. Providence is indeed shining brighter upon us – at least for now."

***

The clock in the tavern struck nine. The revelry was getting underway. A mix of English, Dutch, and Palatinate German dialects bantered back and forth as a dozen farmers, woodcutters, and laborers argued over the week's events. First and foremost, the war was on their minds. But not Creed. He wondered how Pierre and Fleurette made out. *Are they back in Canada?* His thoughts drifted to Emily, sending his heart into a flip.

Morgan's powerful voice broke his thoughts and dreams. "You feeling sick?"

Morgan was wiping his mouth with the tablecloth at a corner table across from Creed. Each had a tankard of ale. Between them lay the remains of a rack of lamb the tavern owner had prepared in their honor. He accompanied it with some local trout and bread pudding.

Morgan reached for his pipe. Creed delighted himself in a glass of *genever*, which the owner kept for special occasions. The waiter scurried in with a small pot of coffee.

Morgan tugged at his pipe. "I agree with you, Mister Creed. This war is far from over. But some believe otherwise. Those who think they should be running the army instead of His Excellency."

"'Tis a sad state for the rebellion if men speak against His Excellency."

"I don't mean the men," Morgan replied.

"You mean officers?"

"Worse, I mean generals." Morgan bit into the pipe.

"Why, that's treason," Creed muttered.

"Only if they fail." Morgan smiled grimly.

"Surely, they would. I mean, they shall."

"Only if good men stand in their way. But sometimes, I'm not sure enough will."

"Surely, His Excellency is the undisputed leader of the cause. Who could take his place? Who would take his place?"

"Spoken like an Irish dreamer. Jeremiah, some question His Excellency's authority and, more to the point, his judgment. They would place others, meaning themselves, in his place." Morgan spat a piece of tobacco across the room.

"Are you among them?" Creed had always seen the rebellion through somewhat rose-colored lenses. His youthful idealism seemed to wane a bit with the tone of the conversation.

"Never! But that scalawag Gates…."

"What, sir?"

"Never mind. Shouldn't be saying such things to a…."

"To an Irishman?" Creed asked.

"No, to a lieutenant. I never liked Gates much. He's peculiar. Well, I disagreed with his strategy – sit back and wait. But we did our duty. And we beat 'em twice in a stand-up fight."

"That we did." Creed took a sip of the *genever*.

"But his Convention. I didn't like the idea. We beat 'em, damn it! I told Gates they should surrender outright, or my riflemen would cut them to pieces by the first snowfall."

"What did he say to that?"

"He shook his head. I think he still feared another fight. A fight he didn't want, couldn't afford to lose if we were to be the new 'indispensable man.'"

"You mean?"

"Yep. Gates offered me a place in his army. I told him my orders were to help him beat Burgoyne and rejoin the commander-in-chief."

"What did he say to that?"

Morgan glanced around and lowered his voice. "He said that was exactly what he had in mind. He said some in Congress sought a new brand of leadership for the cause."

"Who?"

"He mumbled a few names: Conway, Mifflin, and Wilkinson. And then he removed his glasses, placed his fat hand on my fist, and asked if he could count on me."

"By Christ! What did ye say ta him?"

Morgan stared at the smoke spiraling from his pipe. "I said that he could count on me to do my duty. No more. We left the next day."

"The enemy within takes on a new meaning now," Creed said.

Morgan nodded. "Something tells me His Excellency will need your help more than mine if he is to defeat this challenge."

"'Tis as you said, sir."

"What's that, Jeremiah?"

"They'll only succeed if enough good men don't stand in their way. I think His Excellency has those in full measure."

-The End-

The North Spy

S.W. O'Connell

Author's Notes

I should comment on the mix of history used in this fictional story. General George Washington did face a dilemma in the spring of 1777. His attempt to thwart or block General William Howe's move backfired. Meanwhile, the command controversy in the north made for some chaotic shifts on both sides. General Arthur Saint Clair evacuated the vaunted Fort Ticonderoga because his position was untenable. I used the fictional Jeremiah Creed, or James Lawrence, to nudge him.

General John Burgoyne faced a strained supply chain that put him in a desperate situation by late autumn. His incursions eastward in pursuit of the rebels and supplies caused unnecessary delays to a plan that required quick movement and focus to have a chance to succeed. The fictional Lazarus Sinclair was added as his foil. He also lost the valuable services of many of his native, mostly Iroquois, allies. While not decisive, these factors contributed to his failure.

Burgoyne's "three-pronged" strategy was solid, but the difficulties in coordinating over a large, rugged continent made it unfeasible. Adding to the confusion were problems in the chain of command. General Henry Clinton, Guy Carleton, and William Howe were in a political struggle, both among themselves and with Burgoyne. The person responsible was George Germain, Lord Sackville, British Minister for the Colonies, who allowed the chaos in command.

For clarity and brevity, I barely mentioned British Lt. Colonel Barry St. Leger's attack from the west. Had it succeeded, it might have tipped the balance. Thanks to the brave resistance of the Continentals at Fort Stanwix, the sacrifice of the Tryon County militia, and Benedict Arnold's clever and bold move, St. Leger's force was forced to retreat to Canada in defeat.

The controversial surrender of General John Burgoyne began to shift the momentum of the conflict. With effective diplomacy, the Americans aimed to use this event to persuade the French, who were silent partners in the war, to become full allies. However, despite the victory, this was not guaranteed. Many months of diplomacy in Paris still lay ahead.

Congress and public opinion quickly turned against the Saratoga Convention, and although Burgoyne and his officers were granted safe passage home, the British and German soldiers were not. Soon, they were marched from Boston to various prisons from New England as far south as Charlottesville, Virginia.

The fourth year of the war would introduce a new approach to the conflict, filled with intrigue, politics, and posturing on both sides of the Atlantic. The year 1778 would start with questions about the leadership of both armies. However, the defeat, among other things, would eventually cause General Howe, not General Washington, to surrender his command.

Regarding the historical figures, Horatio Gates was indeed a schemer driven by ambition. However, his notable achievement should not be overlooked. He was able to work well with the New Englanders and built a credible force to block Burgoyne's army. His caution was fortunately balanced by aggressive commanders like John Stark, Enoch Poor, and Benedict Arnold.

John Burgoyne was a bon vivant, playwright, and general in his personal life. He engaged in politics, had a mistress, and loved the theater, writing or co-writing plays and librettos. But he was also a student of the military arts and had progressive thinking on leadership. His failure to capitalize on an initial victory at Ticonderoga and to manage the misconduct of his Indian allies helped unify American forces north of Albany, which halted his progress. Upon returning to England, he faced criticism for his handling of the campaign and was barred from holding further active command.

Benedict Arnold was the most tragic figure in the story. Gallant and naturally skilled in battle, he was flawed in many ways. He did have contacts with French collaborators during the invasion of Quebec. This fact provides the basis for the fictional Father Vincennes and his network. Arnold resisted the amputation of his leg and survived the battle with a limp. He never held a field command again in the American Army. Recent information suggests Arnold was not quite so insubordinate and that Horatio Gates may have given him permission to take action. I will wait for more to develop on this.

The shady Lieutenant Colonel James Wilkinson once again crosses Jeremiah Creed's path. After the war, he would rise to prominence and hold a controversial role in the new nation's history. The historical figure Wilkinson was later connected to many contentious events during America's early development.

Colonel Daniel Morgan was a genuine hero of the Revolution. Strict and just, his efforts played a key role in many campaigns along the eastern seaboard.

British General Simon Fraser was a brave and noble officer, and his loss might have been the biggest tragedy in the battle, jeopardizing Britain's future success in America. Fraser is said to have been shot by Private Tim Murphy of Morgan's rifles – I altered the scenario to include the fictional Sergeant Guthrie. I apologize for the confusion about the names, but Captain Alexander Fraser was indeed his cousin and one of the best woodland fighters in the British Army.

Lieutenant Colonel Friedrich Baum was a Brunswick dragoon officer and commander at Bennington, where he was mortally wounded and died while in American captivity. His defeat paved the way for Burgoyne's loss two months later.

Lord George Germain, Clinton, and Howe provide the backdrop to this tragedy. An excellent plan was squandered by their miscommunication, political agendas, and competing egos. In the end, Germain's inability to clearly instruct Howe on his role in supporting Burgoyne was the fundamental blunder that led to the debacle that began to turn the tide. However, over five years of fighting still lay ahead.

S.W. O'Connell

Cast of Characters
(in approximate order of appearance)
(* = Historical figure)

* General George Washington – Continental Army commander-in-chief
* General Sir William, General Howe - British commander-in-chief in North America
*Lord George Germain - Minister for the Colonies
*King George III – British sovereign
*Major General John Burgoyne – Commander of British expedition against New York
*Colonel Robert Fitzgerald – Washington's "Intelligence Advisor"
Lieutenant Jeremiah Creed – Platoon commander 2nd Continental Dragoons and leader of "White Knights"
Captain Harold Martin – Senior surveyor and map maker on Washington's staff
Lieutenant James Tobias - Subaltern working for Martin
Major Benjamin Tallmadge -Washington's chief of intelligence operations and troop commander, 2nd Continental Light Dragoons
Thomas Jeffries – Trooper, 2nd Continental Dragoons
Roy Harry – Sergeant, 2nd Continental Dragoons
Thaddeus O'Quinn – Trooper, 2nd Continental Dragoons
Delbert Greene - Freed slave, line-crosser, and asset
Jonathan Beall – Trooper, 2nd Continental Dragoons
Elias Parker – Trooper, 2nd Continental Dragoons
Simon Beall – Troop Sergeant, 2nd Continental Dragoons
*Colonel Theunis Dey – Commander of Bergen County Militia Regiment
*Missus Hester (Schuyler) Dey – Wife of Theunis Dey
Jan Karcz - Trooper of 2nd Continental Dragoons and former Polish lancer
Thaddeus Quill - Trooper, 2nd Continental Dragoons and a former trooper with the Habsburg Empire's O'Reilly Light Horse
*Brigadier General Benedict Arnold – Led American troops in gallant attacks at Bemis Heights and Freeman's farm
Captain McKay – Loyalist officer
Major General Guy Carleton – British Governor-General of Canada
Claude - Canadian servant to Carleton
*Susan Caufield – General John Burgoyne's mistress
*Lieutenant Colonel Barry St. Leger – commander of British column based in Ontario
Lady Dunning – Matilda Dunning, wealthy Loyalist widow
Lieutenant Colonel Sir Horace Stilton - Second in command of the New York garrison regiment
Major James 'Sandy' Drummond – Chief of British intelligence in New York
Edmund Laseby – Wealthy banker and land speculator
*Major General Sir Henry Clinton – Second in command to General Howe, the British commander-in-chief in North America

Klara Stumpf – Young ward of Sandy Drummond and confidante of Emily Stanley
*Elizabeth Loring – Mistress of General Howe, wife of British quartermaster of prisoners
Lieutenant Stephen Whittington – British officer and suitor of Klara Stumpf
Emily Stanley – Daughter of doctor Reginald Stanley, proprietress of the Stanley boarding house
Mister Smythe – Code name given to Washington's top spy in New York, Emily Stanley
Captain Richard Hawkins – Artillery officer and commander of General Howe's ordnance and artificers
Finn – Jeremiah Creed's horse
Captain Hargrove – Medical officer and colleague of Reginald Stanley
*Joshua Loring – Loyalist head of the commissary for prisoners of war and cuckolded husband of Elizabeth Loring, General Howe's mistress
*James Rivington – Journalist and publisher of Rivington's Royal Gazette
Justin – Attendant to General Burgoyne
Colonel Lazarus Sinclair – Adjutant who directed General Burgoyne's staff
Captain James Lawrence – Cover for identity used by Jeremiah Creed
Sergeant Edgar O'Ballance – Company sergeant of the Royal Americans detachment recruited by Captain James Lawrence (Jeremiah Creed)
Absher – Boarder at the Stanley House
Jellicoe – Boarder at the Stanley House
Major Donald Haddix – British Quartermaster in New York
Coos Dederick – New York underworld figure and owner of Guldner Adler
Cornelius Foch – Shipmaster, owner of Red Hen and Washington's top spy in Brooklyn
Mister Jons – Code name given to Cornelius Foch
Griet – Serving girl
Bartholomew "Bart" Saunders – Young Loyalist ensign with Royal Americans
*Oliver De Lancey – Loyalist leader in New York
Nancy – Servant at the Stanley House
Captain Ezekial Hazard – master of the privateer sloop, Merilea, and friend of Creed
Smitty – First Mate of Merilea
Danny – Cabin boy on Merilea
*General William Heath – commander of American forces in the highlands north of New York City and south of Albany
Etienne Androche – Canadian coureurs du bois who guided Creed's journey south
Pierre – Wyandot warrior whose native name was Tsamehuhi or Eagle
Father Vincennes – French Jesuit priest and leader of a secret movement in Canada
Madame Grouchy – Housekeeper of the rectory
Captain Sidney Baker – Loyalist officer and subordinate of Major Sandy Drummond
Captain Daniel Black – commander of the Scorpions

Fleurette Binoche – Mixed Canadian-Iroquois maiden
Serge Binoche – Canadian coureurs du bois and British agent
Pierre Saint Luc de Lacorne – Leader of Canadian troops with the British
Ensign Framingham – Naval officer who ferries Baker on a secret mission
*Lieutenant Colonel Alexander Hamilton – Senior aide de camp to Washington
*Major General Phillip Schuyler – Commander of the Northern Department of the Continental Army
*Brigadier General Simon Fraser – British general in command of a wing of Burgoyne's army
*Captain Alexander Fraser – Distant cousin of Simon and commander of the elite company of marksmen
Lieutenant Dilley – Loyalist Provincial serving Sidney Baker
Major Stephen Rumson – British liaison officer to the Hessians, one of Emily's suitors
Solomon – Christian name for the leader of a Mohawk war party
*Marquis de Montcalm - French general and commander in the French and Indian War
*Major General Thomas Gage – Commander of British troops at Boston in the run-up to the war in 1775, and lost Boston to the rebels in 1776
*Samuel de Champlain – French explorer of the New World and founder of New France in the 17th century
*Henri the Fourth – King of France
Golden Apple – Codename for a British secret agent sent into the American camp in 1776
Lorie Dale – Friend of Emily Stanley and Mistress of Rip Hyde/Roy Harry
Jonah Dale – Lorie's husband, a gentleman farmer and Loyalist officer
Rip Hyde – Cover name used by Roy Harry
Tom Gordon – Line-crosser recruited by Benjamin Tallmadge to spy on the British
Private Stedman – Soldier in the Royal American Regiment
*Brigadier General Arthur St. Clair – Scottish-born American commander of Fort Ticonderoga
*Colonel Jeduthan Baldwin – New England militia officer and engineer at Fort Ticonderoga
*Colonel Pierse Long – New Hampshire Continental Line regimental commander
*Sergeant Jimmy Heath – Scout for Arthur St. Clair at Fort Ticonderoga
*Colonel Thaddeus Kosciusko – Polish officer serving as Continental Army engineer
*Brigadier General Roche de Fermoy – French mercenary granted a commission in the Continental Army
Tom Salamander – Loyalist cowboy leader in the Jerseys
*General August von Riedesel – German officer whose troops made up a part of Burgoyne's army
*Colonel Ebenezer Francis – American militia leader killed at Hubbardton

*Lieutenant Colonel Friedrich Baum - a German dragoon of Brunswick serving under von Riedesel
*Lieutenant Glich – Aide to Baum
Captain Schroeder – Baum's senior company commander
Ruud Steivers – Dutch smuggler
Mister Smythe – Cover name for General Washington's most important spy in New York
*Brigadier General John Nixon - Commanded a brigade of the Massachusetts Line
*Colonel John Glover – Commander of the Gloucester Regiment
*Colonel Daniel Morgan – Commander of the 11th Virginia Regiment and then the Provisional Rifle Corps at Freeman's Farm and Bemis Heights during the Battle of Saratoga
*Major General Horatio Gates – commander of the Northern Department following Schuyler's removal
*Lieutenant Colonel James Wilkinson – Aide to General Gates
*Brigadier General Benjamin Lincoln – Commander of the New England militia at Saratoga
*Brigadier General Enoch Poor – commander of a New Hampshire brigade at Saratoga
*Brigadier General John Stark – commander of the New Hampshire militia
*Ebeneezer Learned – commander of a brigade of New York and New England troops at Saratoga
Captain Jim Rife – New Hampshire militia company commander
Lieutenant George Beatty of the Queen's Loyal Rangers
Silas Milford – British sailor and Scorpion
Harvey Robson – Royal Marine and Scorpion
Unteroffizier (corporal) Gert Hoffman – Braunschweiger (Brunswick) dragoon
Tom Willets – First Mate on the Red Hen
Niklas – Sailor on the Red Hen
Nys – Able-bodied seamen on the Red Hen
*William Cunningham – Provost of New York City
Major Brown – Quartermaster officer on the tribunal
Colonel Colmes – Loyalist officer on the tribunal
*Billie Lee – enslaved manservant to George Washington
Captain Ebenezer Utley – New Hampshire militia company commander
Sergeant Tom Guthrie - one of Morgan's riflemen assigned to Creed
Thomas Swords – Loyalist owner of the Swords house and estate
*Missus Swords – Proprietress of the estate used as Burgoyne's headquarters
*Luc de La Corne – Canadian leader of the Indian allies
Jean-Paul Tremblay – Coureurs de bois and sidekick of Binoche
Sergeant Barnaby – One of Captain Alexander Fraser's sharpshooters
Tsongas – Iroquois warrior and scout

*Tim Murphy – American rifleman and sniper believed to have shot Simon Fraser
*Major Henry Dearborn – commander of the 300-man elite light infantry assigned to Gates's army at Saratoga
Willy - American rifleman
John Abbot – Vermont militiaman
Tim Stiles – Vermont militiaman
*Jane McCrae – Young woman murdered by the Iroquois
Sergeant Reynolds - light infantryman of the Royal Scots Fusiliers
Lew Emerson – Pennsylvania rifleman under Sergeant Guthrie
*Major John Acland – Commander of the British grenadiers
*Colonel Balcarres – British light infantry commander at Saratoga
* Brigadier General James Hamilton – British infantry commander at Saratoga
Private Jones – Deserter from the 24th Regiment of Foot
*General Johann von Specht – Commander of two brigades of German troops
Freddie – Subaltern under General Simon Fraser

Gazetteer

Adirondack Mountains – large and expansive mountain range south of St. Lawrence River and west of Lake Champlain

Albany, New York – American town at the confluence of the Mohawk and Hudson Rivers

Albany Post Road – highway leading from the City of New York to Albany along the eastern bank of the North (Hudson) River

Batten Kill – tributary flowing west from the hills of Vermont, emptying into the North (Hudson) River in New York

Beacon, New York – small village on the North River

Beekman House – General Howe's Headquarters, a home in the countryside of the Island of New York (Manhattan) north of New York City.

Bemis Heights – farmland north of Albany and the site of the American camp

Bennington – town in southwest Vermont

Block Island – island in the Atlantic off Narragansett Bay in Rhode Island

Boston – port city in Massachusetts and the largest city in New England

Brandywine Creek – tributary of the Delaware, south of Philadelphia, and site of a great battle

Brown's Ferry – a ferry landing across the Hackensack River in New Jersey

Cap-Diamant - cape on the edge of the Promontory of Quebec at the confluence of Saint Lawrence and Saint Charles rivers

Crown Point – an old French post on the west side of Lake Champlain, north of Fort Ticonderoga

Dey House, Preakness, New Jersey – a mansion in central New Jersey belonging to Theunis Dey and used by various officers during the war, including George Washington

Douw's Ferry - ferry landing on the Hackensack River in New Jersey established by John Douw around 1759

East River – salt water tidal estuary in New York City.

East Slip – large and busy wharf in lower New York City

Fisher's Island – island in the Long Island Sound at the far (east) end of Long Island

Fort George - French and Indian war era fort southeast of Lake George

Freeman's Farm – small farm south of Saratoga

Great Ravine – large ravine near Freeman's Farm

Grand Redoubt – most robust defense works at Freeman's Farm

Green Mountains – mountain range in Vermont running from north to south

Hackensack River – a large river extending from upper New Jersey and emptying into Newark Bay

Halifax, Nova Scotia – British port on the Atlantic, north of Massachusetts

Hampshire Grants – the disputed region between the Connecticut River and Lakes George and Champlain, claimed by both New Hampshire and New York that became the self-declared state of Vermont

Hoosick River – tributary of the North (Hudson) River that originates in the mountains of Vermont, New Hampshire, and Massachusetts

Hubbardton – town in the western part of Vermont

Isle la Motte – island in Lake Champlain

Isle de Noix – town on the Richelieu River

Jacob Arnold's Tavern, Morristown, New Jersey – spacious home that served as Washington's residence and headquarters

John Street Theater – first professional theater in New York City

Kébec - Algonquin name for the area around Quebec

Kip's Bay, New York – a small inlet of the East River along the shore of central New York Island

Lake Champlain – long body of water in upper New York stretching north-south to the east of the Adirondack Mountains, separating Vermont and New York

Lake George – major waterway north of Albany stretching to Lake Champlain

Lake Ontario – large body of freshwater between New York and Canada

Lévis - village on the south shore of the St. Lawrence River, opposite Quebec City

Liberty Pole – village in New Jersey's Hackensack Valley

Long Island Sound - extension of the Atlantic Ocean between Long Island and the mainland of New York and Connecticut

Manchester – city in New Hampshire

Massachusetts – critical New England state east of New York and south of Canada

Mill Creek – a ravine near Freeman's Farm

Medoc – region near Bordeaux in southwestern France known for wine

Monongahela – river in western Pennsylvania and site of a French and Indian massacre of a British army during the French and Indian War

Montreal – second-largest city in Canada, on the Saint Lawrence River, north of New York

Morristown, New Jersey – trading center nestled behind the Watchung Mountains west of New York

Mount Hope – large wooded mountain overlooking Fort Ticonderoga and Lake Champlain

New York Island – today's Manhattan

North or Hudson River – major body of water stretching from upper New York Harbor to Lake Tear of Clouds – headwater of the Hudson or North River in the Adirondack Mountains

Paulhus Hook – small port village opposite New York City in New Jersey

Philadelphia – city on the Delaware River, capital of the United States and largest city in North America

Place Royale – central square in Quebec

Pollepel Island – a small island in the North River near Beacon
Portsmouth – coastal town in New Hampshire
Post Road - major highway between the City of New York and Westchester
Princeton – town in New Jersey and the site of the battle
Quai Saint Andre – Saint Andre slip, a dock in Quebec
Quebec – Canadian city along the lower Saint Lawrence River and capital of the province of Quebec
Raritan – a river that runs through New Jersey's central region and empties into Sandy Hook Bay south of Staten Island
Raritan Landing – an inland port on the river of the same name
Richelieu River – body of water connecting Ille aux Noix on Lake Champlain to Sorel on the Saint Lawrence River
Richmond – the county comprised of Staten Island and the name of the hamlet there
Rue Saint Pierre – street in Quebec leading from the river
Saint-Jean sur Richelieu – Canadian village on the Richelieu River south of Montreal and north of Lake Champlain
Saratoga – town 30 miles north of Albany, New York, and site of the British surrender
Skenesborough – village in New York on the lower bay of Lake Champlain and east of Lake George near the Connecticut border
Snake Hill – a mountain promontory in central New Jersey
Swords House – used as Burgoyne's headquarters near Saratoga
Tappan Zee - wide expanse of the North River between Albany and New York City
Ticonderoga – the largest fort in North America, dominating the southern tip of Lake Champlain
Trenton – town in New Jersey and site of two battles
Trois Rivieres – village on the south bank of the St. Lawrence
Verplank's Point – peninsula jutting into the North River
White Marsh – township northeast of Philadelphia
White Plains – largest town in Westchester County, north of the City of New York
Zion Hill – section of high ground near Hubbardton, Vermont

Glossary

Algonquins – an Indian eastern woodland tribe

Allemande – French term for German

Anglais – French Canadian word for English

The Battery – original stone fort built by the Dutch at the lower tip of Manhattan Island

Bostonais – French-Canadian term for all New Englanders

Brig – two-masted square-rigged ship of medium tonnage

Brigade Irlandais – Irish Brigade, Irish soldiers serving the King of France

Carbine – short cavalry musket

Cartouche – a pouch or box used to carry cartridges

Chevaux de Frise – stakes driven into the ground to block the passage of troops or vessels when underwater

Citadelle – large fort in Quebec

Cock – what we today call the hammer of a musket or pistol

Cowboys – Loyalist criminal partisans supporting the British

Coureurs du Bois – literally "runners of the woods," rough and tumble backwoodsmen who traded with and lived with the Indians

Eglise Notre-Dame-des-Victoires – Church of Our Lady of Victories, a small Roman Catholic stone church in the lower town of Old Quebec City

Fusil – a short, light musket but longer than a cavalry carbine

Genever – a white spirit of Dutch origin similar to gin

Gloucester Regiment – American seamen from Marblehead, MA, who doubled as infantry and sailors for General Washington

Grapeshot – bags or nets of musket balls or small shot that fire from cannons like a shotgun

Habitants - local French Canadians also known as Quebecois

Hanger – a short infantry sword

Horse Guards – British military headquarters

Huron – a confederation of native North American tribes formerly living in the region east of Lake Huron

In flagrante delicto – archaic Latin phrase meaning caught red-handed

Iroquois – a confederation of native North American tribes of Mohawk, Seneca, Onondaga, Oneida Tuscarora, and Cayuga that controlled much of upper New York and northern Pennsylvania

Jung (s) – Dutch slang for boy (s)

King William's War – 17th-century conflict an extension of the War of the Grand Alliance of Britain, the Holy Roman Emperor, Netherlands, and German states against Louis XIV of France

Loyalists – Americans who supported the King and resisted rebellion

Meen Heer – a Dutch appellation, meaning roughly, my sir or sir.

Mijneer – Dutch appellation meaning, mister

Patriots – American colonists who favored independence from Great Britain

Privateers - armed merchant vessels that sailed under letters of marque from an authority, allowing them to plunder for the sake of that authority and a share of the booty

Provincials – Loyalist troops raised by the crown and organized as British infantry, not to be confused with Loyalist militia

Red Hen – merchant brig owned by Cornelius Foch

Royal American Regiment – British infantry regiment recruited initially in America, later in Ireland

Royal Marines - sea soldiers of Great Britain

Royal Navy – the maritime service of Great Britain

Sachem – Indian tribal leader, separate from a war chief

Scorpions – fictional British special operations unit

Skinners – patriot criminal partisans supporting the Americans

Sutlers – merchants who followed the armies selling sundry goods to soldiers and officers

Wyandot - North American people, belonging to the Huron nation

27th Foot, the Inniskillens – British infantry regiment recruited in Ireland

About the Author

S.W. O'Connell holds degrees in History (Fordham University) and International Relations (University of Southern California). He is a retired US Army intelligence officer who spent the majority of his service in the field of counterintelligence. Most of his time was spent overseas in US Army Europe and Allied Command Europe, but he does admit to a tour in the Pentagon and a stint at the John F. Kennedy Center for Special Warfare at Fort Bragg.

A native New Yorker, S.W. O'Connell settled in northern Virginia when he returned from his last overseas tour. His long-held love of history made it only natural that he would turn to the historical novel when he finally succumbed to a decades-long urge to craft fiction.

The North Spy is his fourth novel in the "Yankee Doodle Spies" series.

The North Spy